15.00

To C

my lovely friend

T·H·E
Flume Tender's Daughter

Much love,

Deb

DEB MOHR

ISBN: 1453776133
ISBN-13: 9781453776131

CHAPTER 1
HANKSPORT, WASHINGTON STATE
MAY 14, 1905

Just beyond first light Linnie Bede, sixteen-years-old ten days ago, bolted up-right on her thin mattress and cupped her hand to her ear. Flume bell was down. Linnie clambered over two of her sleeping sisters, slipped a moth-eaten flannel dress over her head and wriggled into a heavy wool sweater, too long in the sleeves. Twelve-year Baby stirred in a crude, rough-slated crib and sucked her thumb.

Birdie Mae, a year older than Linnie, left the bed too and dressed quickly. "Be careful," she said.

"Yes." Linnie hurried out to the stoop. Roy Bede, a red-haired, lantern-jawed man on the quiet side and father of the six Bede children, glanced at her, shrugged into a heavy jacket and grabbed a pickaroon.

Linnie pulled on a pair of corks with newspapers stuffed in the toes, threw on a sheepskin coat and clapped on a battered hat. She seized a lantern and the two quit the shanty and broke into a run, Roy, stiff-gaited, but quick and sure footed. Linnie, steady and loose boned.

In thick fog and drizzling rain they followed a path through a thicket of salal and huckleberry to reach a wide, v-shaped wooden chute built in a swift, narrow stretch of the Blackduck River. A large silent bell hung over the chute. Without wasting a moment Roy and his daughter climbed a ladder up to a catwalk alongside the flume and hurried up-stream.

At Camp Five, a small logging camp located on the river's headwaters up on Wildcat Mountain, loggers cut the big timbers, roughly milled them and sent them down the flume. At Roy Bede's place the planks struck the bell causing a steady, but erratic *bong bongbong bong*. A good sound. Silence meant something had gone haywire up stream and it was up to Roy Bede, a flume tender, to fix it. When Roy's bad leg gave him fits, his daughter helped him.

Earlier this morning the choked-up flume caught the attention of a flagman tending the lower chute. He hoisted a red-lighted lantern to alert workers at Camp Five. The men stopped their work. After Roy tended the trouble the flag-man would raise a large white flag and fresh-cut timbers from Five would come hurtling down again.

The flume, supported by a spindle-legged trestle, wormed its way down through tumbled pumice and skree to the meandering river at Tat Meadow. Oh, Lord, thought Linnie. Let the trouble be at Tat and not up on the mountain. That place was far.

She'd been there once when she and her father went up to fix the flume, choked with debris after a fierce wind storm. From there she could see smoke from Strom logging camps and shacks spiraling up above the rug of thick trees. Mt. St. Helens, slick and shiny with ice and snow, lay south. To the west, the Olympic Range loomed like pieces of white jagged glass.

On reaching Tat Meadow Linnie and her father climbed down from the catwalk and loped alongside the chute in which choked up water pooled and spilled over the sides.

Linnie, ahead of her father, held the lantern high. She stopped. "There." She pointed to a scatter of timbers boiled up over the structure.

That wasn't so bad. She and her father would prod those sticks loose, free up the flow and the timbers would tumble downstream, knock against the bell and shoot down-flume to the mill at Hanksport Bay.

But closer to the clogged water Linnie gasped. A corpse, burnt black as deep scorch, bobbled among the trapped timbers.

Roy went to take a close look. "Good God," he said. "Looks like anti-union work." He turned to Linnie, his face tight as a balled-up fist. "Take the short-cut down to Corrigan's. Tell Jim and his boys, whoever's around, to come help me horse this thing out of here. Then get on home."

"Who is it?"

"Only union man I know of around here is Sam Dickerson. Now, get going."

"You keep the lantern. I can see well enough."

Arms flailing, Linnie raced down an old skid-road to Corrigan's sturdy, well-kept place. Lantern light glowed in a front window. Linnie went up to the stoop and pounded on the door. Busby, one of the four Corrigan boys and known as "Buzz," cracked it open. "Linnie Bede. What . . . ?"

"Father and I . . ." She bent to catch her breath. "We found a burnt man. A . . . a corpse up at Tat. Might be Mr. Dickerson. Father needs help."

Buzz yelled, "Dad. Roy found a dead fellow and Linnie . . ."

Jim Corrigan, a small, muscular fellow with graying hair, alert, dark eyes, and a thick mustache, appeared. "You're all right?" he said to Linnie.

"Yes. I guess so. Father told me to come get you. Now . . ." She shivered. "I've got to, got to go home."

Jim Corrigan and Buzz hurried to one of two autos, a fancy Rambler and a shiny black Runabout Sedan, parked in front of the house. They climbed in the Rambler and roared up the narrow skid road toward Tat Meadow.

Linnie, breathless and fearful, raced on down the wet, muddy hill. Whoever killed the burnt man could be most anywhere. Hiding behind any one of the big trees. Crouched down in a hollowed out stump. Waiting to nab anybody who came his way.

Closer to home her fear eased. Lantern light glowed through the grimy windows of scattered, rickety shacks. Smells of smoke coming from wood stoves was strong. But for the Corrigan's two-story substantial home, all of the shacks, including the Bede's, built by Strom, were worn and if not squalid, close to it.

Almost home—Linnie raced past the chicken coop, the garden in which nothing took root, and then the privy. In the pale light of day she collapsed on the stoop. Birdie Mae, a tall, big-boned girl with a blunt face, pursey lips, deep dimples and big teeth, came outside. "Good mercy," she said. "What's happened? Where's Father?"

Fifteen-year old Druscilla followed Birdie.

Linnie gulped for air. "Oh, Lordy, God. What Father and I . . . Oh, Lordy, what we saw. A burnt man. Dead. Scorched. Might be Mr. Dickerson. Buzz and Mr. Corrigan went to help." She shivered and put her head down on her arms. "Mercy, what a sight."

Birdie said, "Come in and I'll make nerve tea. That ought to help settle you."

Inside the chilly house a kerosene lamp allowed dim light. Seven chairs surrounded a round table covered with faded red and white checkered oilcloth. Books and Blue Willow dishes sat on a shelf beyond the reach of Baby, the youngest Bede child.

Meara Bede, a tall, willowy woman, mother of her six living children, and always up from bed just after first light, sat ram-rod straight on a platform rocker beside a window.

Shortly after Baby's birth, her family recognized the child as simple-minded. Meara tried to nurse her, but the baby hard-gummed her mother's nipples bloody. Days on end she'd howled and pounded her fists on her head. Dirtied her diapers until she was seven years old. To this day, if angered or frustrated, she destroyed anything and everything she could lay her hands on.

One day, some years ago, Baby's mother stood stock still and stared at two-year-old Baby flailing on the floor at her feet. "Who is she?" Meara cried. "Take her away. Oh, please take her away." Meara tip-toed into the bedroom she shared with her husband and closed the door.

Since that day, Meara seated in her rocker did little but stare out the small, dirty window and she seldom spoke. In nice weather she might venture outside to sit on a stump close to a small wooden cross. The cross marked the grave of Lily, Meara and Roy Bede's seventh child. Lily was born in the shanty one day and the next day she died.

Now, Linnie, shivering, her teeth chattering, sat at the table and hugged herself to try to stop her awful shaking. Druscilla sat and put her arm around her. "With Buzzie's help, Father will be all right," she said.

"Lord, Dru. I hope so. Too bad Gavin and Newt weren't home to help."

"They're both in Seattle."

"Yes, and Johnny's soon going to work." Linnie had no idea what Buzz did with his time and she wasn't about to ask. She didn't want to listen to Dru talk about him.

Birdie Mae gave her mother and sisters each a cup of hot tea and she said to Linnie, "It's good that you're going to church with Joe this morning. It will take your mind of the sight you saw."

Linnie straightened, sipped her tea and took a deep shaky breath. "I don't know about that. I can't get the danged picture out of my mind."

"In time you will."

"Well, all month Joe has nagged us to go to church with him and yesterday I promised. I just hope that flume bell rings before we leave."

Birdie Mae said, "I hope the dead man isn't Mr. Dickerson. He and Newt had become pretty good friends."

"Father says Mr. Dickerson is union."

"Does that matter?" Birdie slapped pieces of stale bread in a skillet sizzling with bacon grease.

"I don't know," said Linnie. "I didn't know him. Saw him a couple of times at the store. He was a big man and he had a nice smile." She set down her cup and went out to the pitcher-pump on the back stoop. She pumped water into a large, rust-pocked, enameled bowl and reached up into a cupboard for a bar of fine, creamy white soap.

Some years ago, before Baby was born, Meara saw the soap advertised in *The Ladies Home Journal*. She sent for a dozen bars at a time and insisted that her girls use the soap, with their faint, delicious scent, for daily wash-ups and once-a-week bathing.

Finished with washing, Linnie brushed out her hair. She and her oldest brother, 19-year-old Joe, had their father's brown eyes, red hair and fair skin with a sprinkle of freckles. Colin, Linnie's eighteen-year old brother, Birdie Mae, Dru and Baby had their mother's thick, blond wavy hair and blue eyes. But while Colin's and Dru's and Birdie Mae's eyes held thought, Baby's held little.

"Linnie." Joe hailed her. He and Colin came from a shed in which they slept back by a fringe of trees. Joe, wearing a checkered cap, a white shirt and tie, dark pants, shiny in the seat, and a jacket too short in the sleeves, said, "We'll leave for church right after . . ."

"Wait. I'm spooked, Joe. Father and I found a burnt man. In the flume . . ."

"You found *what*?"

"A burnt man. Father said it looks like anti-union work and the man might be Mr. Dickerson."

"Yeah?" said Colin. "Just last week Dickerson was talking I.W.W. up at Camp Six. If that's who it is, maybe union folks will get the message and quit bothering us."

"I don't know," said Linnie. "But the burnt man was awful. Just awful."

The three went inside the house. Linnie poured coffee into thick white china cups. Birdie Mae forked slices of the fried bread onto plates and set one plate in the warming oven for her father. Linnie served her mother and then five of the six Bede offspring sat to eat. Fire crackled in the stove. Forks scraped against plates. Nobody spoke.

Joe and Colin left the table. After the girls cleaned the kitchen, Linnie went to the bedroom and put on a long gray skirt, a white middy blouse and a pair of her worn, but decent lace-up, black boots.

Baby wakened and stood up behind the slats in the crib. "Baby up. Baby up. Up. Up." Her skin was the fairest of the Bede offspring, flawless and clear. When pleased her smile was a bit coy. When displeased, with her chin thrust forward, she was defiant. Her curly blonde hair, cut by her sisters and kept short, sat like a cap on her head.

Linnie helped her climb over the rail. Baby held her arms up. Linnie slipped a worn, blue wool dress over her head. "Good, Baby. Good. Now, let's get your arms into the right holes."

Baby twisted sideways, fought the dress, and cried out, "Baw. Baw."

Linnie straightened her out, Baby emerged from the neck and Linnie guided her pudgy arms through the armholes.

Tears ran down Baby's face. "Baby, no. No."

"It's all right," said Linnie. She gave her a quick hug. "You'll learn. Now, sit down."

Baby sat on a frayed wicker chair and Linnie put a pair of thick wool socks on her feet. "Birdie or Dru will take you to the privy and wash you up," she said. "I'm going to church with Joe."

"Baby go, too."

"No, not today." Baby followed Linnie out to the front room.

Birdie turned from her work in the kitchen. "Thanks for dressing her. I'm almost through re-making those two dresses."

"Good. If we can teach her how to button and unbutton them, she'll be tickled pink."

It had been Linnie's idea to take a couple of her mother's dresses, cut them down the front, sew on big buttons and make buttonholes to fit. If Baby learned how to dress and undress herself, life for her three older sisters would be a bit easier.

None of the girls felt uneasy about altering their mother's clothes. Meara was content wearing a light brown wool dress with a white collar and cuffs, or a black cotton skirt and a white blouse, depending on the weather.

She'd come to this country with clothes fit for a city and for some years she enjoyed wearing them. But after Baby was born most of her clothes stayed neatly packed away in two large steamer trunks, not seeing the light of day until one of her daughters put her garments to good use.

Joe, seated at the table, was drawing a picture of the First National Bank in town. He made sketches of buildings every chance he could grab. "Ready to go?"

Then, and just then, the sharp, clipped irregular tone of the flume bell rang. *BongBong. Bong Bong* Linnie smiled. "Except for the danged corpse, everything is fine up-stream. Yes, Joe. Let's go to church."

The steady drizzle had let up some and shadows from weak sunlight played fitfully on the narrow dirt road that led down to town. Linnie said, "Have you ever seen a burnt man?"

"No. I've seen plenty of dead men though. Last week a fellow at work slipped on a log boom and drowned. I hauled him out. Two years ago, when I worked with Colin and Johnny setting choke, a steel cable line broke loose and sliced a fellow clean in two. That was the worst."

"I remember. You got so sick you couldn't go to work for three days. But the men you saw weren't burnt. I've seen dead people, too. Birdie and I were with Mrs. Corrigan when she had her last baby and they *both* died. And I've seen plenty of dead folks in caskets, but they looked all right. The burnt man was burnt black and his eyes were open and pearly white. Dang it, Joe. I wish I could get the picture of him out of my mind."

"Take your troubles to the Lord. He'll shed light and you'll see truth. If you don't go to the Lord, you'll live in shadows and you don't want to do that, Linnie."

"What's caused you to get so interested in God? I don't think Father is very happy about it. Except for weddings and funerals, none of us ever go to church."

"Father doesn't have a bad temper. I do. Father doesn't believe in God. I do. My temper gets me in trouble. A couple of weeks ago, when Newt and I went hunting, I claimed the buck that went down was mine. He said it was his. I picked a fight and gave him a bloody lip. While he nursed his lip, he reminded me that when the buck went down I was on the other side of the river and couldn't have even seen it. He was right. I felt bad about hurting him and I gave him my hat."

"The one you bought from the catalog?"

"One and the same. And I talked to Preacher at First Baptist about my temper. He said prayer and church would help cure me."

"Well, you might lose your temper quick, but you get over it quick, too."

"I'd rather not lose it at all. Last Saturday, when I took Baby to town I ran into a fellow I work with. He said to Baby, 'Oh, look at that pretty hair bow and all that pretty blond hair. And you sure smell good. How old are you, anyway?' "

Linnie said, "Baby smells good because we use the nice soap to wash her. And when she goes to town, we want her to look nice as can be. The pretty hair bows in her hair helps too. But, mercy buckets, she doesn't know if she's two or twelve, or twenty."

"No, but she knew enough to like what the fellow said. She giggled and blushed up and then the fellow said, 'You're sure gonna have some swell knockers in a couple of years.' He smacked his lips and that's when I lit into him. Socked him pretty good and knocked him down. I said, 'You don't talk like that to my sister.' "

"Good for you. Was Baby upset?"

"No. She liked the attention. I took her to the ice cream parlor before we came home. She loves those ice-cream pies."

"Well, the fellow who smart-lipped Baby got what he deserved. And you don't want to get mad at Newt. He's a real gentleman if I ever saw one." She hit him playfully on his upper arm. "Except for you."

Joe flushed up, ducked his head and smiled.

In the town of Hanksport, built on the banks of The Blackduck River, saws whined, hammers banged, dogs barked. Stumps, set on fire to burn through and rot, glowed and winked like big red eyes. White oak and aspen, a few pine, cedar and fir trees, were spared.

Linnie and Joe passed by Tom Johnson's livery, and the A.D. Calkins Dry-Goods store. In the next block the United States Post Office, Holm's Hardware, and the First National Bank took up two blocks across from the Strom Company Store, Morrison's Funeral Parlor, The Blackduck Saloon, and The Hanksport Hotel. All of the Bede children, except Baby, had attended the two-story grade school tucked in among a stand of fir trees at the end of town. The new brick high school up on Pine Butte boasted a gymnasium and small auditorium.

Mrs. Holm's Ice-Cream Parlor, built beside a grove of aspen, was just north of town and convenient for folks like Joe and Linnie to patronize. Mame Holm, wife of Mayor Ollie Holm, had taught and now supervised her staff of two women who baked treats concocted from Mame's South Carolinian culture. The sweets and treats were served to customers seated in ice-cream parlor chairs at small round tables.

A city park was at the south end of town. The Hanksport Ladies Improvement Club had prevailed upon city officials to clear two acres, build a bandstand and benches, a horseshoe pit and a softball diamond. The park was hot and dusty in summer. In late fall, continuing through winter and spring, it was a mud hole.

A squat, stone, two-cell jailhouse stood across the Blackduck River. Twice, in Linnie's memory, spring run-off from Cougar Mountain had washed out the bridge.

A block from the park Joe and Linnie climbed the hill to First Baptist, went inside and sat on a bench. Again, the swollen, burnt man popped up in Linnie's mind. *Was* it Mr. Dickerson, the widower who lived in the big, shabby place a couple of miles up the road from the Bede's?

Mrs. Dickerson died a couple of years ago and a niece, said to be about Birdie's age, used to come up from Seattle to visit her aunt and uncle, but Linnie had never met her.

If the corpse wasn't Mr. Dickerson, who was it? And who had done the awful thing? Was it the man who lived in a cave somewhere up river? Or was it somebody Linnie had never seen in her life? Well, she would tuck those worries away. She had another worry to pick on and it was a good sight worse.

Two weeks from today Linnie and her family—not Meara—would meet in this same church to witness Birdie Mae's marriage to Newt Corrigan.

It had happened so fast. Six months ago Birdie told Linnie that she liked Newt "more than enough. He's so handsome and he has those nice blue eyes and yesterday after school he was waiting for me in his auto and he drove me home. I let him kiss me and he kisses real nice, too."

Then came a day when she whispered to Linnie that she'd gone to Newt's house and nobody was home and she and Newt lay on a bed and she allowed him to get on top of her. "That felt soooo good," she said.

Two months ago, when Linnie and Birdie Mae were picking pudding berries up on an old logged-over site, Birdie said she'd gone to Newt's house with him and again, nobody was home and she went to bed with him and allowed him to put his poker inside her. "I wanted him to do it," she said. "And I liked it a lot." Her cheeks flamed bright.

Linnie straightened from her picking. "Oh, Birdie. I hope he didn't make a baby inside you."

"It doesn't matter if he did. I love Newt and he loves me."

Well, Birdie stopped having her monthly, but instead of being worried, witless and scared, she was delighted.

"Newt and I are going to get married," she announced to her family one night at supper. "He's building us a nice house with two bedrooms."

Roy Bede and Jim Corrigan were good friend and neither objected, but Linnie was losing her best friend in the world.

Church was about over and Linnie hadn't paid one bit of attention to Preacher's sermon, but she sang, as loud as she could, *Onward Christian Soldiers, marching off to war . . . ."*

Outside the church, folks milled about and visited.

Fishing and hunting. "The catch is pretty good up at Blue Mirror Lake. Got my last buck up there, too."

Work. "Anybody heard anymore about union?"

"What about the hospital Strom said they'd build? We're paying for it. Money docked from our pay every other week. Ought to see something happening up here."

"We need that hospital."

"Didn't Mr. Dickerson come up here to try to see it got built?"

Who had passed on. Who had given birth. Trading recipes. Mame Holm's fine scalloped potatoes. Ella Magilly's delicious baked calico beans. Mary Elser's famous coffee cake. Exchanged among the women. Exchanged again, and again.

Joe and Linnie spoke with Sheriff Chester Mann. Chester, a skinny, tall, bony headed blonde fellow with large blue eyes, was a couple of years older than Joe. He was Joe's friend, as close to a friend as Joe would allow anybody to be.

Joe was a loner. Worked as a bolt puncher, balancing all day on a log floating in a pond among bundles of shingles. Dirt and sticks never clogged bolts under Joe's watch and he guided them, clean as a whistle, to a conveyer belt that carried them into the mill. He worked pretty much alone and that suited him fine.

Chester Mann hadn't heard about the murdered fellow. "I hope it isn't Sam," he said. "But he talked up some pretty radical union ideas around here for the past couple of years."

"Yeah," said Joe. "Can't say I'm much interested in union."

Later, while Linnie and Joe walked along the narrow, dirt road toward home, Joe said, "I see that Birdie is . . . well . . . it looks to me like she's in the family way?"

"She is and it's her business."

"That may be, but I'm shamed by her. She's sinned and she'll go to hell and live in a place of fire and coals forever. I can't carry that thought."

"You'll have to," said Linnie. "She isn't the first girl to hurry to the alter."

"No, but, she's a Bede. She's shaming our family and she's sinned."

"She's Birdie and we all love her. Don't let this religion you've taken to turn you into a person stiff as a stick with no bending."

❦

Sunday nights were bathing nights for Baby and Dru and in spring, when evenings were even a little warm, it meant bathing out on the stoop instead of behind a sheet strung up at the far end of the kitchen.

After Linnie and Joe hauled buckets of hot water from the stove to the big, galvanized washtub, Joe pointed up to the sky. "Look," he said. "I see God."

A full moon, white as chalk, was rising above the dark, rugged trees.

Linnie said, "Oh, for pat's sake Joe. Those moon shadows are mountains. Mother and Father taught us about them a long time ago, before Mother got strange."

"They might be mountains to you, but I see God."

Linnie put her hands on her hips. "All this religion you've taken to makes me wonder. As Father says, 'too much of a good thing can get you in trouble.'"

"A good man or woman or child can't ever get enough good religion."

"Well, I guess I'd rather see God in my mind than that danged burnt man."

CHAPTER 2

Late morning, two days later, a day of spring breezes and bright sunshine, Linnie came from the chicken coop and set a bucket of eggs on the table. Glittery, blue-back flies stitched the air over a pot of beans and fatback on the stove. Baby, seated on the floor, rocked back and forth and banged her spoon. "Knockers. Knockers. Pretty Baa bee. Ma, Ma, Ma, Ma."

Meara, seated in her rocker by the window, seemed oblivious.

Birdie Mae reached up to one of the high shelves, brought down a hatbox and plucked out a wide-brimmed, white straw hat with a pink ostrich plume. She put it on and peered at herself in a piece of cracked mirror. "What do you think?" she said to Linnie. "Is it too fussy to wear for my wedding?"

Linnie shrugged. "Suit yourself. It's your wedding."

Birdie took off the hat. "It's awfully fancy, isn't it. I'll ask Dru to make a couple of daisy chains and I'll wear them like a crown." She licked her finger, twirled a curl, and again eyed herself in the mirror.

"Go ahead and wear Mother's hat," Linnie said. "That would suit you better than one of Dru's daisy chains."

"You're mighty peckish today."

"I've got the gloomies. Feels like I'm full of spiders. I wish I hadn't seen that danged burnt man. And I wish Mother would be like she was a long time ago. I wish Baby was like the rest of us. Most of all, I wish you hadn't let Newt put his thing in you and you weren't getting married and leaving home."

"In time you'll forget that burnt man, but the rest of your wishes are thin as air. Newt put his poker in me because I wanted him to. Mother's not going to change, and neither will Baby. But perk yourself up. You and Parley will have a fine time standing with Newt and me at our wedding. Parley is stuck on you as a bee is to clover and you know that Father wants you to marry him."

Linnie smote her fist in her palm. "I've told Father, and I'll tell you again. I'm not going to marry anybody. Mercy buckets, Parley can't even read or write."

"That doesn't mean he's not a good man. And it's time for all of us to settle. Who knows when Joe, with his shy ways, will show interest in a woman? So, I'll go first. Colin wants to marry Mide and it's clear to anybody who might take notice that Buz and Dru have eyes for each other. But I don't know about you."

"I do. I want to go to Seattle, find work as a stenographer, or maybe be a nanny in a rich lady's house. I'll save my money and go on to school. You've *always* known that I want to be a teacher. Besides, I'd be a bad wife because I don't want babies at all."

"You've said that before and I don't understand." Again, Birdie Mae peered at herself in the piece of mirror. She pinched her cheeks and bit her lips to raise the color. "Know what? Newt says he will give me my own money every month. The first thing I'll do is buy a mirror with a gold frame and a handle. Like the one in the catalog."

Linnie laughed. "You and Dru sure like to look at yourselves."

"You'd do well to spend a little time looking at your own self. Appreciate those high cheek bones and big brown eyes. And why you cut off your hair is beyond thought. Looks like you're wearing a shaggy red cap." She put the hat back in the box and put the box up on the shelf.

"I whacked it off because all that hair was half-way down my back. Ow!" She grabbed the back of her head.

Baby's big, dented cook spoon clattered to the floor at Linnie's feet. Baby rocked and laughed big horsy chuckles. Linnie picked up the spoon and put it on a high shelf. Baby's chuckles turned to throaty barks. "Baw. Baw. Baw."

Meara got up from her rocker and left the house.

Birdie Mae said to Linnie, "I'm worried about how you and Dru will manage without me around. The older Baby gets, the more she's a try. I used to think it would be the other way around, but it isn't."

"I'm not as worried about her as I am about Dru and Buzz. Ever since he heard her sing at Evelyn Potts's funeral two months ago, he's waited for her at school and brought her home in his fancy auto. She *loves* every minute of it, too."

"What fault do you find in that? Buzzie is a good sight better than a lot of other fellows who've been swoony over Dru."

"But, with her fine voice she shouldn't get caught up with anybody right now. She ought to put her mind to becoming a music teacher and teach down in Seattle."

"You've known most of your life that Father doesn't have money to send any of us on to school. All of us will get married, live here, have babies and take care of Mother and Baby until they die. When Father gets old, he'll need looking after, too."

Linnie went to stand in the open doorway. The air smelled of wet woods and smoke. Dru, perched on the edge of the stoop, plucked her father's guitar and hummed a lively tune.

Meara sat on the stump a few yards from the house. Skinny, her graying blond hair pinned up in a knot, she looked hard-bit and old. Yet Linnie's memories of her were of softness. White curtains embroidered with blue and red flowers hung at the clear, clean windows. Sunday dinners were served on the pretty Willow Ware dishes. Evenings, Meara read to her children and later, after Linnie was in bed, she would peek out from behind the blanket, used as a door, and feel warmth and comfort at the sight of her mother reading by the fire.

Meara, who had loved nature and had studied botany at the University of Chicago, liked to pack up picnics and take her brood—Joe, Colin, Birdie Mae, Linnie, and Dru—up to Horsetail Falls. There, atop a high ridge where the sun shone bright as a tin bucket, she taught her children how to identify moss pinks and roseroot trailing out from tumbled boulders. She taught them how to recognize bird calls—the deep, irregular hoot of the great gray owl, the flat, nasal whistle of the white-breasted nuthatch, the rolling call and sharp pecks of the woodpecker.

While eating thick-sliced bread with venison and pickles and a sweet treat of sugar cookies, she pointed to fork-stemmed fairy bells with creamy-white blooms. And she favored clusters of leafless stems on which snow orchids grew. "Don't they look like tiny ghosts?" she said and she and her children laughed and hugged one another.

Twice Meara took her children to the head of the falls and they shouted to be heard over the thundering watery roar. A long lace of water fell to a dark pond far below and Meara said, "This is a dangerous place. Slippery and steep. You can come here, but only with me, or your father."

After Baby was born Meara stopped doing those things and the soft feeling went away. For a time Linnie and Birdie and Dru went up to Tat Meadow to pick flowers for her. On receiving them, she smiled and then she slipped back into her lost place, her eyes like those of a china doll Linnie once shared with Birdie Mae and Dru.

But now, four shrill blasts shattered the air. Faded. Blasted again. Someone was hurt up at Camp Four. Birdie and Linnie moved fast. Linnie grabbed a dinged up dinner bucket, full of medicines and herbs, from a high shelf. Birdie Mae said to Dru, "If Baby behaves, give her back her spoon."

The girls dashed across the smoky, stump-pocked clearing. At a fork in the road they turned east and hurried through a forest of cedar, fir and pine, most of which were over eight feet in girth. Fog and clouds often covered the treetops. But for logged over hills and clearings, a few meadows and escarpments, sunshine was rare.

"I hate it when that whistle toots," said Linnie. "I wish Father and Joe and Colin would quit logging. Seems like more and more men get killed or hurt. Remember the fellow who fell in the river last month? Joe hauled him out all right, but his leg bone poked straight out of his skin and he died."

"That might be, but what can we do about it?"

Linnie kicked at a clod of thick duff. "I don't know, but all that misery isn't fair. At least you won't ever have to worry about Newt. Land-speculating with his father is safe as can be. All they have to worry about is their automobile and making a bundle of money."

"They work hard and it's too bad that Johnny, being the youngest, doesn't join them."

"Does Buzz work with them?"

"I'm not sure. He's in Seattle a lot. Can't say I know what he does."

"Well, Johnny has worked alongside Colin for as long as I can remember," said Linnie. "Doesn't he play the sweetest harmonica you ever did hear?"

"Yes. And he's sweet on *you*. Having two suitors isn't bad. Johnny Corrigan and Parley Hearn."

"I don't give a fig for old Parley Hearn."

"You'd do well to give him thought. He's head sawyer up at Camp Five and he owns his own place up at Blue Mirror Lake. Father says he's well thought of. Doesn't take to whiskey, he's smart and he's fond of his dog. Father thinks he'd make a fine husband."

"Maybe for somebody, but not for me. I don't have to like him just because Father does."

On up ahead a rider astride a horse approached them. Kees Strom, son of Mr. and Mrs. Strom, reined in his mount. He was a well dressed, good-looking, round faced young man with curly, wheat-brown hair and dark eyes. "Nice day isn't it." His smile was hesitant.

"Someone's hurt up at Four," said Birdie Mae. "We're in a hurry."

"I heard the whistle. Hope it's not serious." He tipped his hat, kneed his horse, and was on his way.

"I like Kees," said Linnie. "His eyes are like the color of Mother's brown velvet cape. And I liked sitting next to him at the Fourth of July picnic last year when we listened to Mayor Holm speak and Dru sang so nice. Kees said he enjoyed her songs. He's polite."

"He's a sly one, Linnie."

"How can you say that when you don't even know him? And he's not sly, he's shy."

"I don't care for him, that's all."

At the Dickerson place a chunk of land surrounding the big log house had been cleared of all trees. But two groves of aspen, close to the fringe of trees, had been spared. Last week when Linnie had passed by, a dusty, black sedan automobile was parked in front. Today, the auto was gone.

Another junction lay just east of the house. One road went down to Hanksport, a mile away. Linnie and Birdie Mae stayed on the westbound road they had taken from home.

"I wonder why Mrs. Dickerson never had children," said Linnie.

"Maybe Mr. Dickerson pulled his poker out of her at the right time. Men do that and women won't have babies. I didn't want Newt to do that with me. Loving is lots nicer for husbands when they keep their poker inside their wives and I'm so excited about this baby I could jump right out of my skin."

"You wouldn't be excited, if you already had six or seven."

"Yes, I would. Newt and I want lots of children."

"You can afford it. Newt's got plenty of money. But all the women we know are poor and have way too many children. I pray that none of *us* ever has a child like Baby. Just thinking about it makes my blood run cold."

At Camp Four weak sunlight shot through a veil of smoke and dust. Axes rang. Saws whined. Belching donkey engines pounced on tangles of snarled root wads, stumps, and snags. A locomotive, ready to haul logs down to Hanksport, steamed and chuffed.

"Timber!" a cry went out. A sharp crack split the air and the ground shuddered as an enormous fir tree crashed to the ground. The crew boss, a big-shouldered man, his face wet and red from heat, pointed to a hill. "Over there," he yelled. "I'll go with you."

The three hurried.

A girl who looked to be Birdie's age knelt on one side of Johnny Corrigan. Colin knelt on the other side. "Oh, no," Linnie and Birdie cried. "Not Johnny. Oh, not Johnny."

He lay on his side as if asleep. Blood, thin as wire, trickled from his mouth. Birdie Mae sprung open the dinged-up bucket in which rolls of muslin bandages, camphor, quinine, and small tins of laudanum were neatly packed. "He doesn't look to be too hurt," she said.

"He's badly hurt," said the girl. She stood. She was a short, button-nosed girl with snapping black eyes and bobbed black hair. She had about her a sassy demeanor. "I'm a nurse," she said to the crew boss. She spoke with the voice of authority. "This boy is hurt inside himself. We need to put him on the train and get him down to the doctor in town. The train is faster than my auto."

"Sorry, Miss. Nobody rides down in that locy but my crew."

Colin said, and his voice rose. "But, he's *part* of your crew. Please, let us get him down to town."

"He ain't part of the crew when he ain't working. But laddie, I'll give you the rest of the day off and you can give these ladies a hand."

The girl said, "I'll pay you five silver dollars if you'll let us put him on the train. If we can't get him to a doctor quick, I'm afraid he'll die."

Die? Not Johnny Corrigan who often came to Linnie's house and played his harmonica and sat with Linnie out on the stoop. Not Johnny, Colin's fishing buddy and best friend.

The crew boss shook his head. "Wish I could, but I can't. Rules are rules. If I don't follow them, I'm out of work and I've got nine mouths to feed, soon to be ten. Now, I'll carry him to your auto and I'll be careful as I can be."

The man, with surprisingly gentle hands, lifted Johnny, carried him over the rough, torn up ground to the automobile and eased him down on the back seat. "Good luck," he said.

The girl, while cranking up the auto, looked over the hood and shouted, "I'm Ann Easton. Mr. Dickerson's niece. Came up here to claim my uncle's body and the house. I'll do my best to get this boy to the doctor."

Colin said, "Where's the damned hospital Strom says they're gonna build? We pay on it every month, so where is it when we need it?"

Ann Easton said, "It's not. That's what. My uncle worked hard to try to see it happen. Too hard. That's why he was murdered."

So, the burnt man *was* Mr. Dickerson, but now the question loomed. Who murdered him?

The motor turned over, Ann hopped in the front seat and Birdie Mae took the seat beside her. Linnie and Colin sat on the floor beside Johnny in back. Linnie took hold of one of Johnny's dirty, rough hands. Johnny opened his eyes.

Colin said, "Hey, Johnny. Come Sunday, we're gonna go up to Blue Mirror Lake and hook the biggest danged trout we've ever caught."

A thought of a smile played on Johnny's face. Film covered his eyes. His hand slipped from Linnie's. His breath stopped. Piss leaked from under him.

Tears welled in Colin's eyes and for a moment he rested his head against one of Johnny's legs. He reached up and touched Ann Easton's shoulder. "Miss Easton," he called out. "Johnny passed."

Miss Easton slowed down. "Oh, Lord, I'm sorry. Where shall I . . ." She cleared her throat. "Where shall I take him?"

"His dad's place," said Birdie. "Stay on this road and I'll tell you when to turn off."

"I feel terrible about this. It isn't right. It's another example of capitalists working the labor class to death."

Linnie wondered. Capitalists? Yes. Johnny's death was plain wrong. If Miss Easton had got him to the doctor in town he might have lived. And where *was* the hospital Strom had promised folks for as long as Linnie could remember? Workers like her father and her brothers were docked money from their pay every two weeks to pay for it and there wasn't a hospital in sight.

Nobody was home at the Corrigan's place. Linnie and Colin, Birdie Mae and Ann lifted poor, dear Johnny from the auto, took him into the house and laid him on a bed. Colin offered to wash Ann's auto. Ann, Linnie, and Birdie washed Johnny and dressed him in a clean shirt and trousers.

Laying out the dead was not new. Two years ago they helped Mame Holm lay out her and Ollie's only son, struck down with pneumonia. Last year they helped Mide Finley and her mother lay out one of Mide's brothers, killed while bucking timber.

Finished with the task, Linnie went behind the house and picked white string flowers. She took them in and slipped them into Johnny's shirt pocket. She kept a silent watch over him and she swiped once or twice at her wet eyes.

If Mr. or Mrs. Strom found out about him, they wouldn't give a sugar moon. Cutting the danged trees and getting them down to the mill was more important than getting a boy on the locy and trying to save his life. And in spite of Birdie's mean words, Kees Strom was surely different from his rich, selfish folks.

CHAPTER 3

The following day, a warm day with sluggish gray clouds, Linnie used a shug stick to churn Birdie Mae's clothes—aprons, blouses, a pink flannel nightgown, flannel petticoats and skirts, long black stockings and drawers—in a washtub full of steaming soapy water. Birdie, using another stick, stirred the clothes in a tub of hot rinse. They worked quickly and in silence. With strong hands they wrung the clothes and pinned them on a rope line strung between two pine trees to dry. Birdie would soon take her things to her new home.

An auto came chugging up the road.

The girls smoothed their aprons and their hair before they went around to the front of their place. Ann Easton pulled up and stopped. She leaned out of the window. "Can only stay a minute," she said. "Again, let me say I'm sorry about your friend, Johnny, but I'm glad I've met you two. Friends of mine are coming to visit next Friday. Can you both come for lunch? A social like that might help take your mind off the loss of your friend."

"Thank you," Birdie Mae said. "I'd like to come, but I'm getting married week after next and I'm awfully busy." She turned to Linnie. "Why don't you go?"

"I will. Yes, I'd love to come to your party."

"Good. I'm going home for a few days, but I'll be back mid-week. On Friday I'll drive up around noon to get you.

We'll have a swell time. Toodle Ooo." She waved, and drove off.

"Now, isn't that something," said Birdie Mae. "She drives an auto like she was born to it. *I'm* going to learn to drive, too. Newt will teach me. And *you* are going to eat lunch with city folks at Mrs. Dickerson's house. If Mother was herself, she'd say, 'Isn't it grand.'"

"It is and it isn't. It *is* because I've never done anything like that. It isn't because I don't have any nice clothes. But I want to go more than I don't, so I'll go."

Late that afternoon Linnie and Dru sat at the table and leafed through a dog-eared *Sears Roebuck Catalog*. Dru pointed to a picture of a pair of high-buttoned black boots with pointed toes and high heels. "Aren't those pretty. As soon as I save enough money, I'll send for them. Buzz will like them. He says I'm the prettiest girl in all of Hanksport County."

"Mercy buckets," said Linnie. "Buzzie has turned your head all the way around and sideways. Every day, every *day*, you talk about him."

"I *like* him." She lazied her chin in her hand and gazed out the window. "And he likes me even more. Someday I'm going to marry him and we'll live in Seattle in a painted house." She turned to Linnie. "Do you know that none of us have ever even seen a painted house?"

"That's beside the point, Dru. Young girls like you start keeping company with older fellows and pretty soon the girl swells up. She and the fellow get married and have babies year after year after year and the girl gets old and wrung out quick. Buzz is nineteen years old. Four years older than you."

"That's one reason why I like him. He's grown up and he treats *me* like a grown-up, too."

"Oh, Dru." Linnie left the table and while she set plates and silverware for supper, she tried to consider Buzz on the bright side. He *was* a fine looking fellow. Flashing blue eyes. Black hair combed straight back off his face. Seemed he always had plenty of money, drove a fancy four-seat auto and he gave Dru beautiful presents. A pale blue silk shawl with a black fringe. A box of six linen handkerchiefs trimmed with lace. Last week when he came calling he gave her a silver brooch with a small pink enameled flower.

Dru kept her gifts tucked away in a dresser drawer. Every few days she took them out and displayed them on the table. Baby took particular delight in ogling them, but she minded Dru. She must not touch. Not ever.

And Buzz was right about one thing. Dru, with her thick, curly blond hair, blue eyes, a near perfect nose, and a sweet, full mouth, was favored. And she could sing better than anyone Linnie knew. Why, she could bring tears to the most sour-faced folks with her songs like "Beautiful Dreamer." "When You and I Were Young, Maggie." And she brought laughter with her rollicking "Won't You Come Home, Bill Bailey."

Over the past year or so, folks had paid her in scrip to sing at weddings and funerals. She kept the scrip in a canning jar and the jar was almost full.

Birdie Mae interrupted Linnie's musings. "Supper's ready."

Dru put the catalog aside and helped Birdie Mae dish up boiled beans and venison. Dru wrinkled her nose. "I get tired of eating this every day."

"It's not every day," said Birdie. "Yesterday we had cabbage, so quit nagging."

Linnie's place at table was next to Baby's. Oh, she was a nuisance. Fingernails bit down to the quick on her white, chubby hands. Give her a broom and tell her to sweep the floor, she'd grab the broom, swat at anyone in her way, put it between her legs and gallop around in circles. Ask her to help pluck a chicken, she'd grab it, hold it tight, pet it and put up a fuss when forced to give it over to one of her sisters.

"Help wash the dishes, Baby." She'd snort her big horsey laugh, slap at the dishwater and howl guffaws as water swelled up over the pan onto the floor.

Now, at supper, she kicked her bare feet back and forth. "Bay bee," she said. "Pretty Bay bee. Ma. Ma." She giggled. "Knockers. Bay bee. Knockers."

"Hush," said Linnie. "Hush and listen to Joe."

Joe bowed his head. "May the good Lord bless this house and accept us as sinners. And dear Lord, have mercy on Jim Corrigan and his living sons. Newt, Gavin, and Buzz." Joe's soft voice rose up. "Dear Lord, take Johnny Corrigan into Your arms and into the kingdom of heaven. And dear Lord, have mercy on Birdie Mae. Let her confess her sins and allow her to see Your glorious light. Let her . . ."

"Enough praying," Roy said. "Joe, we need to eat while our food is hot."

"Amen," said Joe. He turned to Birdie. "I believe you're in a family way?"

Birdie said, prim-like, her mouth set straight as a stick, "You know very well that Newt and I are getting married in two weeks."

The clattering racket of an automobile caught everybody's attention. Birdie Mae smiled. "Speaking of Newt, here he is."

Roy said, "Ask him in and serve him supper, daughter. If he wants to talk about Johnny, we need to listen."

The second oldest of the four Corrigan boys, reduced now to three—Buzz, Gavin and Newt—Newt was a tall, rangy fellow with bright blue eyes like his brothers. He had fine features and he, again like his brothers, combed his thick, coal-black hair straight back off his face. His trace of a smile broke easily into a wide grin and his blue eyes crinkled with good humor. Linnie didn't know anyone who disliked Newt Corrigan and in her heart she was proud to soon have him as her brother-in-law.

He parked his Rambler in front of the house and started for the door. Birdie went to meet him. He doffed his cap, took off his driving goggles and, arm-in-arm, the two came inside. "Hello, Mr. Bede," Newt said. He turned and nodded to Meara. "Mrs. Bede. Joe. Colin. Ladies. Well, Johnny passing like he did is tough."

Roy said, "Sit down, Newt. Join us for supper."

"Thank you, sir."

Birdie served up a plate of food, set it in front of him and sat beside him.

Newt said. "Gavin came home with me. I dropped him off and came straight here. Burial is next Saturday." He cleared his throat. No one spoke. Even Baby kept her silence. Newt said, "Well, Johnny wouldn't want us to be glum and . . . oh, good Lord, excuse me. I left something in my auto."

He hurried out and returned with a package wrapped in white tissue and tied with a green ribbon. He offered it to Birdie Mae. "This is for you."

Birdie's eyebrows shot up. "Why Newt, I'm real surprised." She unwrapped the box, carefully folded the tissue and plucked out a hand mirror in a gilded frame. "Oh, Newt." Her hand went to her throat. "For me?"

"For you."

"Why, it's beautiful." She peered into the mirror. "How did you know this is just what I've wanted for a long time?"

He smiled. "I suspected."

"Well, thank you. Oh, thank you."

Now that's nice, thought Linnie. Men always go about their business without giving women a thought except when they wanted to eat, or diddle and poke, but Newt regarded Birdie in a different light and he didn't mind showing it.

"Birdie," he said. "Father says that you and Linnie and Colin and a nurse were with Johnny when he passed."

"Yes. He looked so peaceful you'd have thought he was asleep."

"I don't think he suffered," said Colin. "Got caught in the bight of the line and was knocked clean out. He couldn't have known what hit him."

Linnie said, "The nurse's name is Ann Easton. She's the Dickerson's niece and she came up here to claim her uncle and the house. She said if we'd got Johnny to a doctor in time he might have made it."

"Is that so?" Newt stirred his beans. "It shouldn't have happened." He looked off beyond the stove.

Joe cut into the silence. "How does Gavin like living in Seattle?"

34

"Likes it fine. Likes school at the University. He and I went to a union meeting and I'll tell you, it's time for Strom workers up here to talk about organizing."

Silence, thick as bean stew, settled over the room. Colin said, "If union boys come up here, they'll drive spikes into logs and break our saws and donkey engines."

Joe agreed. "And if they take the notion to blow up the flume, they'll do it and we'd be out of work. Who knows when we'd get back."

Newt leaned across the table. "Who in tarnation told you that malarkey?"

"Fellows we work with," said Colin. "You know that."

"And that's what Strom tells you, too. Let me tell you some truth here. Union boys destroy things *only* as protest when negotiations between workers and owners break down. Union wants to be heard. Needs to be heard. Workers deserve higher wages and cleaner camps. All of you work like slaves for Strom. Yeah, you finally got the five-day-work-week, but hell—excuse me ladies—you took a decrease of four cents an hour to get it. And you deserve the eight-hour-day, not the ten or more you work, five days a week."

Joe stood, hitched his fingers in his suspenders. "I don't like this union talk. Strom keeps us working and we got that five-day work week last year without union help."

Yeah," said Newt. "But Strom feeds you lies. They don't want any of us up here to learn a thing about union. I say it's time we listen."

Joe sat down and wiped his brow with a large red hand-kerchief. "You have your thoughts, I'll keep mine."

Newt leaned across the table. "There are other concerns here. Women." He sat back and put an arm around Birdie

Mae and he spoke with no steam, but with certain force. "Women, like my Birdie Mae, they've got to get the right to vote. And as far as union goes, Dad and my brothers and I, even though we own our own business, should get on a soapbox and get the word out."

Joe said, "You all don't need to learn about it. You don't depend on Strom."

"If Gavin and Buzz and Father and I are going to hire folks who live up here and work for us, we've got to understand this business. And I'm not talking about any old union. I'm talking about the International Workers of the World. The I.W.W. They call themselves the Wobblies and the Wobblies make sense."

Linnie smiled. What a funny name. Wobblies.

Colin said, "Yeah, and they rob folks blind by taking their money every pay-day for union dues."

"Malarkey," said Newt. "Union's not gonna knock you up for dues every pay-day. Only once a month. And not a whole lot at that. Now, down in Seattle I heard a man named Dobbs give a speech. I talked to Dobbs. He knows about us up here. And folks are coming to visit Miss Easton next week to scout things out."

Linnie's heart quickened. "And I'll get to meet them." She told Newt about the invitation.

Newt said, "That's a good thing, Linnie."

Roy said, "Remember what happened to Sam Dickerson when he pushed folks to join? I don't want to see that happen again."

Newt said, "Dickerson's murder won't stop Dobbs. He says you all should get more than two bucks for that ten-hour day. And you should get paid in silver dollars. Not scrip. Those two bits you pay every two weeks for a hospital?"

"Yeah?" Colin said. "For Johnny's sake, I'll listen to what you have to say about that."

"Hospital's a scam. Dobbs says that Strom doesn't have a notion in the world to build it."

Good mercy, thought Linnie. Does Kees Strom know about this ugly business? But Kees with the dimpled smile and sleepy brown eyes couldn't possibly know of such mischief.

"So, what are we supposed to do?" said Colin.

Newt held up a pamphlet. "Read this."

Roy took it, looked it over, returned it and said, "I'll tell you a story I've never told anyone up here and you need to hear it." He took tobacco from his packet, fattened his pipe and leaned back in his chair. "In Chicago, back in 1894, Mrs. Bede and I joined the I.W.P.A. The International Working People's Association. We, like you, were educated people. We, like you, thought we could save the world. And we, too fought for the rights of women getting the vote."

Had Linnie heard right? Her mother had been part of a union? Women could do such a thing? She glanced at her mother who was fishing around in the pots on the stove. Did she even hear her husband, or if she did, did she give a sugar moon?

Colin gave words to her questions. "Father, you say Mother joined union?"

"Yes. We were young and smart and we wanted to help the common man. One day a crowd of us, over a hundred, went to a rally to agitate for an eight-hour day. The I.W.P.A., just like this I.W.W. outfit you're talking about, had all sorts of high-minded ideas. Why we believed that we could solve all the problems in the world for the working class."

Newt said, "That was sixteen years ago and you're still working ten-hour days."

Roy said, "Young man, you listen to the rest of my story."

Newt flushed up. "Yes, sir."

Roy drew on his pipe before he continued. "At that rally we agitated for the eight-hour-day. Well, some screwball threw a bomb into the crowd and all hell broke loose. Buildings were set on fire. Looters ran wild. Yet we fought for what we felt we deserved. We *believed* in union. We would have died for it." He thumped his gimpy leg. "But when some of us got hurt and crippled up for life, union boys turned their back on us. We lost our jobs. The I.W.P.A. blackballed us. Nobody would hire us. Mrs. Bede and I decided to come out here and not have anything to do with the union again. Only job I could find was working in the woods for Strom, a non-union outfit if I ever saw one."

Newt spoke up, his tone soft. "I'm not talking about the same union, Mr. Bede. The I.W.W. stands behind its folks. 'One Big Union.' One big family for workers all over the world."

"Doesn't matter," said Roy. "Big talk, but empty talk. Big dreams, but empty dreams. Union's a scummy bunch of folks who go around talking high and mighty about what they'll do for poor folks. Hell, that's easy. Then trouble comes and they don't do a damned thing to help."

"Well, I won't argue further," Newt said. "Not with Birdie and me getting married real soon." He stood up. "Thanks for supper, Mr. Bede. Come on, Birdie. Let's go for a ride while there's still daylight."

"Hold on just a minute," said Roy. "Newt, in spite of our different views about union, you and Birdie have my blessing. You're a good man, and I know you'll be good to my daughter."

"Thank you, sir. I surely do love her. And you and your family will always be welcome at our house."

Birdie Mae, still holding her mirror, started for the door.

Joe blocked her way. "Birdie," he said softly, "You need to go to church and ask the Lord to forgive you."

"Oh, Joe, stop your preaching."

"No. In the eyes of the Lord, you're a sinner."

"Wait just a minute," Roy said, "You've got no right to talk to your sister like that."

Joe squared his jaw. "I have the right to tell her that she needs to go to church and pray and ask the Lord to forgive her." His voice rose. "If she doesn't, she'll go to hell."

"Aw, dry up, Joe," Newt said.

"No. I won't dry up." He turned back to Birdie. "You, a Bede, allowed yourself to get in the family way before you're married. You've shamed us. You're soiled, Birdie and . . ."

Newt's fist arced high and smacked Joe square in his face.

Joe staggered back. "Well, son-of-a-gun." He rubbed his jaw. He sprang at Newt. The two bumped into Birdie. She fell with a hard thud. Her eyebrows arched with startled surprise and she sat, surrounded by pieces of shattered mirror, her blue skirt skewed above her pudgy knees.

Joe cried out, "Oh, Birdie, I . . ."

Blood pooled under Birdie and seeped into the wooden floor.

"Oh, God," Newt cried. "I'll get Doc Watson. Joe, you can go straight to hell."

Roy said, "Joe, because of your fool temper and med-dling you've brought trouble you didn't intend."

Linnie and Dru helped Birdie to bed. Dru, white faced and silent, swept up the broken mirror. Baby clambered up on the sofa, rocked back and forth and bit her fingernails until they bled. Linnie sat beside Birdie. She clasped and unclasped her hands again and again atop her slightly swollen belly. Tears glinted in her eyes. "I want to keep this baby," she said. "Newt and I already love it so much."

It wasn't long before Doc Watson and Newt came in. Doc set his satchel down, knelt and gently felt Birdie's belly. "What happened here? Newt said you took a bad fall."

"I did."

"That's not quite right," said Newt. "Me and Joe . . ."

"Got to scuffling," Birdie said. "They've scuffled since they were tad poles and this time I got in the way." Her face crumpled. Her voice got small. "Please tell me I can keep this baby."

The doctor took a small bottle filled with clear liquid from his satchel. "Miss Bede," he said to Linnie. "Please make some tea and add ten drops of this. Cramp bark should help relax her." He took a chair and sat down beside Birdie Mae. He spoke quietly. "I have to be honest with you, Miss Bede. I can't promise that you will keep the baby. You took an awfully hard fall."

Birdie's soft sobs almost broke Linnie's heart. She gave the tea to Birdie and in silence she and Dru cleared away the unfinished supper.

Some time later the doctor picked up his satchel. "The bleeding has stopped and sleep is the best thing for her.

When she wakes up she must stay quiet. Help her use the bucket. Wait on her. I'll stop by early tomorrow to see how she's doing."

Roy paid the doctor in scrip.

Before Newt left to take Doc Watson home, he said to Linnie, "If she wakes up, tell her I'll buy her another mirror tomorrow."

Baby plopped down beside Birdie. She ran her fat, clumsy fingers through Birdie's hair. A curious puzzle. Baby, brash, awkward, dumb and difficult most of the time, slipped into a kind of gentle other self when something troubling, like Birdie's anguish, happened.

Roy, Joe, and Colin settled themselves outside out on the stoop. Roy lit his pipe. Colin rolled a cigarette. Joe was slumped in the far corner.

Linnie went to the washtubs behind the house to help Dru wash Birdie's bloody clothes. "Men," Linnie scoffed. "A woman gives birth, or has trouble, and fathers, husbands, brothers, or uncles are either at work, or off fishing or hunting. If they're home they sit and smoke somewhere out of the way. Men are useless creatures."

"Some are," said Dru. "Some aren't."

"On, Lord, Dru. I hope to goodness that none of us Bedes ever has a baby like Baby. And I think of women like Mrs. Corrigan who died while birthing and I think of women who run away and sometimes they use knitting needles to . . ."

Dru slapped at the water. "Stop it. I'm not going to listen to anymore of your prattle." She left Linnie to finish the wash alone.

Questions, thought Linnie. So many questions. What *could* women do to stop babies from coming? And just who might know about things like that? City girls, like Ann Easton, that's who. Girls with city schooling and when Linnie met Ann again, she would ask lots of questions about it. But now, Birdie might lose her baby and Birdie needed her mother and where was *she*? Sitting out on the danged stump.

In the soft velvet twilight of evening Linnie hurried across the reach. "Mother," she said. "Do you hear me?"

"Yes."

"Please come with me to be with Birdie. She's in trouble and she needs you."

"No. A loud, naughty girl lives in my house. I'm afraid of her. She shouts and bangs on pans and breaks things. Someday she'll break my dishes."

"We keep those things up on the high shelf, away from her. And she's yours. Just like Birdie and Dru and me and Joe and Colin are yours. She's ours, Mother. Do you hear me?"

"She *isn't* mine and she's *not* ours and I want her to go away."

"Mother, you birthed her twelve years ago. She didn't ask to be born dim-witted and you need to give her a real name. Next month, on June 2nd she'll turn thirteen. Mercy be. Will we still call her 'Baby?' "

Meara said, her voice small and thin. "I think I once had a baby named 'Alice.' But that naughty girl isn't her. She's not mine. Now go away."

Linnie, her heart heavy as stone, returned to the house.

The men sat quietly visiting a little and smoking. Linnie went to her father, "You get off nice and easy, don't you. It's not Mother's fault that she's the way she is. If you'd stayed off her, she wouldn't have had all of us kids."

Roy frowned, put his pipe aside and said, "You listen to me, daughter and you listen well. I've never done one thing with your mother that she didn't want me to do and you remember that."

Silenced, puzzled, and shamed Linnie went in the house. What had her father meant? Had her mother *wanted* him to get on top of her all those times?

Baby, quiet and watchful, still sat beside Birdie.

Dru had set a bucket of water on the stove to heat. The family would soon come in, silently wash up and go off to bed.

But sudden and quick, Birdie Mae cried out, "Help me. Oh, help me. I'm cramping up fierce." She grunted hard, sharp grunts and she pushed out a lump that looked like a small fish, its head curled inward. Birdie sobbed. "Oh, no. No. No. I lost my baby and I loved it so much."

Linnie picked a soft, clean rag out of a ragbag, wrapped the tiny being and said to Dru, "Ask Joe to make a suitable box and bury this beside Lily. Maybe he'll come to his senses and understand the sorrow he's caused."

Dru, pale and shaken, took the bundle and left the house. Baby started to follow her. Linnie said, "Baby, no. You stay here, inside." Baby sat on the couch and chewed on her bloodied fingers.

Linnie packed thick pieces of flannel between Birdie Mae's legs. When the bleeding eased, Linnie made another cup of tea laced with laudanum. She gave it to Birdie and Birdie slept.

Linnie and Dru got Baby to bed. Meara came in, went to the bedroom and closed the door. She had no idea that she'd lost a grandchild and she had no idea that her oldest daughter grieved deep.

Sunday, mid-morning, Newt came by. Birdie Mae put forth a sunny demeanor, but her eyes held a haunted look. When Newt gave her a pretty mirror set in a shiny black frame she expressed her pleasure, but she was quiet about it. Newt sat with her. "We'll have us a baby, Birdie. Just as soon as we can." He stayed with her and drank tea and then kissed her before going off with his father and brothers to make final arrangements for Johnny's funeral.

Joe, hat in hand, came to Birdie, knelt and again asked her forgiveness. "I'm sorry," he said. "I'd never want to hurt you. But, I can't stand the thought of you burning in hell forever."

Birdie Mae put one hand atop his head. "I know you didn't mean to hurt me." She tousled his red hair. "Don't be so hard on yourself, Joey. I'll be all right. Newt and I can make another baby, as Newt says, 'just as soon as we can.' Now, what happened to my little baby?"

"I buried it next to Baby Lily's grave and I made a little cross and I set it there."

"Thank you."

"I'm moving up to Camp Two, Birdie. I need to live on my own. Kees Strom told me he'd save a bunk for me."

Linnie was startled. "Kees doesn't live at home?"

"Well, I guess not, if he bunks at Two."

Why in the world would Kees, who could live in the big house up on the hill overlooking town and the Blackduck River, want to live in a dirty old bunkhouse?

Roy said to his son, "You'll come around once a week, won't you."

"Sure. And, like always, you'll get a good part of my pay."

Roy gave his son a quick, awkward hug. Joe pecked his mother's cheek, hugged Linnie and Dru and patted Baby's blond curls. He picked up his bindle. "Birdie, if you and Newt need help on your house, let me know."

"Even though you think I'm a sinner, you'd better come to my wedding."

"I'll be there." His tone was stiff as new cardboard.

Linnie watched him from the open door. Tramps, looking for jobs carried bindles from camp to camp. Joe had a job. He had family. She wanted to run after him. *Please, don't leave. With your bad temper, I'm scared you'll get in trouble. I don't want you to live at a camp, Joey. I want you to live at home with us.*

At Camp Two, Kees was waiting for Joe in the two-story bunkhouse. "Hey, Joe. I'm sure glad to see you. I saved the bunk above me. Or, if you want the lower, I'll take the top."

Joe eyed the two rows of straw pallets atop the bunks. "Thanks," he said. "I'll take the one over there." He pointed to an unoccupied bunk at the far end of the place.

"Aw, come on, Joe. I want to be your friend."

Joe shrugged. "I don't know you very well, but I'd say you're my friend." He grinned. "You're sure not my enemy." He flung his bindle atop the bunk, untied the rope and pulled out his Bible.

"I see you like to read in the Good Book," said Kees.

"Read in the Old Testament every day." Joe tucked his Bible under his arm and left.

Kees grabbed his Bible and followed him. "Hey," he shouted. "I'll join you."

Joe stopped. "I'm told that supper's coming up," he said. "I don't mean to hurt your feelings, but I like to be alone. Listen, pal, it's not you. It's just the way I am."

CHAPTER 4

Rain poured from peevish, gray skies on the day Linnie was to have lunch at Ann Easton's house. Birdie Mae had recovered and was up and about, but Linnie was reluctant to leave. "How are you feeling?" she said for the umpteenth time.

"I'm fine and I want you to go to the lunch party. If Mother was herself, she'd want you to go."

Dru said, "I'll loan you my pink sash. You'll look stylish, Linnie. And you can borrow my blouse with the lace collar and cuffs."

"Thank you. And I *will* borrow your things, but I wish you'd come with me."

"Buzz is coming over. Wear my blouse and sash and I wager you'll like how you look."

Late morning, Linnie washed herself with the nice soap, put on Dru's white cotton blouse and fussed with the dark, rose-pink lace-trimmed cuffs.

How did she do it? Dru could take any old dress, a skirt or blouse, add a touch of lace or ribbons, and the garment became fashionable. For this particular sash she'd taken a number of pale pink ribbons from one of her mother's hats and she'd sewed them together and made a graceful bow at the side of the sash. Linnie put it on and Dru was right. Linnie considered herself quite stylish.

She took one of her mother's hats, a white straw hat, festooned with black organdy and long, black feathers. When she heard the rattle of an auto approaching, she plopped on the hat and was out the door before allowing herself time to get nervous jumps in her belly.

"The hat," said Ann. "It's the bees knees, and you look gorgeous."

"Thank you." Linnie's voice wavered. "I've not met many city people. Living up here, like we do, we just . . . don't."

"You'll like my friends and you'll feel easy with all of them." Ann put her attentions to maneuvering her automobile up the rough road and through and around mud puddles. On a smooth stretch, just before coming to the house, she said. "You'll meet my honey-bug, Paul Garibaldi. And Hale Tosstles, who cooks at a union hall in Seattle. He never uses his first name, so just call him 'Tosstles.' Bruns Wald is an attorney. Frank Dobbs, a lively, keen fellow, and his honey-bug, Sophie, had planned to come, but they couldn't make it. We're all Wobblies."

"Wobblies," said Linnie. "Yes. The other night Newt Corrigan, Birdie's sweetie, told us something about Wobblies."

"Good. I like to hear that. We're members of the I.W.W. That means Workers of the World and we believe in equality and brotherhood. It's *good* to know that word about us is getting around."

"What do Wobblies do?"

"For starters, we share a philosophy of a global view. One Big Union. We fight for folks like your father and your brothers. Strom workers up here deserve to be paid higher wages. And Strom bunkhouses are infamous. Awful. Bunks with lice infested straw. Bad food. Spoiled meat. Rancid bacon. We've got plenty of testimony."

"My brother lives in a bunkhouse and I've never heard him, or anyone else, complain."

"You probably won't hear it, either. It's bad up here, Linnie. Jobs are scarce everywhere so it's impossible for men and women who work for Strom to demand better pay. They're trapped. Add to the misery the fact that most women up here have children year after year. They know nothing about 'family limitation.' "

"Landsakes," said Linnie. "So that's what it's called. 'Family Limitation.' Well, I'll tell you that almost every woman I know has too many children. My mother had too many and her last baby, my youngest sister, isn't right in her head. If I knew how to stop all the birthings, I'd go all over Hanksport County and talk about it."

"Now, *that's* an idea. I do know enough to insist that my honey-bug must use a condom."

"What's that?"

"A rubber."

Linnie laughed. "How can rubbers stop babies?"

"Not the kind we wear on our feet. Men put rubbers on their . . . you-know-what."

Linnie frowned. "That doesn't make any sense."

Ann pulled up beside her uncle's house and parked beside one of two automobiles. "I'll try to explain this business later. Now I want you to enjoy the party."

Big rafters. Shiny, varnished log walls. Limp, white curtains hung at tall, many-paned windows. But a fire blazing in a large rock fireplace had not overcome a damp, musty chill. Ann hung Linnie's hat on a hat tree and introduced her to Paul Garibaldi, a short, swarthy fellow with dark eyes and a confident air. His bushy eyebrows looked like black caterpillars. "Miss Bede," he said. "Ann has spoken about you and your sister. I'm so pleased to meet you. And what beautiful country. Ann and I may want to settle up here someday."

"Oh, I hope you *do*."

The attorney, Bruns Wald, a tall, loose-framed man with a big sunny face, curly blonde hair, and a neighborly air, said, "I've never seen timbers like those I've seen up here. Am I right, Miss Bede, in assuming that some folks make a decent living?"

"Strom makes money. Workers like my father and brothers, who work for Strom, make enough to live on."

"What do your people do?"

"My father is a flume tender. Colin, one of my brothers, sets choke. My oldest brother is a bolt puncher."

Tosstles, a big, stocky fellow with carrot-red hair and a great bib of a beard, said, "Well, this surely is beautiful country. Thick forests. I'll bet the pretty rivers are full of fish. I'll wager that in a short time a lot of folks will discover this place and will want to live up here."

Ann excused herself. Linnie found that she was the center of attention.

Mr. Wald said, "It's a capitalist paradise, Miss Bede. Consider the lumber baron, Max Strom, the fellow your family works for."

"Yes. Most folks up here work for Strom."

"Strom and his wife have made, and continue to make fortunes off the backs of laborers, in large part because of the miserably low wages they fork out."

"That's right," said Paul. "And they use the weapon of fear to keep the working class under control. *Fear* of losing jobs. *Fear* of cutting wages. So, the rich get richer and gain power over the poor."

"I believe you, sir," said Linnie.

Ann called her guests to the dining room to eat. On a sideboard a stack of pamphlets lay beside an odd contraption with a long handle and a flat disk. Scarlet creeper in a brown bottle with a blue sheen sat in the middle of the dining table. The pair-shaped bottle was plain odd and Linnie had no idea what the contraption on the sideboard might be.

She was seated between Tosstles and Mr. Wald. Ann passed platters of meat loaf, tomato chutney and cucumber salad. Bruns poured dark red wine into goblets, one at each place. He lifted his glass. "May the Capitalist's wine turn to wormwood. Here's to us Socialists. Here's to us Wobs."

Linnie found the wine a little bitter, but not unpleasant.

Mr. Garibaldi lifted his glass. "The I.W.W. is the most significant social movement happening in America," he said. "We'll change the way people view the working class. We'll change the way people view *women* for women must have the right to vote."

Discussion about union, women's rights and the I.W.W. flowed without let-up. Linnie tried to take in every word. Union fought for the working man. Fought for better pay, better working conditions and decent homes.

Over coffee and a lemon crumb pie, Ann said, "Frank is coming up for a Fourth of July picnic at the park next month. I can't be there. Linnie, I work at Providence Hospital and when I asked for *this* time off, I promised I'd work over the holiday."

Bruns said, "Isn't Sophie coming with Frank?"

"No. She's giving a lecture to a group of women in Seattle. Can any of you be at the park to show Frank support? If he's arrested, as we expect he'll be, somebody will post bail."

Tosstles, Mr. Wald and Mr. Garibaldi had other commitments.

"I'll go," said Linnie. "I'd like to hear him. I think my sister and her husband will want to hear him, too."

"Good," said Ann. "He won't disappoint you. And someday you must meet Sophie. She's a splendid suffragist. A real liberator of women. Because of women like her, we *will* vote someday soon. And we *will* have a *voice* and we *will* be heard on the topic of family limitation."

Late afternoon the party broke up. Tosstles and Bruns went upstairs to work on speeches. Linnie said to Ann, "It's been such a lovely party and thank you. I see it's stopped raining and I'll enjoy the walk home."

"You're sure?"

"Yes."

Ann and Paul saw her to the door. "I must ask," Linnie said. "What is the strange machine on the sideboard?"

Paul said, "It's a small printing press Sam used for printing pamphlets. It will come in handy, believe me." He sniffed the wet air. Out over the reach grasses and lupine and daisies—shone vivid beauty in the fresh, watery sunshine. "This is almost too beautiful to be true," Paul said. "Miss Bede, you are fortunate to live up here."

Ann put her arm around him and hugged him and she said to Linnie, "He's taken with this country. I knew he would be and I've always loved it. We'll be back, but I don't know when. When we do, I'll drive over to see you first thing. You might consider joining us, Linnie. You'd be a swell Wob."

Instead of taking the old skid-road home, Linnie crossed the clearing and followed a little-used trail to a meadow. A couple of years ago she'd hauled a half dozen rocks to a shallow place in the creek and placed them as stepping stones in the busy, rushing water.

On the other side of the meadow a rock, a good three feet high and four feet wide reminded her of a big thimble turned upside down and she'd named the rock, "Thimble Creek Rock," and the meadow, "Thimble Creek Meadow."

She enjoyed coming to this place, and she had never shared it with a soul, not even Birdie Mae. She would bring one of her mother's books with her and she'd sit on the rock and read. Henry James's *Portrait of a Lady* was her favorite. She admired Isabel's spunk and how she dealt with her unhappy marriage. Linnie noted that the luxurious, moneyed world was in fact a troubled world of deceit and sorrow.

The book spurred her to think about what she wanted for herself. She didn't want to get married right away. She wanted to teach.

She crossed the creek and made her way through long strappy grasses and the wildflowers to the rock she considered her own. She sat down. A "liberator of women" had to be someone who brought freedom to women. Freedom to vote. Freedom to have a say about life.

A thread of an idea caught her thoughts. A woman's place in the world meant marriage, obeying a husband. Didn't marriage vows say a woman should love, honor and obey a husband? The husband might want lots of children and give no thought to what his wife might want. So, a "liberator of women" must believe in a woman's freedom to make decisions of her own. And there *were* ways to help women from having too many children. Linnie must learn about it, but tomorrow Ann would leave and Linnie had no idea when she'd be back.

CHAPTER 5

Early afternoon on the day of Johnny Corrigan's funeral, Parley Hearn came by the Bede's house. This was the fourth time in the past month he'd made his presence known. Some six months ago he'd stopped by to introduce himself to Roy. He'd had a small, runty brown dog with him. Linnie was not impressed with the bean-pole of a man with a strong, hooked nose, coarse dark hair, high color and black eyes.

On the day of the funeral he offered Linnie a limp bouquet of grass pinks. "Miss Bede, it's my pleasure to offer these and accompany you to the funeral."

"Thank you."

He leaned down and patted his dog. He straightened and his smile was open and genuine. "I call him 'Pal,'"

Linnie set the flowers in a canning jar. She cared not one whit about the name of the man's dog.

Dru, who was brushing Baby's hair, tied a wide pink ribbon around Baby's head and fashioned it into a bow. "Pretty Baby," she said.

Baby smiled. "Pretty Baby. Pretty Baby knockers."

Pal went to Meara and curled up at her feet. Meara leaned over and petted him and a smile played on her face. Baby lumbered over to her mother. She pointed to herself and to the pink hair bow. "Bay bee," she said. "Pretty Bay bee." She plopped down and tried to pick up the dog. The dog scrambled away.

"Baby, get up," Linnie said. "You're going to town with us and we're leaving in about five minutes."

Baby jumped up and smiled. "Bay bee go. Bay bee knockers go."

But for Meara, the family and Parley started walking down the road to town. Parley, walking alongside Linnie, said, "It's a sad day, going to Johnny's funeral, but I'm proud to be with you, Miss Bede. Say, may I call you 'Linnie,' and would you mind calling me, 'Parley?' "

She shrugged. "No harm in that."

"Thank you. Now, I think your father has something to say."

Roy stepped back to walk with Linnie and Parley. "Daughter," he said, "Parley has asked me for permission to ask you for your hand in marriage. Now, you'd look for a long time and not find a man as fine as he is. I gave him my consent and it's time you set a date."

Linnie caught her breath. "But . . . Father. I . . . I'm not looking to find a man. I've told you a hundred times, I want to go to Seattle and find a job, work and go on to school."

"Your dreams of going to Seattle are pipedreams and nothing more. What it boils down to is this. It's time you get married."

"If Mother was herself, she'd understand my feelings. You plain don't and . . ." She turned to Parley. "No offense, but I don't want to marry anybody."

"I'm standing firm on this," said Roy. "Now, you settle yourself."

Linnie knew that tone. She was as trapped as a beaver caught in one of her father's traps, but she would have a word or two about it before it was done. "I have something to say," she said.

"And what's that?" said Roy.

"That will be my own business with Parley and I'll talk to him when I decide to and when we're alone."

Linnie, seated on one of the long benches in First Baptist Church, craned her neck and scanned the crowd. Buzz sat with his father and brothers, a handsome lot who took after their mother. Mrs. Corrigan, now deceased, had been a beautiful woman with dark hair and startling blue eyes. Linnie's father said Jim Corrigan still grieved over his loss of her and the baby girl.

Kees Strom, with his pal Soapy Metzler, sat across the aisle and down two rows. The back of Kees's neck looked so nice she wanted to touch it and run her fingers up through his curly brown hair. He was the most handsome, polite boy she'd ever known. His hair was always neatly combed and he had those sleepy, brown eyes and he always wore nice vests and knickers and caps.

She didn't know him well. He'd been three years ahead of her in school and the first time she met him was at the Company Store in town three—no four years ago.

"Hello there," he'd said and he tipped his cap. "It's Linnie Bede, the flume tender's daughter, isn't it?"

"Yes."

"Well, I'm pleased to meet you, Miss Bede."

"Thank you."

He smiled and went on his way.

She saw him again at the Fourth of July picnic last summer. And last fall at a wedding, with dancing afterwards, he asked her to dance. He wasn't a good dancer, but he spoke lively about his work that past year over in Idaho.

Now, seated in church, she wondered how he regarded her and her family. Her own navy blue, ankle length skirt and white blouse with a navy blue bow at the neck were acceptable. Dru's frock with the pink ribboned sash was fashionable and a wreath of daisies she'd made and tucked in her hair was pretty. Baby's dark skirt and white middy were fine and every now and then Baby, her face wreathed in a smile, touched the pink hair bow on top of her curls as if to see that it was still there.

Birdie Mae's sky blue cotton dress with a tucked bodice was nice. And Linnie's father and Joe and Colin, wearing clean white shirts and serge suits—even though the suits were worn—were passable. Kees would surely consider the Bede family in a favorable light.

Dru, called on to sing, went up front and her rich-throated voice soared out over the room. "Rock of ages, cleft for me . . ."

Preacher talked about Johnny living in heaven and how fortunate he was to be in the arms of the Lord. Linnie didn't believe Johnny was in anybody's arms. But maybe his soul was in a better place than in the dark, wet woods of Hanksport County.

After the service the Bede family and Parley walked back up the narrow road home.

Parley asked to speak to Linnie's father and the two went out on the back stoop. Linnie felt wrung out and old. If they were talking about her and her marriage to Parley, there was nothing in the world she could do about it.

❦

Two days later Parley arrived at the Bede house with a handsome mare and a spanking new wagon. He turned the reins of the horse over to Roy. "I hope you find this useful," he said. "It's my pleasure to give it to you and your family."

"We will find it useful and I thank you."

Without another word, Parley went walking up the road.

Roy, as tight-lipped as Linnie had ever seen him, told his children that Parley had insisted on buying the horse and wagon. "He says we need it and he wants us to enjoy it. I'm a proud man, but I couldn't argue with that."

Linnie gave thought to the matter. Parley must have means. It had been hard for her father to accept the gift, but if she was Parley's wife, who knows what Parley might do for the Bede family? The notion stuck in Linnie's mind and she couldn't find peace with it, yet it was a good sight better to think about that, than think about the burnt man.

❦

A week later Roy drove his children and Parley in the wagon to First Baptist for Birdie Mae and Newt's wedding. Birdie had never looked so happy and her curls shone like gold under the garland of daisies and bleeding hearts.

Dru sang, "Let Me Call You Sweetheart" and her eyes and sweet smile lingered on Buzz. To Linnie, it was a mystery. Dru, smitten with Buzz. Birdie Mae, nuts about Newt. Linnie considered Parley a nice enough man, but nothing more than that.

After the wedding, when Newt and Birdie waved and drove off in the Corrigan's automobile, a dry, unsettled lone-liness gripped Linnie and she said to Parley, "I already miss her. I'd like to walk home. Alone. I hope you understand."

"Well, I suppose I'll have to, but when do you want to talk to me?"

"Maybe at the Fourth of July picnic."

"The Fourth of July is a ways away."

"It is. Well, it was nice of you to give us the horse and wagon, but remember, please. I'm not looking to marrying anybody at all."

CHAPTER 6

One morning in mid-June, after the men left for work, Linnie eyed a slab of elk meat on the table, picked up a butcher knife and sliced the meat clean through.

Dru, humming a tune while washing the breakfast dishes, turned to Linnie and said, "Buzz is coming by today. We're driving over to Coldsprings to look at the new hotel. Someday soon, Buzz will take me over there for dinner."

Linnie set her knife aside. "That's nice, but on all of these little outings you take with Buzz, you don't allow him to diddle you, do you?"

Dru's chin went up. "That's none of your business."

"It is my business. You allow Buzz to love you up, you'll end up having a baby and then, you're trapped. You'll have another baby, and another and you'll never get out of here."

"This is *my* business. I love Buzzie and he loves me and we love our loving each other a lot."

"Oh, Lord, Dru. You allow him to drop his seed inside you?"

Her cheeks flamed. "Yes. He didn't want to . . . leave me. And I didn't want him to. We're going to get married and so are Colin and Mide and we'll all go to Seattle and Buzzie and I will live in painted house with a white picket fence."

"That's what he tells you?"

"Yes. He promised."

"And that's what Colin told Mide?"

"I don't know. She doesn't want children right away, but I *want* to have Buzzie's babies."

Linnie slammed her fist down on the table. "No."

Dru's eyes got wide as a cat's yawn.

"You're digging your own grave. Look at you. Hardly grown and allowing that fellow to love you up. Where is it going to get you? Nowhere. You're smart and you're pretty and you have a beautiful voice and you love music. *Please* finish high school. Do the two years left in one like I did. Then *go* to Seattle. Find a job and go on to school at the university. Please, don't believe that devilish chap who makes promises he'll probably never keep."

"He's *not* a devilish chap. I don't *want* to finish school and you know that you can't get in the family way the first few times you love each other."

"Buzzie tells you *that*?"

"Yes. And it's true."

"That's a bald-faced lie." Linnie's voice rose. "You'll have one baby. Then another. And another. And another. Six. Seven. Ten. A dozen. Look at Mother. She shouldn't have had all of us and after Baby was born, she went nuts."

Dru set her chin. "I'm going to marry Buzzie and you can't stop me."

"And you'll be old and worn out before you're twenty."

"Don't talk to me like that. *You* don't love Parley. *I* love my man and *I* love his loving me, but *you* don't understand that."

"How I feel about Parley doesn't have a thing to do with you." Tears welled in Linnie's eyes. She and Dru might argue now and then, but they had never said cruel words to each other. And now, even Baby's constant yammer was quiet. When Linnie turned to see what she was up to, Baby's eyes, bright as blue nails, were fixed on her and Dru.

CHAPTER 7

Baby turned thirteen on June 2. A couple of days later, when Linnie was out hoeing in the weed-choked garden, Baby lumbered out.

"Baww!"

Tears coursed down her face. Blood ran down her legs.

Birdie Mae, Dru and Linnie had tried to explain "women's monthlies" to Baby. They had shown her the bag of rags kept in their bedroom. They had shown her the scrubbing and drying the rags and putting them back in the bag. They couldn't have spoken any more close and personal about this touchy subject, but Baby had fidgeted and got cross and it was plain to see that she didn't understand.

Now, she was terrified. "Batty loon. Batty loon."

Linnie took hold of her shoulders. "It's alright." She pointed to herself and nodded her head. "Me, too. It's all right. Dru. Birdie Mae. Mide. All of us women. Women." She nodded. "It's all right. Blood comes and we *can now* have babies. Yes. Blood comes once a month. Like has happened to you. When that happens we know we're old enough to have babies."

Linnie put her hands on her belly and softly sang, "Rock-a-bye, Baby. In the treetop."

Baby laughed. She folded her arms. "Rock Baa bee. Rock . . . Baa bee."

Linnie nodded. "Yes. Now, if the blood *stops* coming, we women know that we *will* have a baby. A baby is growing inside us." Again, she put her hands on her belly and sang the lullaby.

She took Baby's hand, led her inside and showed her how to pin rags between her legs. She sat with her at the table and again tried to explain the cycle. Baby's brow wrinkled up and her mouth turned down. Linnie said, "Don't worry about that. You must be married before you have a baby."

That afternoon Birdie dropped by for a visit. Linnie said to her and Dru, "I *think* Baby understood a little about monthlies."

"She's growing up," said Birdie. "Newt suggests that we try to teach her the alphabet. Teach her something to keep her busy."

Linnie and Dru agreed and a week later Birdie Mae bought Baby a big writing tablet and two fat pencils. Every day one of Baby's sisters sat with her at the table and guided her pudgy hands around A and B. Baby took to her task and sat for hours laboriously writing the two letters.

As time went on, one of her sisters added two more. C and D. And later, E and F.

CHAPTER 8

At one end of Strom's front room a hefty Bible sat on a large oak table. Three straight-back chairs sat in precise order around a polished dining table. A four-foot high papal cross inscribed in Latin, INRI, hung on one of the dull gray walls. Three tall windows overlooked the Blackduck River, the town of Hanksport and the bay. There were no other furnishings, decorative touches, or rugs.

On The Fourth of July, Kees Strom's mother, Inga Strom, stood in front of the fireplace in which a meager fire sputtered. She recited prayers. Kees stood beside his father who was confined to a wheelchair. After Inga pronounced, "Amen," Kees went to stand at one of the windows.

Inga joined him. "Last week I put out notice for help up here," she said. "Yesterday I hired a young man, Joe Bede, to work on Thursdays. And on Sunday afternoons after church. He'll continue to work for the company three days a week."

"Why did you hire Joe?"

"He was the best applicant. And smart."

"He'll do a good job, Mother, but he likes to be alone."

"That's fine. He wants to be paid in silver, not scrip. And he and I struck a bargain."

Kees laughed. "Joe put *you* in the position of having to bargain?"

"I can do that when necessary. In case our workers join union and go out on a strike—God forbid—Joe won't go along with it. He starts up here next week." She picked up a pair of binoculars and peered down at the town. "People are going to the park," she said. "I loathe holidays."

"You only allow two. Christmas and this one."

"God put less intelligent creatures on this earth to work for those of us smart enough to make money. I think back to the one-wagon operation your father and I brought up here almost twenty years ago. We had no thought of taking a day off. The only time I took a holiday was when you were born. And that was hardly a holiday."

"There are times, Mother, when I think you shouldn't have had me."

"Well, I'm glad I did. And now, with your father, sick as he is, you are the only one I can talk to. This looming problem with union bothers me."

Kees shrugged. "Union has spread the word. Workers today believe they're owed. Not owned."

"I loathe their selfish demands. If we're forced to go to the eight-hour-day, we stand to lose a lot of money. You'd think that the five-day-work-week would satisfy them. Their wages are reasonable and as for improving their living conditions, that's nonsense. The places we provide are far better than what they had before they came to work for us. Their complaints about the pittance we dock from their pay once a month is ridiculous. We need that money to upgrade our operations and build a hospital."

"Your workers know they're being cheated and they're irked."

"That's what you hear?"

"Of course it is."

"I'll fight them every inch of the way."

"You might fight them, but I'm not sure you'll win."

"I'll win. And Kees. I hate to think of you sleeping in a bunkhouse with those common men. I wish you'd sleep here at home. You know very well that your father would want you to work in the office with me."

"Up here I'm isolated and shut off from town."

"You should be isolated. You aren't one of them. But, let's not argue. How's Soapy? I haven't seen him for a while."

"The funeral business is good. Last month four people died, including a young fellow who worked for us. I went to his funeral. Soapy plans to buy out Mr. Morrison and pay you back by the end of the year."

"I'm not worried. Soapy is good on his word. He's got a good head for business."

Inga went to her husband. After wiping drool from his mouth and chin, she tied a clean bib around his neck and re-tucked the blanket around his knees.

Inga—tall and slender with fine features and brown eyes, her honey colored hair coiled in a smooth thick bun, her plain black dress buttoned high on her graceful throat—bore herself well. Her long, tapered fingers with a gold wedding band on her left hand were beautiful, but Kees could not imagine those hands cuddling him, as an infant, to give comfort.

Years ago, when nightmares of a wall of black dogs with yellow eyes and tiny ears cornered him and he cried out, "Mother, help me, Mother," her pale face floated above a candle and she whispered, "Hush. Hush. Don't be a cry-baby, Kees. Your father and I need our rest."

As Kees grew older he became interested in plants. He spent hours tramping through the woods along the Blackduck

River while looking for trapper's tea, fringe cups and bar-
berries. When finding these treasures, he dug them up and
took them to school. A teacher interested in botany at the
Hanksport grade school identified them and was pleased to
allow eleven-year old Kees the time and place to study the
plants under his microscope.

Kees spent long hours studying the trapper's tea white
petals and fragile stems, the texture of fringe cups' rich green
foliage and slender wands of dark pink petals. He learned that
the stout stalk of Bear Grass supported a large knob of tiny
white flowers. And Indians used the tough leaves to weave
clothing and baskets and they roasted and ate the rootstock.

As Kees got older he sensed his father's disapproval, but
he continued with his studies, reading as much as he could
find about the plants he found in the world around him.
Someday he would leave Hanksport and his parents' business, in which he had no interest. He would go to Seattle,
attend the University of Washington and pursue a career in
botany.

But Kees's father had something to say about that. "Prissy
Sissy. Sissy Prissy," he taunted him. "You spend your spare
time studying flowers? Next thing you'll tell me you want to
go to University and study bugs."

"Yes, sir. That's exactly what I want to do. I want to
become a botanist."

"Don't go against me, Prissy Sissy. Sissy Prissy. Prissy
Sissy. You'll stay right here and run this logging operation.
Understand?"

From that day on Kees's father failed to call Kees by his
given name. "Sissy Prissy," or "Prissy Sissy" was his habit of
speaking.

Now, Inga bent again to her husband, her tone anxious. "Are you warm enough?"

He shook his head.

"Kees," Inga said, "Please bring in some wood and build up the fire."

"I can't believe he's cold on such a warm day."

"Nor can I, but he is."

In the kitchen the Strom's cook and housekeeper was preparing supper. Kees said, "Marta, people are gathering down in the park. Can you put together a picnic basket for me?"

"Of course. Ham sandwiches and fried potato balls? And how about the rest of last night's baked beans?"

"That will be nice. What do you have for desert?"

"I made the chocolate potato cake for supper tonight."

"Can you make something else for Mother? I'd love to take the cake to the picnic. I want to share your good food with all of my friends. I have quite a number you know."

"Yes. Your mother loves my nut roll. The chocolate cake is yours."

"Thank you, Marta."

Kees considered Marta his friend. She'd been with the family all of Kees's life. She was a thin woman of forty some years. She wore her blond hair braided in plaits on top of her head. She only went to town to shop for food at the Company Store and she rarely mingled with town folk. Kees wondered if it was because the little and third fingers on both of her hands were webbed. It didn't seem to matter with her work, but Kees figured she must be shy about showing herself too much in public.

Now, he hoped to share his basket of her good food with Linnie Bede and her family. He wanted so much to be their friend.

He crossed the back-porch and went out to the woodshed.

Five years ago, loneliness drove thirteen year old Kees down the hill, through town and up to Camp 4 where he claimed a spare bunk. Many boys his age worked in the woods and at the mill, but when he tried to talk with them and befriend him, they eyed him suspiciously, ignored him, or walked away and more than once he heard himself tagged with a snicker as "Strom's pretty boy."

As he got older he came to view the boys and young men as clannish, hard drinking, godless louts who sought whores, did not believe in God, and broke the Ten Commandments. But when Joe came to live at the bunkhouse, Kees was sure that he and Joe would become friends. Like Kees, Joe was smart, nice looking and religious. But Joe had gone his own way.

Now, his only friend was Soapy Metzler. And nobody in the world knew Soapy like Kees did. Yet, Soapy was the person with whom Kees did bad things. Kees yearned to break away from him, but he couldn't seem to do it.

They had met in seventh grade. Soapy, a fat, unruly boy, sixth of eleven children in the Metzler family, was often locked in the woodshed for one or two days at a time and given nothing but water and a cold boiled potato to eat.

When Soapy was thirteen years old, the Metzler shanty caught on fire and Soapy's folks, pie-eyed on moonshine, were trapped inside.

"I burnt it down," Soapy told Kees. "I watched it burn and I felt good."

Soapy's confession allowed Kees to feel better about himself and his own fantasies. Chores on his parents' property did not please him, but after he learned to set fire to piles of debris, the pictures he saw in the shivering flames aroused him. Naked women knelt at his feet. Licked his legs. His thighs. His penis and scrotum. Naked men petted him and brought him to the white heat of ejaculation.

Guilt and anxiety plagued him. What was wrong with him? Why did he feel these exhilarating, but sinful thoughts? What part of him provoked the thrilling, but unholy pictures?

After Soapy told him about the pictures *he'd* seen in flames and the things *he'd* done, Kees felt better about himself. He peppered Soapy for details. What did it feel like to strangle a bird? To feel the faint, kicking protest of the feathered body and clawing feet? What was it like to drown a kitten, or a puppy?

Soapy's deeds kindled exciting ideas and the two boys enjoyed each other. Finding sex exciting in firelight they set fire to abandoned shacks and outhouses, but they were careful to keep the flames under control. Forest fire was the great fear and dread held by everybody who lived in Hanksport County and Kees and Soapy were no exceptions.

The clincher came last summer. The two were jawing with loggers at one of the camps one night when Mr. Dickerson came around to talk about the I.W.W. Dickerson, a well-spoken fellow, polite and educated, wasn't felt to be welcome and when he appeared ready to leave, Soapy and Kees said they would walk with him. Mr. Dickerson said he would enjoy their company.

A half-mile from camp the three came upon a stump on the banks of the Blackduck River. Soapy took from the ample hidey-hole a long-necked, brown bottle and a .32 revolver. He held the gun to Mr. Dickerson's back, forced him to kneel, and Soapy shot him without batting an eye. He and Kees flopped the body on a log that lay on the river bank. Kees pulled the stopper out of the bottle and soused the corpse with kerosene. The boys pushed the log out onto the river, Soapy tossed a piece of flaming bark atop it and the boys stared, wide-eyed, at the beautiful flames atop the dead man floating down-stream.

The two took off their pants. Soapy got down on his hands and knees. While Kees rode his butt the lurid flames prompted a vision of red-haired Linnie Bede caressing him and the vision of her prompted ejaculation. "Ah, Soapy," Kees panted. "I love your sweet ass."

Later, the two whistled and sang, "Down by the Old Mill Stream" while walking home.

Kees carried the load of cut wood into the house, built up the fire and went to stand with his mother at the window. No matter the season, Kees found joy in the view. In spring, the greening of pale, purple teasel and yellow milk vetch pleased his eye. Summer brought shrubby white heath, blue lupine, and bright yellow buck bean. In fall, pink clusters of water smartweed showed their pretty heads in quiet back-waters. And in winter the ice-crusted river rushed through a forest, clothed in snow. Now, mid-summer, the burst of deep blue gentian was in bloom.

He picked up the binoculars and peered through them. Linnie Bede, swinging a dinner bucket, walked with Parley Hearn. "Excuse me," said Kees to his mother. "I'm going down to town. Marta packed a picnic basket and I won't be home for dinner."

CHAPTER 9

Red, white, and blue bunting draped the bandstand. A group of folks played, "You're a Grand Old Flag," on assorted fiddles, an accordion, and a drum.

Boys hollered while playing tug-of-war and football. Over at the horseshoe pit, horseshoes pinged against stakes. A softball game, in which Newt was pitching, held a good number of folks' attention.

Birdie and Linnie draped an old quilt over one of three eight-foot wide stumps they'd staked for their picnic site. There were a good number of the big stumps throughout the park for folks to claim. The park had once been part of a great forest. But white oak and aspen trees still flourised and provided welcome shade in summer and red and gold beauty in fall.

Linnie said to Birdie, "Mr. Dobbs is supposed to make a speech today and I'd like to hear him."

Birdie said, "That's the fifth time you've told me that these past two days."

"Well, dang it, Birdie. I think about that and it takes my mind off the burnt man. Does Newt know if Mr. Dobbs is coming?"

"He hasn't said."

Colin and eighteen-year old Mide Finley strolled by. Mide, a soft-spoken girl with long dark hair, a bow shaped mouth and heavy, dark eyebrows, was known for her sweet nature. Buzz and Dru joined them and the two smiling couples mingled into the crowd.

Baby, wearing a pretty blue dress, galumphed here and there, but never far from her family. Every now and then she touched her big white hair bow. "Pretty Baa Bee here. Pretty Baa bee knockers." She flashed her smile, pointed to herself and sang out, "Baa bee rockabye. Rockabye Baa bee knockers." One or more members of the Bede family kept her in sight and if she got to be a bother, one of them fetched and settled her.

Parley, now at Linnie's elbow, said, "Looking for somebody?"

"Yes. Mr. Dobbs from the I.W.W. is supposed to give a speech."

Parley nodded. "We'll watch for him. How about walking to the bridge with me? I've got something to say, and I think you have something to say to me, too."

Linnie's dread held her tight, but she went with Parley through the celebrating crowd to the Blackduck Bridge. She leaned over the rail. The river, low and easy at this time of year, seemed almost hushed.

"I like river sounds," she said. "Even low as this is now, I can't imagine living anywhere without it. But, even this pretty sight won't take that burnt man out of my mind."

"That's tough, Linnie. I wish you hadn't seen it, but in time the thought will ease."

"How do you know?"

He went to stand beside her and they both leaned over the rail. "We see good things," he said. "Like the river here. And we do good things. And good things happen to us and we forget bad things. It's just the way humans are."

"I like those words, Parley. I want to remember them."

He straightened and so did she and they faced each other. He said, "This is what I want to say, and I'll say it plain. I know you don't love me, but I'll work hard to be a good husband to you and a good father for our children. I hope you can learn to love me. Will you give it a try?"

She didn't flinch. "From what I know, you're a good man, Parley Hearn. But, all my life I've wanted to get schooling beyond high school. Unlike most girls, I haven't wanted to get married. I still don't. And I'll tell you this, straight out. I don't want children. Please, think about this. I *could* have a baby like Baby, my sister."

A deep frown creased his brow. "Having children . . . that's a big part of marriage. I've always thought I'd have children after I marry."

"I learned from a friend that . . ." *Mercy buckets, this was hard to say, but Parley must understand.* "I *think* there are some ways to stop babies from coming. And I *think* I can learn about it. You might not know this, but if you . . . if you leave me. . ."

He held up one hand. "I know what you're talking about and a husband shouldn't have to do that. Husbands and wives should enjoy their loving. When I'm your husband, if I do as you ask, neither of us will enjoy our loving as we should."

Her wildest dreams couldn't bring her to imagine enjoying the act and she had no answer, so she changed the subject. "Birdie says you live up at Blue Mirror Lake. That's far."

"Not really. Six miles up Wildcat Mountain. I've bought an automobile. A fine Runabout and it's coming into Coldsprings next week. I'll teach you how to drive and you can drive down to see your family and go to town anytime you want. A fellow, who lives a couple of miles from me, works with me. He drives his auto, picks me up and drops me off. So, our auto is yours."

"That's generous, and it's nice to know that we'll have it, but I don't want to live far."

He turned from her and again, he leaned over the rail. Neither he nor Linnie spoke. Laughter and shouts floated from the park. He straightened and turned back to her. "Arguing won't get us anywhere. As for our loving, I'll do as you ask, but I want you to learn what you think we need to learn, quick."

"My friend, Ann Dickerson, is coming up here soon and she knows more about this than anybody I know. I promise I'll ask her."

"The mayor's about to speak and I'd like to hear him."

The two returned to the park and sat on a bench. Ollie Holm, a short trim man with a fine mustache and lively blue eyes, was one of the nicest men Linnie knew, but she didn't hear one word of his reading *The Declaration of Independence*. As to Parley and marriage, she had set the rules, Parley had agreed and now she must hold up her end of the bargain.

The afternoon brightened for Linnie when Dru, accompanied by two fellows on fiddles and one strumming a washboard, took the stage and launched into "Yankee Doodle Dandy."

"Come on, everybody," Dru called out. "You all know this song. Sing along with me. 'Caught a feather in his cap and called it Macaroni.' " She slapped her thighs and clapped her hands. Two verses. Three. Finished, men whistled and some threw their caps in the air.

Buzz jumped up on the platform, grabbed Dru and swung her around. "Hey," he shouted. "She's my girl. And isn't she the prettiest peacherino you'll ever see?"

Dru, answering cries for more songs, led the crowd again. "Take Me Out To the Ballgame." And, "It's a Grand Old Flag." Again, folks clamored for more.

"One more, then," said Dru. "Everybody is hungry, so just one more."

After she sang, "Amazing Grace," Linnie and Parley made their way to the Bede picnic site. A number of folks brushed wet eyes and spoke of Dru.

"Druscilla Bede has a fine voice."

"The Bede girl ought to go on stage."

"You ever hear anybody like her?"

"No. And she's a real beauty."

Linnie and Birdie Mae set out fried chicken, baked beans, string beans and three apple pies. Colin and Mide joined them and Mide added two loaves of fresh baked bread and a potato spice cake to the feast.

Colin said, "Hey, Newt, any more thoughts about union?"

Newt laughed. "Tying the knot makes a man think of different things, but I've not forgot about union. Not by a long shot."

Linnie was laying silverware out on a neighboring stump when Kees appeared. "Hello, there." He held up a large wicker basket. "I'd like to share my picnic with you. Ham sandwiches, fried potato balls, baked beans and the best chocolate cake you'll find."

"Sure," said Newt. "Come join us."

Linnie pointed to the food-laden stump. "Set your basket right there, Kees. And thank you." A rush of pleasure gladdened her heart. The reason for Kee's interest in her family had to be herself and nobody else.

Birdie Mae noisily flapped two old quilts and spread them on the ground. Linnie said, "Here, Birdie. Let me help."

"You tend to your company."

Linnie sidled close to Birdie. "Don't be rude. Mother wouldn't like it. He's our guest and he brought some real nice food."

"I'll do my best," said Birdie under her breath.

Parley said, "Well, Mr. Strom. Union talk is . . ."

Kees raised his hand. "Please, don't call me 'Mr. Strom.' Call me 'Kees.' "

"Alright. I hear that union is interested in us up here. I say it's high time. Logging outfits over in Idaho organized just last year."

"Yes. I worked up there last year. Pretty country, isn't it."

"Sure is. Where'd you work?"

"Up in Coeur d'Alene," said Kees. "Bunker Hill to be exact."

"Make good money?"

"Two-fifty a day."

"Signed the yellow-dog contract?"

"The what?"

"The contract saying you weren't a union member and had no intention to join."

"No," said Kees. "I . . . I didn't sign it."

"So you went with union?"

"Sure did."

"It's unusual," said Parley. "You, the son of timber owners, sympathetic to union."

Kees's left cheek twitched. A red spot blossomed on his forehead. "That's just the way I am," he said. "No reason to get sore about it."

"Hey, Kees. I'm not sore. It's just unusual. No hard feelings on this fine day." He smiled. "Come on. Let's dish up."

Folks heaped their plates. Some sat on quilts, some perched on stumps. Linnie wanted to set beside Kees, but Joe beat her to him. Parley, with his plate heaped high, firmly took Linnie's arm and guided her to a stump on which Buzz and Dru sat.

Joe offered thanks and praise to the Lord, but nobody except Kees paid attention.

"Union man!" Someone shouted. "Union man's in jail."

Banter, laughter and camaraderie ceased. Picnic plates, laden with food, were set aside. Folks streamed across the bridge and hurried up the road to the squat jailhouse. Mr. Finley, Mide's father, a quiet man who liked to visit Roy from time to time, kicked the tires on a black, mud-spattered, open-air automobile. Two men with baseball bats bashed the windshield. Splinters of glass spewed out like an opened fan. A knot of men and two young women beat their fists on the hood of the auto. "No union," they yelled. "No union."

Folks picked up the chant. "No union. No union."

"You know who it is?" Parley shouted to Newt.

"Yeah. Dobbs. Frank Dobbs."

"Why was he arrested?"

"Trespassing. This is a company town."

Newt shouldered his way through the crowd to the auto. "Hey!" He cupped his hands. "Listen to me. Please." The crowd quieted some. "We don't want trouble," Newt said. "Let this fellow leave peaceably."

"Why?" Mr. Dolce shouted. "He's a god . . ."

"Bert, this fellow's got the right to express his ideas," said Newt. "And he's not caused trouble at all."

"He will, if he sticks around."

"If we'd listen to him, we might learn a thing or two," said Newt.

"I'd rot in jail before listening to a union man," said Bert Dolce.

Linnie stood on her tiptoes and craned her neck. What did this union man, Mr. Dobbs, look like? She worked her way through the crowd to a favorable place close to the door.

Sheriff Chester Mann came out. "Folks, I don't want trouble, understand? Bail's been posted and I'm gonna bring this man out and you all are gonna let him leave in peace." He ducked back inside.

He returned and he had with him a tall, lean, strong-faced fellow with dark, wide-set eyes and thick, tousled nut-brown hair. The sleeves of his white shirt were rolled up. His red necktie was loose. Sheriff Mann handed him a suit coat and a fedora. Dobbs set the hat rakishly on his head and draped his suit coat over one shoulder and held it there. His hands were slender, his fingers long and tapered and he had about him a confident air. For a moment his eyes rested on Linnie.

"Clear the way, folks," said the sheriff. And to Dobbs, "Get outta' here, bub. You don't want to end up like the last Wob who came around trying to organize union. That fella was shot and dumped in a flume."

"Yeah," said Dobbs. "I know about him." He went to his automobile and thrashed his coat across the front seat. Shattered glass spurted out on the ground. He cranked up the auto and put on his driving goggles, but before he drove off he raised his left fist high. "No Gods," he shouted. "No Masters. No Surrender. *Organize*."

Linnie's spine tingled. The union man's words rang in her ears. She wanted to stand up to Mrs. Strom. Tell her about Johnny. Tell her that when loggers got hurt they should be able to ride on the locy down to the doctor in town. But, she also sensed the crowd's anger and unease.

Mr. Dolce, his voice high-pitched and shrill, yelled, "That sonuvabitch travels all over the place preaching union. And he lives with a woman who ain't even his wife. He oughta' be tarred and feathered and hanged."

The crowd muttered among themselves, crossed the bridge back to the park and returned to their quilts and picnics.

Day began to fade. Children got cranky. Yet folks drifted about, not ready to go home, but not knowing what else to do.

Kees gathered up his bowls and set them in his basket. "Thank you," he said to Newt and to Parley. "Thank you, Linnie. I enjoyed myself." With a peculiar awkward gesture he offered his hand to Parley. The two shook hands. He offered his hand to Linnie. She shook it and was taken aback by its odd, limp feel.

Buzz and Dru and Mide and Collin piled into Buzz's sedan and drove off. Their high spirits and laughter echoed in Linnie's ears. Those four were happy and in love.

Birdie Mae and Newt got in their auto, Birdie snuggled close to Newt and they called out their good-byes. They too, were happy and in love.

Linnie was anything but happy. Not only were her dreams dashed to smithereens, she would soon marry a man she didn't love. But she'd better make the best of it. She had no choice.

She and Parley, Roy, Joe, and Baby climbed into the wagon. Roy took the reins.

"I wonder who paid Mr. Dobbs' bail," said Linnie.

"Newt did," said Joe. "Chester told me he had Dobbs in jail. Said Newt would pungle up the cash. Asked me not to say anything about it. No point in getting folks riled, but word got out."

Parley said, "I wish he'd stick around. Maybe folks up here would learn a thing or two.' "

Roy said nothing at all.

Baby chortled. "Pretty Baa bee home. Bay Bee home knockers."

Parley, speaking softly to Linnie, said, "I don't think Kees Strom worked over at the Coeur d' Alenes. At least not when he said he did. I worked up there the same time he claims he did. Bunker Hill wouldn't go union and management paid their muckers only a dollar-fifty a day. Kees said he worked for two-fifty."

"You're accusing him of lying?" Her tone was cold.

Parley shrugged. "His story doesn't add up. Well, it doesn't matter. I've had another thought about our talk on the bridge. I've heard there's an Indian woman over in Sunnydale who might have answers for us. I'd ask you to call on her. Soon."

"I will."

"Linnie, darlin,' " said Parley. "We've got a big job ahead."

CHAPTER 10

In late August, Dru and Linnie were busy in the kitchen cutting up chunks of chicken fat to use in making soap for laundry and scrubbing. They took the chunks outside and dropped them into a kettle of lye water hung on a pole rigged over a burning stump in front of the house. While the two stirred the mess Dru said, "Buzz is coming over this afternoon. We're going fishing over at Tat Meadow."

"Well, cool your heels until I get home from town. Mame Holm pickled up a batch of pig's feet the other day. I'll trade some of our sauerkraut for one of her jars and we'll give it to Father on his birthday. I won't be gone long."

"All right. I had a tussle with Baby earlier today." She pulled up the sleeve of her blouse. An ugly purple splotch with two dark teeth marks bruised her forearm.

"Lord, heaven! What riled her?"

"You were out at the coop. Mother started out for her stump and Baby ran after her. I stopped her and she bit me."

Linnie turned to glance at Baby who sat, big and hump-shouldered, on the stoop. "She's batty as a loon," Linnie said. "And a real try. But she's ours and . . ."

"I know," said Dru and in a sing-song tone—"And we take care of her the best we can."

When the soap mess thickened, Dru held the mouth of a muslin bag wide and Linnie, using a small pan, scooped the mix into the bag. Dru lugged the bag to a tree and hung it on a limb to harden and cool. She and Linnie went in the house.

Baby came to Linnie. "Batty loon Bay Bee go. Pretty batty baby go."

"Lord, heaven," Linnie said to Dru. "Now she's picked up 'batty loon.' I wish she'd pick up useful words." To Baby she said, "You can't go with me today, but in October you can come to my wedding."

Baby chortled. "Batty loon go. Batty knockers Baby go. Knockers Go."

Dru said, "You've set a date?"

"Father wants me to marry Parley soon. I told him October. I try not to think about it."

"Don't be surprised if I beat you to the alter." Dru's blue eyes glinted with happiness. "I was going to wait and tell you later, but I can't wait. Buzz wants to marry me and he talked to Father and Father is pleased."

Linnie grimaced. "You know I'm against it."

"I love him, Linnie. He loves me and we want to be together."

"I know that and I don't feel good about it, but right now I've got to get to town." She clapped on her old felt hat and left. She hurried.

No Gods. No Masters. No Surrender. Organize. For the past two weeks Mr. Dobbs's defiant words had rung in her ears. Dobbs, thrashing the broken glass with his coat. Raising his fist. Shouting words of defiance. Would she ever see him again? Probably not.

But troubled thoughts plagued her. In two months she'd be a married woman and live at Parley's house up at Blue Mirror Lake. She would scrub clothes and cook and keep his house clean and grow a garden and put food by. She would do all the things expected of her and she wouldn't complain, but the act of coupling, resulting in babies, terrified her. She'd made her feelings known to Parley, and she had to trust him.

In town, she stopped by the Holm's house. Ollie's wife, Mame, was a small, busy woman who wore her blond hair piled up on her head in a nest of curls. But for losing her son to pneumonia a few years back, her blue eyes sparkled and her round face was usually flushed with smiles.

Without fail, when Birdie, or Linnie or Dru dropped by, Mame invited them in for refreshments. During the frigid, dark winter days, a fire blazed in the front parlor's fireplace. Ruby-pink wallpaper covered the walls. Heavy, fringed damask swags hung at two large bay windows. A burled walnut sofa and large, cut-glass lamps gave the room a feel of Mame's Southern prosperity. She served small cups of hot coffee or tea. Her assortment of treats—johnny cakes, beignets, fried pies, pound cake, sweet potato pie—were served on beautiful cut-glass plates.

In summer she offered tall glasses of lemonade along with her assortment of sweets and these she served out on the large, screened back porch.

On this summer day she said, "Linnie, dear, please come in. I've made lemonade and you'll surely enjoy my lemon-ribbon ice-cream pie."

"Thank you. I'd love to visit, but I can only stay a short time."

The two sat out on the back porch. Shadows from two enormous fir trees played on the floor. A fat orange cat snoozed on one of two wicker chairs. Mame inquired about Linnie's family. Linnie resisted telling her about Buzz courting Dru, but she mentioned her own plans to marry Parley Hearn.

"I have no feelings for him," she said. "He's a nice man, but I . . . I just have no feelings for him at all."

Mame said. "You're a sensible girl, Linnie. With time you will no doubt come to appreciate Mr. Hearn. Love can follow and I understand he's is a fine man."

Mame's words didn't help the sinking feeling in Linnie's belly. She said, "I enjoyed the Fourth of July picnic. Do you by chance know Mr. Dobbs?"

"Ollie has known him for some time. He's the person we need up here if Strom workers are going to go union."

"Is he coming back?"

"I don't know. He travels all over the Northwest."

The big standing clock chimed noon and Linnie said, "I have to run my errands and get on home. Thank you for the nice sweet and the lemonade and the visit."

"Come again, Linnie. You know you are welcome to stop by any time."

◯◯

At the company store she hurried past a knot of men and older boys out on the porch. Kees was among them. He tipped his cap. Linnie, aware that she looked a sight in her faded and worn cotton dress, ignored him, bought what she needed and paid for her purchases. She left the store, slipped past the men again and started home.

Kees fell in step beside her. "Where are you going in such a hurry on this hot day?"

"I'm going home." Oh, my. Didn't he look snappy. Checkered knickers. Dark blue vest. A good looking cap that matched his knickers.

"Let me buy you one of Mrs. Holm's treats at the ice-cream parlor."

"Thank you, and I'd like to, but I'm not dressed right. And it wouldn't be proper. I'm . . . well, I'm going to marry Parley Hearn quite soon."

He stopped in his tracks. She did, too. They stared at each other. "Yes," she said. "I'm getting married in October."

His eyes widened. His eyebrows arched. "I'd not thought that of you, Linnie Bede. Getting married so young. But, engaged or not, we can still be friends. Let me buy you a sweet before you get to be an old married woman. Please." His shy smile won her over.

They sat at one of the small, round tables. Kees ordered two lemonade drinks and two small, peach fried pies. He twiddled his thumbs.

Linnie said, "I'm sorry to hear about your father passing."

He shrugged. "He was sick for a long time. Will you and Parley live here after you're married?"

"Yes. But, if I had my way, I'd leave this place. Wouldn't you?"

"No." Again, the dimpled smile. "I'd be away from the girl I love more than anyone in the world."

Linnie's spoonful of peach pie stopped in mid-air. Kees hadn't had a girl with him at the picnic and Linnie hadn't heard a whisper about him having a girl. That kind of news would move fast as forest fire. But, maybe his girl lived over in Coldsprings. "Where does your girl live?" she said.

"In a barn."

"In a barn?"

"Yes."

She laughed. "You're teasing me, aren't you?"

He nodded. "My best girl is my horse. Her big sister is my mother's horse."

"Joe told us about those beautiful animals."

"Hey. Joe is doing a good job. Seems to like what he does, too. I talk with him sometimes, but he's a quiet sort, isn't he."

"He's always liked to go his own way." She took the bite of her fried pie. "M'mmm this is good. Mame Holm is the best cook I've ever known. The lemonade is good, too. Thank you."

"Thank *you*, Linnie Bede. Say, remember Mr. Dickerson, the burnt man you and your father found?"

"Of course I remember. It was awful."

He leaned to her. "What did it look like?"

"Scary. Burnt. Ghost eyes wide open. And whoever did it never got caught."

His left cheek twitched. "What came to your mind when you first saw it?"

"I . . . I don't know. I wanted to get away from it. Fast. And now I don't want to talk about it."

He took a bite of his pie, set his spoon aside and leaned across the table close to her. "Soapy lets me look at cadavers in the funeral parlor." He twiddled his thumbs fast.

Linnie drew back away from him. "You like to do *that*?"

"Yes. I don't know why, but I do."

Linnie found herself flummoxed and tongue-tied. Kees liked to look at dead folks? Goose bumps, like pin-pricks, slid over her.

He said, "What do *you* like to do more than anything in the whole world?"

"I . . . I . . ." She would *not* tell him about her rock at Thimble Creek Meadow. "Well, I don't know, but I don't want to talk about corpses, so I'll say this. Parley doesn't think you ever worked up in the . . . . wherever you said you did. The lanes? Parley said he worked at that place the same time you said you did."

Kees looked down at his twiddling thumbs. He leaned across the table, closer to her. "Parley's right," he said in a soft voice, almost a whisper. "My folks own a couple of mines over at Coeur d'Alene. They own a logging operation over there, too. I've been there, but I made up the rest. I want Parley to like me. Respect me. I want you and your family to like me and respect me. Please, Linnie. Keep this a secret. Please."

"But, why would you . . .?" She jumped up. "Jeepers. I've gotta go. I told Dru I'd be right back and I've been gone way too long." She picked up her things. "Thanks for the treat."

He stood. "I enjoyed it, too. And I like to think of you as my friend."

Linnie had no answer to that.

At about the same time that Linnie sat down with Kees to enjoy lemonade and fried pie, Buzz drove his bright yellow Runabout up to the Bede's house. Hot-eyed and eager, he tickled Dru's neck, grabbed her and kissed her. "Hey, Peacherino. Come on, let's go for a ride and catch a few smooches at Tat Meadow. Maybe do a little fishing."

"Oh, drat. I've got to wait for Linnie to come home. What a bother."

He glanced at Baby. "Can't you leave her alone for just a little while? Linnie should be home shortly."

"I shouldn't."

"Well, *I* don't have to wait for Linnie. And when I move to Seattle I won't have time to go fishing."

"And I'll bet that all the pretty girls you'll meet will take your mind off fishing. And off of me, too."

"Aw, come on, Dru. That's not fair. I won't forget you for one minute. Now, if you're of a mind to wait for Linnie, that's fine. I'll walk over to Tat and wait for you." He left the house and started across the clearing.

Oh, how she wanted to go with him. She was so eager to love him and allow him to love her. Drat, Linnie. She'd said she wouldn't be gone long and here she'd been gone for almost two hours. But, Baby had been good as pie and if Dru tied her to the stove, as happened once in a great while, it couldn't hurt to leave her alone for a short time. Mother, sitting off in the corner, wouldn't know the difference and if Baby was tied up, she couldn't get to her and pester her.

Dru touched the stove. Good. Cold as could be.

She worked fast. After tying a rope around the stove leg she looped it around Baby and tied it into a knot. She grabbed three cookies from the big, dented cookie tin and gave them to Baby. She snatched her hat and fishing pole. She raced across the reach after Buzz. "Wait for me," she called. "Hey, wait for me."

❀

Meara watched the naughty girl eat. If she got loose and came close, Meara would push her away and go up to the falls. The naughty girl had never been up there. The naughty girl gobbled her cookies. She worked her fingers at the knot. Her smile was broad while she continued to work the knot. The knot came loose. The naughty girl dropped the rope. Again, she looked at Meara. She pointed to herself. "Ma. Ma, Batty loon Bay bee ." She lumbered across the room, sat at Meara's feet and leaned her head against Meara's skirt.

Meara pushed her away.

The naughty girl got up and tried to hug Meara. Again, Meara pushed her away. "Get away from me," she said. "You're a naughty, naughty girl."

The naughty girl gave Meara a good long look. The naughty girl frowned and she carried a chair over to the bookcase. She climbed up on the chair. She pushed all the pretty dishes off the shelf. CRASH. CRASH. CRASH. The naughty girl got down from the chair. She kicked the broken dishes. She looked at Meara.

Meara started to cry.

The naughty girl went to her. Again, she tried to hug her. Meara shoved her. "Get away from me," she said. "You're a naughty, naughty girl."

The naughty girl went to the window and ripped off the curtains. Meara picked up a piece of kindling. She went after the naughty girl. She swatted at the naughty girl. The naughty girl ducked and dodged around the room. "Ma Ma," she cried. "Ma Ma."

Meara went out the open door.

The naughty girl stood in the doorway. "Ma Ma. Batty loon Bay bee home. Ma Ma gone. Ma Ma all gone."

Linnie high-tailed it up the road. Dust hung in the air. Blue bottle flies swarmed on bear scat, deer droppings and horse flops. Mosquitoes zinged. And, in spite of Linnie's hat, a welt the size of a quarter swelled on her forehead.

Kees Strom, not the likeable, smooth-talking fellow she'd thought him to be, was awkward, nervous and interested in dead people. A creepy fellow who had few friends and made up stories to try to make himself look important. Linnie no longer wanted his friendship and she was glad that Joe kept his distance.

Once home she was surprised to see nobody around. Dru, for all of her vanity, was a busy soul who did her share of work and more. If she had any free time on sunny days, such as this, she liked to sit out on the porch, strum her father's guitar, and sing.

"Dru?" Linnie called. "I'm home."

Silence.

"Dru?"

Baby appeared in the open doorway. "Batty loon Bay bee home. Knockers batty loon home. Ma Ma gone. All gone."

Linnie jumped up on the stoop and went in the house. She clapped her hand to her mouth. Torn curtains lay on the floor. Pieces of her mother's beautiful Willow Ware dishes were smashed to smithereens. "Oh, my Lord," Linnie said. "My Lord, my Lord."

Baby pulled on Linnie's arm. Tears rolled down Baby's face. "Ma Ma gone," she cried. "Ma Ma all gone."

Linnie quit the house and raced across the clearing. Logic told her that her mother had gone up to Horsetail Falls, a place where Baby had never been. She started up the trail. *Please, Mother, please be at the falls. I promise I won't belly-ache anymore about marrying Parley and I'll try to be a good wife and I won't think about the union man ever again.*

Hurrying, hurrying. *Baby wants Mother's love. Mother won't give it to her. Baby turned mean. Baby tore up the house.*

Hurrying, hurrying. Linnie's breath came short. Up on the high ridge she stopped for a moment to catch her breath. The thing that happened today must not happen again. Her mother must understand that Baby was her daughter and Baby needed her mother's love.

At the falls Linnie, weak with relief, found her mother sitting on a log. Linnie sat down beside her, put her arm around her and said, "I was scared something terrible had happened to you."

"We're leaving here," said her mother, her voice high and clear. "A naughty, naughty girl lives in my house. We'll go back to Chicago. I'll put you chicks in a fine school and I'll sew clothes and make pretty hats."

"Mother, that girl you think is naughty is yours. She's ours. She needs us. Especially you. She wouldn't be mean if she knew you loved her."

"That naughty girl is *not* mine and I *don't* love her and I *don't* want her around." She bent her head and wept.

Linnie took her mother's hand and after a few minutes she said, her tone soft, "Come on, Mother. We have to go home."

CHAPTER 11

On a morning of heavy, gray mist and steady rain, Birdie drove Newt's Rambler over to Mide Finley's house and picked up Mide. The two drove to Birdie's father's house to sew, darn and mend with Dru and Linnie. They had all graduated from Hanksport High and this once-a-month get-together provided some sociability.

Birdie had finished re-making one of Meara's pretty pink dresses and she had made wide buttonholes and sewed big buttons all down the front. She, Linnie and Dru had spent a fair amount of time showing Baby how to push the buttons in and out of the button holes. When Baby finally got it, she chortled and ran around in circles and called out, "buttons, buttons."

Today Birdie had with her another dress for Baby. She'd made it from lavender cotton cloth she'd bought at The A & D Dry Goods Store. She'd trimmed the dress with white organza lace at the neckline and wrists. Today, when she took the dress out of the bag and gave it to Baby, Baby held the dress against her cheek. "Buttons. Buttons," she said.

Birdie allowed Baby to hold it for awhile. She showed Baby the large, purple buttons she planned to sew on the dress. Baby thrust the dress to her and Birdie set to the task of finishing it.

Baby, seated at the big round table with her sisters and Mide, worked a large, blunt unthreaded needle in and out of a piece of coarse lace, once part of a cuff on one of Meara's dresses. She smiled while she worked.

Mide deftly moved her needle and blue thread in and out of bleached flour sacking. She liked the effect of the pale yellow tulips and light green leaves on what would soon be pillowcases. She paused with her work, set it aside and sipped her tea. "I want to talk about something," she said. "Something . . . delicate. Something we don't ever talk about, but maybe we should."

She had a captive audience. Work was set aside. Dru said, "Yes?"

"I'm not interested in having a large family and it's become a problem for Colin and me. I want to enjoy life for a couple of years before we have children."

Birdie Mae said, "And Colin has other ideas?"

"Yes. I haven't allowed him to have his way with me. And I won't, until after we're married. We've quarreled. If we stay up here, Colin will work for Strom and we'll be poor forever. I'd like to move to Seattle, like Buzz and Dru plan to do. I'd find work as a stenographer or a seamstress. Colin would find work with good wages. We'd save money and buy a house. I want two children. Not one. Not three. Two. That would be a nice life."

Linnie agreed with Mide. "But I don't want children at all," she said. "Parley and I had a discussion. It was hard to talk about, but I made myself clear. He didn't like it, but he agreed."

Dru picked up the sock she was darning. She kept her head low and she said, "I love Buzz so much and I *want* to have his baby. I feel sorry for you, Linnie, marrying Parley when you don't really give a sugar moon about him."

"Parley is a very kind man, but I don't want to marry anybody." She pointed to Baby, laboriously working the needle with the empty eye on the piece of lace. "Any one of us Bedes could have a child like her. That thought makes me shudder."

Birdie, bent to her task of sewing the buttonholes, said, "I'm different from all of you. Newt and I want a big family and I'm disappointed every time I have my monthly."

"You and Newt have plenty of money," said Mide. "We *won't* if we stay up here. And isn't it true that a couple can stop a baby from coming if the husband leaves the woman in time?"

"I think so," said Linnie. "That's what Parley agreed to do, but as I say, he's not happy about it. And I'm supposed to go over to Sunnydale Valley and talk to a Makkah woman. Parley says she might be able to help us."

Mide picked up her sewing. "I've heard about her. I've tried to talk to Colin about her, but he isn't interested. I love him to pieces and he knows that, too. Linnie, would you talk to him, as a favor for me?"

"I don't know that it's my business, Mide."

"I'll soon be your sister-in-law so it *is* a bit of your business. If Colin gets angry, he can take it out on me."

"He's stubborn as a mule."

"He's stubborn and spoiled. He always gets his own way, but with this, he hasn't and he won't until we're married."

Birdie shook her head. "You two have strange ideas."

That evening after supper Linnie said to Colin, "Can we talk for a bit? Out on the stoop?"

The two went outside. A chilly, but gentle breeze moved the boughs of the two large pine trees beside the house. Linnie told Colin, in her direct way, about Mide's concerns. "She loves you so much, but please, Colin, try to understand." She went on to tell him about the agreement she and Parley had reached.

Colin said, "Your agreement with Parley isn't anybody's business but your own. Mide had no right to air our business to you. I'd appreciate it if you mind your own affairs and I'll say the same to Mide."

CHAPTER 12

On a Saturday in mid-September, sunshine brought long inky shadows to the forest, to the meadows, rivers and creeks, with the chill of fall in the air.

The prattle in town and throughout the camps and shanties sizzled. Colin Bede and Mide Finley, Druscilla Bede and Busby Corrigan had eloped.

They had left notes for their families. The two couples drove over to the Hanksport County Courthouse in Coldsprings on Saturday morning and tied the knot. They would spend the night at the new Snoqualmie Hotel. They'd be home Sunday afternoon.

Late Sunday afternoon, shortly after the Bede family had finished supper at Birdie and Newt's tidy new house, Buzz and Dru drove up. Buzz picked up a valise from the back seat and the two, arm in arm, came inside. Roy and Joe greeted Buzz with a polite manner and shook his hand. Birdie Mae and Linnie gave Dru a warm hug.

Dru bubbled with happiness as she talked about the "swanky hotel we stayed in. They serve their food in a beautiful dining room and one is waited on as if you're a queen. Or a king. Oh, we had a fine time, didn't we Buzzie."

"We sure did." He put his arm around her. "Mr. Bede, sir. I'm leaving my beautiful Peacherino here for a short time. I want to find a nice place for us and I'll work hard to give her a good life."

Roy nodded. "You do that, young man. And I expect you to take good care of her."

Buzz flashed his broad, handsome smile. "I surely will, sir." He reached in his wallet and took out a fistful of dollar bills. "Peacherino, use this for whatever you might fancy." After he gave her a nice kiss and a hug, she saw him out to his automobile and he got in, waved and drove off.

Shortly, before Linnie, Joe, Roy and Baby left, Dru told her family that she was two months along with a child.

Joe slowly shook his head. "What's happened to us? Birdie, Dru. How can you act in defiance of the Lord?"

Roy said, "Joe, stop punishing yourself for acts you think are made in sin. We're all sinners in one way or another, so no more preaching to your sisters."

Linnie said, and she kept her tone soft, "Mide is pregnant too?"

"No."

"Are they going to live in Seattle?"

"No. Tomorrow Colin goes back to work for Strom."

CHAPTER 13

Parley Hearn had worked hard all his life. Before coming to Hanks Port he and his father worked on the Mendocino Coast in California. For three years they helped build trestles out to moored schooners that sailed the Pacific Ocean between Vancouver, British Columbia and San Diego. They worked the gold mines in Tonopah, Nevada and the copper mines in the Coeur d' Alenes of Idaho.

But every year, late summer, Parley and his father went up to Alaska to visit the Tsimshian village in which Parley was born. There, paying close attention to his elders, Parley learned the craft of wood carving. A piece he held in the highest regard was a small owl his grandfather made for him when Parley turned thirteen.

During the ceremony, held in recognition of Parley coming into manhood, his grandfather put the little piece around Parley's neck and Parley had not, and would not give one thought to taking it off.

After Parley's mother and father died, Parley continued to make his yearly trips north. But when Strom Logging hired him, as head sawyer at Camp Five, he could no longer take the time to make his visit. And he heeded his father's advice. "Because of me, people consider you white. Don't say otherwise. Don't borrow trouble."

But Parley was proud of his mother's people. And when the time was right, he would tell Linnie about them.

CHAPTER 14

On a late October day of wind and gray drizzle, Linnie put on a dark blue skirt and a white blouse with not one piece of decorative lace, ribbon or embroidery. After she set her mother's deep-brimmed, brown straw hat on her head, Birdie Mae said, "Why are you wearing such dull clothes? And that hat is plain ugly."

"Why should I do otherwise? Oh, Birdie, I don't want to get married."

"You're being foolish. Heaven's to Betsy. Parley replaced our old rotten stoop and he built the root-cellar, and the barn. Things father didn't know how to do at all. And he bought the horse and wagon. And that snazzy Runabout auto, mainly for you, I might add. There aren't many men like him. He'll be a good husband and a fine father. As Father said, 'you'd have to look far and wide to find a better man than Parley.' "

"I'm not saying he won't be a good husband, but I plain don't love him. And he won't have a chance to be a good father because I won't have babies and he knows it and that's that."

Birdie's eyes got hard. "I've never been really mad at you," she said. "But if you stop him from loving you, like he's got a right to do and is going to want to do, you'll be sorry some day."

"What about me? What if I don't want to love him at all? And why should I have babies if I don't want them?"

"Because wives *do* have babies. Because most of us love our husband's loving us. Land sakes, Linnie, at least give Parley a chance."

Linnie, accompanied by her family, went into a big, drafty room on the second floor of the County Courthouse. Parley, wearing a brown suit that looked stiff as cardboard, waited. His smile was warm and his dark eyes held a softness Linnie had not seen in a man. But, the soft look didn't help.

A Judge performed the ceremony and when he pronounced Linnie and Parley "man and wife," Linnie wanted to plug her ears. Parley bent to kiss her and her hat fell off and she kept her lips pressed tight.

She'd balked at the notion of a party, but Birdie Mae, who had not had means for a party after her own wedding, talked it over with Newt. "If Linnie is going to act like a brat, so be it," she said. "But I want folks to have a good time."

"A real party might help Linnie feel better," said Newt. "And I'm sure that Parley will enjoy it. Do whatever you want, Birdie. Hire Mame. She'll know what to do."

Mame and her help prepared a feast of black-eyed peas, roast ham, fried chicken, cole slaw, bread pudding with bourbon sauce and pound cake. Most of the guests had never been to such a scrumptious party. They enjoyed the good food and they remarked on it.

After the table was cleared, Jim Corrigan picked up his banjo, Gavin tuned up his fiddle, Roy picked at his guitar and Buzz found a washboard. It wasn't long before folks were dancing the Polka and Two-Step and even Joe, who considered dancing a sin, clapped his hands to the beat. Parley, whirling Linnie around, said, "Linnie, darlin,' quit your sulking and try to have a good time."

Late afternoon Parley, wearing a brown bowler hat the same color as his suit, helped Linnie into his shiny black sedan. He put on his goggles and handed a pair to Linnie. She slipped them on, but she didn't like them and she took them off.

Buzz, Colin and Newt had tied a good number of empty cans on the rear of the auto and when the bride and groom drove out of town the cans clanged and Linnie likened it to the dreadful beating of her own heart.

She had never been on the steep, winding road that wound up beyond Camp Five. The deep forest she was familiar with gave way to a forest of thin, spare pines. Parley shifted gears for the climb.

"This is far." She leaned to him and shouted to be heard above the wind, the roar of the auto's engine and the clattering cans.

He put his hand on her knee and smiled. "Not with our auto. Six miles isn't that far."

She moved away from him. "Will we have neighbors?"

"The fellow I told you about lives half a mile east of us. A few families live across the lake at Sunshine Bay. Nice folks."

"Why do you live way up here?"

"The place belonged to my father and I spent a lot of time here when I was young. I like it. I think you will too. On nice days the lake is a beautiful deep blue. It freezes over in winter and we can snowshoe out on it and have a picnic."

Linnie made no attempt to make further conversation over the noise of the auto climbing the steep grade and the awful clattering cans.

Parley steered the auto off the road and followed a wide path through tall, spindly pines to the lake. Mist hovered over sunless water. A small, sturdy, house, painted white with a dark green door, wasn't far from the rocky shoreline. A wide porch wrapped the house. A woodshed and privy, both painted white with the dark green trim, stood off behind the house.

"I've never seen anything like this," Linnie said.

"Linnie, darling,' you'll like it after the weather clears. I want you to see it as pretty as it can be." He pointed to a large grove of aspen just north of the house. "Have you ever seen a more beautiful sight than that?"

"It's pretty."

He got out of the auto and she did, too. He came to her and put his arms around her and held her close. He was aroused and she drew away from him. "I'd like to see the house."

He carried her valise and the two went inside. A tidy room with two sparkling clean windows, a table, two chairs, a stove, a sink and a bed was what it was.

He set down the valise and again, he came to her and tried to envelope her. She ducked away. "I find myself listening for the flume bell," she said, while standing at one of the windows. "But all I hear is wind."

"Yes, it's windy today. But it certainly isn't windy all the time."

He built a crackling fire in the stove and then he went to stand beside her. He put an arm around her.

She stiffened, but allowed it. "Are we going to live here forever?"

He turned her to him. "No. It's small, even for the two of us. I'm thinking of selling it, buying land and building a new house, just for us. Do you like that idea?"

"Yes." *Let's keep talking. Let's talk all night.* Refusing to look at the bed on which an act would happen to her that she didn't want, she kept her eyes locked on Parley. "Where would we build it?"

"I'd thought we'd live somewhere up here, but where would you like to live?" His brow was creased, his dark eyes troubled.

"Close to my family." Tears welled and her words tumbled out before she could stop them. "This is far from all I know. Dang it, Parley. I can't hear the flume bell. Or the river. Until our house is built, I want to live at Father's place. We can sleep in Joe and Collin's shed. They're both gone now and yes, we can sleep there."

She went to stand beside the stove. The shed behind her father's house had two narrow bunks, but she'd be *home* and she'd sleep in one bunk and Parley would sleep in the other and she'd hear the flume bell and the river. She'd be close to Birdie and Dru and even being in the same house with Baby wouldn't bother her. Living up here in this gray, windy place beside a misty lake with nobody around and far, far from home would be awful.

Parley stayed at the window. She could read his mind if she cared to. He wasn't pleased. The Bede's house was crowded. Baby would be a nuisance. Linnie and Parley would never be alone, except out in the cold, dark shed.

He turned to her. "Linnie, darlin,' I want you to be happy and we're on pretty shaky ground here. I'll talk to your father about adding a room onto his house. A room just for us. And I'll try to build our own house next year. Would you like that?"

"Yes. Oh, yes. I'd like that a lot. Will our own house be close to Father or to Birdie and Newt?"

"I'll have to see." He came to her and put his hands on her shoulders. "I didn't think this through very well. I thought you'd like it up here. When the sun is out, it's so pretty and I find it pretty even when it's like this." He pulled her to him and whispered in her ear. "Give us a chance, Linnie. Please give us a chance."

She accepted his embrace, but she said, "I'll try, but I don't like being so far."

"We'll talk about it tomorrow. It's been a long day for you."

Dark was coming on. He left and he was gone for a few minutes and when he returned he lighted two lanterns. "Do you want to use the privy first?"

Sickening dread churned in her belly.

"Yes."

"A lantern is hanging by the door."

She picked up the valise and one of the lanterns and she quit the house. Bucking the wind she followed a path through the thin scatter of trees. The glowing light of the lantern led her to the privy and she ought to feel grateful to Parley for thinking of her. She didn't.

The privy door, caught by a gust, banged open and shut. There, in that awful, chilly place, sure to have spiders and snakes, she put the lantern on a small bench and she shed her clothes and slipped her night shift on over her under-shirt and drawers.

On the way back to the house she stopped in the windy place with so few trees. She felt exposed. She set down her valise and lantern and she smote her fist into her palm. *No Gods. No Masters.* Parley was not her God. He was not her master. She should not be forced to go through something she did not want, but what could she do about it? Nothing.

The flame in her lantern guttered and died. Shivering and cold, she blinked back her tears, picked up her valise and the lantern and made her way toward the orange glow in the window just up ahead.

Parley, wearing a night shirt, took the other lantern and went outside.

Linnie got in bed and pulled the blankets up under her chin. *The awful thing will soon happen to me.*

The pitcher pump on the back stoop squeaked. Oh, Lord. Mortified in confused agitation she'd forgotten to wash. And early this morning she had put a bar of the nice soap and fresh underclothes and aprons, skirts and blouses in her valise.

Parley came back in, snuffed out the lanterns and climbed into bed. He smelled. It wasn't a bad smell. Maybe like salt and wet moss.

He slid one hand under her head and cupped it gently. He leaned over her. "Linnie, darlin,' we're going to make love."

"I don't know how."

"I'll teach you. It's . . ."

"You can teach me someday, but not now."

"Darlin,' this is what happens between husband and wife. And you are my wife and I love you and I hope you'll learn to love me. We'll start tonight."

He tugged at her drawers. "Take these off," he said, his breath hot and close. "Take them off."

"No."

"Darlin', this is one of the most important parts of marriage. You need to take off your underthings. We made promises and I intend to keep mine."

Mortified, Linnie got out of bed and did as Parley asked her to do. Fear settled over her skin like cold oil. She crept back into bed and pulled the blanket around herself and hugged her goose-bumped skin.

Parley unwrapped her and pulled her to him. His breathing was fast and hard and he smoothed back her hair and he whispered in her ear about his love for her.

"I don't like this," she said.

"If you'd let yourself go a little, you might be surprised and enjoy our loving."

He kissed her cheeks, her neck and breasts. He gently, ever so gently touched her private place and it was all right. Her awful stiffness and fright ebbed a little and she appreciated his gentleness and she began to feel a stirring in her loins she'd not felt in her life.

With infinite patience he nuzzled her and he put his poker inside her. A prick of hurt jabbed her and she feared him dropping his seed and she whispered, "Don't drop your juice in me."

"I promised and I won't." His breathing was hard and he stayed on her and stayed and stayed and finally he pulled out of her, sudden, and he moaned and she turned from him and vowed not to let him do that to her ever again.

☯

The next day, another gray day with mist hovering over the lake, Linnie and Parley drove down to Roy's house and

Linnie made her requests known to her father. "It's far," she said. "We're going to build our own house, but I want to live here until its ready. We'll sleep out in the shed."

Parley told Roy about his plans. Roy said they were welcome.

Parley drove back up to Blue Mirror Lake and came back with his clothes and tools. Linnie kept her clothes in the bedroom she shared with Baby and Dru, as if she had never left home. At night she slept out in the shed on the lower bunk, Parley slept on the upper and on the rare occasion that she gave in to his want of her, she fretted. "Don't drop your seed in me."

On week-ends, and after work, no matter the hour, Parley was busy framing and building a bedroom on one end of the house. He didn't have time to finish the room before blustering winds brought slate-gray clouds and blizzards whipped through the mountains.

Through November, December, January and February thick, hard-driving snow bore down on the land. Enormous limbs on the towering trees bent, snapped and fell. On some days, roads were closed. Schools and sawmills shut down. Logging operations came to a halt.

Axes rang. Late afternoon and far into the night wolf packs whined, at times close to people. The people shoveled paths and tunnels out to their root cellars and privies and gave thanks for the providence of meat from elk, deer, pheasant and wild turkeys, salted and cured, and for the occasional beef, or pork purchased at the Company Store, and thank God for chickens.

In spite of the long dark days, Dru brimmed with happiness. When the mail came through she had letters from Buzz. He would come home to her when the roads cleared and she must take good care of herself.

While doing her chores she sang, "My Gal Sal," and "I've Got Rings on My Fingers." In evenings, sitting close to the circle of lamplight, she hemmed flannel baby blankets. She used the money Buzzie had given her to buy a sewing machine and seated at it, her feet working the treadle, she sewed rompers, a bunting, and gowns.

In March icicles hanging from the eaves began to thaw. Linnie and Dru scraped frost off the windows and peered through the watery glass to see trees across the reach drop great chunks of snow.

Parley finished the room. In late March he drove the wagon over to Coldsprings, purchased a spooled bed and springs and a thick feather mattress. Linnie was happy with the bed, but in the bedroom they would have for themselves, he would expect her to allow him to love her as he wanted to do. She wasn't inclined.

One night, a week after he'd brought the bed home, a full moon shone high and bright into their bedroom and Parley, leaned on his elbow toward Linnie, said, "If you have any feelings for me at all, maybe you could try to show it?"

"I think you're a very kind man," she said. "And I appreciate your care for me and for my family. I . . . I don't know what else to say."

"You can try to allow me to love you right. Without leaving you. If you do that, you might learn to love me."

"We made promises," she said. "Ann hasn't come back, so I'll drive over to Sunnydale and talk to the Makkah woman just as soon as I can. I promise."

"You do that," he said and he turned away from her.

∞

In early April, Gavin Corrigan drove up to Roy's house and delivered a cherry wood cradle to Dru. "Buzz thinks it's the most beautiful cradle he's ever seen," he said. He handed Dru an envelope. She opened it and found two ten dollar bills with a card. "Buy whatever you want, my beautiful Peacherino. I'll be home soon."

She was pleased with the money, but it was the cradle that caught her up with delight. She ran her hands over the beautifully smooth rich-polished wood and she made it up with the soft, flannel blankets for her baby and she set the cradle next to her bed.

Birdie stopped by every day to see how Dru was doing and to be on hand for the birthing. The arrival of the cradle heralded the baby's birth, for on April 15 Dru felt the first sharp spasms of childbirth.

Hour after hour she clamped her teeth down hard on the hard knots of a rag and she arched her back, and then she eased. Sweat beaded her face. Pain showed in her eyes. She was in labor until mid-afternoon.

Baby, who tried to help Dru by patting her head, was sent out of the room. She sat on the sofa and held her arms in the rockabye way of hers and sang, "Rockababy rock rock rockababy rock . . ."

Late afternoon Dru cried out, "Is this baby ever going to come out of me?"

Linnie said, "Let's go walking." She and Birdie walked Dru from one room to another and back and forth and forth and back. Dru's pains increased and came faster. Faster and faster. Linnie put two pillows on the floor beside the bed and covered the pillows with a quilt. Birdie said, "Squat over the blanket, Dru. Squat." She and Linnie held on to Dru. "Push," the women shouted, "Push, Dru. Push."

Dru, hanging on to Linnie and Birdie's arms, pushed, grunted and screamed, "Never again. You hear me, Buzzie wherever you are? You're never getting on me again." Then, with two enormous grunts, she dropped a baby boy on one of the pillows.

Birdie cut the umbilical cord and picked up the infant. She bathed him, dried and oiled him and took him to Dru. Dru raised her arms and she took the child to her swollen breasts. She smiled. "Thank you," she whispered to Birdie and Linnie. "His name is Hugh." She and her son slept.

The following day birth fever came. Dru's breasts got hard as rocks, her nipples cracked and bled.

Linnie put hot baked potatoes inside clean wool socks, pounded the socks with a hammer and applied them to the infection. The sickness eased, but Dru wasn't interested in nursing her boy. "I want to be pretty when Buzzy comes home," she said. "And Hugh has taken to the bottle just fine."

Linnie, quite taken with the child, wondered if Dru would stick to her vow and not allow Buzzie to make another baby. She didn't think it was likely.

Birdie Mae's eyes spoke of hunger for a baby of her own. On days when she wasn't off with Newt speculating, she came to her father's house and stayed until late afternoon. She hovered over Hugh, bathed him, fed him, rocked him, cooed and sang to him.

Baby sat beside his cradle for long periods of time. When Dru bathed him, she tried to help, but Dru shooed her away. "You don't know how to take care of a baby and you'll never have one of your own, so you don't need to learn. Now, leave him alone."

Baby bawled. "Rockabye batty baa bee. Knockers." She sat on the sofa and she rocked and hugged herself hard.

Two months after Hugh's birth, Linnie and Birdie helped Mide deliver a healthy, robust girl she named Emma. It was a difficult birth for Mide, labor lasting well into the second day and leaving Mide exhausted. Birdie stayed at Mide and Colin's house for two days to help.

Linnie recalled Mide's wishes to hold off on having children. Evidently Colin hadn't paid her mind attention at all.

CHAPTER 15

Parley sold his place up at Blue Mirror Lake. Aware of Linnie's desire to live close to her family, he spent weeks negotiating with Inga Strom and he ended up buying Roy's place and an adjoining ten acres. Linnie thought he must have paid a dear price and she wondered where the money came, but it was not her place to ask. Nor was she eager for him to build the new house. She was quite content living with her father, her two sisters, and the baby, Hugh.

But guilt plagued her. She wasn't treating Parley right and she recalled Birdie Mae's words of caution. *If you refuse to allow him to love you like he's going to want to do and like he's got a right to do, you'll be sorry.*

One day she asked him, "When do you intend to build your house? And where on your property?"

"I'll build it next year," he said. "I spent quite a bit of money buying the land. Now, I have money coming in, and I'll have enough to build next year. It's not *my* property, Linnie. It's *ours*. And the house isn't *mine*. It's *ours*. In the meantime I'm building a workshop on the far northeast corner."

"That's good," said Linnie. "I remember you told me once that you enjoy carving wood."

He built it where he said he would, out on the far northeast corner a good distance from Roy's house. To get there one took the old skid road for a quarter of a mile and then cut through a thick understory of salal, huckleberry and fern.

The shop was close to the river and from the one window Parley could see the big timbers coursing down-flume. He installed a wood-stove with a round glass eye and he made a wide bench on which he often sat while he worked. He enjoyed settling in, smoking his pipe and honing his wood-carving skills. Linnie never went to his shop. It was his and she preferred to give him time alone.

During that spring and summer Baby's nature improved. She brushed her hair over and over for long minutes and while she couldn't tie her hair-bows, she sat still while Dru or Linnie tied one in her blonde curls. She fussed when food spots stained her dresses and she tried to keep herself clean and not so dependant on her sisters. She liked to soap her hands over and over and she smelled her hands and she smiled and whispered, "Pretty Baa bee. Pretty, pretty loon knockers. Buttons. Buttons, too."

As long as she had one of her three button-front dresses clean and available, she took a fierce pride in dressing and undressing herself. Her favorite dress was the lavender dress with lace at the collar and cuffs. She still needed help with her shoes and stockings, but she managed her own underthings.

She enjoyed, beyond measure, looking at the pretty things Buzz sent to Dru. One day when Dru slipped the pretty blue shawl around Baby's shoulders, Baby sighed. "Oh," and she gently touched the soft silk.

She still had a mean temper, but it didn't flare as often, and when Parley was around she seemed to try hard to be as good as good could be. She made it her habit to sit next to him at supper. Parley didn't seem to take notice and if he did, he wasn't bothered.

One Sunday when Baby was down on her knees at her mother's feet trying to polish her mother's shoes, Meara got up and started for her bedroom. Baby tried to follow her. Linnie stopped Baby and Baby, her face beet-red with anger, screamed and fought Linnie off. She threw pots and pans and books—anything she could get her hands on—until Parley, who had been outside tending the garden, grabbed her and held her arms pinned down tight to her sides. "No," he said. "You mustn't do that. You're hurting everybody who loves you."

She settled some, but she chewed on her fingernails until blood came. That afternoon her rage still seethed and Linnie knew she'd be a handful for the rest of the day.

Parley said, "Baby, come with me." He took her hand and led her across the reach to the road and from there to his workshop. Her eyes widened and she plopped herself down on a log beside the river and she watched the big sticks tumbling downstream for the rest of the day until Parley took her home.

Her trip to Parley's shop became a habit. As long as she didn't demand his attentions he didn't mind. Sometimes she examined his tools. She picked up the planer. The chisel. Rabbet. And T-square. She didn't touch his handsaws, but for days she worked at his folding measure stick and after she figured out how to unfold it, she smiled and said, "Oh, Pawley."

One day she sidled up to him while he was working and she pointed to the object he held in his hands. Parley told her he was making a set of wooden bowls for the family. Her presence didn't bother him, but he was at odds with himself. In a peculiar way he enjoyed her and her scent.

CHAPTER 16

On a hot day in August Buzz wheeled his shiny automobile up in front of the house, got out, jumped up on the porch and gave his startled, delighted wife a hug and a fine kiss. She hadn't seen him now for close to a year and he, of course, had not had a peek at his son.

He brought presents. A spinning top for Hugh. A pair of high-buttoned black leather boots with pointed toes for Dru, who was almost beside herself with delight. But Buzzie wasn't much taken with the baby. He held him briefly and casually passed him back to Dru.

At supper he talked of nothing but Seattle. "It's just a swell place," he said. "And I've had some palmy days. Went roller skating at the Dreamland. Saw a play in a fancy theater. And get this, Dru. One night I was down on Yesler Way when the Salvation Army came by. What a sight. They sang 'Onward Christian Soldiers' and carried flags and torches. Hey, Peacherino, I've got my eye on a nice house, too and after I buy it, I'll come get you and we'll have a fine time."

Dru, with sappy love-eyes, clung to every word Buzz uttered and she hung at his side like a burr. At night Linnie couldn't help hearing the heavy breathing and Dru's sharp little yelps of pleasure coming from her and Buzz's back bedroom.

He stayed for three days.

Six weeks later Dru told Linnie that she was expecting again. "That's all right," she said. "You heard Buzzie. The next time he comes home he'll take us to Seattle and we'll live like a real family. I figure this baby will be born right around the time of your birthday, May 4th."

"We'll celebrate together," said Linnie.

Fall, always beautiful, gave in to the dark, cold winter that seemed to last forever. Battling deep snows and freeze. Knocking icicles as big as small logs off the house. Smoke spiraling up from thin stove-pipes on the shanty's roofs held a feel of cold. The only warm rooms in Roy's house were the kitchen and living room. The back bedroom, in which Parley and Linnie slept, was as cold as outdoors.

Once in a blue moon Linnie grit her teeth and allowed Parley to perform on her the act of loving, but she continued to fight the battle of him leaving her in time. It was not pleasant for either of them and more and more frequently during that winter Parley left her alone.

ᏣᎤ

One afternoon in early spring, when Hugh was sleeping in his cradle and Dru and Linnie were hanging laundry at one end of the kitchen, Hugh's high-pitched scream shattered the otherwise quiet air.

Dru dropped the soapy drawers she'd been scrubbing and raced into her bedroom. Hugh, his face red with screams of anger and fear, lay on the floor. Baby, on her knees beside him, was trying to pick him up.

Dru yelled. "You dropped him! Idiot girl! I've told you again and again that you're not to touch him." She scooped up Hugh and cuddled him. Baby reached out to try to touch him. Dru pushed her. Hard.

Baby tumbled in a heap on the floor.

Dru said, "Bad girl. Bad, bad girl. Don't you ever touch him."

Baby's face screwed up and she bawled and went to the front room and sat on the sofa. She rocked and hugged herself hard and she sang in her monotone, flat voice, "Rockaby Bay beee. Knockers. Batty Bay beee. Loon."

From that day on Baby did not touch Hugh. But every now and then she stood beside his cradle when he was sleeping and she hugged herself and sang the tune that Linnie and Dru now called, "Baby's rockabye song."

Spring—and folks up in Hanksport County could begin to claim the outdoors.

Parley bought a hand mirror and on the back he carved a likeness of Blue Mirror Lake and he gave it to Linnie for her 18th birthday.

"Oh, Parley. It's lovely," she said.

"On a nice summer Sunday, let's pack up a picnic and drive up to the lake. I want you to see it when the sun is shining."

"Let's do that." She kept the mirror on top of a small dresser drawer Parley had made for her.

Parley had other talents and he put them to good use. Vegetable gardens up in Hanksport County were hard to come·by, but Parley turned the thin, acid soil, mixed it with horse and chicken manure and in late spring, at the time of the waxing moon, he planted carrots, lettuce, and cabbage. When the moon waned, onions, turnips, and potatoes went in. A sturdy fence protected his garden from deer.

One spring day after the pale green vegetable shoots had begun to show, Baby, in one of her fits of temper, uprooted and scattered them. Parley grabbed her and again he held her arms down stiff against her body. "You leave the plants in the ground so they can grow," he said. "If you pull them up, they'll die. Here." He gave her two of the uprooted plants. "Help me plant these and *you* will help them grow."

Parley knelt. Baby knelt beside him and paid attention while Parley replanted the plants and patted the earth around them. "Now you plant yours."

She planted slowly and when she'd finished she stood and clapped her hands. "Oh, Pawley."

Parley filled a water can and taught her how to water the plants. "Now, you can watch them grow."

She smiled. "Baby knockers loon grow. Grow. Grow."

Baby seemed content to tend the plants and she kept them watered and she showed a fierce pride in what she did. Parley showed her the difference between plants to eat and weeds to pull and Baby spent long hours tending the vegetables and she did it with a fair bit of proper care.

On May 5, Dru gave birth to a little girl and she named her Stella. Stella and Hugh were thirteen months apart. And Mide gave birth to her and Colin's second child, Ted.

Every few months Buzz sent gifts to Dru and the babies. Extravagant things. Jewelry—necklaces, bracelets and rings for Dru. Toys—dolls and teddy bears, rubber balls, marbles, and jacks for the children. Most of the toys were far beyond the children's years and Dru tucked them away with her own treasures.

And Buzz wrote to his family. Stella was seven months old when Dru shared one of his letters with Linnie. *I'm coming home soon and let's talk about BUILDING our own home.*

But it was shortly before Stella's first birthday when Buzz arrived with flair and drama in his beautiful auto and, as always, he had gifts. He seemed anxious and uneasy, he stayed only two days, but before he left he gave Dru a ten dollar bill.

That evening, after the children were tucked into bed, Linnie and Dru settled down by the lantern to mend and darn and Linnie said, "What does Buzzie do in Seattle? What is his line of work?"

"He's I.W.W. Secretary and spends time in the Ballard Union Hall. I know he's got lots of meetings and he's plenty busy."

"Where does he get the money to buy all the fancy gifts?"

"I don't know. It's his business, Linnie. Not ours."

❦

On a bright summer morning Linnie chanked open the firebox to feed the fire. She would bake bread today. Baby, seated at the table, practiced her letters. Dru, carrying Stella on her hip, called out the door to Hugh who was playing in a sand-box Parley had built. "I'll come out in a minute," she said. "I'll bring Stella and we'll make sand-pies and we'll pick flowers and give the pies pretty hats."

Once again, Dru's belly had swelled. She drew a bath in the baby tub and while she soaped Stella with the nice soap, she said to Linnie, "If I knew how to get rid of this baby, I'd do it. Buzzie doesn't take much to the kiddies and that's why he doesn't come home very often."

"You're not thinking straight, Dru. It's not a good idea to try to get rid of a baby once it's started. In fact, it's plain wrong. But every time Buzz comes home, you let him make another baby. Keep him off of you."

Anguish pooled in Dru's eyes. "I did that the last time, but then he starts loving me and I don't want him to stop."

"Then don't complain. He should at least pull out of you in time."

"I tell him that and he gets mad. Mide is having another one, too."

"Colin and Buzz are selfish. They don't think about their wives as they should. Mide has a hard time birthing. Too hard for comfort. Buzz comes up here to visit, gets you in the family way, stays two or three days, then merrily goes back to Seattle and you don't see him for months. But, you put thoughts about getting rid of a baby out of your mind. Once this new one is here, you'll love it to pieces."

"I suppose you're right." Dru finished bathing Stella, dressed her in a pretty yellow dress with a smocked bodice and, with Stella again on her hip, she went outside to join Hugh. Shortly she was singing, "Cuddle up a little closer, lovey, mine," with Hugh and Stella and dancing around the mud-pies with flower hats.

On February 16 of the following spring Dru birthed another girl. Nellie was a quiet baby who seemed to study shadows and light. Dru, sure that Buzz would enjoy this little girl with his own blue eyes and dark hair, wrote to him. *Please come to see the children. Nellie looks like you and she's beautiful.*

CHAPTER 17

Except for one thing, Linnie considered this summer delightful with very little rain. Now, on a bright morning in mid-June she drove to the Blackduck Bridge, parked on the other side, returned to the bridge and stood by the rail. She looked down at the surging, chalk-white river. It would be three years this July since she and Parley had spoken of their private concerns to each other. Parley had lived up to his. She had not. Now she was on her way over to Sunnydale to try to see the Makkah Indian woman.

The hoot of a great gray owl brought to her mind a late afternoon with her mother. The sun was low that day. Shadows were deep and her mother pointed to a bird gliding above the trees. "It's an owl and it's hunting, Linnie. Its big yellow eyes see the world all around him."

Parley wore a small carved owl around his neck. Linnie might ask him why he wore it and what did it mean. She knew nothing about his family. Where did they live? What was in the brown envelope that came in the mail every month? But she doubted she would ask those questions. His life and family didn't matter to her one whit.

But he'd surely been good to her and her family. Not only had he built the bedroom for themselves, he'd also built the room for Dru, and a new front room. The old front room was now a dining room and, because of Parley, the once miserable shack was a home.

But, while Parley was responsible for all of those good things, Linnie had done nothing to fulfill her pledge of three years ago. Guilt pecked her. Last night, after refusing once again to allow Parley to love her as he wanted to do, she said, "I promise that tomorrow I'll drive over to the valley and talk to the Makah woman."

"You do that," Parley said. "If you'd even give me a chance to love you right, and knowing you as I do now, you would enjoy it."

"Not if I feared you started a baby inside me."

Parley turned from her and she sensed a chill about him she'd not sensed before.

She returned to her auto and drove up past Strom's big, boxy, two-story house, its shingled roof faded to silvery-grey. A large front window must have a fine view of the river and town. A blaze of sunshine shone off one of three second story windows.

Occasionally Linnie ran into Kees in town and she always spoke to him, but she hurried on. And Joe never spoke of his work for Mrs. Strom, but Joe rarely spoke about much of anything, except God and church.

Linnie drove on, climbing up and up through a dark forest where mushrooms, big as plates, sprouted from massive rotting logs. A bit further she came to open space and Canyon Road, a narrow road skirting a deep canyon. Linnie was cautious. If an auto should come from the opposite direction, traveling west, the driver must pull over to allow the east-bound traveler room to pass. Otherwise the east-bound vehicle would fall over the edge and crash down the canyon.

Linnie was relieved to reach the valley, the air warm and sweet with blooming lilac and apple trees. She pulled over and basked in the sun for a few moments. From somewhere, not far, a cow bawled. A dog barked. Just up ahead a man wearing a floppy straw hat pushed a wheelbarrow toward her. She hailed him. "Good morning. Do you know where the Makah woman lives?"

"That way." He pointed up the road to a small house covered with thick shakes. Linnie thanked him, drove to the place and parked. A spotted pony grazed beside the house. A strange sight caught her attention. Brown bottles with a peculiar blue sheen hung on the limbs of an apple tree. The tree was in full bloom and the bottles, moved by a slight breeze, made a pleasing sound while reflecting a splintered brilliance. The pear shaped bottles were identical to the one Linnie had seen at the Dickerson place three years ago. How had Mr. or Mrs. Dickerson, or their niece Ann, come to have one?

Linnie went up on the porch of the little house and knocked on the door. Sensing nobody was home and thinking that perhaps the woman was working in her garden, Linnie took a path through tall spiky, cream-white flowers and a tangle of plants. Spider webs, damp with morning dew, brushed against her face. Emerging into a clearing, she came upon a woman busy with her hoe.

"Hello," Linnie called out.

The woman, wearing a long dress the color of green apples, straightened. She shaded her eyes and she approached Linnie. Her nose was broad; her egg-shaped eyes the color of elk.

Linnie smiled. "Are you Brown Hon?"

"I am."

"I need your help."

"What kind of help?"

"My name is Mrs. Hearn. Mrs. Parley Hearn. I'm a married woman and I've heard that you know how to stop children from being born. Can you tell me what my husband and I should do to . . . to stop them?"

Brown Hon's dark eyes seemed to probe Linnie. "No," she said. "You'll have to learn about that from your own people. We have our ways and if I shared them with you, I could get into trouble."

"Why would you get into trouble?"

"White people have strong feelings about this business. Your people believe in a God who won't allow a woman to use her own mind. Your people believe that if your God wants you to have children, you must obey him. Women who speak out against this belief are sent to jail. No. I can't help you." Brown Hon turned and went back to her hoeing.

Linnie, empty of any knowledge she had sought, left Sunnydale. While driving home she pondered her situation. She couldn't learn a thing in the valley, or in Hanksport. She must go to a city to learn about this business and the closest city was Seattle.

That evening, just before supper, Linnie took Parley aside in the front room. "Dang it, Parley. Brown Hon won't help us." She told him about her journey and about her thoughts of going to Seattle."

"Yes," said Parley. "You should go. I'll . . ."

Baby came clumping into the room, sat down on the sofa, rocked back and forth and sang, "Baa bee knockers. Baa bee rockabye. Hoo loon knockers."

Parley said, "We'll talk about it later, when we won't be interrupted." He ran his fingers through his hair. "God knows when that might be."

Later, after Parley had gone to bed, Linnie sat out on the stoop. *Your people believe in a God who won't allow a woman to use her own mind. Your people believe that if your God want you to have children, you must obey him. Women who speak out against this belief are sent to jail.*

What did Wobblies know about this? If Linnie joined the I.W.W. she would learn something about it and hadn't Ann said that she'd be a "swell Wob?" What would she have to do, to become a 'liberator of women?' A 'suffragist?'

She leaned back against the step. The *bong bong bong bong* of the flume bell echoed. It was nice to know that there was no trouble upstream, but the burnt man flashed in her mind. Nobody had been charged with Mr. Dickerson's murder. The person who did it was somewhere around, and probably not far. And while Parley was right about Linnie slowly forgetting the sight, she still thought about it and felt uneasy.

The air was chilly and she went inside, undressed, put on her night shift and got into bed.

Parley said in a soft voice, "Don't give up on the Makah woman. Let's both go visit her next Saturday."

"Yes. It's a beautiful drive. But, I've been thinking about all of this. I'm sure that Wobblies know about this business. If I was a Wob, I know I'd be a liberator of women. I think that has everything in the world to do with what we need to know."

He slipped an arm around her and pulled her to him. "I'm behind you in whatever you want to do, and I've always been favorable toward union. We'll both join."

"Strom workers are leaning toward the I.W.W.?"

"Yes. Word is getting out. It might be a battle, but it will happen." He turned his back to her.

CHAPTER 18
FRANK DOBBS
AUGUST, 1914

Frank Dobbs clung to the weed-slick piling in the high, slack tide and considered his fate. He was cold. His limbs were numb, his mind dazed and it would soon be dark.

He narrowed his eyes and set his sight on a railroad trestle spanning two or so miles of mud flats. He knew where he was. He'd grown up in the town of Wiley, ten miles south in this Northern California country. He also knew what he had to do.

By the position of the moon he figured it to be about six o'clock in the evening. Around seven o'clock the north-bound Southern Pacific train would barrel across the trestle. A half-mile south an east-west bound road intersected the north-south route of the line. At that intersection a blinking red light warned automobiles, wagons, drays and people on foot to stop. It warned trains to slow down. Dobbs had to get to that light and he didn't have a whole lot of time.

To get to dry land he must swim a good hundred yards in the murky tide waters, slog through mud flats to a steep grade and climb the grade. Then, on solid, firm ground he must press on south to the signal light and hope to God that authorities weren't around. If he missed that rattler heading north, he'd have to wait for another train and that meant killing time for another twenty-four hours in country known to be hostile to men with bindles slung around their shoulders, men combing the countryside looking for work, and men, like Dobbs, spreading the word about the I.W.W.

He blamed himself for his predicament. Crimps aboard lumber ships moored, in this case, out on Humboldt Bay, were hired to shanghai chumps like Frank. Best places to find them? Saloons. Hell, they'd buy you a drink, drag your hapless, floppy self to rowboats, row you out to the waiting ships and see that you got on board. The crimp would catch four bits tied in a rag from one of the deck hands and row back to shore. Three or four runs, day or night, got the crimp pretty good pay.

Mooney's Saloon, built on pilings north of Wiley was notorious for crimps. Notorious for drunken, bleary-eyed roustabouts throwing thick bladed knives at the bull's eye pinned on one of the greasy walls. Notorious for thieves whose glittering sharp eyes took note of anyone and everyone who came through the heavy bat-winged doors. Notorious for the five or six ladies-of-the-night with bright-painted faces, their hair curled and fashioned, laughing and teasing before disappearing with a gent.

Dobbs usually avoided such places, but after spending six days riding the rails and camping in rain-soaked hobo jungles, the soft glowing light of the smoky saloon beckoned. He pushed open those double-hung doors and went inside. A blonde, blue-eyed fellow with a friendly smile held out his hand. "Friend, let me buy you a drink."

Seated at the bar with fellow drinkers, Dobbs coddled his shot of throat-burning whiskey. "Where're you from?" he asked his pal.

"California. You bet I'm a union man. Joined the I.W.W. couple of years back. Hell, I've picked hops down in the Sacramento Valley for a goddamned two-bit day. Logging camps might be bad, but they're a lot better . . ."

Dobbs' ears rang. His pal's face got swimmy and stretched tall as a twenty-foot tree. Dobbs's smiling friend had doped Dobbs up and there wasn't a goddamned thing Dobbs could do about it.

Dazed, limp as a rag doll, he slumped to the floor along with two other fools. With no time to waste—time meant money—the three were dragged through the back of the saloon and dumped into a dinghy moored in the cold lapping waters below. Two crimps rowed them out to one of the waiting ships.

But Dobbs' bad luck changed. The ship's captain took two of the men, but didn't need a third. "I ain't gonna feed a man I don't need," he yelled and he tossed the crimps their pay. The crimps rowed Frank back to the tide flat and dumped him close to the pilings.

Dobbs took a deep breath and struck out. Using a strong side stroke he swam to the mud-flats and splashed through slime and mud to dry land. After resting a moment he pushed on to reach the grade and clawed his way through muck up to the top. He lay, panting, exhausted, and he longed for sleep.

"Don't be a fool again," he said aloud.

He got up. Loping along beside the tracks he kept his eyes on the glow of the red signal light and once there he knelt and put one hand on the rail. Not much of a vibration, but it was good. The approaching train would take him to Seattle, the one place he wanted to be.

He set his bindle down. He sniffed the air. Salt marsh land and fish. Out on the mud flats the calm still water reflected a silver-white moon.

From the south came the long, keening whistle and a pinprick of light. Dobbs picked up his bindle and slung it across his back. The train slowed. It belched steam. The steady red glimmer of the firebox flashed and Dobbs was plunged into a blast of iron-smell and hot oil. Hammering drivers. Screeching brakes. Dobbs, running alongside the slowing train, reached up, grabbed the door handle of a rattling box car and swung himself up inside. Six, maybe eight men were slumped against their bindles. He slung his own bindle down against the wall to claim his place. No one spoke. Frank hunkered down, leaned back and closed his eyes.

It had been twelve years since he'd been in this country, once his home. Even as a child he'd disliked his parents' house that bristled with fancy lattice work, gables, richly carved redwood, stained glass windows and marble fireplaces. When he decided to leave home, he doubted he'd be back. He had no desire to go into business with his father, who made millions harvesting giant Redwood trees.

While attending Columbia University in New York he became interested in people on the lower East Side. One night he dropped by a saloon and listened to a big, red-haired man speak about the injustices the working class had to endure. Hale Tosstles became Dobbs' good friend.

Dobbs started going to I.W.W. rallies. He listened to street speakers. He read *The Industrial Worker,* and work written by Big Bill Haywood, Joe Hill, and Elizabeth Gurley Flynn. What he read made sense. Dobbs dropped out of school and went to work on behalf of the vast numbers of the underclass.

After joining the I.W.W., Dobbs and Tosstles made their way out to the West Coast. In Seattle they met a fellow Wobblie, Maude Easton, daughter of an East Coast shipping magnate. Maude's husband was murdered in Seattle following a protest rally aimed at capitalists when Ann, the Easton's only child, was four years old.

Maude continued her work with Union. She offered rooms in her spacious home up on Queen Anne Hill to union folks who needed a place to stay. Dobbs, Tosstles, Paul Garibaldi, Bruns Wald, and fellow Wobs, men and women and Maude's daughter, Ann, seated at Maude's dinner table, held lively conversations about American politics, education, social justice, music and religion. They enjoyed themselves.

"I'm an old Wob," Maude liked to say. "My husband and I joined the I.W.W. as members of *The Dill Pickle Club* back in Chicago. Capitalists called us a dangerous bunch of radicals who would destroy this country. But we knew that union wasn't destroying our nation. Neither was the working class. Capitalists were, and are, bringing this country to its knees."

While in Seattle, Dobbs took to the streets, harangued and attracted a considerable crowd. "Who owns those buildings?" he'd call out and point to either Smith Tower, or in the direction of the palatial Union Pacific Railroad Station on King Street.

"Millionaires uptown," the crowd yelled.

Dobbs struck his palm with his fist and cried out, "Who works in the woods? Who goes down in the mines?"

"We do. We do."

"Who builds the great railroads? Hauls fish from the seas? Harvests crops?"

"We do."

"You're right," Dobbs answered. "*You* made those fellows millionaires who are now uptown at the Rainier Club. *You* work in his highball logging camps. His mills. His coal mines. *You* work in his wheat fields. His orchards. And for all your hard work you're treated like scum and paid next to nothing."

Dobbs didn't stop his haranguing on the streets. He carried it into the hobo camps. "Join union. One Big Union. Join the I.W.W." A few men raised their fists and joined the chants, but it was hard to reach hungry men who had no jobs. No money. No home or hope.

The train slowed and Dobbs let go of his tangled half-dreams. A number of matters came to mind. First, he'd go home to Sophie Krueger, his lover and comrade. My God, he was proud of her. Against all odds, experiencing arrests, incarceration in the infamous Crooked Neck Workhouse for Women, hunger strikes and frightening threats, she had established a clinic in Spokane in which to educate women about family limitation. She wanted now to establish one in Seattle.

Tomorrow Dobbs would stop by the Ballard Union Hall to see Tosstles and the two would pay Maude a visit. Word was out. Some time ago Newt Corrigan alerted the I.W.W. that most all of Strom workers were ready to organize, but they needed a voice. Dobbs would provide it.

He recalled the red-haired girl he'd seen some years back when he was released from the Hanksport jail. A pretty girl with high cheek bones and large, dark eyes. No doubt a logger's daughter, dirt poor with a slew of brothers and sisters and she no doubt lived a bleak life. Married young, had too many babies, and in all probability would die young. Too bad Sophie couldn't find time to set up a clinic up in Hanksport.

The train slowed and approached the station. Dobbs smiled. Wouldn't Sophie, Maude, Ann and Tosstles be surprised to learn he'd been shanghaied by two goddamned crimps.

CHAPTER 19

September with shots of sunshine through mist and fog.

Before the sun was high Linnie took to her task of peeling, slicing, and packing peaches into hot, scalding quart jars, adding sugar and a pinch of cinnamon and setting them in a boiling hot water bath atop the fire blazing in the stove.

Nellie was sleeping. Dru and four-year old Hugh and three-year old Stella were out in the garden.

Baby, seated at the table, was working on her letters and softly singing in her tuneless voice, "Rockabye Ba bee. Rockabye . . ."

At sixteen years old she was a soft, pillowy girl of medium height with a simpering smile. She was a callow girl, girlish and fastidious, paying great attention to herself and forever brushing her hair, grown long after fighting her sisters' attempts to keep it cut short.

An automobile came grinding up the road.

Dru came to the open door and called out. "Linnie. We have company. I don't know who it is, but it isn't Buzzie."

Linnie, with Baby clomping along behind her, hurried outside.

Ann stopped the auto and got out. "My heavens!" She hugged Linnie. "It's been over four years. I can't believe it's been that long. Why, you look fit as a fiddle." She turned to Dru. "And you look peachy keen, too. Did you two know that my honey bug, Paul, and I got married last year? I'm still trying to get used to my name, Ann Easton Garibaldi. I don't want to give up my maiden name."

"No," said Linnie. "We didn't know and I'm pleased for both of you."

"Thank you. We're holding a meeting at my house next Sunday. Mr. Dobbs will speak and we're getting the word out. It's time to organize. Both of you please come to the meeting."

Dru said, "Thank you, but I have my kiddies to tend to."

"Bring them," said Ann. "Children are always welcome."

"Somebody has to stay home with our mother. And her." Dru indicated Baby with a nod of her head.

"I'll gladly come," said Linnie. "I'm sure that my husband will come with me and I'll tell Birdie and Newt about it."

"They'll be there," said Ann. "And Linnie, I'll look forward to meeting your husband."

"Hoo rah Bay beee go," Baby chortled. "Hoo rah batty loon Bay bee go. Knockers."

"No," said Linnie. "I'll take you another time."

"Knockers go. Pawley go." She smiled and ran around and around in circles. "Buttons. Buttons."

Ann gave Baby brief, but close scrutiny. "I used to work in a place that takes care of people like her."

Dru said, "What kind of place are you talking about?"

"Down in Seattle a very rich man had a daughter who wasn't right in her head." She watched Baby, still running in circles. "What's her name?"

Dru said, "We call her 'Baby.' Our mother never gave her a name."

Ann frowned. "No name? Well, this man in Seattle built *The Denise Harvey Institution*. If a family member, like Baby, needs care and looking after, he or she is brought into this place and the family no longer has that worry. So, if you took Baby down to *The Harvey*, you wouldn't have to worry about her. You wouldn't have to pay for her care, either. The foundation takes care of that."

Dru said, "That sounds too good to be true. If Baby wasn't living here, I'd have some ease of mind. She hurt Hugh once when he was just a few months old. Whenever she's close to my kiddies I watch her like a hawk and I'll soon have another one to worry about."

Linnie said, "Last year Birdie and Newt wanted to take her to live with them. At first she was excited to go. Then she balked. Now, Birdie and Newt want to take her again. If she'll go, that will give us some ease."

"She won't," said Dru. "If she did, she couldn't go to Parley's shop. But, I'll talk to Father about this place in Seattle. The Harvey?"

"Yes," said Ann. "My Lord, I don't want to cause any trouble. I just thought you ought to know about it."

Linnie said, "It's good that you told us. And we *will* talk to Father."

Dru said, "Mrs. Garibaldi, are *you* in the family way?"

"No. We don't plan on having children."

Linnie said, "Do you *not* have children in the same way Parley and I don't have them? Your . . . your husband leaves you early?"

"No. That wouldn't be fair to him. Or to me. Paul uses a rubber. A condom. Linnie, I think we talked about that the first time we met. I didn't know much about all of that business back then. I'll find some pamphlets about this and get them to you. Now, I've got to run. See you Sunday. Tootle ooo." She hopped back into her auto, waved and drove off.

All sorts of ideas tumbled through Linnie's mind. Mr. Dobbs hadn't forgotten the people up at Hanksport and she would get to hear him speak. She might even meet him. The A&D in town now carried women's hats. Linnie would ask Parley for a little money and she would buy herself a hat.

At supper that evening Dru spoke up about the notion of sending Baby away. "Ann says we wouldn't have to pay a dime, Father. Baby would get good care and it would . . ."

"That sounds like a fine idea and the sooner, the better."

"Hoo loon Bay bee home," Baby shouted. She pounded her fist on the table. "Pawley. Pawley. Buttons. Buttons. Hoo loon home."

"Hush, Baby," said Roy, "I'm not putting you into any house of charity." He turned to Linnie, Dru and Parley. "Birdie and Newt have spoken to me again about taking Baby for awhile. That's fine. We look after our own and I won't listen to another word about this other matter."

"Hoo loon home, Pawley," Baby said. "Batty hoo loon home."

CHAPTER 20

On Sunday afternoon, the day of the I.W.W. rally up at the Dickerson place, Kees Strom stood on the porch not far from Mr. Dobbs. Dobbs was speaking with men Kees had seen around, but he didn't know them. He kept his eyes on folks coming up the road.

As was his habit, he wore tweed knickers. A cap to match. The chain of his gold pocket watch gleamed against his white shirt. His mission was to share his picnic lunch with Linnie and Parley.

Linnie, wearing a jaunty, dark blue sailor hat, strode with purpose up the road alongside her husband.

Kees picked up the picnic basket and went to greet them. "Hello there," he said. "I've brought a fine picnic to share with you, just as I did on the Fourth of July some years back. You enjoyed it, so today I have pork sandwiches, herring salad, apples and ginger cookies."

"Sorry," said Parley. "We can't stay to eat. But we thank you all the same."

The red spot on Kee's forehead bloomed. "You can't stay for a short time to share a picnic with me?"

Linnie said, "No. And thank you, but right after Mr. Dobbs speaks, we need to go home." She went off to join her sister—wasn't her name Birdie? And fellow loggers hailed Parley.

Questions and shame picked at Kees. What had happened? Why had Linnie, at one time so friendly and kind, become haughty and one who barely spoke to him?

For the next two hours Kees did not allow her out of his sight. A tingle raced up his spine when she, responding to Dobbs's shout, "This is a true class war, a class war we Wobs will win," pumped her fist high and shouted with the crowd, "Union! One Big Union."

"This isn't just an ordinary meeting," Dobbs said, his tone strong and defiant. "This is one great rally of working families who know it's time to organize. We *need* union up here. We *need* you. *Now.*"

Whistles. Cheers. Linnie chanted with the rest. "O. B. U. One Big Union. O. B. U. One Big Union."

Dobbs continued. "Now, I want to recognize a fellow Wob-volunteer. A Wob you'll see a lot of during this campaign. A Wob who wants to see Strom workers get *paid* what they deserve. *Live* and eat in decent houses and clean camps. *Work* decent hours. So let's give a hand to Lester Knef."

Les Knef, a big, swarthy man Kees had seen from time to time, jumped up on the porch, took the bull horn and waved his hat. "We'll break the backs of management up here," he called out. "We'll get our eight-hour-day. We'll get decent pay. Join up. Join up, folks. It's time."

Again, Linnie joined the crowd in cheers. "OBU. OBU."

With the speeches over, folks chatted, shared pamphlets and asked questions. Parley and Linnie, Birdie Mae and Newt visited with Paul Garibaldi, union treasurer. And they visited with Dobbs. Dobbs appeared to be interested in them. There was laughter and talk among them. Mr. Dobbs paid some attentions to Linnie alone, and then he turned to

Parley before moving on to speak with other folks. Linnie and Parley, both with broad smiles, paid their dues and left.

A peculiar ache knit Kees's belly. Linnie Hearn, the flume tender's daughter, had no reason to give him the brush off when he'd always treated her with respect. And he didn't know anyone else in the crowd well enough to approach with an invitation to share his picnic. He picked up the basket. A knot of anger gnawed at him and he left the Dickerson house and went walking down the road to town.

On the way home Parley said to Linnie, "It was nice, meeting Mr. Dobbs, wasn't it."

"It was."

"I feel sorry for Kees Strom. If we hadn't promised Dru we'd be home early, we would have shared his food with him, like he asked us to do."

Linnie told Parley about the afternoon, some years back, when Kees bought her lemonade and a fried pie at the ice-cream parlor. "There's something odd about him," she said. "He wanted to talk about the burnt man. He wanted to hear more about it than is natural. He likes to look at dead people at Soapy's mortuary." She took hold of his arm. "I don't like him and the more I see of him, the more I find him creepy."

"He's strange," said Parley. "An odd duck."

Linnie had enjoyed the meeting and listening to Mr. Dobbs. He seemed to be interested in Parley. The two had talked about the International Longshoremen Association and Parley told Mr. Dobbs he had once belonged to the ILA while working in Eureka, California.

Linnie was surprised and flattered when Mr. Dobbs had turned to her. "Don't I remember you standing by the jail some years ago?"

"Yes." Linnie felt heat rise in her face. "I was curious about you."

He'd laughed. "Well, I hope I didn't disappoint you," he said. "Nice meeting both of you." And he'd turned his attentions to Max Knef and other folks waiting to meet with him.

But aside from the pleasure in meeting Mr. Dobbs in the flesh, of late Linnie had found comfort in talking to Parley. She trusted him and he listened and he gave her words thought. But now, out of the blue, he said, "I'm mighty glad that Birdie Mae and Newt want to take Baby off our hands. I'd like to see her live with them, permanently."

"So would I, but I don't know that she'll go. You remember how she balked up a storm last winter when Birdie and Newt offered to take her. Dru says she won't go because if she does, she can't go to your shop."

"She's become a nuisance. If she balks about going to Birdie's again, I'll talk to your father again about taking her to Seattle."

"He won't agree to it."

"He should. We all have to live together and she's causing trouble."

"You sound sore as a picked scab."

"We ought to live in our own place a good distance from her. Or she ought to be with folks her own age, folks like herself."

"Well, we'll live in our own place someday. But Father won't ever agree to send her away. You might as well talk to the moon."

After supper that evening Parley lugged a bucket of hot water from the stove and set it in front of Roy's chair. Roy, barefoot, rolled up his left pants leg and swung his gimpy, deep-veined limb into the water. His face, stiff with pain, relaxed.

Parley sat on the sofa and lit his pipe. Linnie sat next to him.

Roy said, "What in tarnation do you two think you're going to get out of joining the I.W.W.?"

"Decent wages," said Parley. "Clean camps and an eight-hour day."

"I doubt it. I see that the I.W.W. is getting a toe hold up here and I won't fight it, but don't ask me to join."

Parley nodded. "Fair enough. While we're on subjects we don't agree on, I'd ask you to think again about sending Baby to the place in Seattle. I've got means to pay for her keep. Or I'd like to make a fair arrangement with Birdie and Newt to take her."

Roy said, his tone stern, "You can have your opinions about union. You can join and that's your business and I won't fault you. But I won't allow Baby to live under any roof but her own. That includes Birdie's and Newt's. If she doesn't want to live with them, and I don't think she does, she doesn't have to."

Linnie said, "She's a handful, Father. You and Parley see the best side of her. Day after day Dru and I have to manage her and she's a real try."

"Linnie's right," said Parley. "And she's not behaving proper."

Roy frowned. "What do you mean?"

"She comes to my shop and makes a nuisance of herself."

"Send her home. She respects you and will do as you say."

"I've tried, but she won't leave."

"I'll talk to her," said Roy. "But, Linnie it's up to you and Dru to keep her here and I don't want to hear another word about sending her to live in some kind of charity institution."

Parley was stopped in his tracks, but he'd die rather than tell anybody that Baby had developed a bad habit. Increasingly these days, when she came to his shop, she'd sidle up and stick her big bubs against him. A couple of times he'd given her a rough hug and he was hot and shamed of his stiff poker.

❦

A month after the organizing picnic, the spindle-legged flume up on Wildcat Mountain was blown to smithereens and Lester Knef went missing. Mrs. Strom closed the mill up at Camp 5 and once again, with all the trouble up-stream, the flume bell fell silent.

Roy said to Linnie and Parley, "You see what happens when union boys come around? If I were you I'd put those cards and buttons away."

"Tommyrot," said Linnie. Parley agreed.

The sheriff deputized six men, including Kees Strom, Colin and Joe Bede to search for Les. Joe and Kees found him in the Blackduck River. Like Mr. Dickerson, Les was burnt to a crisp. Joe got so sick at the sight he couldn't work for two days.

With the flume and Camp Five out of commission, Roy took a job as a sawyer with Thurson Brothers Logging, an outfit over in Coldsprings. Parley would wait to see what happened before taking another job. He had plenty of money for food and necessities. Linnie might wonder where the money came from, but it wasn't her business and she didn't ask.

Four days after finding Les Knef, Parley said to Roy, "Tomorrow we're meeting with Mrs. Strom and we hope to reach an agreement about our concerns."

"Good luck," said Roy. "Higher wages? Clean camps and decent food? Anytime you try to negotiate with capitalists you've got a real fight on your hands."

Roy was right. Inga Strom refused to consider the I.W.W.'s requests.

❧

One week later, on Sunday afternoon Frank Dobbs and Paul Garibaldi met with Parley at the Dickerson house. While seated at the dining table Paul poured whiskey into three small glasses. Parley took two sips and set the glass aside.

Paul said, "We have to leave next week, Parley. The West Coast I.L.A.needs our help in Seattle. You have a good grasp on the problems up here and if anyone can successfully negotiate with Mrs. Strom, it's you."

Frank said, "How about serving as leader on a bargaining team?"

"I'm pleased to be asked and I'll be pleased to serve," said Parley.

But when Frank and Paul, Parley, along with three more·Strom workers, met with Inga Strom, she refused to negotiate.

Paul and Ann packed up their things. Ann said to Linnie, "After we see this struggle between the big west coast longshoremen settled, we'll see what's going on up here. In the meantime, why don't you come to visit us? Our apartment is small, but it's only two blocks from Mother's house and you could stay with her. If Sophie Krueger happens to be in town, we'd go to one of her lectures."

"I'd love to, and I've thought about it and I've talked to Parley about it. Dru can't handle her kiddies and Baby by herself for long periods of time. I'll talk to Birdie. Maybe we can work it out. But please send the pamphlets you told us about. Dru and I need to read them. And I'll pass them out to all the women I can reach. We have to educate ourselves."

"I'll send them as soon as I can. Now, heed me, Linnie. You told me you're feeling more comfortable with Parley and you enjoy his company. It shows and you've learned how to smile, so use it. It's beautiful."

❧❧

The Seattle team left Hanksport and Parley was on his own. He decided to wait for a couple of months before asking Mrs. Strom to meet with his team again. If she refused to meet, or if she agreed to meet, but refused to agree to the workers' concerns, Parley might encourage the workers to go out on strike. The I.W.W. had funds to support it, but not for a prolonged period of time.

"We'll work it out," he said to the workers and their families gathered up at the Dickerson house. "We want to do it peaceably and we want to do it right."

❀

Two weeks passed before Linnie had a letter with the pamphlets enclosed from Ann. She brewed up a pot of coffee and, in great anticipation she sat down to read the material.

The courts of America reject any notion of allowing contraceptive information to be sent in the U.S. mail.

What in the world did mail have to do with women having babies?

The term 'birth control' is replacing the classical terminology of Neo-Malthusianism and the inexorable economic laws of Malthus.

What was to be made of all that? How could she understand words she'd never seen? Abortion. Puberty. Ovaries. Uterus. Sexual emancipation. Venereal disease. Gynecologist. Diaphragm. Pessaries.

Ann wrote: *This information is what Sophie Krueger uses to teach women who plan to work at her clinic. Some of it is beyond me, but it's all I could find. You need to come to Seattle. Sophie can tell you what you need to know.*

Linnie, feeling pangs of frustration and touched with anger at her own ignorance, put the pamphlets in a box up on the high shelf. Until she could get to Seattle, the information she needed would continue to elude her.

In the meantime she would work with Parley, planning logistics of a possible strike. This was new for Inga Strom. Workers might become restless and threaten to strike, but a strike had never happened.

CHAPTER 21

One evening when Dru was putting her children to bed, Roy said to Linnie and Parley, "Jim Corrigan went down to Seattle to visit his sons. He and Gavin lit into Buzz for ignoring his family. Buzz promised to come home soon, but don't say anything to Dru. No point in disappointing her again. Too often she hears that he's coming home and he doesn't show up."

Linnie said, "And each time he does, she ends up with a swollen belly."

"That's not our business," said Roy. "But, I'm not pleased to see it happen."

The following week Buzz surprised the dickens out of Dru by driving up in a snazzy, open-air Packard sedan. He had on a beautiful, grey pin-stripe suit. His shoes were polished to a shine. A stylish grey fedora sat atop his fine looking head.

Of course he had presents. Toy soldiers for Hugh. More Teddy bears and dolls for Nellie and Stella. And for Dru, a luscious, blue silk blouse. He took delight in taking the entire family for a ride in his automobile, but the marvel of all was his Cameo camera.

"It's made of rosewood," he told the family. "And look at the fine nickel plate." He pushed a button and out popped folded maroon material. "Billows," he said. "Here. Here. I'll take photos of all of you. Dru, you and Birdie and Linnie, first."

Click. Click. "Joe's coming down for dinner?" he asked.

"Yes," said Dru. "Colin and Mide are coming over, too."

"Good. I'll take photos of the whole family, have them processed and mail them to you."

"I want one of you and me and the kiddies," said Dru.

Buzz showed Colin how to operate the camera and he and Dru and their three children stood beside Buzz's fancy auto. *Click. Click. Click.* "Done," said Buzz. "You'll all have a high old time with the photos I'll send."

After supper that evening, Buzz instructed the family to stand straight and tall and *smile, smile smile smile* into the camera's eye. *Click. Click Click. Click. Click. Click.*

Linnie was pleased to see that the camera gave him such joy, but did he ever consider giving his wife the greatest of pleasure by living with her and their children as a family?

For the next two days, mid-afternoon, Buzz and Dru went to the back bedroom, not to emerge until shortly before supper. Dru looked her young self again, fresh and spirited.

Following breakfast, on the third day of his visit, Buzz told his children and his wife good-bye, got in his shiny, open-air Packard and with a wave of one hand, he was gone.

CHAPTER 22

Inga Strom was in trouble. She had rebuilt the spindle-legged flume up on Wildcat Mountain and work had resumed. Her workers had not gone out on strike that fall, but they were close to doing it. She still had not given an inch.

One day she drove up to Camp Five to speak to Parley. The two sat down at a table inside the tender's hut beside the flume and conversed, in a limited way. She offered her workers a raise of five cents an hour, but refused to grant the requested twelve cents, or the eight-hour day, or going to the expense of cleaning up her camps.

"I'm losing money, as is," she said. "Is it possible to meet and re-negotiate?"

"I'll take your request to your workers," Parley said.

Two days later, on a Saturday afternoon, I.W.W. members met in the smoky, chilly back room of the Blackduck Saloon. Parley bought a couple of rounds of whiskey and while consuming the welcome beverage—welcome to most of the men, and Parley took a sip or two—he counseled them not to go out on strike. "We'll keep up the pressure. We'll see if she won't agree to something we can manage," he said.

The men agreed.

Parley related the news to Linnie and she said, "I'm proud of you." And she smiled and touched his cheek.

Following Buzzie's last visit, once again Dru's belly swelled. But over the months she lost her spunk. Shadows appeared below her eyes. Her skin took on a look and color of old wax.

One day she said to Linnie, "I don't think the children and I will ever live with Buzzie. He says he loves me. He says that all the time. And he brings us presents. I've begged him to take us with him, so we can be a family. He says we'll all be together soon, but it never happens."

"And what's his excuse?"

"Finding a nice house. I've told him a thousand times the house doesn't matter. I only want us to live as a family. And now I'm worried that something bad is going to happen to me. If it does, please take care of Hugh and Stella and Nellie and the baby I've got inside me now."

"Oh, Dru, of course we would. But nothing bad will happen to you. You're just having too many babies, one after another. Three, going on four in five years is a lot."

"Yes. How could Mide and I have known that we'd be in this pickle?"

"How is Mide? I haven't seen her for some time."

"She's sick a lot and Colin is worried."

The letter from Buzzie contained the photos. The family gathered around and passed the photos and gazed and exclaimed at the splendid likenesses. Dru and Buzz and their three lovely children and the photo of the entire family were, as Dru put it, "marvelous."

Baby looked closely at the family photos. She frowned. "Baby," she said. Her voice rose. "Baby gone? All gone?"

Linnie peered at the family photo. The top of Baby's blond hair could be seen behind Colin and Mide. "But, you're there, Baby. You're there with all of us." That appeared to mollify her and she paid them no further attention.

Those of Dru, alone, and of Dru with her children were especially lovely. Linnie put one on the dresser in her and Parley's bedroom. Birdie Mae took two for herself and Newt, and Dru kept the rest. She set those of her and Buzz and their children on a shelf in the living room. The photos pleased her and seemed to bring her out of her low feelings.

Using money Buzz gave her, she bought cloth from the A. & D. She made a clever baby bunting for her new baby. For her little girls she made dresses and pinafores to which she added a touch of whimsy. A bit of smocking. A collar and a small pocket trimmed with bright rickrack. She made handsome, wool shirts for Hugh. Evenings, spent close to the glow of lantern light, working her needle in and out of the fabric she held in her graceful hands, she seemed happy.

But the birth of her fourth child, a boy she named Will, was difficult and left her exhausted. The tiny baby had blue-white skin, his eyelids like rose petals not yet ready to bloom. He lived for three days and never did open his eyes.

At the Hanksport cemetery Parley and Colin lowered the small wooden box Parley had made, down into the ground. Dru, pinch-faced and thin, planted pansies atop the grave and sprinkled water from a bucket over them.

Buzz had said he'd come up for the service, but he didn't. Linnie thought the baby's death was all for the best. If he'd lived, he would have been one more for Dru to care for, a child who probably would not have known his father. A boy with spare choice in life.

While Joe said long prayers, Linnie put her arm around Dru's sharp-boned shoulders. And for supper that night she made Dru's favorite soup of barley and meaty beef bones and made sure that Dru got the coveted marrow.

CHAPTER 23

Two months passed before Buzz came to see his family again. With his handsome smile and flashing blue eyes, he came in the house, picked up Dru, swung her around and took her and the children for a spin in his automobile.

At supper he seemed agitated and he had little to say to his children. They, sensing something askew, withdrew from him.

Dru boldly put the question to him, in front of her family. "I want to come to see you," she said. "You are my husband and I, as your wife, want to know where you live."

"Hey, Peacherino. I'll give you a thumbs up real soon and we'll go house hunting together."

"I'll hold you to it," she said with spunk.

But that night his complaints wakened Linnie. "I come home and you treat me like this?"

"Every time you come home, you make another baby," Dru's tone was high and whispery. "And our last baby didn't live. I don't want another one. I don't want your loving again until we live together."

"Goddamn!" A door slammed. Buzz's footsteps. Dru's pattering behind. Whispers. Footsteps back to the bedroom.

The following morning, while Dru was feeding the children breakfast, Buzz, valise in hand, went out to his automobile and cranked it up.

Linnie, carrying a basket of clothes out to the clothes-line, stopped and said, "Leaving so soon?"

"Got to get back to the city. There's an important union meeting tonight and I'm secretary. I gave Dru plenty of money and when I find a nice house, I'll come get her and the kiddies."

"Will you really?"

"Yes."

"It's easy, isn't it. Larking around in the city while your wife and children are miles away."

"It's our business, Linnie. And I'm doing the best I can."

Dru came out. Her tone was chilly. "Good-bye Buzzie. You said you'd come home for Christmas. It's not necessary that you come home at all."

Buzzie got in his automobile, waved his cap, and drove off.

"Linnie," said Dru. "I'll help hang up the laundry."

CHAPTER 24

Strike!

In October, sixty-five Strom workers, all I.W.W. men, walked out. Scabs, including Joe Bede, crossed the picket line and continued to work.

Parley said to Linnie, "If the I.W.W. can send our local two hundred dollars, we can stay out. But now, Linnie, darlin,' this would be a good time for me to learn to read and write. Can you take the time to teach me?"

"I can."

He was an eager student, plenty quick and he caught on fast. Mornings, at first light and in the deep chill of winter coming on, he'd chank up the fire and sit at the kitchen table. Linnie would find him deep in study in the lantern's soft glow. She'd go to him and put a hand on his shoulder. "I'm proud of you," she said, more than once.

For some unexplained reason Meara began to come out of her shell. She helped Dru with the children. She combed their hair and helped them wash up, but she'd have nothing to do with Baby.

Now that Dru had her mother's help, Linnie was free to go to union meetings with Parley. A fine pride stirred in her for him. Folks listened to him with respect and looked to him as a genuine leader.

"Read everything you can," he'd call out while holding up a publication written by Eugene Debs, Vincent St. John, or Elizabeth Gurly Fynn. Or he would lead the workers in a song composed by Joe Hill, who had been executed just a year ago on November 19.

"Spread the word," he'd call out. "We want *change* for the working class. Stop greedy corporate ownership. Stop slave labor. We want equality in this great land of America. We're the backbone of this country. Think about that when you're out on the line. Wear your red buttons! Pity the scab."

During November strikers and sympathizers held their home-made placards in mittened hands, stayed on the line and chanted: "Union. Union. We'll stay on the line. Union. Union." Tempers flared between union and scabs. Fights were frequent and bloody. Union dollars ran out. Union men wrapped their feet in burlap, stuffed newspapers into the thinning soles of their caulks and work boots and continued to stump the line. Women joined them when they could and they brought them hot soup and bread.

Linnie and Parley and the family never spoke of Joe, but Linnie fretted about him. He was a likely target of nasty insults and fights. But, he appeared undisturbed and he never spoke about the strike, his work at the mill, or his work for Mrs. Strom up at her house...

On Sundays he always came home to his family. After supper he and Linnie and Parley huddled over the table in the soft glow of the lantern light to study Joe's renderings for Linnie and Parley's house. Parley wanted two bedrooms and big casement windows throughout. "Linnie wants to hear the river and the bell," he said. "And I hope that someday a child of ours will sleep in one of the bedrooms."

"A wrap-around porch," said Linnie. "And a view of the river from the front room and kitchen." She said nothing about a child sleeping in a second bedroom.

Parley would start building the place next spring and finish it before winter. Linnie couldn't recall a time when she'd been so happy. She would soon have a light, bright home of her own with a front parlor, a dining room, a nice kitchen and a large, wrap-around porch.

But the thought of having a child continued to jar her. She and Parley had been married for almost five years, and they were no closer to finding an answer to the rigid request she'd made of him, than they were on their first night of marriage.

It was agreed between them—come spring, Linnie would take the train to Seattle, stay at Ann's mother's house if convenient, and visit Sophie Krueger.

❧

Ten days before Christmas heavy snows brought logging operations to a halt. Dru had a letter from Buzz telling her that he and Gavin were coming home on Christmas day. "We'll see," said Dru. "I'm not going to hold my breath."

Jim Corrigan was always included in holiday dinners, held at Birdie and Newt's or at Roy's. This year they would gather at Roy's. "The roads will be a mess," Linnie told Jim. "But, we'll wait for Buzz and Gavin to eat, so come over anytime."

Jim said he'd wait for his sons and they would come over together.

On a bright morning, two days before Christmas, Parley took hold of Hugh's mittened hand and the two waded through the snow to the other side of the clearing. They came home with a small fir tree. Parley set it in place in the front room. Dru fished green and red buttons from her button box and she cut ribbons and lace from her mother's hats and the children used these treasures to decorate the tree. Linnie helped Baby drape two garlands over the dark green branches. Baby laughed and she walked around and around in circles, chortling. "Pawley home. Batty loon knockers Baby home. Buttons. Buttons."

Mid-afternoon, as it began to get dark, Linnie warmed milk on the stove and added a little honey. She poured the sweetened milk into thick cups and she and Dru, Baby, Parley, Roy and the children sat at the table and enjoyed the winter treat.

Mid-morning, on Christmas day, Newt and Birdie set four mincemeat pies, a scalloped potatoes casserole and two jars of sweet pickles in a large basket, chanked up their automobile and drove to Roy's house. Joe snow- shoed down from Camp Two, stood the shoes on their tails and went in the house. He set four small cloth bags underneath the tree, one for Hugh, one for Stella, one for Nell and one for Baby. Inside each bag he'd placed one shiny fifty-cent piece and he'd tell the children and Baby they could use the silver money for whatever they might want to buy.

Dru, Birdie, and Linnie prepared roast venison, mashed potatoes, baked onions and squash to add to the feast. At noon, when the sun was high and bright, Parley, Joe, Newt, Dru, Baby and the children went outside to make a snowman. Dru told her children that very small and very pretty fairies with gold wings came early that morning and sprin-kled tiny sugared diamonds all over the snow and that was what gave the snow its sparkle.

The little girls wanted to eat it. Hugh laughed and went along with the fantasy.

Joe, Parley, Newt, and Dru rolled snowballs. Baby and the children, laughing to beat the band, tried their hand at it, too. Hugh and Stella made small snowballs, but while Baby tried, she couldn't quite do it. Instead of being frustrated, she ran around and around the stacked balls of snow that became sizeable. Joe dug up small rocks and stuck them into the top ball. The snowman now had a face.

Dru, her blue eyes dancing in spite of her skepticism about Buzz coming home, went inside the house and returned with a big piece of cardboard on which she'd printed blocky letters. WELCOME HOME BUZZIE. She propped the sign on the ground against the base of the snowman.

Roy stood at the kitchen window and watched the cavorting. To Linnie's amazement, he picked up one of his pipes, took it outside and stuck it in the snowman's mouth. Parley came up with a battered, red felt hat that he set atop the head. Birdie and Linnie—Linnie holding Nell—went outside to join the family. The children nearly collapsed with laughter and Baby ran around and around the creation and laughed and called out, "Pretty Baby home, knockers home, Pawley home," until everybody got tired and cold and went inside the warm, cozy house.

At four o'clock, when darkness wrapped the land, the women set the table and the family waited. Linnie and Parley, Birdie Mae and Newt took turns reading Meara's book, "*A Christmas Carol,*" aloud.

Twice Dru went outside to listen for the chuffing rattle of Buzzie's auto. All she heard was the high-pitched howl of wolves echoing through the silent, snow-bound forest.

At a quarter to five an auto finally came churning up the road. Dru, with an expectant smile, went to open the door. Jim and Gavin stomped snow off their boots and came inside.

Dru said, "Buzzie . . . ?"

"He couldn't get away," Gavin said. He handed Dru a package. "I'm sorry."

"Get away from what? Why . . .?"

"I don't know. It was rough coming up the mountain and I'm mighty glad to be here."

Dru's blue eyes spoke of keen disappointment, but she brightened. "Linnie, aren't we ready to eat?"

After dinner, during the exchange of gifts, Dru opened a card from Buzz, silently read it, and then waved it in the air. "Listen, please. Here's what he says. 'The roads are bad and I can't make it home. Peacherino, you'll look beautiful wearing these things. You'll see me after the roads are cleared. I love you. Buzzie' "

She opened the box and picked a white rabbit fur muff with a matching scarf from the white tissue. She wrapped the scarf around her neck, put one hand into the muff, picked up Nellie and pranced around the room. "Come on, Hugh and Stella." She sang, *"Jingle Bells, jingle bells, jingle all the way. . . ."*

Linnie wished Buzzie could see the joy his gifts brought to his beautiful wife. But had a cad ever been born worse than Busby Corrigan?

When it was Parley's turn to open his gift from Linnie, he picked Jack London's *The Son of the Wolf* from the wrapping tissue. He leafed through the book and he smiled. "I own a book, darlin,' and I can read. That makes me feel pretty good about myself. And I thank you again for teaching me."

He handed her a heavy package about six inches square. She opened it to find a beautiful wooden box and inside the box two wide, silver haircombs decorated with tiny pearls lay on a bed of white velvet. She caught her breath. "Oh, Parley." She held up the box and the combs. "These are grand. Oh, so grand. And the box, too. Well . . . what finery."

"You always pin up your hair with little bitty combs and I figured big, pretty combs like those would be just fine."

She put her hand to her throat. "Just fine?" She laughed. "Yes, I believe they will be just fine. They are beautiful and grand and I'll wear them with pride." She went to him and kissed his cheek.

Baby shouted. "Hoo loon Bay bee, too. Knockers Bay Bee, too." She stomped over to Linnie. Her hand, quick as a whip, grabbed the box.

"No," said Parley. "Give the box back to Linnie. The haircombs are hers."

Baby shook her head. "Hoo loon home. Pawley. Knockers home."

Parley said, "Baby. Give the box to me and I'll give you your own present."

She gave the box over to him and he handed her a package wrapped with a red ribbon. She opened it and found a box of new crayolas and a writing tablet. She threw the crayolas down on the floor and she stomped in circles around the room. "Pawley. Hoo loon Bat Bay bee. Hoo loon knockers Bat bay bee."

"Baby," said Roy. "Here's another present for you. Why don't you open it and see what it is."

She ripped off the tissue and picked up a pair of long, black stockings. She frowned. She threw the stockings down. "Hoo loon Bat Baybee. Knockers. Hoo loon home."

Parley shook his head and muttered, "Lord, she's a try."

He gave Meara a gift and he hoped she'd enjoy his carving of Pal, but Meara, her eyes on Baby, took the unopened package, went to her bedroom and quietly closed the door.

❦

On December 31st howling winds brought more snow. Temperatures plummeted to 15 degrees. Nobody could endure walking the picket line.

That evening Parley was huddled in front of the stove with Linnie and Roy. Dru was in bed with her children. Meara was also in bed. Baby, wrapped in a quilt, sat at the table and worked her letters. In recent months, with help from Birdie, Linnie and Parley, she'd learned how to form names. B A B Y D R U M A M A. She had not mastered "Linnie" or "Parley." She worked with a quiet intensity and was allowed to stay up if she stayed quiet.

Parley said, "I don't know how much longer we can stay out on strike. People are running out of food. Colin killed one of his chickens and gave it to Mide's folks."

Linnie said, "Birdie and I took some canned tomatoes and peaches over to the Dolce's place. It's a wretched house and they have ten children. I told Mr. Dolce we've got potatoes and squash in the root cellar and we'd bring them over."

Parley nodded. "Good. We're fine and we need to share."

During January and February negotiations with Inga Strom continued and while Parley enjoyed serving as leader on the bargaining team, he was frustrated when nothing came of the meetings. He and the team worked hard and spent hours trying to reach agreement, but Parley continued to come home with a creased brow and worried eyes.

Linnie, with a steady calm, worked hard to keep his spirits up. "After all we've gone through, we can't let her win. We can't give in. We *won't* give in. She's a tough nut to crack, but we'll do it."

Late afternoon of March 4th Parley went to yet another meeting and he came home with a smile. "She's agreed to give us a ten-cent an hour pay increase," he said. "Ten, not the twelve we've wanted, but it's better than five. It's a fair compromise and she'll clean up the camps next summer. She won't give in on the ten-hour-work day, but by God, Linnie, darlin,' we've won a small victory."

On March 5 notices posted at the mills and throughout the town read: ATTENTION STROM WORKERS: EFFECTIVE APRIL 1, 1915 YOU WILL SEE AN INCREASE OF TEN CENTS (10c) AN HOUR IN YOUR WAGES, PAID IN SCRIP. YOU WILL CONTINUE TO WORK A FIVE-DAY WEEK, TEN HOURS A DAY, WITH SATURDAYS AND SUNDAYS AS HOLIDAYS. ANYONE NOT SATISFIED WITH THESE TERMS MAY LEAVE MY EMPLOYMENT. INGA STROM.

Parley said to Linnie, "As you said, 'she's a tough nut to crack.' But we did it."

"It's a start. I look forward to spring when we build our new house and I'll take that trip to Seattle."

CHAPTER 25

Spring in Hanksport County. Along the moist, shady banks of the Blackduck River blue fringed kittentails burst into bloom. Rotting snow trickled and seeped deep into the earth. Violets and blue toadflax emerged at Tat and Thimble Creek Meadows. Bubble throated birdsong returned to the cold, dark, wet land and instead of gray skies and snow, billowing clouds brought rain and watery sunshine.

In town, Maxwell's furniture store, Mrs. Barker's Bakery, and Elton Clark's Drugstore rose from the mud. Soapy Metzler built a fancy funeral parlor. Mame and Ollie bought The Hanksport Hotel in which Mame opened a restaurant. Membership in the I.W.W. increased and on South Main a new union hall opened its doors.

As soon as the roads became passable Parley hired a crew to haul five wagons loaded with fieldstone from a Seattle quarry up to the site of what would be his and Linnie's new home.

One evening after a brief downpour of rain, the sun came from behind tattered grey clouds and shone a clear, watery light. Linnie and Parley sat out on the stoop; Parley fattened his pipe, lit it and settled back against the step. Linnie pointed to a rainbow stretched across the reach toward what would soon be their home. "A symbol of good fortune for us," she said. "Our own house. And I had a letter from Ann today. In two weeks Sophie Krueger is holding a workshop for women. This will happen while I'm in Seattle. Her speech is about 'family limitation.' "

Parley nodded. "Luck won't hurt us and I'm glad you're going. I expect you to come home with good news."

"I plan to do that."

Parley often went off to bed before she did and he slept with his broad back toward her. Her relief of not having to reject him was great, but what was it that Birdie said on the day of her marriage? *If you don't let him love you like he's going to want to do, and he's got a right to do, you'll be sorry some day.*

She leaned close to him. "You asked me once, before we were married, to try to learn to love you."

"U'mm."

"I'm not sure I know what love is, but I feel differently about you than I once did. And I promise that after I learn about family limitation, you can have your way with me."

"I don't want to 'have' my way with you. I want you to love me and want me, too."

The two fell silent. Then Parley said, "While you're in Seattle, take a look at the place Mrs. Garibaldi told you about some years ago."

"The place for people like Baby? Mercy buckets, Parley. Father won't bend."

"That doesn't mean that you can't look into it. Baby shouldn't keep coming to my shop. I don't want her there. She needs to be with people like herself. People her own age. Fifteen, sixteen, seventeen years old." He stood. "But, come with me. I have something to show you."

The two went inside. Baby, hunkered over her tablet at the table, stood up and hit herself on her breast. "Hoo loon batt Bay bee home," she said.

"Lord, yes," Linnie said. "You know you're home and so do we."

She and Parley went into their bedroom; Parley closed the door and lifted up one end of the big feather mattress. Atop the bedsprings lay a thick canvas purse. "Take it," he said. "Take it and look inside."

Linnie picked up the purse and opened it. Her fingers ticked through twenty dollar bills. Her eyes widened and she sucked in her breath. "Mercy buckets, Parley. Money. Lots of it. Where did it come from?"

"It comes in the brown envelope every month. I figure you need to know. I used a lot of it to buy the land and I've had to wait to save it up again before I could start building our house. Now, I have enough to pay for it and then some."

"Who sends it?"

"A bank in San Francisco. Pops owned property down in California. Gold country. He sold the property before he passed and every month, for the rest of my life, money comes to me. Last week I wired the bank and made sure that if I should die, the money comes to you. It's usually around twenty-five dollars a month."

"But, you aren't going to die."

"I don't plan to, but I want it settled this way. And I want you to take some of that money and buy something nice for yourself in Seattle."

Linnie took hold of Parley's hand. "You're a good man, Parley. You're good to us, and you're awfully good to me."

Three days later Linnie had another letter from Ann. *This is terrible news for all of us. Day before yesterday Sophie Kreuger's clinic was destroyed. Windows smashed. Furniture broken up. Files stolen. Some people accuse Sophie of murder. Next week she leaves for Europe and I don't know when she'll return. I'm so disappointed for you and me and I'm scared for Sophie. Everyone needs to know about family limitation. How can people be so hateful and deny women this right?*

Paul is taking me on a trip up to Canada. A much delayed honeymoon and we'll be gone for a month. After we get home, can you come to visit? If Sophie isn't back, we'll find another suffragist you can talk to. There are a fair number of us around.

Another disappointment. But, the month would go fast and Linnie would take her trip to Seattle whether Sophie Krueger was there or not.

CHAPTER 26

After supper, on a balmy evening when the first long, warm fingers of June touched the dark forest, Dru, her children and her mother went for a walk. The old hounddog, Pal, tagged at their heels.

Parley went to his workshop. Baby, who had on her lavender dress, worked on her letters at the dining table.

Linnie picked up a pamphlet Parley had brought home from work. *Political Parties and the I.W.W.* Mr. Vincent St. John wrote an article about the importance of people uniting to gain power.

She set the pamphlet aside. If Mr. St. John could reach people like herself through a pamphlet, why couldn't she write about family limitation? Why couldn't she learn how to talk about it, too? Most older folks up in Hanksport County couldn't read, but Linnie could reach the few who could. Working together, why couldn't they spread the word?

She stood and smote her fist into the palm of her hand. A printing press sat idle up at the old Dickerson place. Who might teach her how to use it?

Baby left her letters, stepped outside and started across the reach toward the road that led to Parley's shop.

Linnie ran out on the porch. "Baby. Come back. Parley wants to work alone."

Baby plowed on as if she were deaf.

Linnie let her go. It was getting on toward late evening and Baby wouldn't have much time to bother Parley. Linnie went inside, sat down and picked up her book. She smiled. For some time now, she had found life and her husband enjoyable.

Parley examined the ten-inch fir carving of Linnie's bust he'd worked on for the past three months. Her long hair was coiled up into a chignon and a few fine strokes of his knife in the wood resembled the haircombs he'd given her last Christmas. He thought he'd caught an expression of calm that he liked. During their years together—five years now—he had rarely seen this expression, but now when the two of them spoke of their house he sensed it in her.

He should be feeling keen pleasure in his work. He didn't. Once again he'd witnessed Linnie's keen disappointment in not being able to take the trip to Seattle. And with all of her wordy pronouncements of her feelings for him, she didn't love him. For years it had been easy for her to deny him pleasure with her. And going to Seattle was fine, but after she claimed to know the answers, would she allow him to complete the act of loving her, or would she continue to put him off?

Beyond that concern, a dark fantasy he'd had for some time continued to nag him. Baby. Years ago he'd asked Roy to send her away. He'd hoped Roy would understand. He hadn't. Parley had asked Linnie and Dru to keep Baby from coming to his shop. They couldn't do it.

He'd become obsessed with her. He dreamed about her curly blond hair. Her scent. Her odd smile. He'd bury his face between her soft breasts and she'd be willing and hot and eager for him and he'd plunge inside her and feel her hot well of want for him. Those dreams plagued him and he waked and he left his and Linnie's bed and went out to the privy and he wanted to beat his drooping penis, which moments before had been rigid, throbbing and dripping.

Baby would never leave home. When Parley and Linnie had their own home, he, as master, would forbid her to come inside, but would that solve the problem?

And now, just as he'd expected, the understory of salal and huckleberry outside his shop rustled. He turned from his workbench. "Go home, Baby. I've got work to do."

She kept her eyes on him. "Buttons," she whispered. "Buttons." She unbuttoned her dress and she pressed against him and the swell of her, the feel of her warm body aroused him. She stood back and she opened her dress and thrust her shoulders back and her full white breasts, like pearly mounds with fat pink flowers, seemed to bloom. She was without drawers and her naked, smooth belly gleamed above her mound of thick, curly hair. And the scent of her, sweet and sensuous.

She laughed and she took one of his hands and put it on her breasts. "Knockers," she whispered. "Knockers."

He caressed her warm, pillowy breasts and her dimpled belly button and he touched her moist, hot place. She nuzzled him. "Pawley," she whispered. "Oh, Pawley."

With trembling hands he unbuttoned his pants and dropped them. He pulled her down with him, got atop her, plunged inside and pumped on her. For just one moment her

185

eyes widened and she took a sharp breath. But then her hands found his butt and she kneaded it and she heaved her body up to him. Again. And again and he, washed with his awful hunger, had no thought until after the intense high of release.

"Pawley," she said. Her laugh was raspy and low, her hands were gentle in his hair. "Pawley. Oh, Pawley."

He lay, stunned.

She nuzzled him, again and again. "Oh, Pawley. Pawley."

He got off her and stood. Rubbery knees. Unsteady hands. He pulled on his pants.

She got up and buttoned her dress.

He grabbed her hand, pulled her behind him and bush-whacked through the salal and huckleberry. The hem of her dress caught on a thorny branch of a bush. She turned and yanked her skirt free, leaving a scrap of the pale lavender material stuck fast to the limb. She caught up with Parley and she clumped up the road and when they came to the clearing he said, "Go in the house. Now."

She galloped across the reach.

Parley, his senses foggy, took the trail leading up to Horsetail Falls. Once, twice, three times he stopped and smacked himself on his head so hard he saw pinpricks of light. At the base of a tree, he hunkered down. His sin could not be undone. If Linnie learned of it, he couldn't imagine what she would do. If Baby found herself in a family way, word would get around like wild fire. He, who had coupled with the idiot girl, would be the fool of Hanksport County. An unwanted cur. He bent his head low between his knees. Tears dropped on his big clasped hands. His shoulders shook.

CHAPTER 27

A month, six weeks passed. Parley no longer went to his workshop. Evenings he set strings and stakes marking the foundation for the new house. He and Linnie read aloud to each other, but Baby's rocking back and forth, ogling him and saying, "Pawley. Oh, Pawley," irritated both of them.

"Shush," he'd say. "Shush your mouth."

Baby, never an early riser, was now up at first light and at breakfast she insisted on sitting next to Parley. Parley ate with frenzy and left the house.

A terrible dark thing came to Linnie's mind. She pushed it away, but one evening she said to Parley, "She acts downright swoony about you. And I'm worried. She puked these past mornings and I don't know what's got hold of her. None of us are sick. And strangest of all, she hasn't had her monthly."

Parley's face, usually of high color, paled and he looked undone and before Linnie could say another word, he quit the house.

The dark thing began to take shape. She denied it.

In bed one night Linnie said, "What's troubling you? You're cross as a bear and all froze up. You've been this way for weeks."

"We need to build our house, quick as we can. After we move in, I don't want Baby coming around." He rolled over, away from her.

The following evening, after Dru, the children, Meara, and Pal went for their walk and Roy had gone fishing with Jim Corrigan, Linnie listened to Parley read. She liked his thoughtful dark eyes and well defined nose—a face with purpose and strong feelings.

He read, "The working class and the employing class have nothing in common." He stopped, got up from his chair and went to the window. "Why don't you read for awhile?"

Sensing his nervous restlessness, she took the book. "There can be no peace as long as hunger and want are found among millions of working people and . . ."

"Linnie, darling,' " He came to her and took hold of her hands. "I've got to talk to you." His tone was soft but uneven, his eyes anguished. "Just you and me. Soon as I get home from work tomorrow, let's go off by ourselves."

"Let's go for a walk, now. We have time."

Baby, who had been sitting quietly working on her letters, got up and went to Parley. "Bay bee," she said. "Rockabye Bay bee."

Parley said, "For God's sakes, keep her here." He slammed out of the house.

Linnie said to Baby, "Leave Parley alone, Baby. You're bothering him."

Baby clumped out to the stoop. "Pawley," she bawled. "Bay bee." She headed off toward Parley's shop.

Linnie started after her. Baby quickened her pace. Linnie broke into a run, caught up with her and grabbed her arm. Baby turned, reared back and kicked Linnie's shins. A sickening pain shot up Linnie's leg. Baby lumbered off toward the road leading to the shop.

Dru, the children, Meara, and Pal had just returned from their walk. Dru ran out to help Linnie chase down Baby. After catching up with her, Dru grabbed her and hung on to her skirt, but Baby broke loose, stopped, picked up a rock and took aim. The rock struck Linnie's left cheek. Hot pain seared her face. She sank to her knees.

The dark thing stood in front of her. Why had Baby turned against her? Why had she deliberately hurt her?

Dru helped her back to the house and applied a soothing burdock poultice.

Roy came home. Dru told him what had happened. Roy worked his jaw, said nothing and went out on the stoop. Dru followed him. "You can't walk away from this," she said. "Someday Baby will hurt one of us worse than she's hurt Linnie. And it better not be any of my chicks. Or me."

Parley, trailed by Baby, came in. He gave Linnie a quick look. "Good God. What's happened here?"

After Dru told him, Parley turned to Baby. He took hold of her chin and yanked her head around to face Linnie. "Look what you did," he shouted. "You hurt her." He paced the room. Smacked one fist in his palm. Again and yet again. He spun around and said to Baby, "You're going to that place in Seattle. You can't live here anymore. Understand?"

He went out on the stoop. "Roy, because of your god-damned stubborn pride, Baby's become a real danger. For all of us. As soon as I can, I'm taking Linnie and we're leaving your cursed house."

Dru started to cry. The children cried. Meara left the house. Tears rolled down Baby's cheeks. "Pawley," she wailed and pointed to herself. "Bay bee. Bay bee." Parley stormed out the door. Baby started after him, but this time Roy stopped her.

◕◑◑

Parley had walked in deep woods alone all of his life. The road over to Sunnydale Valley was somewhat familiar to him—he'd been over there a couple of times—but now he would go cross-country and it would take all night and into day for him to get there, but he would do it. If he paid Brown Hon lots of money, would she tell him how Baby could rid herself of a child?

After crossing the Blackduck River he stopped and looked up at the star-encrusted sky. "Linnie, darlin,' " he whispered. "You told me about the bottle tree at Brown Hon's house. If I can find it, I'll know I'm there." He walked on, stopped again and gazed up into the sky. "Oh, Lord, darlin,' I've dirtied myself and torn up our marriage and torn up my heart. When you find out, you'll be torn up, too. There's no decency left in me. I've lost it and I'll lose you, too."

He pressed on, his voice thick and choked. "I'd say this to you if I could. You always get on folks who talk bad about Indians. I don't think it would have mattered if you'd known about me. And darlin,' that little baby Baby will have, is part Indian. Part Tsimshian. Part me."

A chill wind took hold of him and he recalled the story of the Tsimshian ghost. A small, round ghost without arms or legs, it rolled through the woods, up and down hills and across rivers and lakes. Silver tears spilled down its round face and if a Tsimshian caught sight of the tears, the Tsimshian knew he would soon die.

Parley, using the stars for direction, thrashed on into the woods. At the south fork of the Blackduck River he sat down on a log. Scattered thoughts spun in his head. He was up north, at Nootka Bay, and ghosts of his father and grandfather played among the trees. He rose from the log and cried out. "Oh, look. Look!"

There, on the other side of the river, a little white ghost rolled down the steep bank, crossed the river and rolled up close to Parley. Silver tears spilled from its big, round eyes. .It turned from Parley and started to go back to the river.

"Wait," Parley cried. "I'm coming." He followed the ghost and splashed into the river's wild current. The great ripe moon riding high in the sky made him think, not of Linnie's belly which he had never seen, but of Baby's. He bent his head and in the luminous water the little round ghost with its dazzling tears smiled. A noise roared inside Parley's head, his ears popped and moments later, bubbles rose and floated for a moment in the busy, moon-sliced water.

Parley had never stayed out all night and the family feared he might be a victim of anti-union work. That didn't square with Linnie. His behavior during the past two months was caused by something personal and strange and it had the shape of the dark thing.

Still, she looked for clues. The auto was parked in its usual place alongside the house. His 12-gauge was behind the bedroom door. The family asked around. "You've seen Parley yesterday or today?"

Jim Corrigan saw him pass by his place late last evening, after Jim got home from fishing with Roy. Seemed a bit out of the way, but Jim hadn't given it much thought. Up river folks hadn't seen him at all. Some time ago he'd bought a sack of six-penny nails from Ollie Holm. "He was in high spirits," said Ollie. "Told me life was pretty good."

Sheriff Chester Mann offered to send out his deputies, but Joe thanked the sheriff and said he didn't think Parley would appreciate it. "He'll show up in a day or two," Joe said.

He didn't.

Linnie went out to his workshop. A likeness of her, complete with the beautiful hair combs carved into the wood, looked to be completed and his tools were in good order. She left everything as he'd left it. Surely he would return to the work he enjoyed, and to her, whom she thought he loved.

Baby became silent. Almost mute. She sat at the dining table, but she didn't eat and the lavender dress had disappeared. Linnie left Baby alone.

On the third day of Parley's disappearance, Linnie drove up Wildcat Mountain to Blue Mirror Lake. The man who had bought Parley's house said he hadn't seen him in years. The once tidy place was paint-peeled, shabby and unkempt. Trash—empty boxes and tin cans, an old caulk boot, a rusty pickaroon—lay scattered beside the place.

The lake, a deep azure blue with a dark reflection of the trees mirrored in the water, was beautiful. *It's a pretty lake,* he'd said.

Why hadn't she had the courage and gumption to rise to the challenge in making this place their home? If she and Parley had lived here these past five years, he would not have had Baby's grating presence day after day, year after year.

But, no. She had been selfish and fearful. She had thought only about herself. She had not given her husband a second thought and she had continued to do that all during their marriage.

Sleep eluded her. During the night she'd get out of bed, pace the house and try to recall what she and Parley had talked of and done over the weeks before he disappeared. Again and again, she asked herself what had happened to turn her husband of good, gentle humor into a sullen, angry man. But one day she no longer asked herself those questions. She knew. She waited.

⊙⊙

Ten days after Parley disappeared Linnie was working out in the garden with Dru and the children when Birdie and Newt drove up and parked. Linnie went to greet them. Tears pooled in Birdie Mae's eyes. She put her arm around Linnie, but she didn't speak.

Newt put his arms around both women. "Trapper up the south fork of Blackduck River found him caught on a snag. Said it looked like Parley lost his footing."

Linnie's first thought was that Parley would never know how much she had come to enjoy and regard him. Furthermore she didn't believe he had slipped and drowned. The dark thing was now stuck fast in her mind.

⊙⊙

Linnie refused to hold a church service for Parley. Instead folks came to pay their respects at the I.W.W. Hall.

The Hall filled quickly. Tributes, many from men Linnie did not know, were numerous.

At the cemetery, before Parley was laid to rest, Baby, in her newly mute silence, put a torn piece of her lavender dress into the coffin.

Linnie took the small carved owl from Parley's neck, slipped it over her head and it rested at her throat.

CHAPTER 28

In mid-July Linnie had a letter from Ann.

Paul and I are home and we've just learned about Parley's death. I didn't know him well, but thought of him as a fine man. My heart is heavy for you.

I.W.W. folks are coming back up to Hanksport to shore up the fight for the clean camps and eight-hour-day campaign. I'm needed here where the I.W.W. General Timber Strike is in full swing. Workers are sticking to their guns, but employers won't give an inch. If the Lumberman's Protective Assoc., (the LPA who protect rich industrialists like Inga Strom,) won't agree to the 8-hour day, our strategy is for a slow-down. Frank and Bruns will urge Strom workers to use this tactic, but keep this information under your hat.

Sophie Krueger is back and would be glad to talk to you, BUT, you should come down before the end of the year. Next year she's going to Portland to set up another clinic and it's hard to tell when she'll be back. You can have the nicest room in Mother's house. Look out the window and you'll see ships out on Puget Sound. How's that for bait to entice you???? Love, Ann.

Linnie slipped the letter back into the envelope. Yes, she wanted to go, but there were problems. She had promised Mide that she would be with her for the birth of her fifth child and the child was due any day now. During Mide's previous births, Birdie took Mide and Collin's children home with her while Linnie helped Mide.

Secondly, an important I.W.W. meeting was coming up the last Saturday in July followed by a rally on Sunday. Mr. Dobbs, Tosstles, and Bruns were expected to speak. Linnie wanted to go for Parley's sake, and for her own. After these two events occurred, she would go to Seattle and learn what had eluded her all these years.

CHAPTER 29

L innie did not want to be late for the I.W.W. meeting, but she couldn't find her pretty hair combs, or the box in which she kept them. She went to the kitchen. "Where's Baby?" she said to Dru who was bathing Nellie in the small washtub.

"She left awhile ago. Headed for Parley's shop."

"My haircombs and the box are missing. I'm sure she took them."

"Use mine. They aren't as pretty as yours, but they should do."

"Thanks. I'll search for mine after I get home."

Linnie arranged her hair in the wide pompadour Parley had liked, grabbed her straw hat and drove to town.

She parked in front of Ollie and Mame's hardware store and stepped lively down Main Street. A block from the Union Hall, Kees fell in step with her. "Hello, Linnie. Say, I'm sorry to hear about your husband. I thought he was a good man and I wish he had liked me."

"He liked you. He liked most all people" She picked up her pace.

Posters hung in the front windows of the hall read: AN INJURY TO ONE IS THE CONCERN OF ALL. JOIN ONE BIG UNION. Kees followed Linnie inside. He grabbed her elbow. "Excuse me," he said.

She shook her arm free. "Please. I'd like to find a place to sit."

"Yes. I want to, too, and I know it's not proper for you to consider this now, but after a fair amount of time has gone by, will you . . . will you allow me to buy you a treat?"

"It's kind of you to ask, but no."

"Why not?" The red spot bloomed on his forehead.

"I'm not interested in having a treat with anyone." She turned, found a seat between two women, sat down and took a deep breath. Kees Strom was a nuisance and a creepy fellow who paid no attention to boundaries.

She was delighted to see Mr. Dobbs leap up onto a raised platform. He scanned the crowd. He spotted Linnie, jumped down and went to greet her. After expressing his sympathies about Parley, he said, "With your permission I'd like to say a few words about your husband."

"He'd be pleased. And so will I."

Mr. Dobbs returned to the platform and grabbed a bull-horn. The crowd quieted. Mr. Dobbs noted Parley Hearn's contributions to union. "Last year he successfully bargained with Mrs. Strom to grant most of the pay increase we'd been fighting for and she promised to clean up her camps. Parley Hearn was a good man. He fit in the mould of the best."

Several folks spoke well of Parley. Then a number of men and women raised issues of other concerns. Pitched battles against wealthy industrialists in Spokane, San Diego, and Los Angeles. Strikes. Six, ten-hour working days per week with miserably low pay. Men *and* women gave fiery proclamations defending free speech.

"One Big Union," the crowd chanted. "O.B.U. O.B.U. Stamp out capitalism. Return the country to the people. Rally here tomorrow. Rally here. Everyone come."

Mr. Dobbs, again using the bullhorn, spoke to all of the expressed concerns. His primary thrust was that of free speech. "We will go to jail rather than give up our right to speak. Speak on the streets. Recruit new members. Speak out about reform in our lumber camps and industries."

The crowd chanted: "One Big Union." A dozen or so large I.W.W. cans were passed out among the folks for contributions. Linnie dug around in her purse and put a dollar in scrip into the can.

Mr. Dobbs, again, using the bullhorn, said, "We expect a large turnout tomorrow, but we need help. Bruns Wald, one of our comrades, will be up at the Dickerson place printing material to distribute throughout the county. If there's trouble here in town, someone has to get word to him. He'll drive over to Coldsprings to wire newspapers and get the word out. Whatever might come our way, the country needs to know. Will someone volunteer to get word to Mr. Wald?"

"I'll do it." Linnie stood, shouted and waved her hand. "Yes, I'll do it."

Mr. Dobbs said, "Mrs. Hearn, you're sure you want to take this on?"

"Yes."

The meeting ended with the crowd singing, "Workers, Shall the Masters Rule Us?"

Linnie was making her way out of the building when Mr. Dobbs caught up with her and thanked her for taking on the task of informant.

"I want to help," she said. "Parley would want me to."

Mr. Dobbs smiled. "Some time ago Ann told me you'd make a fine Wob. Ann was right."

"Thank you, Mr. Dobbs. I'll do my best."

Close to home and acting on a hunch, Linnie took the road that led to Parley's shop. She went inside. Her knees weakened. Her breath came short. "What . . . ?"

Remnants of Baby's lavender dress, neatly folded, lay on Parley's work bench. The beautiful wooden box Parley had given Linnie was perched on a ledge beside the likeness of Linnie. The haircombs were missing.

The dark thing hovered close. It had a shape. *Parley! Baby! Baby, vomiting. No bloody monthlies. Baby, gaining weight. I'll talk to Birdie. No. Speaking of it would admit light.* Linnie pushed the dark thing—like a great wad of wool—from her mind. She took the box and left the shop.

At the edge of the clearing she stopped. Across the reach Baby sat on the edge of the stoop and swung her bare feet, carefree as a child. At the end of the stoop Dru was reading to her children. Meara, sitting between Stella and Nell, had her arms around both of them. Roy was hoeing out in the garden.

Linnie strode across the clearing. She went to Baby and stood in front of her. She snatched the sparkling haircombs from Baby's hair. "You stole these. I would have allowed you to wear them if you had asked."

Baby stood. She wrapped her arms around herself. "Bay bee," she cried. "Bay bee."

"Great God," Linnie screamed. "I *know* who you are."

When Roy put one hand on Linnie's shoulder, she ducked. "Get away from me. Parley was right. Baby can't live here anymore."

Baby whapped Linnie's face. "Bay bee," she screamed and again she hugged herself.

Roy came running. He grabbed Baby. "Don't you *ever* hit her again. Ever. You understand?"

Baby's big face crumpled and while she clomped off toward Parley's shop she sobbed, "Bay bee. Bay bee."

Dru made a soothing poultice of oxalis and applied it to Linnie's bruised face. "Oh, just one day. One day away from her." She started to weep. "Don't know," she whispered. She put her hands to her face and bowed her head. "I'm scared of her. I don't know what I'd do if she hurt one of my . . . I need time to think. Time to think."

Linnie cried, "I need time to think, too." She went to her bedroom and she took one of Parley's shirts from a hook and she buried her face into the rough wool. It smelled like him. A good, clean smell. *Dru hasn't had easy years, Darlin.' Take the children to town tomorrow. Give Dru a day for herself with her mama. Take Baby, too. She . . .*

Calm settled over Linnie. She would face whatever lay before her and it would no doubt be the most difficult path she could imagine. Would she go to Seattle? Probably not.

While fixing supper she said, her tone calm and even, "Dru, let me take Hugh and Stella and Nellie to town tomorrow. And being angry with Baby only makes things worse, so I'll take her, too. She loves to go and she always behaves herself. If I have to get word to Mr. Wald, I'll take the kiddies with me."

Dru's smile was thin. "If Father won't get Baby out of the house, I'll take my chicks and go to Seattle."

"We'll talk about this later, when we're not so frazzled."

"Yes. But, thank you for giving me a day to myself with Mother."

Linnie put her arm around her. "You deserve it."

After supper Linnie sat out on the stoop. Her father sat down beside her. Linnie fought the dark thing and kept it at bay. She said, "Dru and I can't handle Baby anymore. She's hurt me for the second time. Who's next? Me again? Dru? Stella? Hugh? Little Nel?"

"I think . . ."

"No. You should have *thought* a long time ago.

She left her father and went inside to go to bed. The dark thing hovered close. *Tomorrow, after the rally, buy the kiddies and Baby treats. On the way home, have Baby sit up front with you. Ask her questions. Why does she hug herself and say 'Bay Bee'? You see what she has to say.*

CHAPTER 30

Baby learned of the plan to go to town and she chortled and ran around in circles. "Hoo loon bat Bay bee go. Hoo loon bat Bay knockers bee go. Buttons. Buttons."

Shortly before they were to leave, she soaped her hands and her face and brushed out her hair. As was her habit, she took one of her hair ribbons to Dru. Dru refused to help her. She took the ribbon to Linnie. Linnie tied the ribbon around her head and into a bow on top. Baby smiled and patted the bow. "Pretty Bay bee. Hoo loon. Pretty."

Linnie put on a navy blue skirt and a long-sleeved white blouse. Her deep-brimmed straw hat shaded her bruised face.

Birdie and Newt stopped by. "Good mercy," said Birdie to Linnie. She touched her cheek. "What happened?"

"Baby hit me. I'll tell you about it later."

"Newt, you drive on into town. I'll go with Linnie."

Linnie said, "Newt, wait a minute, please. Birdie, if there's trouble at the rally, will you bring the kiddies home in my auto? I'll walk up to get word to Mr. Wald."

Newt said, "Good idea. If it gets rowdy in town, neither of you should stick around. Linnie, you'll be all right going up to Dickerson's place?"

"Of course."

"Good," said Newt. "Birdie, I'll pick you up here." He waved and drove off.

Baby lumbered out to the auto and sat in the back seat. After Dru settled her children, she said to Linnie and Birdie, "Father is going fishing with Mr. Corrigan. So it will be Mama and Pal and me. Thank you, for doing this."

Birdie said, "We'll buy treats at Mame's before we come home."

Baby prattled. "Baby go. Pretty Baby go. Buttons. Buttons." Hugh and Stella joined in with the gibberish, while Nellie, wide-eyed and somber, stared at them.

Linnie shifted into gear and got under way.

Gritty dust hung in tinder-dry heat without a breath of breeze. Satin-white clouds piled off to the east looked like the meringue Mame put on her lemon and chocolate pies.

In town a sizeable crowd had gathered in front of the Union Hall and a six-man band played a rousing, "Stars and Stripes Forever." Linnie parked in front of Mame's parlor. Mame came out to greet Linnie and Birdie. "Tosstles stopped by last night," she said. "Bruns and Paul got here early this morning. We've got a good turn out."

Birdie scrutinized the sky. "Smells like rain. I hope it holds off until after our rally."

Baby scrambled out of the auto. She stood in front of Mame and pointed to herself. "Bay bee. Bay bee."

Mame smiled and patted Baby's blond curls. "Yes. And how is Baby today?"

Baby shook her head and she hugged herself. "Bay bee," she cried.

Birdie Mae said, "Baby. Get in the auto and sit down. After the rally we'll stop by and I'll buy ice-cream cones."

Baby minded. Mame went back into her ice-cream parlor.

Linnie gave Birdie a short account about what had happened between her and Baby. She said nothing about the lavender dress she'd found in Parley's shop.

"She's getting harder to handle, Birdie. Dru is almost at the end of her rope. So am I. We've got to send her away."

"That's a lousy idea. After this rally, Newt and I will take her home with us. We won't ask her. We won't ask Father. We'll just take her."

"Let's wish ourselves good luck. Where's Newt?"

"Probably going over Union business with Ollie."

"I'm glad he's taken over Parley's role in all of this."

Birdie Mae shrugged. "I wish Parley was still doing the job. Funny thing, him slipping like he did."

"He didn't slip. Something went haywire. For the past month or so, he was touchy as a spooked cat."

Mr. Dobbs's crisp voice, amplified by the bullhorn, soared out over the crowd. "Fellow workers. Hear. Hear. Last night our bargaining team met to discuss our strategy."

The crowd quieted.

"Comrades," he said, "Hear this, please. If Mrs. Strom refuses to clean up the camps, we will NOT go for a slow down. We'll go out on another strike."

Loud whistles. Cheers.

A call from the crowd. "Anarchists." An egg grazed Mr. Dobbs's head and splattered at his feet. He ignored it. "We will continue to . . ."

"Arrest the bastard. Throw him in jail."

Sheriff Chester Mann and two deputies jumped up on the platform. "Dobbs," said Mann. "I'm arresting you for trying to incite a riot."

"I have the right to speak out," said Mr. Dobbs. "I'm try-ing to give information to Strom workers and they . . ."

Sheriff Mann slapped cuffs on Mr. Dobbs and started to hustle him off the stage. Mr. Dobbs resisted.

The crowd shouted, "Down with tyranny. Down with Strom."

Countered by, "Throw the union scum in jail. Let 'em rot."

Two deputies joined Sheriff Mann, hustled Mr. Dobbs and shoved him into the sheriff's automobile.

Tosstles took Mr. Dobbs's place. "Comrades." His voice boomed out. "We have the right to protest the lousy camps and report the rotten food. And for years you workers, you who work for Strom have had money deducted from your pay for a hospital. That hospital has never been built."

"Strike! Down with Strom! Strike! Strike!"

Deputies, accusing Tosstles of inciting a riot, scuttled him away.

Paul Garibaldi picked up the bullhorn. "Just as we fought in Spokane and Portland, we'll continue our fight up here. You *need* clean camps. You *deserve* good food. You . . ."

Another arrest.

Shouts. Loud. Loud and louder. "Strike. Strike." Fists pumped the air. "Union. Union."

A gunshot rang out.

Sheriff Mann again took the bullhorn. "Ladies and gen-tlemen, clear the streets. Now. Clear the streets."

Newt came running up to Linnie's auto. "Get going, Birdie," he yelled. "Get the kids out of here. I'll pick you up later at Roy's. Linnie, you'll be alright?"

"Yes." She gave the keys to Birdie and got out of the auto. She said to the kiddies, "You mind Aunt Birdie."

Pushing and elbowing her way through the crowd she walked with a fast pace up Main Street to the end of town and started up the road toward the Dickerson house. It was some time before the din of the uprising in town faded and died.

Without stopping she took off her hat and ran her fingers through her hair, damp with sweat. She skirted deer scat and horse flops. She swatted her hat at whining mosquitoes and droning flies. Her bruised face burned. But, this was not the time to think about herself. Yet, twice, she turned, sure that somebody was behind her. A doe with two fawns drank from a creek, but she hurried.

At the Dickerson place Mr. Wald met her and insisted that she sit down and he'd pour her a glass of lemonade. She accepted his offer and recounted to him all that had happened in town.

"Good report," he said.

She eyed the small printing press. "Is there anything I can do to help?"

"Would you mind folding and stacking the flyers over there?" He pointed to the printed material. "I've just taken them off the press. And if you don't mind stamping them, they'll be ready to go when I get back."

"I'm pleased to help."

Mr. Wald went outside, cranked up his car and drove off.

Linnie set her empty glass on the sideboard. The same bottle she'd seen at Ann's party some years ago stood beside the press. Where had it come from? Had Mr. or Mrs. Dickerson known Brown Hon?

She folded the flyers, stamped them and stacked them, making sure they were straight and neat. She examined the press. Only about a foot square, it printed the single-sheet flyers she had stamped and folded. The flyers carried a lot of information. Date, time and place of the next I.W.W. meetings. The news was put out with short, quick sentences. Strikes possible in Yakima and Centralia, Washington. An important meeting in Spokane later this summer.

Someday Linnie would put that press to work, but now, free from her tasks, she could go home. She didn't want to go home. She didn't want to fight the dark thing. She wanted to go over to Thimble Creek Meadow and sit on her rock and think.

The sweltering air, so still one could hear needles drop from the trees, was the color of copper. Thunder rumbled. Linnie took the narrow, overgrown trail to the creek. She stopped. Someone had set two by four planks—six of them—across the water and on the other side of the meadow a large white tent enveloped her rock. Who had done these things? Who had trespassed on property she considered hers? Who might be inside that tent right now? She cupped her hands. "Hello? Hello?"

Throaty burbles of birdsong ceased. High reedy grasses rustled like whispers. A frog croaked.

She crossed the bridge. She called out again, "Hello?" A small cook stove stood beside the tent. She opened the flap of canvas. "Hello, in there?" Silence. She ducked inside. A stack of books and pamphlets lay atop the rock. A small, but sturdy table, a stove, a chair and a dark blue carpet allowed a feel of comfort. A gray wool blanket covered a mattress in front of a steamer trunk and a valise.

She opened a book. Bold letters printed on the inside page. FRANK DOBBS. She picked up another book. It had the same name. So, Mr. Dobbs had made the bridge and pitched the tent and in doing so he'd taken the rock—her rock—away from her. She slammed the book down on the table. But wait just a minute. This place didn't belong to her anymore than it belonged to him.

A cartoon drawing of a man standing in front of a crowd of folks was pinned on the canvas wall. The man held a bull horn. Words, floating on a cloud – *Workers of the World—Unite—One Big Union for all* – came from the man's mouth.

At one time Linnie had known nothing about that world, but now she knew something about the overall sense of it. Workers of the world must unite to fight off the greed of Capitalists. And it was Capitalists of the World, like Mrs. Strom, who kept workers under her fist poor, powerless and as ignorant as possible.

She set the paper aside and picked up a pamphlet in which a woman named Elizabeth Gurley Flynn had written a piece. *Sabotage. The Conscious Withdrawal of the Worker's Industrial Efficiency.* She glanced through it. She liked the fact that a woman had written the piece.

But, enough of this. She had no business being in this tent and going through Mr. Dobbs's things.

She returned to the house to retrieve her hat and go home. Thoughts churned in her mind. Capitalists, like Mrs. Strom, were willing to kill people seeking good wages and a decent life. Most poor people didn't know how to fight back. They'd had little or no schooling. The women had too

many babies. Husbands, unable to leave poor paying employment, were trapped. People, like Mr. Dobbs and Ann and
Paul Garibaldi and Tosstles and Bruns Wald risked their lives
fighting for poor people.

But Linnie and her family weren't like other families.
Linnie's mother and father had had schooling and had seen
to it that Linnie and her brothers and sisters learned beyond
what they learned in school. But still, Linnie, a flume tender's daughter, was one of the poor and she shouldn't forget
it.

She put on her hat and was about to leave when somebody came up on the porch.

"Hello, Linnie." Kees leaned against the door jam of the
open doorway. The crotch of his knickers bulged. He smiled.
"Mr. Dobbs thought you might need some help." He came
toward her.

A wave of revulsion nearly knocked her over. "I'm leaving," she said.

He rubbed his crotch. His eyes, bright and glittery, were
fixed on her. "Let's say *I* thought you might need a little help.
You're too pretty and too young to be a widow. And I like
you. I've always liked you. Did you know that? I dream about
you kissing me."

A hot, metallic taste of fear rose in her throat.

He came to her and grabbed her arm. She twisted out of
his grasp and backed up against the side table. He lunged at
her, grabbed her again and held her in a vise-like grip. "Why
don't you like me?" he whispered, his face a hair's breath
away from hers. "Don't you understand that all these years
I've wanted to be your friend? Your special friend? And all
these years you've treated me badly."

She raised one foot and slammed it down hard on his shoe. He howled and let her go. She picked up the brown bottle, darted behind the dining table and held the bottle high. "Don't come near me. You do and I'll smash your face bloody."

Eyes narrowed with disdain, he sneered, "I'll leave. But, you'll hear from me again. Remember, Mrs. Hearn. Linnie Bede. You have no station up here. A flume tender's daughter? Hah! Someday you'll be sorry for the way you've treated me."

"It doesn't matter who I am. You don't present yourself to me and you don't force yourself on me. Now, leave! Mr. Wald will soon be home and I don't think you want him to find you here."

Kees turned and left.

Linnie went out on the porch. She watched him. He walked stiff as a stick, turned once, and walked on. Relief came when he did not take the east-bound junction toward Linnie's house, but the south-bound junction to town.

A dull ache angled up her back and neck and lodged steady in her head. She lowered her face into her hands and leaned back against the big log wall of the house. Her legs felt like loose mud. How dare that man come at her and force himself on her. Sickening. Degrading. She feared that if Mr. Wald came home, she would blurt out the dreadful scene to him. She put on her hat, left the house and started home.

Thunder rumbled close. Big drops of rain splotched the dust. On down the road a ways she stopped to sit on a mossy rock and catch her breath. Nausea rippled through her. She leaned over and wretched at the thought—the image—of Kees in the doorway.

She left the road and made her way up a hill to the south fork of the Blackduck River. Her mother had once taken her, Dru, Birdie Mae, Joe and Colin to this place for a picnic. They'd made dams and small castles with pebbles surrounded by pools of quiet water. Oh, Lord, Linnie wished she could talk to her mother right now and she wished that her mother would understand.

She knelt and submerged her aching face into the stream's icy-cold water. Had Parley felt water this cold when he drowned? She sat up. "Yes," she whispered. "He knew what he was doing, even though I didn't. And I still don't. Not yet."

She got up, picked up a stout walking stick and she hurried, eager to be rid of this horrid day.

At home she crossed the clearing to the garden. She stopped. "What!" Half-ripened tomatoes stripped from their vines lay strewn among smashed squash, carrot, and potato plants.

"Baby?" she called. "Mother? Dru?"

She found it hard to breathe. She went up to the stoop and she grabbed a broom. If Baby attacked her, she would fight back.

"Dru? Mother?" She peered in the open doorway. Baby, her face contorted with tears, held her arms up to Linnie. "Bay Bee." She cried. She pointed to herself. "Bay Bee. Ma Ma gone. All gone."

Linnie shook Baby. Shook her and shook her. "Where's Mother? Where? Where?"

"Gone. Ma Ma all gone."

Linnie quit the house. Should she go to Birdie's place? No. The children were safe with Birdie and Newt. But, where was Mother? Horsetail Falls, the place to which Baby had never been.

Linnie ran up the trail. She hurried. Thunder rolled. Not far from the falls Pal yelped and came tearing down the trail toward her. Linnie hurried. Pal turned and ran ahead of her and back to her. Back and ahead. Linnie's throat tightened. At the top of the overlook one of Meara's shoes was caught on a thick root and far below the great lacy falls Meara lay, splayed on the shore.

Late that night steady, hard rain drummed on the roof of Roy Bede's house. Forked lightening flashed. Thunder cracked hard and loud. Dru's children and Baby were in bed. Roy, Joe, Linnie, Birdie, Newt and Dru sat at the table. Linnie fought her urge to scream at her stoney-faced, silent father. Joe, his freckles paled in his chalk-white face, sat tight-lipped, his brown eyes, sat tight-lipped, his brown eyes brimmed with sorrow.

Birdie Mae said, "Baby kept hollering for ice cream. When she saw I wasn't going to stop to buy it, she raised a ruckus. I got out of town, stopped, and settled her down by telling her I'd take her to town tomorrow and buy her ice-cream. We came by here. Dru wouldn't allow her chicks to be here with Baby, so I took Dru and the kiddies with me. Left Baby here."

Newt said, in a nervous, stiff way, "I stopped by here, thinking I'd pick up Birdie. Nobody was here. Except Baby. She was sitting out on the porch crying like a little kid. Pointing to herself. Saying her name over and over. I was crazy with worry about Birdie and the little ones. Figured I'd deal with Baby and Meara later, so I drove home."

Tears brimmed Dru's eyes, "I'm taking my chicks to Seattle and we'll find Buzz."

"That's nuts," said Birdie. "You haven't heard from him . . . I don't know when."

Dru set her chin. Her blue eyes got hard. "I'll find him. He won't let me and our children go unattended. He's connected with the Ballard Union Hall and I'll find him."

Linnie said, "Father, none of these things would have happened if you'd let us send Baby away a long time ago." Her voice rose. "But, no. Because of you, Mother is dead. Because of you, Dru is leaving home. Because of you, I can't follow my own dreams. But, I'll build my own house and move out of here as fast as I can. And if you allow Baby to be at Mother's funeral, Dru and the children and I won't be there. And Mother did right by not giving her a name. She's a nobody, hear? A nobody."

Joe, solemn looking and disturbed, said, "I don't know what to think except the Lord has surely cursed this house." He put on his cap and his coat and left.

CHAPTER 31

Roy made arrangements for Baby to stay at Ollie and Mame Holm's house while the rest of the family went to Meara's service.

Under frowzy gray skies and skittering rain the family trudged up to the cemetery. There, beside a newly dug grave Joe read scriptures, said prayers and insisted that the family sing, "Leaning on the Everlasting Arms."

Linnie didn't believe that her mother was leaning on anyone's arms, but she hoped that wherever her soul and spirit might be, it was a place of music and sunshine. And she knew she would always wonder if her mother had killed herself, or had she tripped and accidentally fallen over the falls.

Before she left the cemetery, she stood for some time beside Parley's grave and she touched the small, carved owl that lay at her throat.

The following day weak sunlight shot through a gray mist hovering over the forest and at Roy's house the flume bell clanged its never-ceasing, erratic *bong bong bong bong*.

Dru said to Linnie, "I'm taking the kiddies to town. I'll send a wire to Buzzie at the Ballard Union Hall. I'll stop to buy goods at the A & D to sew myself and the children new clothes."

Linnie said, "that's all very well and good, but you can't fill your head with dreams like you've been doing for the past six years."

"I know him. You don't. He might be a cad in a lot of ways, but he's not going to allow me or his children to go hungry."

Mid-morning she harnessed the horse to the wagon, helped her children up into the bed and drove off.

Linnie got busy. The past few hours had been heavenly without Baby around, but she had to work and stay busy to keep her mind from wandering off to a place where she did not want to go.

A new, fresh idea took hold. She and Dru would take the children to Seattle. Using Parley's money she could afford to rent a decent house and she would find a job. Secretary, Saleswoman, Seamstress, Nanny, Nurses aid. Surely, Ann, or Mr. Dobbs, or Mr. Wald, or Tosstles would put in a good word and help her find employment.

She and Dru would raise the children and see that they went to good schools. If Buzz and Dru came together as husband and wife, mother and father, that would be fine. Linnie would build a new life, save her money, go on to school and learn to teach. Mercy buckets! She'd be free to follow the dreams she'd been denied because of her marriage to Parley.

She trimmed wicks and washed the chimneys. She was getting ready to wash the windows when Birdie Mae drove up and came in.

Linnie set her rags and ammonia water aside. "Mercy buckets, you look white as paste. What's wrong now?"

Birdie, pale, her blue eyes distraught, sat down on the sofa. "The worst thing has happened. The very worst of all."

She rooted around in her skirt pocket, took out a handker-chief and blew her nose. Her chin wobbled. Tears filled her eyes.

Linnie said, "I don't know what could be any worse than what's happened, unless something's wrong with you. If it's something to do with Baby, I don't give a Tinker's Damn."

"Come and sit down," Birdie said. "Here, on the sofa."

The dark thing hovered close. *You know what's coming. You do. You do.* "I might as well hear it, straight out," she said.

"Baby's going to have a baby."

Linnie fought the dark thing. "You know that's not possible."

"You're wrong. Early this morning Mame brought Baby home to Newt and me. They're over at our house now. Mame figured it out when Baby kept pointing to herself and saying, 'Bay bee.' Linnie, Baby knows she's going to have a child and she told me and Mame who the father is."

Linnie did not move. Parley, standing at the front win-dow, his back to Linnie. Parley, eating with agitation when Baby sat beside him. Parley, distracted, pacing the floor, shouting at Baby. *You can't live here anymore.* The piece of Baby's lavender dress Baby put inside the casket. The rem-nants out at Parley's shop. Baby, sick. Missing her monthly.

"Parley." Linnie whispered.

"Yes. Baby knew, but she didn't know what to do about it. She tried to tell us—all of us—the best she could, but none of us understood her."

Linnie bent over and Birdie Mae took hold of her. Some time passed before Linnie whispered, "Baby and her child can't ever live with me. Not ever."

"No. Of course not. Newt and I will take them. There's no other place for them to go. Early this morning Newt went over to Colin's and Mide's and told them what happened. We'll tell folks who ask about the child that a cousin in Portland died giving birth and we're pleased to be able to raise it."

"Yes," Linnie whispered. "I suppose we should do that." Questions jammed her mind. Would the child be dim-witted? What would it look like? But, it didn't matter, did it? She wasn't bound to its care.

She got up from the sofa and went out on the stoop. Across the reach the image of the large, log house she and Parley had planned to build came to mind. It was to have been such a fine place and from it she could see mist rising from the river and she could hear the rush of it and the irregular *bong, bong bong* of the bell.

But now, neither the thought of her house, or the pale, watery sun shining through misty splinters of light brought her a ray of comfort. She bent and retched. Again and then again. Birdie came to her and put her arm around her. "You'll be all right," she said. "We'll all be all right."

"How do you know that?" Linnie cried. "How can you say that to me?"

"I say it because it's true. We'll be all right. We have to be. But we need to tend to business and we need to start now. Come in, and I'll fix nerve tea."

The two sat at the table and Birdie said, "When *did* Dru last hear from Buzz?"

"Dang it, Birdie. Why must we talk about Buzzie when our own lives have been torn up so bad?" She paused. "Two months, maybe. Whenever it was, she didn't say much about it."

"Just last week Newt asked Jim about him. Jim said he'd quit sending Buzz money some time ago and he doesn't know where he is now. Hugh and Stella and Nellie shouldn't have to suffer because of their father. Dru must not take her chicks to Seattle until she learns something about Buzz."

Linnie said, "Dru and I will go together." She told Birdie about her plan.

Birdie said, "You shouldn't get mixed up in her trouble. She should go alone, find Buzz and decide what's best for her and her kiddies. You've got your union work up here. Folks depend on you."

Linnie sipped her tea. Fiddled with the sugar spoon. "So it's up to me to look after Dru's chicks, isn't it. By myself."

"If you will, yes. I'll tell Father about Baby. If Dru leaves, there's no point in telling her right now."

"You've got to understand that I'll have nothing to do with Baby's child."

"You won't. Newt and I will take care of it and Baby. They have no other place to go."

Roy Bede took the news with somber stoicism. Linnie had nothing to do with him.

Two days later Buzz wired Dru about his pleasure at having her come to see him. He sent money for train fare. One way for one passenger. *We'll get settled send for the kiddies Look for me at train station Love, B.*

Dru became her old self, busy and full of fun and laughter. She had color in her face, light in her eyes, and a lilt in her voice. "Cuddle Up a Little Closer," she sang and Stella, who had a voice much like her mother's, sang with her.

For herself, Dru fashioned a blouse out of creamy white cotton with tucks across the bodice. She made new dresses for Stella and Nell. At the A&D she bought knickers and two caps for Hugh. "When Buzzie and I come get the kiddies, I want them to look nice as can be," she said. "And they'll have new clothes to wear to school in the city."

Linnie said, "All of this sounds fine and dandy, but you don't know what to expect from Buzz. And be careful. Plenty of people are waiting to take advantage of pretty girls like you."

"Don't fret. I'll be with Buzzie."

"You've got plenty of money?"

"Yes. Buzz sent fifty dollars."

The day before she was to leave, she packed her clothes and all of the gifts Buzzie had given her over the years in a valise. She put the valise in a far corner of her bedroom.

At the Coldsprings train station on a foggy, gray morning, all but one of Roy's children went to see Dru off. Newt stayed home with Baby. Dru hugged her children and told them she'd soon be back with their father. "And the back seat of our automobile will be stuffed with presents," she said. She smiled her beautiful smile, boarded the train, turned, waved to her family and was gone.

❧

Two weeks later, Linnie picked up a letter from Dru at the post office. Perhaps her news would help ease dark questions from Linnie's mind. Questions that never left her. How many times had Parley and Baby coupled? When had it started? Had he finally been able to love a woman the way he'd wanted to love her, his wife? Had Baby loved him, the way Dru loved Buzzie, and Birdie loved Newt? Questions, over and over and over again. But, no answers and there never would be.

With the letter in hand, Linnie went to the ice-cream parlor, ordered a cup of tea, and opened the envelope.

Dear Family;

I found Buzzie right away. Tosstles knew where he lived. Buzzie moved out of his place and we found an apartment on Fourth Street. We might get electricity soon. I spend most of my time looking for a house. Buzz sometimes comes with me, but he's awfully busy. Yesterday I found a gray painted house with a picket fence. It has four bedrooms and the living room has a pretty fireplace and leaded glass windows. Buzzie hasn't seen it yet, but I hope he'll go with me tomorrow to look at it. If we buy it, we'll drive home and get Hugh and Stella and Nell. I want them to go to school here, in the city. I'll write again, soon. Love to all, Dru.

CHAPTER 32

Union negotiations with Mrs. Strom failed. Once again, Strom workers went out on strike. Their demands: Ten-hour days reduced to eight. Clean camps. Decent food. Once again folks walked the picket line. But this time, when scrip ran out and Mrs. Strom refused to negotiate, the workers caved and went back to work.

Linnie did not attend the meetings. She went to town only through necessity. She was kept plenty busy tending the children, cooking, housekeeping, laundry, mending, and caring for the vegetable garden. When, on occasion, a letter came from Dru, she read it aloud to the children.

She had little to say to her father and he, with his gimpy leg continued to carry himself with stiff dignity and he treated her accordingly.

From the get-go, Linnie made it clear to him that Baby was not welcome in his house. He kept his silence. Birdie's habit of coming over to visit four to five times a week stopped. Birdie was free to leave home only when Newt agreed to stay with Baby.

While Linnie continued to fight the dark thing of fantasies, questions and realities, she tried to put her mind to her new house. In time she succeeded fairly well. She walked the foundation Parley had marked. She studied tree shadows and angles of the sun at different times of day and into the evening.

Instinct told her that Dru would not return any time soon and she asked Joe to design two more bedrooms. "One for each child and one for me," she said.

That summer Joe, Roy, Newt and Colin built the foundation and framed the house. From the large front-window frames Linnie had a fine view of the swift, wild river and she smelled its wetness and she listened to the erratic *bong bong bong* of the bell and all of it—the sights, smells and sounds—brought to her chaotic mind a sense of strength.

By late fall, sturdy-hewn logs sat solidly on the foundation. The thick-shingled roof was steep; the wrap-around porch wide. Joe crafted beautiful maple kitchen cupboards. The counters he crafted were wide and a large breadboard slid out of sight underneath. A glazier from Coldsprings set the casement windows and sunlight spangled the front room, the kitchen and the front bedrooms and when one swung the windows wide, fresh air and sound came in.

At Ollie Holm's hardware store Linnie bought two wood stoves—one for her kitchen and one for her front room. At Maxwell's Furniture Store she bought a dark blue carpet and a dining table, six chairs and two brown wicker arm-chairs. Without a word to her father, she took her mother's platform rocker, some of her books and the photos Buzz had snapped of the family. She ordered handsome frames from the catalog and she put the photos up on the mantel of the stone fireplace.

One day, amidst the first squall of wind and snow, Linnie, Hugh, Stella, and Nell moved into Linnie's home. It smelled of fir and pine and had about it a sense of pride.

Two days before Christmas Linnie, able to drive into town, in spite of deep snows, stopped by the post office. She was pleased to pick up a package and a card from Dru.

On Christmas morning the children, with great excitement, opened the package. Hugh picked up a Santa Clause puppet—an odd contraption with faded paint and dirty, thin strings. Dru's note read: *Merry Christmas to my chicks. Buzzie and I bought this and I hope you like it. I love all of you. Mother.*

The following day the puppet disappeared.

CHAPTER 33

Late February brought a thaw. On a morning when snow still spit in a haphazard way from dull, gray skies, Birdie Mae drove to Linnie's house. Linnie was hanging crisp, pale yellow curtains at the windows and while she was pleased to see Birdie, she suspected the reason behind her visit was to ask her for help when Baby's time came for delivering the child.

Through the long, dark winter Linnie had given the dilemma much thought. She would do as Birdie asked her to do and together, they would do it right.

Two weeks later Birdie Mae and Linnie helped Baby deliver a girl. Baby seemed to know what to do and she didn't cry out or make much fuss. Immediately following the birth, she let out a great sigh. "Pawley," she whispered. "Oh, Pawley." She turned and pointed to Linnie. "Ma Ma," she said. "Ma Ma."

Birdie held the child to her own breast to try to show Baby what she must do. "You must nurse her," Birdie said. "She's hungry."

Baby shook her head. Again, she pointed to Linnie. "Ma Ma. Ma Ma."

Linnie went to the kitchen. She warmed goat's milk in a pan, poured the milk into a nursing bottle and took it Baby. Baby wouldn't touch it. Birdie Mae, still holding the screaming child, sat down beside Baby. "You must help her eat. You are her mother. You must help her."

Baby shook her head and once again and pointed to Linnie. "Ma Ma."

Birdie, fighting tears, handed the child to Linnie. "At least take her for now."

Late afternoon Linnie took the baby home. Hugh, Stella and Nell were beside themselves with excitement and wanted to hold the child.

"What's her name?" said Stella.

"Well," said Linnie, "Let's think of a name. Come sit by the fire and you can take turns holding her."

The children plopped down on the sofa, all three next to each other. Linnie showed Hugh how to hold her. "And what do you think we should name her?" she said.

"Annie," said Stella. "Let's name her Annie."

"That's a nice name," said Linnie. "My best friend's name is Ann."

"I like it, too," said Nellie.

"Margaret?" said Hugh. "I like that name."

"Yes. Yes." His sisters agreed.

"That's a beautiful name," said Linnie. "Perhaps we could call her 'Meggie?' "

"Yes," the children chimed. "Meggie. We'll name her Meggie."

Hugh passed the baby on to Stella. And after Stella had her turn, she carefully passed the little bundle to Nell. "Does Meggie sleep all the time?" said Nell.

"No," said Linnie. "You'll see her wide awake tomorrow."

After the children had gone to bed, Linnie took the baby and, while giving her a bottle of lukewarm milk, she studied her. She had Baby's blue eyes and she appeared to be studying *her*. Linnie laughed. "You're a curious one, aren't you."

She caressed the baby's soft, round cheek. "And your name is Meggie."

The child slept well into the deep night and during that time Linnie stayed beside her. Just as the first silver streaks of day showed over the trees to the east, Linnie whispered to the baby, "Your mama wants me to be your mama. I think your father would want me to do that, too. So, I'll raise you as if you were mine and nobody outside the family needs to know who is your birth-mother. If we find it necessary, we'll tell folks you're the daughter of a cousin who passed. But, I promise that when you're old enough to understand, I'll tell you the truth. And you're my blood, too."

CHAPTER 34

Over the following year Dru's letters became less frequent. While she didn't complain, she no longer wrote about looking for places to live. *Buzz and I have moved to another apartment. It's small, but the rent is cheap. I've got a job singing in a nice club downtown, so I'm making a little money. Linnie, someday I'll make this up to you, I promise.*

Linnie wasn't surprised by this turn of events, but the irony was that she, who had never wanted children, was now raising four.

The months passed. Dru's infrequent letters told the family nothing, but uneasy, scattered news. She liked her job, singing at The Comiqiue. Buzz was away a lot. *On Union business. He's very involved. Goes to Spokane and Portland a lot. If the kiddies were with me they wouldn't see much of him and with me working nights, it wouldn't work*

At times it occurred to Linnie that Dru knew nothing about Baby's child and it was best to let the matter rest. Her pique at her father began to fade. He'd done what he'd thought was best and there was little to be gained with festering anger. She willed herself to let it go. She put her energies into raising the four children. At times it astounded Linnie to realize that Meggie's presence had eased Linnie's resentment of Baby. At times she considered it as simply as the way it was.

Once in awhile Linnie took Meggie over to Birdie and Newt's house. Baby was now an enormous woman who no longer burst into temper tantrums and babble. When Linnie happened to be in her presence she sat off by herself. When Meggie was around, Baby, in silence, watched her.

As Meggie grew older the two enjoyed each other. Meggie shared her first book with her. *An Alphabet* was Baby's favorite and the two spent long periods of time looking at the pictures. They also liked to color in coloring books.

A strange blessing. For the child, a deceptive joy. For the child's birth-mother, an attentive playmate. And any thought of putting Baby into an institution had faded and died some time ago.

CHAPTER 35

Another two years passed. On January 3rd, a day of Christmas vacation for the children, Linnie allowed them to take the wash tub up behind the house and slide down the hill. She stood out on the porch and watched them. Dru's children, sturdy, nice looking children, no longer asked about their mother and Dru hadn't written now, in over a year.

She would be proud of them. Hugh, in fourth grade, looked like his father, handsome with dark hair and blue eyes. He often said that when he grew up, he wanted to write stories for newspapers. Stella, the image of her beautiful mother, loved music. Nell, a quiet little girl, content to be alone and float in another world, reminded Linnie of Joe.

And Parley would be popping with pride over Meggie. She was a curious, bubbly child who asked questions about people she met. Where did they live? Did they have enough to eat? Did they like to read as much as she did? And she had a love for books.

"Hello. Hello."

Linnie shaded her eyes against the bright sun. Emma, Mide and Collin's oldest daughter, came walking on snowshoes through the snow. Once again her mother needed help with birthing. "I'll stay here and look after the kiddies," she said. "Aunt Birdie is already with Mother. She asked me to come and get you. Dad's at work."

Linnie gathered up her things, loaded them into her auto and slipped and slide over the road to Mide and Colin's house.

Colin had added a new bedroom on to their place and Mide's appreciation for a touch of beauty gave the room a graceful touch. She'd embroidered bright blue flowers on the white curtains and she'd painted tiny white daisies on the lemon-yellow chamber pot that matched the commode. But, with this sixth child, as with the five before, she was having difficulties.

Linnie and Birdie walked her from the bedroom out to the kitchen, to the two other bedrooms and back. Forth and back. Back and forth. They helped her sit in a tub of warm water. Nothing alleviated the pain. Back in bed her screams, like shattering glass, split the air. "I've never had one like this. I've never had it hurt so bad. Oh, Lord, Lord, I want to die."

Mid-afternoon she birthed a boy and his weak, mew-like cry was like that of a new born kitten. Quickly, Linnie cleaned him and tried to avert her eyes from the baby's face. Thank God, Mide had fallen into a deep sleep, induced by tea Birdie laced heavily with laudanum.

Birdie wrapped the infant in a baby blanket and beckoned to Linnie. "Come," she said, softly. "We'll do this together before Colin comes home."

Down at the Blackduck River, not far from the house, the two plunged the infant into the water and held him down. Birdie Mae wept and she choked on her words. "Mide told me she took poke root and tansy to try to get rid of him."

"I can't think what his life might have been," Linnie said.

She and Birdie took the baby from the water and listened for a heart beat. None. Quickly, they wrapped him in the blanket, returned to the house and laid him in a shoe box. Using a shovel, an axe and a pickaroon they hacked through the ice-crusted snow and they dug into the earth over a good two feet before they buried the boy. Out of respect to Mide, who never missed a Sunday at First Baptist, the two made a crude wooden cross with scraps of wood and Linnie used a black crayola and printed on the arm of it. *Baby Boy Bede. Born Jan. 3. 1916. Died Jan. 3. 1916.*

Linnie and Birdie sat for a few moments in front of the fire in Colin and Mide's front room. They both wept a little, and then dried their tears. Birdie said, "Like it or not, we've got to finish supper. Emma got it going earlier today. Colin's favorite. Chicken and dumplings."

Fire in the wood stove snapped. The old hound dog out on the porch howled. Birdie let him inside. Linnie said, "I can't think about what we did."

"Then don't. Think about how we're going to tell Colin."

Mide called out. "My baby?"

Birdie Mae and Linnie went to her and took hold of her hands. "He died," said Birdie Mae, her tone flat as a board. "Linnie and I buried him and we made a nice cross and put it on his grave."

Mide nodded. "It's just as well. I don't have much feeling for life anymore. He didn't have any at all." And she slept.

Colin came home and after supper Birdie Mae and Linnie sat with him. Birdie said, "He'd of been a monster. Two holes for a nose. Little stubs of arms. Twisted, gray body."

Colin leaned over and covered his face in his hands. "Did she see him?"

"No," said Linnie.

"Don't tell her. Don't tell anyone. Linnie, can you tell us *anything* about how to stop having babies?"

"No."

"I've slept outside," he said.

"Good," said Linnie. "Mide once said she wanted two children. Two. Did you ever consider that?"

"Good God, Linnie. I've never, ever . . . forced myself on Mide. In fact, sometimes I've refused to . . . love her. Like she's wanted me to. We know about the coitus inter-ruptis business. We tried it. It didn't work for either of us. You tried to give me advice once, but now you don't have anything to say?"

"No. I'll never again advise a husband to leave his wife before the loving is complete. You surely understand that."

Colin lit a cigarette and paced the room. "You've got to go to Seattle and learn about family limitation. You've got to do it, Linnie. If Mide has another baby, she's sure to die."

Birdie Mae agreed. "We can manage. The kiddies can stay with us. You have to go, not just to get answers, but to find Dru. We haven't heard from her for a long time."

"Yes," said Colin. Please. Mide, once my pretty girl with a spring in her step and a sparkle in her eyes, is fading and we've got to help her."

"I'll think about it," said Linnie. "And I'll stay the night to help."

Birdie drove to Linnie's house to stay with the children for the night. Linnie and Colin stayed up late and before Linnie snugged down under a blanket on the sofa she prom-ised Colin she'd go to Seattle, find Dru and bring her home. And she would try to speak with Sophie Krueger or with somebody who could give her answers. She didn't want to be gone any longer than one week.

While driving home mid-morning of the next day, a sift of powdery snow and a sudden burst of sunlight came through the dark canopy of trees and a voice Linnie had not heard in a long time whispered, *Linnie, darlin,' you let Newt and Birdie take care of the children and you go on down to Seattle and learn the secret that can save women like Mide. And yes, you need to find Dru. You haven't heard from her for a long time.*

Linnie smiled. Joe once said that he'd seen God. Well, Linnie had heard from Parley and that was a good sight better.

CHAPTER 36

Ann's telegram read: *Glad you're coming Meet you at station Jan. 7. Sophie Krueger giving lecture day after you arrive.*

Linnie studied a catalog and ordered things she felt to be suitable for the city. The packages arrived and the children were eager for Linnie to open them. Meggie said, "You won't be gone long will you, Mama?"

"One week. Just seven days. And while I'm gone you'll have a fine time living with Aunt Birdie and Uncle Newt."

"And Aunt Baby. Don't forget her."

"Of course not. Time will fly so fast you'll hardly know I'm gone."

"No," said Meggie. "I'll know you're not here."

Hugh, Stella and Nell said, "We want you to have a good time."

Meggie said, "I do, too."

Stella said, "Can we see you in your new clothes?"

"Of course. I'll put them on right now."

Dressed in her new finery, she took a look at herself in the mirror. Parley hadn't known a thing about fashion, but he would surely approve of her black skirt that chopped smartly at her ankles. And he'd be pleased with her snow-white blouse with its high neck and long sleeves and he'd consider her black boots fashionable. Maybe he'd smile in his straight-forward way and admire her long, stylish gray coat, gray gloves and black cloche hat.

Linnie presented herself to the children. Stella and Nell clapped their hands and Meggie hugged her and laughed. "Oh, Mama. You look so pretty."

"Why, thank you."

Birdie knocked at the kitchen door and let herself in, the children ran off to amuse themselves. Birdie appraised Linnie. "Oh, my," she said. "Why, you'll have heads turning your way every where you go."

"Thank you, but I'm not interested in turning heads. I'm interested in finding Dru, and persuading her to come home with me. I'm interested in finding out what Buzz does for a living. And, of course I'm interested in Miss Krueger's lecture and whatever else I can learn while I'm there." She took off her coat, her hat and gloves.

Birdie's smile faded. "As far as Dru goes, prepare yourself. I'm afraid she's caught up in bad business and I doubt that she and Buzz are living together."

"Yes. I dread what I might find."

"We all do. Now, think about this. Newt and I figure you can't get a whole lot done in one week. If you want to stay on, and if it's convenient for Ann's mother, you should. You know we're looking forward to having the kiddies and we've got plenty of room with the new bedroom Newt built."

"I can't imagine being away for more than a week."

"Well, our offer stands and you know how much we love the chicks."

At the Coldsprings train station, on a dark gray morning with leaden skies, Linnie kissed the children's cold cheeks and hugged them hard before she boarded the train.

The long wail of the whistle blew and the train began to chuff down the mountain. Linnie settled back against the scratchy, green plush seat and closed her eyes. This was her first train trip and her first trip away from home. She was nervous. Finding Dru was her most important task and if she missed Miss Krueger's speech tomorrow, so be it. With those thoughts in mind, the rhythmic sway of the coach and the click on the tracks lulled her into a half-sleep.

Parley, years ago while standing on the Blackduck Bridge. *A husband shouldn't have to do that. Husbands and wives should enjoy their loving. When I'm your husband, if I do as you ask, neither of us will enjoy our loving as we should.*

I didn't ever do anything with your mother that she didn't want me to do. And you remember that.

Lots of us love our men, and love their loving and don't you forget it.

I love my man and I love his loving, but you wouldn't understand.

There have been times when I've refused to love Mide even though she's wanted me to.

What did Parley and her father and Birdie and Dru and Mide and even Linnie's late mother know that she didn't know? Why did they find coupling so delightful when she'd found it sickening? Was there something wrong with her? Maybe she lacked something. Maybe it was impossible for her to love a husband the way a wife should.

She wakened in the dim winter light of mid-afternoon. The train slowed. When a young man across the aisle said something about being close to Seattle, Linnie peered out the window. Off in the snowy countryside people were huddled around flickering bonfires. Hobo camps. Places where folks who had no home could find a warm fire and a cup of hot soup. Mr. Dobbs and Tosstles had talked a little about that kind of life.

A conductor came up the aisle. "Ladies and gentlemen," he said. "We're coming into Seattle, right on time." The train chuffed on past shanties, sawmills and shadows of big buildings. Then, small glowing lights. That must be electricity!

Linnie reached into her purse and took out a slip of paper on which she'd written Ann's telephone number and the address of the Ballard Union Hall. She had memorized both.

The train chugged into the station and stopped. Linnie picked up her valise and made her way down the aisle. A porter helped her step off the train and she found herself in swirling snow with throngs of people. Laughter, greetings, shouts, whistles. People hurrying, hurrying. No sign of Ann.

Inside the station she looked in stunned wonder at the massive columns with the enormous lamps that glowed like moons. Yes. Electricity!

"Linnie!" Ann, a dust of snow on her hat, her hair and her coat, waved and hurried to her. With laughter and wet eyes the two greeted each other.

Linnie said, "This building is grand."

"Capitalist money. Railroad tycoons, who make their riches on the backs of the poor, built these fancy places all over America. Oh, don't get me started. Come on, let's go."

Out on the street, horse drawn carriages and automobiles slogged through dirty snow and piles of steaming dung. Teams of draft horses, breathing clouds of air, strained while pulling electric trolley cars. Liberty Bond posters—*Sweep Hohenzollern and Hapsburg into the Garbage Heap*—blossomed in windows and on lamp posts. From inside a saloon came the sound of a piano and song. "It's a Long Way to Tipperary."

Streetcars clanged. Newsboys shouted, "Extra! Extra! Germans reject President Wilson's Peace Note. Read all about it!"

A clutch of women standing on boxes held up signs reading, IN 1917 WE WANT THE VOTE. And they chanted: IN 1917 WE WANT THE VOTE. Ann dropped money into a pail. "Keep it up," she called out. "I'll join you next week."

After Linnie and Ann got into Ann's automobile, Ann said, "You wrote that finding Dru is your most important task. I went to see Tosstles. Before we go to Mother's, we'll stop by the union hall in Ballard. He can tell you more about your sister than I can."

At the I.W.W. hall a woman lifted tarnished, tinseled garlands from a dried out Christmas tree. Beside the tree a hand-painted sign read, *A Tribute to the Carpenter of Nazareth.* Two men took clothes from a wash tub atop a wood stove, wrung the clothes, and slung them over a rope stretched across the room.

Tosstles came from the kitchen. He stuck out his hand and smiled. "Sit down," he said. The three sat at a long, trestle table covered with faded red oilcloth. Tosstles poured hot coffee into three mugs. "Linnie," he said. "This isn't going to be easy for you. I met your sister a couple of times, but she and Buzz haven't been together for years. Yesterday I learned you were coming and I asked around. She still might be singing at The Comique down on Fourth Street. About a block from Bailey's Tavern."

A tavern? Linnie would go into a tavern? To find Dru— of course she would.

"And Buzz?" said Linnie. "Do you know anything about him?"

"No. I haven't seen him in over a year."

Ann parked on Fourth and Pine. She and Linnie wrapped their mufflers around their necks and struck out. Men, women and children, huddled in doorways, begged for money. A sign hung in a foggy storefront window read, THE HOUSE OF THE LORD COME IN. Behind the murky light men and women slapped their hands to the rhythmic beat of tambourines.

Bailey's Tavern, a dark, smoky place, smelled of fish, whiskey, and cigar smoke. Cue sticks cracked against balls. A man at the piano played, "When You Wore a Tulip." Men pestered Ann and Linnie. "Ladies, let me buy you a drink. Aw, come on. Won't you let me buy you pretty ladies a whiskey?"

"Get on," said Ann, friendly, yet firm. She went to stand at the end of the bar. She held up one hand. "Does anyone here know Druscilla Corrigan?"

"Dru?" said a bearded, heavy-set man. "Yeah, I know Dru. Best damned singer I've ever heard. Sang over at The Comique. She was the reason I went to the shows."

Linnie said, "You know where she lives?"

"Yeah. Lives in that place on down the street. Number 32." He winked. "I've been there a few times."

Linnie's suspicions and dread grew.

Back out on the street she and Ann passed a lamp lighter holding his long flare to the wick of a street lamp. Ann said, "Electricity hasn't come to this part of the city yet. Rich people get it. Poor people don't. Now, if we find Dru in bad shape I suggest that we take her to Mother's. You'll be there, and Mother has nursed a number of women who have taken a bad turn. She'll know what to do."

"That's a good idea, but I'm afraid of what we're going to find."

At the end of the block the two went into a four-story, brick building. Two oil lanterns hung from the ceiling lit a narrow hall. Linnie flinched at smells of cooked cabbage, fowled, damp flannel and cigarette smoke. At the end of the hall empty bottles and cigar butts littered a flight of stairs. On the second-floor landing a man clutching a whiskey bottle was slumped against the wall. Up on the third floor, crying babies, angry voices and occasional laughter came from behind closed doors. The scratchy tune of "Mary's a Grand Old Name," came from a gramophone.

Linnie knocked on apartment 32. She knocked twice more. A wedge-faced girl wearing a coat cracked the door open. "Yeah?"

"Is Druscilla Corrigan here?" said Linnie.

The girl regarded her and Ann. "Who are you?"

"Dru's sister. This is my friend, Ann Garibaldi."

"Yeah. Sure, you're Dru's sister." She started to close the door.

Linnie jammed her boot in front of the stop. "I'm Linnie Hearn. From Hanksport. Dru's husband is Buzz Corrigan. They've got three children and I've come to see my sister."

The girl stood aside and allowed them in. Shadows from a kerosene lamp flickered on water stained walls. Newspapers covered the windows. A black hole gaped in the floor. The girl pointed to a figure on a thin mattress. "She's either corked or nuts. I never know which."

Linnie went to the mattress and knelt. She gagged at the sour stench of vomit. Dru, her back to Linnie, lay under a gray blanket. Linnie put her hand on Dru's shoulder. "Dru, it's me. Linnie."

Dru turned. The blanket fell away, exposing Dru's stick-thin arms. With glazed, unfocused eyes, she raised her head. "Linnie?" Her tongue clacked against the roof of her mouth. "How'd you get here?" She fell back and groaned.

Linnie stood and said to the girl, "How long has she been like this?"

"Maybe a year. She and me worked at The Comique. She had a swell voice. After her man left her, she tried to find him. Couldn't. Then he agreed to see her and she was real happy."

The girl paused to light a cigarette. "So, she gets the night off. I help her get dolled up and she leaves and I don't see her for two days. Thought she and her fella had patched things up. But when she don't show up at work, she got the boot."

"How long did she and Buzz live together?"

"Two years, maybe. On and off. He'd stick around for awhile. Then he'd go off gambling. Last time they was together, they lived just down the street. Got kicked out 'cause they wasn't paying the rent. Then Dru heard her man had another woman. God a'mighty, she went nuts. Found the woman. Beat her up. Cops slammed Dru in the can. Fellow down at Bailey's posted bail. But she sure could sing. Folks loved her. Too bad her man told her to get lost. I tell you she bawled something awful. Wasn't nothing I could do about it. Told her if she was gonna live here, she'd have to help pay rent."

Linnie said, "Did you know Buzz?"

"Yeah. Won big money and couldn't give it away fast enough. Automobiles. Clothes. Presents. All of this for his pals. Got a real kick out of it. Then he'd go broke."

"Where does he live?"

"Last I knew he lived in a boarding house on Yesler Way. Sally's. Yeah. Sally's Boarding House."

"Did Dru ever live there with him?"

"Nah." The girl took a long pull on her cigarette. "Last year she took to the streets. Brought home money and a bad habit. Opium. Learnt she was gonna have a kid. I tried to talk her out of getting rid of it. She done that before while living with her man. This second time, I says, 'Dru, you go ahead and have that baby and we'll put it in a orphanage. You let some quack work on you and you're gonna get real sick again. Maybe die."

"Again?" said Linnie.

"Yeah. Again. Like I said, she got rid of one kid when she was with her man. Now she ain't with him and she wants to get rid of this one. Well, my arguing don't do no good. And now, like I say, she's corked or nuts. Half the time she don't know me, or where she's at. But I take care of her, best I can. I mean, I can't just throw her out on the streets."

Again, Linnie knelt. She stroked Dru's dirty, matted hair. "Dru, do you hear me?"

Dru, her voice high and thin, said, "Yes."

"I want to take you to Mrs. Easton's house. Ann's mother will help you get well."

Dru shifted on the mattress and tried to pull the blanket tighter. Again, the blanket slipped. Pieces of soured, dried vomit were stuck to the once beautiful tucked bodice of the blouse she had made. Her thin shoulders jutted out like broken wings.

Linnie bent to her. "Dru. Let me help you. Please."

"Huh uh."

"We'll be at Mrs. Easton's for just a short time. Then, I'll take you home."

"Don't wanna go."

"Hugh and Stella and Nellie miss you. We all miss you."

Ann whispered, "Linnie, tomorrow, we'll ask Tosstles to come here with us. He's good at this kind of thing."

Once again, Linnie knelt close to Dru. "I've got to go," she said. "But please think about coming home. Hugh, Nellie, and Stella—all of us will be so happy to have you home again."

Silence.

Linnie gave the girl money and said she'd be back the next day.

Once in Ann's automobile, Linnie said, "What time is Miss Kreuger's lecture tomorrow?"

"One o'clock at a friend's place just down the hill from mother's. We won't have far to go."

"I have to see to Dru first."

"Yes. We'll go back to the hall right now and ask Tosstles if he'll go with us tomorrow morning."

"Oh, Lord, she's sick. She's had a terrible life here in the city. We all came to suspect that, but I didn't know . . . I just didn't know."

Without hesitating Tosstles agreed to go with Linnie and Ann the following morning.

Linnie and Ann left the union hall, drove up Queen Ann Hill and Ann parked in front of a large, shingled house that stood back off the street. Snow-covered gardens and trees surrounded the place. Soft lights glowed from the first-floor windows and from two wide gables up on a second floor. Chimneys, one at each end of the roof, loomed up against the night sky.

"I've never seen such a grand house," said Linnie.

"It's nice. Mother's family had money and Mother scandalized the East Coast when she ran off with Bill Easton, the gardener. He was murdered after a rally down by the wharves. He was I.W.W. true and blue. He and my mother."

A short, round woman with lively blue eyes, dark hair and a wide smile greeted Linnie. "Come in, oh do come in." She put her hand out. "I've heard so much about you."

Linnie shook her hand. "Thank you, Mrs. Easton. I'm grateful to you and to Ann for having me here."

"My dear, it's our pleasure. And I hope you'll be pleased with your room. It looks out over Puget Sound."

"Thank you."

"Freshen yourself, and come down for dinner. Ann has told me a little about your sister and we can visit for as long as you want." She turned to Ann. "Paul telephoned. He'll be here any moment."

Ann led Linnie up a long, wide stairway lit by bronze wall sconces with sparkling crystal baubles. Linnie set her valise down in a spacious bedroom with a sitting room and fireplace. "I've never *seen* anything so beautiful and grand," she said. "And you grew up here?"

"I did. Come down whenever you like. Mother has a good listening ear and sound advice. A woman working for her now, was once like Dru. Lorene. Mother and Tosstles worked with her, persuaded her to come here and Mother got her into some kind of treatment. She often pays to help educate girls like Lorenc. She'll give you hope, Linnie, and that's what you need."

A short time later, Paul greeted Linnie at the foot of the stairs. "It's so good to see you, Linnie. Ann told me about your sister and we all hope for the best. You're going to hear Sophie Krueger tomorrow?"

"It depends on my sister. If she'll agree to come here, I don't know if I'll go to the lecture. I've got to help Dru."

"Yes. I understand."

They sat at a large, round oak table in a breakfast room off the kitchen. Bronze sconces, like those lighting the stairway, upstairs hall, and Linnie's bedroom cast flickering light and shadows. A bookcase stuffed with books stood at one end of the room. A telephone sat on a desk bristling with papers.

Lorene, a large girl with thick, curly dark hair and a shy smile, served bowls of rich, potato soup and plates of sausage, sliced apples and sauerkraut.

To Linnie, this was a puzzle. Mrs. Easton had a lot of money and she lived in a beautiful house and she had help from girls like Lorene. She helped educate girls like Lorene. She was also prepared to help Dru. And Maude Easton was a Wobblie. Ann was a Wobblie. Were Paul and Ann rich Wobblies? What about Mr. Dobbs? And Bruns Wald and Tosstles? Were they rich, too? And . . .

"Linnie, dear," Mrs. Easton interrupted her thoughts. "I understand that first thing tomorrow, you and Ann and Tosstles will go see Druscilla. I hope you can convince her to come here to recover. I'll do all I can to help her."

"Thank you, Mrs. Easton."

"You're more than welcome. If your family wants to come to see her, they're welcome to stay here, too. I have plenty of room."

Paul asked about Newt and Birdie Mae. "They're good people," he said. "And I liked Colin. Good thinking folks. Good union folks."

Conversation turned to the I.W.W. In March, Paul, Ann, Frank Dobbs and Bruns would drive to Spokane to organize a Free Speech rally. In June, Bruns, Frank and Tosstles would be off to Eastern Washington, Walla Walla, the Palouse Country and Yakima to organize migrant field workers.

It was eleven o'clock when Ann and Paul left to go home. After Mrs. Easton closed the heavy front door, she took Linnie's hand. "You've had a difficult day," she said. "I hope you'll sleep well. I always enjoy the bleating fog horns out on the Sound."

Up in the pleasant bedroom a fire crackled in the fireplace and the bedspread on the four-poster had been turned back. Luxury Linnie had never dreamed she'd see in her life lay before her. And a woman she had just met would do all she could to help Dru.

Dear, heart-broken Dru whose dreams of Buzzie and the painted house with the picket fence, had kept her going for years. But, then she learned that she'd never have the house and she lost her man. If she returned to Hanksport she'd be hard-bit without spirit. Now, unless she agreed to come to Mrs. Easton's house and accept help, or unless a miracle came her way, she would die. A few hours ago she had refused help and Linnie knew that she herself was not the miracle.

CHAPTER 37

At eight o'clock the next morning Tosstles, Linnie, and Ann picked their way along the icy sidewalks to the building in which Dru lived. Up on the third floor Linnie knocked on number 32.

The girl opened the door. She put her hand on Linnie's arm. "I'm real sorry. Your sister left last night and didn't come back. Early today a fella found her froze dead in the street."

Linnie cried out. "No. Oh, no. How could she have left here? When I saw her, she didn't have the strength to sit up."

"When she needed her stuff, she'd find a way. I come home late, she ain't here and I figured she'd gone to get it." She handed Linnie a box. "Here," she said. "She sold a bunch of real pretty things Buzz gave her. This was all she kept."

"Thank you."

Tosstles went back to work. Ann took Linnie to meet with the coroner, identify the wasted body, visit the funeral parlor, and wire Linnie's family. Dru would be properly buried in Seattle, not up in cold, dank and Isolated Hanksport County. Linnie asked Birdie and Newt to bring the children. Could Ollie and Mame take Baby for a couple of days?

During lunch at the union hall, numbness settled over Linnie. She had waited too long before taking the first step in helping women, like her sister, snared in the nightmare of unwanted pregnancies. And Dru, along with countless, unknown women, had paid the price.

Ann, aware of Linnie's pensiveness, said, "Try to look at Dru's death as means to give you strength in what you want to do."

Tosstles agreed. "Learn about family limitation. Start your lectures. If you do it in her name that should give you a good sense of yourself and a good sense of her, too."

Linnie smiled. "I like that idea. And I have to tell myself that my once beautiful sister no longer suffers. She's given me a big job to do and I'd better do it right."

Ann said, "How do you feel about going to Sophie Krueger's lecture?"

"It's a first step and I'll take it."

Just down the street from Mrs. Easton's house and inside the vestibule of another large home, a blackboard read: <u>Frank Dobbs and Covington Hall to speak in public library on March 2.</u>

In a spacious front parlor Linnie and Ann joined a dozen other straight-spined women who sat on stiff backed chairs and kept their eyes focused on something straight ahead. But for an occasional whisper, or nervous cough, the room was silent. The woman in front of Linnie wore her blond hair pulled high and arranged with hairpins like Dru once used. Linnie blinked back against tears and tried to fix her mind on Sophie Krueger's up-coming lecture.

A woman entered the room. Plain of face, she had wide intelligent eyes. Her dark hair, sprinkled with gray, was worn in an upsweep. Wearing a mid-calf skirt and a long, gray, loose fitting sweater, she greeted Ann. Ann introduced her to Linnie. Miss Krueger put out her hand. Her smile was genuine. "Ann has told me about you. She's wanted us to meet for some time."

"Thank you. There's so much I need to learn," said Linnie. "And I've got to learn *how* to teach."

"You caught me at a bad time and I'm sorry. Tomorrow I'm going to Portland to help my sister set up a clinic. But you've met Frank Dobbs, haven't you? He's been up to Hanksport a couple of times."

"Yes. I've met him a couple of times."

"I'll ask him to call you. Perhaps he can meet with you. He can certainly give you material and tell you as much about family limitation as I can."

"Miss Krueger, I can't talk about this to a man."

Miss Krueger put a hand on Linnie's arm. "If you take on this battle, and that's what it is, you'll have to speak to women *and* men. Men MUST be part of your audience. Frank often speaks publicly about these issues and he'll set you at ease. Now, please excuse me and I look forward to meeting you again."

After welcoming the women, Miss Krueger said, "I want to share a wonderful story about Margaret Sanger, our courageous ally. When the socialist magazine, *The New York Call,* published Mrs. Sanger's column, 'What Every Girl Should Know,' the article was banned under the Comstock law. Put another way, the government is attempting to silence Mrs. Sanger. She responded in *The Call.* Under the heading of: 'What Every Girl Should Know,' she wrote nine words: 'Nothing. By order of the United States Post Office.' "

The women's spontaneous laughter broke the nervous silence.

"Now," said Miss Krueger. "You're here to learn, and I'm here to teach you about what we call 'pregnancy.' A woman, who finds herself in the family way, or expecting, is said to be pregnant. How many of you have more than three children?"

But for Linnie and Ann every woman in the room put up a hand. Miss Krueger pointed to a woman sitting up front. "You look as if you're about to birth another. How many do you have now?"

"Seven."

Responses to the same question—one woman had six children, another ten, a woman sitting behind Ann and Linnie, eleven—gave clear indication of women desperate to find help. Miss Krueger asked the mother of eleven children her age. "Thirty-one," the woman said. "I birth 'em like cats."

A pretty woman wearing a cloche hat similar to Linnie's said, in a straightforward way, "My name is Jean. I've been married to my Bill for ten years and we've got eight kiddies. I work for folks up on Queen Anne Hill. They've been married for ten years and have only two. Two. I figure this has something to do with the secret. Rich folks know about it, but we don't."

Miss Krueger nodded. "And that's why we're here. To learn about 'family limitation,' or 'birth control.' " She picked up a book and held it high. "This is written for women like you. How many of you know how to read?"

A few, including Jean, held up their hands.

Miss Krueger nodded. "Good," she said. "The name of this book is *The Woman Rebel*. Written by Mrs. Sanger. I have six copies and am glad to loan them out. For those of you who can't read, I'll try to pair you with someone who can. But, it's up to you, as a pair, to get together and read the book. Now, this is very important for you to understand. You're here to learn how to *prevent* pregnancy. You are *not* here to learn how to *stop* pregnancy once it's started. I ask you to remember that."

A murmur rippled through the room.

"One method of prevention," Miss Krueger continued, "used since Biblical times, is what we call 'coitus interruptus.' It isn't always successful and it's difficult for the male to experience a heightened climax when he has to pull his penis, the male organ, out of the female. You see, climax is the height of enjoyment for both male and female."

Parley had said something so similar all those years ago when he and Linnie had stood on the Blackduck Bridge. And this "interruptus" was what she and Parley had done. Colin had mentioned it, too. So, Parley was right. He had never experienced the enjoyment he'd longed to have with her. She had never experienced it either, But she suspected both Parley and Baby experienced it.

"Climax," Miss Krueger continued, "during the act of coupling with your mate, or 'intercourse,' as we call it, should be every bit as enjoyable to a woman, to *you*, as it is to him." Again, hadn't Parley said something similar? And Dru and Birdie, who had expressed such pleasure in loving their men, knew about this thing called 'climax.'

Miss Krueger held up a strange looking object. "This is known as a condom. It's like a close fitting cap that fits over the male penis. It's made of very thin rubber, allowing you and your husband to experience the pleasure of climax. It's this condom that stops the male sperm from fertilizing the female eggs. Now, this is important for you to understand. When your husband's sperm is stopped from fertilizing your eggs, you will not get pregnant. And that, ladies, is the answer. It's as simple as that."

Ripples of surprise. Skepticism.

"Oh, my . . ."

"How could that be . . ."

"Well, my stars."

Ann whispered to Linnie, "Some of us call those condoms, 'rubbers.' Remember I told you about them some years back?"

"Yes. Yes, I do."

The woman in front of Linnie raised her hand. "Is this con . . .condom new?"

"No. An Englishman developed it some thirty years ago. In America its use to protect women from getting pregnant *is illegal*. Its only legality is to protect males from venereal disease. Isn't that irony for you?" She handed the cap to a woman in the front row. "Look it over and pass it along. You need to become familiar with it."

"You say it's illegal," a woman asked. "So, will my husband and I go to jail if we use one?"

Miss Krueger shook her head. "Not likely. Fortunately, this silly law isn't easily enforced. Now, the last method I want to discuss is the diaphragm pessary. Like the condom, it's a thin device. But it fits inside *you* to stop your husband's sperm from fertilizing your eggs. It's highly effective, but a licensed nurse or doctor must properly fit you and teach you how to use it."

Linnie tried to grasp this new information. How could one be fit for something inside your private parts? Heat rose in her face at the very thought of it. She wasn't the only uncomfortable woman in the room. Three women picked up their purses and left.

To those remaining, Miss Krueger said, "It's not easy to discuss such matters and it's all right to be embarrassed. But our goal is to work together and learn how to stop unwanted babies. Unwanted pregnancies. Questions?"

"Where do we find those things?" Jean asked.

"I have enough condoms for everyone who wants one." She held up a small brown package tied with a string.

"What if my husband won't use it?" a woman asked.

"Most men use them willingly. If not, a man will eventually come around. But there is always the douche." She held up what appeared to be a hot water bottle with a small hose. "Directly after intercourse, you use this to insert a solution of water and soda inside yourself. While it's more of a nuisance and not as successful as the condom, it's better than nothing."

Over half the women, including Linnie, asked for one of the small brown packages. Jean held up hers and laughed. "Imagine not having to worry about having another baby every time your husband wants some loving. And who knows? I might even learn to like his loving again."

Uncertainty swept over Linnie. Miss Krueger had come to the end of her lecture and Linnie still knew next to nothing about this business. Yes, women had eggs and after the eggs were fertilized, the woman was pregnant. But, how in the world would a husband know how to put on a flat little rubber called a 'condom'? And while he did that, what did the wife do? And those other methods Miss Krueger spoke of didn't make sense. Maybe Linnie's dreams were too lofty.

Maybe she wouldn't be able to do the work she wanted to do. Instead of feeling uplifted by Miss Krueger's lecture, she felt witless.

❧

That evening Ann drove Linnie to the train station to meet her family. Hugh looked stern. Tears flooded Stella's and Nell's eyes. Meggie solemnly said, "Their mama died, but mine didn't."

Linnie gathered the children close. "Stella, Nellie, Hugh. She loved you all so much. But then she got sick and she couldn't come home."

Meggie said, "Didn't she love me, too?"

"You weren't born yet, Meggie."

Hugh kicked at a post. "I don't ever want to see my father. He ran out on her and on us."

Linnie said, "I doubt you'll have much reason to see him, but you must be cordial at the funeral. Your mother would want that of you."

Gavin, who had come to meet the family, took his father and Colin and Mide home with him. Roy, Joe, the children and Linnie squeezed into Ann's automobile. Newt, who was acquainted with the city, said he and Birdie would take a trolley up the hill to Mrs. Easton's house.

Lorene served Mrs. Easton, her family and guests tomato bouillon, shepherd pie, glazed carrots, an apple onion salad, and chocolate pudding topped with whipped cream. After supper, Mrs. Easton, Paul, and Ann excused themselves. "You need time alone," said Mrs. Easton.

Joe was quietly unhappy when he learned that Linnie had arranged for burial without a priest and a church service. "She'll go straight to hell," he argued. "We can't let that happen to her."

"She's already been in hell," said Linnie. "But if it means that much to you, go ahead and find a preacher. I doubt Dru would care one way or the other."

The following morning, after Linnie and Joe, Birdie, Newt and Roy were comfortable with funeral arrangements, they decided to take the children and explore the city. Bundled in coats, stocking caps, scarves, boots and mittens, they struck out. Joe, who had read about some of the newer buildings, took them to see Smith Tower. Standing next to Hugh, Joe put one arm around the boy. "Look closely," he said. "You won't see another building this tall outside of New York City."

"It's touching clouds," said Meggie. The family laughed a little.

Inside the new First National Bank the children ran their fingers along the marble columns and gazed in wonder at the enormous windows, the shiny marble floors and brass spittoons.

Then, off they went to the University of Washington campus. Joe explained the "cantilevered roof" on the new stadium. Didn't Thompson Hall look grand and imagine studying in those two tall, brick buildings, known as Simson Hall and Bryan Hall.

"Gavin is just finishing school here," Newt said. "He's applied for a job up at home. Wants to be Superintendent of Hanksport schools."

"Really?" Linnie said. "Why would anybody in their right mind want to live in that cold, dank place?"

Newt said, "That's his home and his intent."

Mid-afternoon the tourists went down to the wharves and watched boats ply the waters out in Puget Sound. Late afternoon, just as it started to snow, they found a restaurant on the wharf and had a supper of hot chicken soup and sandwiches. It had been quite a day and Linnie was pleased to see sparks of pleasure in the children's eyes.

The following afternoon a small number of people drove automobiles up the muddy road to the cemetery. Linnie had chosen a grave site on top of the hill, open to sunshine and light. She did not want Dru buried in the shade of cedar and fir trees scattered throughout the graveyard.

Buzz, driving a nifty automobile, arrived. He got out and went straight to Linnie. "I'm awfully sorry," he said. "I didn't do right by her."

"No," said Linnie. "You didn't." She turned from him and engaged Ann in conversation.

Buzz tousled Hugh's hair. "Hello there, son."

"Hello." Hugh turned his back and went off to join his grandfather. Stella and Nell followed.

Buzz made no further attempts to speak with his children and Linnie thought it was just as well.

While the preacher, a dour-faced man, spoke of sin and redemption, Linnie recalled the beauty Dru had created in her short life. She'd found joy with her singing, her love of music, growing flowers and making wreaths and pretty clothes. Before the terrible demons got hold of her, she'd been full of love for her children. Today, she would have found beauty in the gulls wheeling overhead. Those thoughts gave strength to Linnie's resolve. Druscilla would not be forgotten.

Back at Mrs. Easton's house Linnie asked Colin and Mide to meet with her in Mrs. Easton's back parlor. This would be Linnie's first attempt to speak on this subject and she had such meager knowledge, but she must try.

She handed Colin the small brown package. "Miss Kruger gave it to me," she said. "It's called a condom. It stops babies from starting and that's all I know."

Colin smiled. "Thank you, Linnie. I've heard about them and have asked around. We can't get them at home."

Mide went to Linnie and gave her a soft kiss on her cheek. "Thank you," she said.

Linnie said, "I won't allow Dru's death to be forgotten. I went to the lecture as a first step. Now I've got a lot of work to do."

Late that evening at Mrs. Easton's house Linnie and Birdie sat beside the fire in the front parlor. Birdie said, "Tell me about Miss Krueger's lecture. You haven't said a word."

"Well, I learned that a man's seed is called 'sperm,' and the sperm fertilizes a woman's eggs. Being in a family way is called 'pregnancy.' You like coupling, or loving your man because you feel something called 'climax.' You must know about that. Dru did. Parley must have had that with Baby. Maybe Baby did. I don't know what it is. I've never known.

I don't know much more than that. Miss Krueger is leaving town and she said she'd ask Mr. Dobbs to call me and talk to me about all of this. But, mercy, Birdie, I can't talk about this with a man."

"If you're bent on learning about it, you will. Now, listen to me. Newt and I love having the kiddies with us. And after all these years, you're finally here and you should take the time you need to learn. Stay for a month."

"I don't know that I have what it takes to learn how to teach this business."

"You've always wanted to teach. But if you don't learn your subject, you won't do it."

The clock out in the front hall chimed eleven. "All right, Birdie. I'll do it. I'll stay for one month."

"Good. Let's consider it settled."

Later, after Linnie was upstairs in her bedroom, she opened the box the girl at the apartment had given to her. She picked up the white fur muff and scarf. Had Dru ever worn them? They looked like new. One day Linnie would give the muff to one of Dru's daughters, and the scarf to her other daughter. It was, as the girl said, "all she kept."

The following morning Linnie saw her family off on the train. She would stay in Seattle for one month, work hard and return to Hanksport prepared to teach women about 'family limitation,' or 'birth control.'

CHAPTER 38

Mid-morning, the phone in Mrs. Easton's breakfast room rang. Mrs. Easton spoke with Mr. Dobbs for a moment before she called Linnie to the phone.

Linnie put the receiver to her ear.

"Mrs. Hearn. This is Mr. Dobbs. Yes. Sophie told me about her conversation with you. Is it convenient for me to come by tomorrow afternoon?"

You've always wanted to teach. But if you don't learn your subject, you won't do it.

"Yes. Of course it is. One-thirty? Two?"

"One-thirty and I look forward to seeing you, Mrs. Hearn."

The following afternoon Lorene answered the knock on Mrs. Easton's front door. She took care of his coat, hat and gloves, and led him into the front parlor. A cheery fire snapped in the fireplace. Linnie and Mrs. Easton were seated on the sofa.

Mr. Dobbs smiled and said, "Mrs. Hearn. Delighted to see you again. Maude, it's always a pleasure."

"Frank, it's always good to see you, too. Tea or coffee?"

"Whatever you and Mrs. Hearn are having will be fine."

A short time later, Lorene came in with a tray of sweets, a pot of tea and three cups. Maude Easton poured the tea and excused herself. Linnie, seated on a straight-backed chair, offered Frank the plate of chocolates.

He said. "Thank you. I'm so sorry to hear about your sister. If she'd been able to hear even one of Sophie's lectures, it might have made a difference."

"Perhaps. I enjoyed meeting Miss Krueger, but I didn't understand a lot of what she said. Women like us—Dru and I—we don't know a thing about this business called . . . family limitation. Or birth control."

She told him about Dru and her husband and their three children. She told him about Dru's fourth child who had died and about Buzzie's abandonment. She described the tenement in which Dru had lived. "She died a horrible death. And when she was young, she was beautiful and loving and smart and she had a gift for music. If she'd been educated, she might have taught music. IF, Mr. Dobbs. If."

"You're correct and I admire you for wanting to take this on. As Sophie might have told you, it's a tremendous undertaking."

"I don't need to be reminded, Mr. Dobbs. I've seen the results that come from ignorance about this family limitation business all my life. My youngest sister, Baby, is simple minded. Four years ago she had a child. I'm raising that child. My mother couldn't stand the sight of Baby. My mother killed herself or died from a terrible accident. My sister-in-law, once a very pretty young woman who wanted two children, has born five. She's beat down and old and when she birthed a sixth, a monster child, Birdie Mae and I . . . we drowned him. His mother doesn't know."

"I'm sorry," he said. "But the child, if badly deformed, probably wouldn't have lived very long. You no doubt spared the rest of your family a lot of pain."

"I tell myself that. And I, myself, when I married Parley, I feared having a child like Baby. It was difficult for Parley. And me. We never did . . . reach an . . . agreement."

He hesitated for just a moment before he said, "The important thing is that you want to help solve these kinds of problems."

"But women at home wouldn't understand one thing Miss Krueger talked about. It's like poor folks are locked in dark rooms and can't get out. This place." She made a sweeping gesture of the room. "The tasseled lamp shades. The settee and the table and the piano and books. Books all over the house. Beautiful paintings on the walls. Beautiful carpets on the floors. None of the women I know own anything beautiful. There is nothing pretty in their poor little shanties. Most of them don't even know about this kind of life. Ignorance, Mr. Dobbs, is our enemy."

She got up, went to a bookcase and pulled out a book. She held it up. "I looked at this early this morning. *Studies in the Psychology of Sex*, written by somebody named Havelock Ellis." She flipped through the pages and paused to read, *"Sex lies at the root of life, and we can never learn to respect and revere life until we understand sex."*

She set the book aside. "Those are nice words, but how can we understand this business called, 'sex?'" Again she picked up the book. "Malthus. Sexual Inversion, Social Evolution, Erotic Symbolism. What in the world do those words mean to me, or to anyone I know?"

"Right now, nothing. But you can learn, Mrs. Hearn. And I want to help you."

"You? Mr. Dobbs, excuse me, but you are a very busy man. Let me tell you this. Early this morning I went out for a walk. On down the street—this street with beautiful houses—I passed a woman and two children making a snow man. The woman set a fedora atop the snowman's head and she and the children laughed and had such a good time. I recalled a Christmas when Dru and her kiddies and most all of my family built a snowman. Parley set a cap on its head and Father put his own pipe in its mouth. Their laughter still echoes in my mind. But, what's the great difference between these pictures? The woman down the street is married to an architect. According to Mrs. Easton he does very nice work. He's educated. The men in my own story, Parley and Joe and Newt, were not educated. The family down the street has two children. Dru, the woman in my story, had three children in five years. She lost one and she got rid of two. Opium and the last abortion killed her."

Mr. Dobbs set his cup down. "And now, you want to educate people of your concern. Of Sophie's concern. And mine. I'll do anything I can to help. But I must warn you of the fact that this will not be easy. Many people, the majority of people here in America, consider this subject a vice. You will no doubt be heckled. You might be incarcerated."

"If I take this on I'll be prepared. The Hanksport County jail isn't far from home."

"No, Mrs. Hearn. If you break laws, such as the Comstock Laws, set out to prevent spreading the word on this subject through the mail, and if you are found guilty you'll no doubt be incarcerated in The Crooked Neck Workhouse for Women. It's north of Seattle on a high, narrow, crooked spit of land. Thus its name. Sophie spent a month there last year. It isn't a pleasant place."

"I'd be prepared for that." She went to one of the windows. The winter garden of trees, their bare limbs etched against the dreary, gray skies held a bleak, but strange beauty. She turned. "Mr. Dobbs, how in the world does Miss Kreuger reach people who haven't had schooling and don't know how to read?"

"She gets on her soap box. Street speaks. Hands out information. Goes to meetings. Organizes meetings. At first, only a few women—five, six—came to her classes. Information is the key. Written, or by word. If people can't read, she asks that they find someone who can read to them. You can do this, Mrs. Hearn." He stood. His eyes were intense. "I'll be your teacher. I'll make the time. Teaching you, so you can teach women up in Hanksport County, is important to me, too. How long will you be in the city?"

"A month. But I don't know how, or where to begin."

"Leave that to me. You mentioned doing this for your sister, Druscilla. You could give her no finer tribute. I can meet with you wherever you want. The public library would be a good place to start, so why not give yourself a chance?"

You've always wanted to teach. If you don't learn about your subject, you won't do it.

He did not need to ask her again.

CHAPTER 39

Mid-morning of the following day Linnie caught a street-car down the hill to The Carnegie Public Library. Mr. Dobbs was waiting just inside the door. He guided her through the building and taught her how to use the file drawers and the Dewey Decimal System.

"Try to find something about a woman named Margaret Sanger," he said. "Tomorrow, I'd be happy to meet with you, say early-afternoon at Mrs. Easton's house?"

"Yes. That will be fine."

"We can discuss anything you want and I'll hope to be able to answer your questions."

Linnie was left to browse and read. She wandered through rooms of books with reading tables and green-shaded electric lights. She liked the smell. She liked the quiet. An occasional whisper. A cough. A soft laugh. She browsed through the newspaper room. She liked the smell of newsprint and the display of the papers on the racks. She was pleased to find *The Hanksport Gazette* of a few days ago.

In one of the book galleries she found a small, thin paper-bound pamphlet about Margaret Sanger, author of *The Woman Rebel,* a monthly publication. She went to the front desk. "Where might I find a copy of Mrs. Sanger's work?"

"We don't have that in our collection."

"May I ask why not?"

"The Comstock Law, Miss. It sets public morality high here in America."

"Can you tell me where I might buy it?"

"I doubt you can find it anywhere. It's 'obscene litera- ture,' Miss. Outlawed here in America."

Information is the key. . . . It's like we're in a dark room and can't get out.

❧

During the following weeks Linnie often took the trol- ley down the hill to the library. She found little information she was seeking, but she discovered authors, Edith Wharton and Theodore Dreiser. Willa Cather and Sinclair Lewis. She read Jane Hull's *Twenty Years at Hull House* twice.

During the afternoons Mr. Dobbs met her at Mrs. Easton's house. There, seated at the dining room table, he and Maude Easton, often with Ann and Tosstles, talked about Margaret Sanger's work with birth control. Linnie learned that the Comstock Laws, powerful laws enacted by Congress in 1873, were meant to "legislate public morality."

"An insane law, designed to 'keep women in their place,' " said Ann.

The group hailed the passage of the Workman's Compensation act, enacted by Congress a year earlier, as an important victory.

At times Linnie and her new friends attended lectures about poverty, illiteracy and the great divide between the rich and poor of America. Linnie studied the manners of public speaking. She noticed movements that emphasized thoughts and words. It pleased her to learn that a certain Jeannette Rankin of Montana was the first woman to be elected to the House of Representatives.

During the evenings, conversation around Maude Easton's dining room table might focus on *how* to provide meaningful information about ignorance, poverty and birth control to a population who had no schooling.

One afternoon Bruns, who came from Boston and admired art, held up a book about a French painter, Jean-Francois Millet. He flipped through the pages and spoke about Millet's painting, *Man with a Hoe*. "The poet, Edwin Markham, said of this painting, 'How will the future reckon with this Man?' Now," Bruns said, "I ask, how can we answer that question today?"

He put the book on the table, opened at the picture of the painting.

Mr. Dobbs said, "The man represents a hopeless, joyless life with labor that will never stop. I predict that overworked, under-paid workers, the labor class we have today, will change this nation and become part of a solid, middle class. But only with the help of strong unions. Preferably one. The I.W.W."

"Capitalism and industrialism," said Paul. "Today our country has powers with industries unheard of even fifty years ago."

"True," said Mr. Dobbs. "But all of this industrialism and rise of capitalism is accompanied by great masses of people living in poverty."

Linnie found her voice. "What about women? I've read about Wobblies on strike at a mill somewhere in Massachusetts. It was in 1912. Women led that strike. If women can do that, we can help change a lot of things. We can put up a real fight for birth control."

"You're right," said Ann. "Someday we women will have the right of control over our own bodies *and* we'll have the right to vote."

Tosstles stood and lifted his glass of wine. "Get the vote! That's the answer to lots of the problems. Here's to women. To birth control and to women getting the vote."

Glasses clicked.

Mr. Dobbs said, "Free speech and debate among men and women are two of our most powerful tools. And we all need to try to view the world with tempered optimism. Mrs. Hearn . . ." He leaned across the table toward her. "May I call you Linnie?"

"Why . . . yes. . . . of course you can."

"Good. And will you call me 'Frank?'"

She smiled. "Yes. And Frank, what were you saying . . .?"

"I was saying . . . oh, yes. You surely know that teaching men and women about birth control will raise ugly emotions."

"Yes," she said. "And those who oppose us have the right to speak out."

"They do. This journey you've chosen will take time, a lot of work and commitment."

She wanted to tell him that she had that passion and commitment and she would find the time. But she would let him find that out for himself.

This group and five or six of Maude Easton's friends often gathered at her house for potluck dinners. Conversation never lagged. Wasn't the I.W.W. the most important movement going on in America? What was America's role in the war raging in Europe? Was President Wilson doing the right thing by keeping America out of the war? Wilson was a Democrat, but with capitalists in charge, America was in trouble. Capitalism was to blame. Education of the masses was a major concern. Concern was expressed about an Immigration Act requiring a literacy test for immigrants, excluding Asiatic workers other than Japanese. Hadn't every American who lived on this soil at one time come from immigrants?

A week before Linnie was to go home she received a letter and two photographs from Birdie Mae. In one of the photos Meggie, bundled in her coat and cap, sat astride a brown pony. Her expression was one of delight. The second photo was taken in Birdie and Newt's living room. The children looked fit and proper. Hugh had on his white shirt, knickers and a checkered cap. Stella, dressed in a white middy blouse, her skirt just at her knees, looked much like her mother. And Nell, somber in her blue "school" dress, wore a large hair bow on top of her head. Meggie, wearing a pinafore, long white stockings, and a hair bow like Nell's, stood in front of her cousins.

Linnie propped the snapshots on her dresser and read Birdie's letter. *Two weeks ago a man with a camera and a pony came through. Meggie loved the pony. Now, she spends as much time as I allow her down at the barn. She's taken on the care of Newt's horse and likes nothing better than to ride. Don't worry. She doesn't ever ride alone. Hugh or Newt ride with her. And aren't the photos nice!*

Last Saturday I took the children and Baby to town. At The Company store we ran into Kees Strom. He commented on how much

Meggie resembled Baby. I said that Meggie's mother, our late cousin, and Baby looked much alike. Meggie didn't hear any of this. She was busy picking out candy at the front counter. But someday, when she's old enough to understand, we must tell her the truth.

If you need more time in Seattle, take it. We're all doing just fine.

That evening Frank telephoned Linnie. "Time has gone by so fast and you leave in only one week. Are you free to meet me tomorrow afternoon for tea at the café just down the street from the library?"

"I'd like that. Two o'clock?"

"Good. I'll look forward to it."

The next morning Linnie, wearing her coat, a white wool scarf, her hat and gloves, took the trolley down the hill to town. At the library she found a book about architects. She sat at one of the reading tables and studied the drawings of Frank Furness and Richard Morris Hunt. If Joe had had education, he might have become an architect. The idea sparked another idea. If Dru had gone on to school, she might have become a music teacher. Why not set Parley's money aside to send Dru's children and Meggie to college? If they had that advantage, they would be far ahead in the world.

With her family in mind, she went shopping.

At one-forty-five she hurried through a squall of snow to the café. Frank was waiting. The two sat at a table beside a big, pot-bellied stove in which flames shivered behind the round glass eye. Up on a shelf a large, black cat blinked its green eyes, stretched and snoozed.

While sipping tea and nibbling on short-bread cookies, Linnie described the books she'd seen at the library. "I wish

Joe had gone to college," she said. "Did you?" She ducked her head. "Silly question. Of course, you did."

"Not a silly question. We've never talked about it. But yes, I went to Columbia in New York City."

"That's where you're from?"

"No. I'm from Northern California."

"Will you tell me about yourself? You know almost all there is to know about me, but I don't know anything about you."

He said he'd left home right after graduating from high school. "Went to medical school in New York," he said. "Thought I'd be a doctor. Then I read a book, *Elements of Social Science* that claimed the major problem facing modern society is the act of sex."

She smiled. "And you didn't become a doctor."

"No. I wanted to help poor, uneducated people learn about family limitation. Or, as we now say, 'birth control.' And I'd always been interested in helping people less fortunate than me. So, I hung around taverns and docks. Hobnobbed with the labor class and unemployed. One evening I met a big, red-haired fellow." He smiled. "Guess who that was?"

"Tosstles."

"Yes. He took me to an I.W.W. meeting and I heard Bill Haywood talk about a labor strike that defeated the political powers of France and Germany. Haywood used that strike to illustrate the powerful weapon of the working class. The threat of a strike. I joined the I.W.W. and took to the road. Harangued every chance I had. Talked about Wobs. Talked about the injustices the poor folks suffer."

"I've read all I can find about Elizabeth Gurley Flynn and Margaret Sanger. They've worked so hard to reach people. Does Miss Krueger know them?"

"We both do. Those women will have a great influence on this country. Elizabeth's work with founding the ACLU alone is monumental."

"You and Miss Krueger know famous people."

He shrugged. "I don't view them as 'famous.' They work hard. They're curious. They ask lots of questions in our society."

Linnie wondered if she was capable of working hard and asking questions. Did she have a curious mind? She'd never thought about it. Yes, maybe she did. Yes, she certainly did.

"How did you meet Miss Krueger?"

"At one of her rallies a number of years ago."

"If I wasn't here, would you be in Portland with her?"

"I don't know. We've always done what's important to each of us. Sometimes together. Often apart. Right now she's involved with her sister's clinic."

Linnie wanted to ask what Sophie, the strong-willed suffragist, would do if she knew about Linnie's presence in Frank's life during these past weeks. But, Sophie was sophisticated, smart and educated. She probably wouldn't give much thought at all to Frank spending time with a flume tender's daughter from Hanksport.

But, the question popped out. "If Sophie knew about how much time you spend with me, how would she feel?"

"She'd be pleased to know that I have a very bright student who is eager to learn."

"Do you love her?"

He frowned and regarded her for a moment. "I think that love is the essential ingredient of life. I admire Sophie. We've been together for a long time. But I'm not *in* love with her and I don't think she's in love with me. It's something we've never discussed."

"I'm sorry. My questions weren't proper."

"It's all right."

In the dim winter light of mid-afternoon they left the café and, in a frenzy of falling snow, they went to Frank's auto. "I love new snow," he said. He put his head back and sniffed. "I love the smell of it."

She laughed. "The smell of snow? What's that?"

"Clean. Falling snow is beautiful and clean. I like it."

He drove her home and she asked him to come in. They sat together in front of the fire and Maude joined them and poured each of them a snifter of brandy. After Linnie saw Frank out the front door she wondered if she would ever again in her life spend such a splendid day.

But later that evening she came down on herself. Hard. Shame. Her nosy questions about Sophie weren't proper. She had tried to pry into Frank and Sophie's private world and she must not do it again. But her feelings for him transcended logic. With him she'd found a harmony of mind with fine-woven thoughts moving between them. But, while she had fallen in love with him, she, in his eyes, was his pupil and nothing more.

And now, she would soon go home. There would be no library. No lessons or interesting conversations around Mrs. Easton's breakfast room or dining table. No lectures. No tea with Frank in a café with a sleeping cat up on a shelf. And there would be no Frank.

On Sunday afternoon, the day before Linnie was to leave, most of the people Linnie had met, dropped by Mrs. Easton's house. The dining table was laden with deserts, tea, coffee and wine.

Much talk and interchanging ideas. Union talk. Talk about the ACLU and Elizabeth Gurley Flynn, Emma Goldman, President Wilson. Charlie Chaplin movies and weren't they a scream? Books. Who hadn't read Willa Cather's *Song of the Lark,* Somerset Maugham's *Of Human Bondage* or Theodore Dreiser's *The Genius?* Linnie had not and she made mental note of the titles.

At one point Frank said, "Linnie, I hope you find the books I'm giving you helpful."

"I'm sure I will. Are you coming up to Hanksport any time soon?"

"If there's work to do, yes."

She stopped short of asking him if he was going to Portland. If he was, she didn't want to know about it.

It was late evening when the guests bid Linnie good-bye. Frank was the last to leave. After he shrugged into his coat, Linnie handed him his hat. He said, "Paul tells me that he and Ann may move up to Hanksport." His tone was stiff, almost cold. "They love that country and I hope they do. You and Ann would make a fine team. In any event, I wish you good luck."

"I hope they come up. I remember when I first met Paul, he said he and Ann might want to settle up there someday. And yes. Ann and I would make a very good team."

"Well, goodbye, Linnie. It's been my pleasure to have worked with you."

"And thank you for your help. Good-bye, Frank."

He put on his fedora and left.

❦

At the train station the next morning, Ann and her mother saw Linnie off. When the train chuffed slowly out of the station Linnie wondered if Frank was on his way to Portland. Would she ever see him again? Maybe not and it was just as well. He came from money. She had none. He and Sophie had been together for a long time. Linnie had known Frank Dobbs, her teacher, for one month.

In the dull light of mid-afternoon the train chugged slowly up through the snow-burdened forest. Linnie thought it was like moving through a long, dark tunnel toward the barren, grim logging towns of Coldsprings and Hanksport with little or no light.

Not far from Coldsprings the wail of the train ebbed like a dying sigh before chuffing to the station. Linnie picked up her valise, disembarked and after folding Hugh, Stella, Nell, and Meggie into her arms, she smiled at her father, at Newt, Colin and Joe.

"Did you bring presents?" said Meggie, dancing and hopping around Linnie.

Linnie tweaked her nose. "Wait and see."

They piled in Newt's automobile—the children sitting on each other's laps—bound for Linnie's house.

Smoke and drizzle hovered over the narrow, muddy, deep-rutted road. Linnie shivered. This dark, ignorant, ugly place smelled of smoke and mud. She feigned interest in her father's news. Ollie and Mame Holm's hardware store was doing well and Mame's refurbished dining room in the Hanksport Hotel was considered stylish. Soapy Metzler's undertaking business had prospered and Soapy now lived in a fancy house up on Fir Butte. The Hanksport school board had hired Gavin Corrigan as Superintendent of Schools.

Linnie had no thought, one way or another about Holm's store, or Soapy's business, or about Gavin's success, or Mame's restaurant. She wanted to teach what she'd learned, but she must use plain words, overcome her hesitant manner and explain with ease, that a woman's vagina was a canal between the uterus and vulva.

What would that mean to people living up here? How might she explain the cervix as the neck of the womb? How could she describe "climax" when she had never experienced it? Syringes. Sponges. Condoms? Those words carried no meaning. Linnie wanted to teach about the modern methods of birth control, but she had never used them. All she had known was "coitus interruptis," an act Parley resented and, because of her own stubborn ignorance, he died.

Newt pulled up in front of Linnie's house. That afternoon Birdie had taken the children's things back to their own bedrooms, built the fires and cooked dinner.

A fire crackled in the fireplace. Birdie Mae came from the kitchen and greeted Linnie with a hug and her dimpled smile. "It's so good to have you home."

"And it's good to be home."

Linnie gathered her family around, opened her valise and pulled out a large, cloth bag. Baby sat quietly and kept her gaze on Meggie.

Linnie took from the bag Jack London's *Call of the Wild* and gave it to Hugh. A songbook for Stella. Charlotte Bronte's

Wuthering Heights for Nell. And a small, bronze statue of a horse for Meggie. Baby smiled and held up the pretty bottle of scented lotion. The men and boys in the family were tickled pink with new fishing flies. Pale blue handkerchiefs trimmed with lace pleased Birdie and Mide, and a book about architecture brought a smile and a quick duck of Joe's head.

During a boisterous dinner Linnie spoke about some of her adventures. She tried to describe the library with its books and reading tables. The café in which the cat snoozed by the stove. "Someday," she said, "We'll all go back to Seattle and plant flowers beside Dru's grave."

"Yes. Yes," said Stella. "She loved lilacs."

After part of the family had left, Linnie sat with the children and asked them about school and about themselves. Hugh was pleased to tell her that he played forward on the grade school's basketball team. Stella had been chosen to play the lead in a school play in the spring. Nell's teacher had loaned her a book about African children.

Meggie had made friends with twins her own age who lived up the road. She gave Linnie a big hug and a smacking wet kiss. "Mama, I'm so glad you're home."

"So am I," the other three echoed.

"And I'm glad to be home with all of you," said Linnie.

She sat by the fire late into the night. The erratic *bong bong* of the flume bell disturbed her. The bell, symbol of a loggers' life. A hard, dangerous life. Filthy camps. Mud and smoke. Ignorance and poverty. The bell, a badge of her own identity, a flume tender's daughter with four children to raise up, brought her to her senses. She, a cheeky woman with lofty notions to teach people about birth control, was deluded, had been played the fool, and Frank Dobbs had no doubt been happy to see her leave.

CHAPTER 40

The following morning Linnie felt somewhat better about herself. She had Frank's books to read, she would get at them, study, take notes, and learn how to teach.

Birdie Mae came over to visit. "Newt is with Baby," Birdie said. "I can't stay long, but what did you learn about helping us make a baby?" She pressed her lips tight. Tears glinted in her eyes. "We want our own chicks so bad."

Linnie picked up a pencil and paper. "Sit down," she said. She drew a picture of the male sperm moving to fertilize the female egg and she said, "If Newt's sperm fertilizes your eggs, you'll get pregnant."

"Yes, I know that. But, what can we do to *make* it happen?"

"I don't know. There's so much I don't know or understand it makes me dizzy. Frank loaned me books to study, but I don't know if I can learn enough to teach this subject well. Last night I had terrible doubts."

She went to the stove and poured two cups of strong coffee. "Family news we didn't go over last night? How's Joe doing?"

"Fine. Just fine."

"And Baby?"

"She's fine. The older Meggie gets, the closer she and Baby seem to be."

"I suppose that's good. But it's strange and we need to tell her the truth when we feel she can understand."

"Yes. When she's . . . sixteen, maybe seventeen."

"Maybe. I don't have a good feeling about it, Birdie. What's going on with union?"

"Weekly meetings. How did you do with Mr. Dobbs?"

Linnie tried to describe the lectures she'd heard and the conversations at Mrs. Easton's table, but her voice trailed off. "I don't know that there's much more to tell you."

"You like Mr. Dobbs, don't you," said Birdie.

"Of course I liked him. He tried to teach me a lot, but I doubt I'll see him again."

☙❧

Spring thaw. Squalls. Gray skies with sudden bursts of sunshine. Melting snow. Mud. Always lots of mud. The Blackduck River's turbulent, swollen waters turned white with run-off from Cougar Mountain.

Linnie spent every spare moment trying to study the books Frank gave her. She took copious notes, filling two notebooks. She read aloud to herself. When the children were away at school she pretended to teach an audience seated in her front room. She heard her own voice. High. Anxious. Wavering. Stumbling over words and not making any sense. At times, in frustration and anger at herself, she slammed her books down and went out for a brisk walk.

In mid-April she had a letter from Ann. *Hang on to your hat, Linnie. In June, Paul and I are coming up to Hanksport to live. He's going into the Real Estate business. I'm so excited about this I could eat my hat. You and I can start teaching classes at my old house and we'll drive my auto all over the county to reach women who can't attend our classes. Those women may not have the means to get to us.*

Or their husbands and family might forbid it. One way or another we'll reach them. See you in June. Toodle ooo. Love, Ann.

Linnie was delighted. She and Ann would work as partners. Teach together. Drive out to reach folks who couldn't attend classes. Write and distribute a newsletter. But as the days passed, she found herself overwhelmed and short tempered. She wanted to be a good mother and pay close attention to the children. She also wanted to learn *how* to teach and do it well.

Birdie Mae, sensing her distractions, suggested that the children come to her house after school and on week-ends. This would allow Linnie additional time for her studies.

On a Saturday afternoon, when thin rain fell from gunmetal skies, Linnie trudged over to visit Birdie. Her kitchen smelled of fresh baked bread. Hugh was helping Newt build a new front porch. Nell was curled up on the sofa reading. Stella was playing a tune at the piano. Meggie had taught Baby how to punch tidily-winks and when, at an odd moment Baby punched a wink up in the air, she sat back and laughed her big, horsy laugh.

Birdie Mae poured two cups of coffee, sliced her bread and after she and Linnie had settled themselves at the dining table, she said, "Folks on this earth are meant to do different things. Like you and me. You're not cut out to do most of the things I do."

"Lord, Birdie. There's so many times I've wished I was like you, I can't count them all. You're always in good humor. You and Newt are still crazy in love, and your heart is big as a barn."

"That might be. But for having a family of my own, I do what I was cut out to do. Now, down in Seattle you started to learn about what you're cut out to do. Teach. But you only had a smatter of learning for a short time. Now, we managed just fine while you were gone, so why not let us keep the kiddies and you can get on with your work."

Linnie toyed with her spoon. "I'll have to think about this. And I'd want to ask the children. I *want* them with me, but it's not good for them when I get impatient and frazzled."

"The offer stands."

A week later Linnie was taking notes from an article written by Margaret Sanger. *No woman can call herself free if she does not own and control her own body; no woman can call herself free until she can choose . . .*

Hugh burst through the door. "Auntie, here's a story about Mr. Dobbs." He held up an edition of *The Seattle Post Intelligencer.* "Can I read a . . ."

Linnie slammed down her notebook. "I'm studying, Hugh. Can't you see that?"

Hugh backed away. "I'm sorry. I'm awfully sorry."

Later that afternoon Linnie took Hugh aside. "I'm the one to apologize. I had no business losing my temper with you, and I *am* sorry. Let me ask you something. Aunt Birdie has suggested that you, Stella, Nell, and Meggie stay with her and Uncle Newt for a while. What do you think about that?"

"They're awfully good to us and you'd have a lot more time for your work."

"Let's talk about it at supper."

"Sure."

"Do you still have the article about Mr. Dobbs?"

"Yes."

"Will you read it to me?"

The story was a brief account about I.W.W. members organizing a strike in Butte, Montana. Guards fired on Wobblies marching in protest at the Neversweat Mine. Three men were killed. Half a dozen were injured. Hugh read the names of the casualties. Frank Dobbs was not among them. Linnie sat still for a moment before she could breathe with comfort.

At supper that evening Linnie told the children about Birdie's suggestion. "How do you feel about this?" she said.

Stella said, "How long would we stay over there?"

"Oh, maybe a couple of months. But every day after school I want you to stop by here before you go over there."

"What are you going to teach people?" said Nell.

"Ideas about family."

"I think we should go," said Stella. "That will give you time to study." Hugh and Nell agreed.

"But you're not going away?" said Meggie.

"No. I'll be right here in our house."

After the older children had gone off to their rooms, Linnie tucked Meggie into bed. "Mama," said Meggie. "When I grow up I want to be just like you." She turned and giggled into her pillow.

CHAPTER 41

One afternoon, while reading in the *Maryland's Woman Citizen*, a publication Linnie and Ann had subscribed to, Linnie was engrossed in a story about a conflict within the suffrage movement. Susan B. Anthony and Elizabeth Cady Stanton refused to endorse the proposed 15th Amendment, giving the vote to Negro men because the amendment did not give women the ballot, too. Other suffragists, including Lucy Stone and Julia Ward Howe, supported the amendment arguing that once Negro men were enfranchised, women would reach their goal.

This was new and exciting material and Linnie took copious notes. She did not appreciate the interruption of an auto rattling up the road. She was not expecting company. The children wouldn't be by for another two hours.

She left her desk and glanced out the window. Frank pulled up and parked. Her heart skipped. Calm down, she counseled herself. There's union work to do up here and he's stopping by to say hello.

She grabbed a shawl and went out to greet him. "Frank. How nice to see you." Oh, Lord, her hair was a mess and she had on a threadbare skirt and an old ratty sweater Birdie had knit for Joe years ago.

He smiled his crinkly smile. "Hello, Linnie." He got out of the car and took off his hat. "How are you? How is your work coming along?"

She found herself stammering. "Well," she said. "Lots . . . lots of . . . lots of studying. Yes. But, I . . . I haven't taught any classes yet. I'm waiting for Ann. She and Paul are coming up next month. Come in. Yes, please come in. I'll fix tea. Will you be here long?"

"It depends. Bruns came with me. He's staying at the Dickerson place until he finds a house big enough for his law practice."

"So, he's moving up here, too?"

"Yes."

"And you?"

"I'll pitch my tent later today."

"In the meadow?"

"Yes. How did you know?"

"I . . . well, I guess if anybody is going to pitch a tent around here, it would be in the meadow across the way from the old Dickerson place. I found it when I was quite young and I named it Thimble Meadow. And the rock, I called Thimble Rock. It reminded me of a thimble turned upside down."

It was easy to talk about the beautiful meadow and she had calmed.

He laughed. "I like your feelings about the place. I enjoy it, too."

The two went inside. Frank looked around. "What a nice place."

She put the kettle on and stoked the fire. "Thank you. The men in my family built it."

"It's delightful." He cocked his head. "I hear the flume bell, don't I?"

She was surprised and pleased. She'd told him about it one afternoon in Seattle. "Yes. If it stops ringing we know there's trouble upstream."

Again, his crinkly smile. "When it rings, as it does now, we know there's no trouble today."

"That's right." While she was delighted with his presence, she was also distracted. School would be dismissed at three o'clock and the children, puzzled by the stranger's presence might speak of it to folks, including Linnie's father. Roy would not approve of Linnie's visitor. And women of high reputation did not entertain gentlemen in their homes without the presence of family and friends.

She set a plate of Birdie Mae's oatmeal cookies on the table.

Frank picked up the photo of Dru and her children. "This must be Druscilla and her family."

"Yes."

"She was very pretty and her girls are, too. Her son is a handsome boy, isn't he." He picked up the photo of Meggie on the horse. "And this is Meggie?"

"Yes."

"I'd like to meet them."

"They're still at school. They're staying at Birdie Mae and Newt's for awhile. This gives me time to study. It's fine for right now, but as soon as I feel a little more confident and ready to teach, I'll want them home again. Please sit down." She sat across from him. "How's Tosstles?"

"He's fine. Can you come for dinner tonight at the Dickerson house? Bruns and I will fix a fine meal."

"What a nice invitation. Of course, I'd love to come."

He went to one of the front windows. He raked one hand through his tousled dark hair and he turned to her. "I have to ask this and I don't know how. So, I'll say it plain. Do you . .. do you have a suitor? You've never mentioned it, but frankly I . . . I'd guess that you do."

She laughed. She was on sure ground here and she observed, rightly so, that he was the one who was rattled. "No. I don't have any suitors. In all honesty, there is nobody up here I'd be interested in. Nice people, yes. But suitors, no."

"I . . . I'll look forward to seeing you this evening."

He didn't stay much longer and she was grateful. But her joy of having him in her life, even for a short time, gave a new light in her soul.

Late afternoon, after the children stopped by on their way to Newt and Birdie's, Linnie went over to see her father. "I've been invited up to the Dickerson place for dinner," she said.

"I saw his auto parked in front of your house. Watch yourself, daughter. Tongues wag up here faster than the tail of an excited dog."

Bruns and Frank presented a fine meal of roast chicken, mashed potatoes, and roast carrots and beets. Over dinner, Bruns related his adventures as a passenger on *The Queen Bee*, a peace vessel that plied the waters of the West Coast in protest of the United States entering the war. Over a lively debate the three argued about American's role in defending Europe against German totalitarianism. Frank felt that the United States had such an obligation. Bruns and Linnie countered that the I.W.W.'s class war was the most important issue in the world.

A dessert of coffee and one of Mame Holm's blueberrie pies was delicious. The brown bottle on the sideboard caught Linnie's eye. A shiver coursed through her, but she quelled the ugly memory. "Bruns," she said. "Frank. Do either of you know where that bottle came from?"

"No," said Bruns. "It's always been there."

Frank didn't know anything about it, either. "I'll bet Ann will know. But say, I'm working on an article about a potential West Coast Longshoremen strike. Delegates to the I.L.A. Convention contend that shipping profits have escalated because of the war, and the opening of the Panama Canal. The I.W.W., in support of the I.L.A., is asking for an increase of fifty-five cents an hour. It's classic. Linnie, would you have time to come over and read it before you go home?"

"Of course. I'm pleased to be asked. I'll help Bruns clean the kitchen and then come over. I'm eager to see your tent in the place I've always liked. And it won't be dark until around eight o'clock."

"Good."

Linnie told Frank and Bruns about the rift between Susan B. Anthony and Elizabeth Cady Stanton on one hand, and Lucy Stone and Julia Ward Howe on the other. Debate was lively among the three, with Frank and Linnie in support of Anthony and Stanton, and Bruns supporting Stone and Howe.

Frank then cleared the table and excused himself.

Linnie helped Bruns clean the kitchen and Bruns spoke about his decision to move to Hanksport. "There's always need for an attorney in a growing community of this size," he said. "And I love this country."

Linnie said, "I'm happy to know that you and Paul and Ann will live up here. We need people like you. And what a fine dinner. You must enjoy cooking."

"I do. Especially for appreciative people."

"Well, I'm plenty appreciative. And Frank flattered me plenty by asking me to read his work."

Bruns smiled. "Well, he admires you." He saw her to the door.

On down the road, some twenty yards from the house, she took the overgrown path to the bridge. Frank was waiting. The two went to the white tent. It was set up as she remembered it to be the first time she saw it. This time a typewriter stood on a small, sturdy table.

Linnie said, "This is so nice. I don't blame you for wanting to stay out here."

He smiled and handed her a manuscript. "Ten pages," he said. "I'll be interested to hear what you think." He picked up a book and settled himself in a canvas chair.

She took her time reading Frank's work. Finished, she said, "I expected this to be good and it is. But, you might emphasize the fact that dock workers have spent years in fruitless negotiations with those huge corporations. And point out that right now, longshoreman are prepared to strike all along the West Coast. That's awfully important." She handed him the manuscript and stood.

He put his book aside and came to her. "Thank you. Excellent suggestions." His eyes were somber. Anxious. He took hold of her hand. "It's been two and a half months since you left Seattle. I wanted to think I wouldn't miss you. I tried not to miss you. It didn't work. I missed you every moment of every day. I couldn't even see you off properly because I was afraid I'd blurt out something foolish."

"Thank you," she whispered.

He drew her to him. "I've not known anyone who moves me as much as you do. The first time I saw you, years ago when I came out of the jail, I was drawn to your lovely but unhappy face. Now, your face is even lovelier and not at all unhappy." He kissed her throat. "I want to make love to you, Linnie. I want you to make love to me, too."

He undressed her. Surprised at her lack of modesty, she saw herself as he might. A lithe body with round, firm breasts and flat belly. He shed his clothes and with deft fingers he slipped on a condom. They lay on the blue rug.

Roused, wet and hot between her legs, she arched herself up to him and he entered her with one long, fine penetrating stroke. His movements were measured. He pulled out of her, just as Parley had done.

"No," she said. "Don't leave me. Please."

He smoothed her hair back off her face. "Let's cool off," he said. "Just a little."

Again, he entered her and he took her to an exquisite high. Again, he left her. Then, once more he entered her and took her to a place to which she had not been. Swept up on a tide of sweet aching pleasure, she cried out and he too, pulsed and trembled and they lay still for a time.

So this fine, intense feeling was "climax" and there was nothing wrong with her and she loved this man, *this man* and he loved her. She understood why Birdie felt as she did about Newt and why Dru felt as she did about Buzzie. But, the thought she couldn't abide was that Frank, so smooth and practiced, no doubt gave Sophie this much pleasure, too. The awful green stone of jealousy struck her hard.

He propped himself up on one elbow and looked at her. "When you were in Seattle, I wanted to tell you that I'd fallen in love with you." He smiled. "It was a hard fall. And I didn't know if you had somebody in your life up here. But the time wasn't right to tell you all of that. Now, it is."

She reached up and ruffled his hair. "Do you give Sophie this much pleasure?"

He hesitated. He frowned. "That's not a good question. I didn't expect it of you."

"I didn't either, but I had to ask."

He drew back. "Don't. It's not fair to you or to me. Or to Sophie."

"I'm sorry. I have to guard against jealousy."

"You have nothing to be jealous about," he said and he gently kissed her.

CHAPTER 42

In order to try to stop wagging tongues Linnie seldom invited Frank to visit her at home and when she did, she made sure that her father was around. At first Roy barely tolerated him, but Frank treated Roy with respect and after a week or so, the two became friends.

Linnie spent some afternoons, some evenings and nights with Frank in his airy, white tent. Measured time. Time she considered so fine and centered, both of them easy with each other. After she told him about her feelings in owning the rock he cleared off his books. "Can we consider this ours?"

She laughed. "I'm delighted to share it with you."

When she stayed the night, she woke with the warmth of him close and in the cool, quiet place in the meadow, she mused on all she had learned. Absent the fear of pregnancy and enjoying control of her own body, she was free to love Frank with immense pleasure.

One late summer day when Frank and Roy sat out on Linnie's porch and read aloud from Jack London's *John Barleycorn,* Linnie, busy in the kitchen, listened to their reading and conversation about London's prophesy of revolution and the rise of Fascism. Linnie joined them and expressed her own opinion. "Sometimes 'revolution' is necessary," she said. "This country had its own in the fight for independence. Now, it seems that we're having a revolution for women's rights. Women *must* have the right of say-so over their own bodies. And women *must* gain the right to vote. Soon."

Frank said, "You speak like that, and you've got a captive audience."

In the weeks to follow Roy, Frank, and Linnie discussed The Great War, which Roy and Linnie opposed and Frank supported. Often Birdie Mae and Newt, Bruns, and Colin and Mide came by and the lively group discussed Socialists, Republicans, and Democrats. Linnie enjoyed the intense discussions and, as in most everything she did, her purpose was to learn how to speak well, become a good teacher and a good listener.

One Sunday afternoon when a group of them were discussing the women's campaign against President Wilson's refusal to support the woman's suffrage amendment, Linnie said, "Bruns, when you have time will you teach me how to run the printing press? After Ann arrives we want to print flyers about our classes and meetings. What better way to get the word out."

"Anytime you're ready, just let me know."

Time, elusive and fleeting. She spent her days studying and trying to catch on to the knack of speaking. Lecturing. She worked either in Frank's tent, or in her house and often far into the night.

Frank was busy meeting with Strom workers, with Mrs. Strom, with union folks over in Coldsprings and twice he and Bruns drove over to Spokane to meet with the I.W.W. But he and Linnie always found time for each other. They took long walks. They read aloud to each other. Linnie enjoyed cooking on the camp stove. Frank was appreciative beyond measure. On Sundays he joined the Bede family for picnics in the park, or dinner at Linnie's, or at Birdie's and Newt's.

Baby ogled him, but she didn't pester him. The children enjoyed his attentions. He taught Hugh how to tie a square knot and he helped him pitch a better baseball. He listened to Meggie and Nell read aloud and he applauded Stella's singing. But, it was clear to see that "his soul," as Birdie said more than once, was with Linnie.

At times Linnie's guilt in denying Parley the loving he had longed for bothered her, but she reminded herself of her own ignorance and fears. Now, her fear was Sophie. Frank never mentioned her, but Linnie battled jealousy about Sophie's role in Frank's life, and she had no idea what that was.

CHAPTER 43

In mid-June Ann and Paul moved to Hanksport. Ann and Linnie co-authored and published their first issue of their newsletter, *The Women's Informer*. Wasting no time, they bundled the pamphlets, along with notice of their first class to be held on July 16 at the Dickerson place.

On a Wednesday morning, when the great forest of firs, cedar and pines stood tall against a clear, blue sky, Birdie, Linnie and Ann packed carrots, beans and potatoes from Linnie's and Birdie's gardens in heavy cloth bags. Birdie had made a dozen such bags and had embroidered each one in red and black: ONE BIG UNION. WORKERS OF THE WORLD UNITE.

The information about the meetings along with the food and useful bags would be offered to all families. Frank, Newt, and Paul warned the women. "Don't expect welcome arms. You won't be seen as angels of mercy. You need to brace yourselves for trouble."

Ann and Linnie had other ideas. Some men might be unappreciative, but once they heard the message of 'family limitation' they would see the light. Most all women would greet them, listen to them and appreciate them. Linnie and Ann would be seen as angels of mercy.

They planned to visit four, possibly five families, each day and meet with the woman of the house to discuss the time, place and subject of the important up-coming meeting.

After leaving a pamphlet and a bag of food, the two would be on their way.

Their first stop was at the Dolce's place. As far as Linnie knew the Dolce's had ten children. Linnie had heard that more than half of them had left home. The shanty was small. One of two windows was broken out. There was no stoop. And one of three steps leading up into the place was missing.

In front of the house three shirtless boys—eight, maybe ten and eleven years—wearing ragged overalls fought viciously, slapping and using their fists on each other for a turn on a knotted rope swing. The oldest boy stopped his fighting and swiped one hand through his dirty blonde hair. "You here to talk devil talk to Ma?"

Linnie said, "We've come to visit your mother."

"That ain't what Pa says. He says you're teachin' devil talk."

Ann knocked on the door.

"Door's open," a woman called out.

Smells assailed Linnie. Kerosene. Dirty diapers. Sour milk. Six children, from perhaps one year to twelve, sat on a rump-busted sofa, or one the floor. A girl with long, blond braids—she appeared to be the oldest—stopped picking on two strings of a broken guitar. The younger children sucked their thumbs. A boy with odd, cat-shaped eyes and a strange half-smile giggled and didn't stop. A thin, blue-pale baby tried to suckle at Mrs. Dolce's sagging breasts. She gave the child an old sugar teat.

"Oughtn't to come," she lisped. She had no front teeth. Her eyes held the exhausted look of defeat.

Linnie set the bag of food on a greasy piece of oilcloth atop a table. "Mrs. Dolce, these vegetables are for you and your family."

"Pleased."

Linnie and Ann told her about their up-coming classes. "Sunday next," said Ann. "At one-thirty. This gives folks time to get home from church."

"Bert's heard of you. He ain't a gonna let me go hear what you got to say. Says you're teachin' devil's talk."

Ann said, "Excuse me, but your husband hasn't ever heard us speak. Surely, he'll bring you and stay to listen to what we have to say."

"Not Bert."

The older boys came inside.

Linnie turned to them. "Can any of you read?"

The boys shook their heads. "We don't have schooling. Dora does." He pointed to the older girl.

Mrs. Dolce said, "Dora don't read when Burt's around. She does, he's gonna beat the tar outa' her."

Ann held up a copy of *The Women's Informer.* "We'll leave this."

Dora stood and held out one hand. "I'll take it," she said. "He won't find it."

Mrs. Dolce said to the children, "Any of you tell your pa, then you ain't gonna eat for a time."

All day and into early evening Linnie and Ann met angry, hostile men and women. "She devils. Preaching against God's word. Something that ain't natural."

Men tore up the pamphlets. A woman threw the offered bag of food on the ground. "We don't want your food. Pick it up and go back to your house and husband where you belong."

"Murderers," a woman screamed.

A young man about Joe's age yelled, "Teaching women how to kill babies. Your souls are gonna rot in hell."

Ann and Linnie persisted. "Come to just one meeting and hear what we have to say."

"Pack of lies," a man yelled. "It's against God's teaching. You come around here again and you'll be looking at the end of a rifle barrel. Understand?"

That evening Ann, Paul, Linnie, Frank and Roy gathered around Birdie's and Newt's dinner table. Roy said, "You've got a lot of work to do. You've started something that will either take you down, or raise you up. It's going to be hard and dirty, but I'm with you all the way."

Frank said, "You've got fine courage. Get your classes going and don't give up. Don't surrender."

CHAPTER 44

On Sundays, in nice weather, before Jim Corrigan and Roy went fishing, Roy liked to sit on the porch, soak his gimpy leg in a tub of hot water and read. One Sunday, in early August, he'd settled himself when Joe called out, "Hey, Father."

Roy raised an arm and hailed him. He enjoyed his son as long as he didn't get carried away with religion. The two exchanged pleasantries. Joe sat down. "We've got to stop Linnie and Mrs. Garibaldi from going around preaching to decent, God-fearing folks," he said. "It's spelled out in the Bible, Father. A man and his wife are supposed to make man in His own image. And here we've got Linnie and her friend speaking against the Lord."

Roy said, "They're *not* saying a woman should stop a baby that's already started. They're talking about stopping a baby from getting started in the first place. There's a whole world of difference in that."

"But, she's telling folks to do things that are wrong. Stopping that baby . . . that seed from becoming a baby is wrong. That is not God's image. And there's this other thing. She's committing a terrible sin, living with Dobbs. She's being talked about and you've got to stop her."

"She's not living with Dobbs." Roy pointed over to Linnie's house. "She lives over there, in her own place. And what she does or doesn't do, on her own time, isn't your business, or mine or anybody's at all."

Joe held up one of Linnie and Ann's pamphlets. "You've seen this?"

"Sure, I've seen it. It's well written."

"I tell you, this family is cursed. Birdie Mae strayed with Newt before she was his wife. Dru did the same with Buzz and then sold her soul to the devil. Now we've got Linnie going around preaching against God's will and committing adultery." He waved the pamphlet. "And she's advertising what she's talking about. She's holding those meetings up at the Dickerson place on the Lord's day."

"I'm not stepping in," said Roy.

"Something awful is going to happen, Father. And I can't stop it."

"There are a lot of things that happen in this world that we can't stop," said Roy.

After Joe left, Roy dumped the water, pulled on a pair of thick, clean socks and went inside. He picked up one of Linnie's pamphlets. LEARN ABOUT FAMILY LIMITATION. COME TO A MEETING AT THE DICKERSON PLACE ON SUNDAY, AUGUST 16 AT 1:00. Roy chuckled. You bet he'd be there. Years ago, if he and Meara had known about this business, Meara might be alive and herself.

That evening Joe knocked on Linnie's door. "You've got to stop this teaching," he said. "You and Mrs. Garibaldi are spreading dangerous ideas."

"You're wrong, Joe. Ann and I have the right to teach women the truth. We have the right to educate women. And men. We are not spreading dangerous ideas. That's pure poppycock."

"Truth as you see it," said Joe. "Not as Christians see it. If you keep on doing this, you'll go to jail. I can't stand that thought. I don't know what I'd do, if that happened."

"I do. Contribute to bail funds."

"I won't give money for someone whose thoughts about our Lord are wrong."

"Then don't worry about me. I'll be just fine."

CHAPTER 45

Linnie, wearing an ankle length, navy-blue skirt, a white, long-sleeved blouse and a navy blue shawl, stood in front of the Dickerson place to view the blackboard Frank had propped on the front porch. INFORMATION! LEARN ABOUT FAMILY LIMITATION. Bold words, but not threatening.

Linnie and Ann moved among and greeted a small group of women. Quiet, their faces expectant and anxious, they waited. Mrs. Dolce was not among them. A few men, including Mr. Dolce, Roy, Paul, Mr. Finley—Mide's father—stood a little apart from the women. Colin and Mide, Birdie and Newt had staked their places close to the porch.

In a whopping cloud of dust an automobile careened up the road, stopped and Sheriff Chester Mann and four deputies, including Joe, got out. They stood off a ways by themselves as if they didn't quite know what to do.

Ann and Linnie went up on the porch and once again made sure that the pamphlets and copies of *The Woman's Informer* were neatly stacked and ready to be passed out. Ann said to Linnie, "Are we surprised to see the sheriff?"

"No. But, I'm sick to see that Joe is with him. Let's get started." She turned to the crowd. "Thank you, ladies and gentlemen. Thank you for coming today." Her voice broke. She took a deep breath and clasped her trembling hands behind her. "Many of you have met my friend, Mrs.

Garibaldi, from Seattle. She and her husband are now citizens of Hanksport County."

A scatter of clapping hands.

"Don't do this Linnie," Joe's cry was sharp. "Don't. . . ."

Linnie continued, her tone high, halting, and unsteady. "You've . . . yes, you've come here today . . . you've come to learn how to *stop* what we call . . . well, we call it 'conception.'" Heat rose in her face. "Conception is . . . it's the process of starting . . . *starting* to make a baby."

"This is wrong," Joe shouted. "What you're doing is wrong."

Anger sparked Linnie. She raised one arm and pointed to Joe. "I've never interfered with your beliefs, and I'd appreciate it if you wouldn't interfere with mine." To the crowd, she said, "The greatest . . ." Again, her voice wavered. "The greatest . . ." She stumbled over words she had practiced day after day, often with Frank's coaching.

A woman coughed. A baby started to cry.

"Yes," Linnie said. "The greatest freedom a woman deserves to have is the right to *decide* if she wants to have a child. This is her . . . her own right of control over her body."

A man called out, "You don't have no right to tell us married folks what to do. Not when you're living in sin."

"Sinner! Sinner." A chorus of voices swelled.

Mide's face stood out from the rest. The deformed baby, drowned . . . And Collin's anguished eyes. *Don't tell her. Please.*

Linnie looked straight at the hecklers, most of them decent men she'd seen around town for years. She strode the length of the porch toward them. "Mrs. Garibaldi and I are *not* here today . . ." she struck her fist into her palm, "to try to persuade you *to have, or not to have* a child." Good. This was better. Nice flow of words that made sense. "That's your business," she said. "It's not mine. It's not your pal's. It's not your sister's or your brother's. It belongs to you and to your wife. *Only* to you and your wife."

She found eye contact with two women who had a great number of children. "Understand, please. If you, Mrs. Elser. And you, Mrs. Magilly. If you and your husband don't want another child, Mrs. Garibaldi and I can teach you *how* that can be done. You *can* prevent the start of a child. We are *not* here to teach you how to end an unborn child's life. But you can stop the *start* of a child. *This* is what we call 'family limitation.' Or 'birth control.'"

"Murderers," Mr. Dolce, his eyes sharp as knives, pushed through the crowd to stand directly in front of Linnie. "Baby killers."

"Mr. Dolce," said Linnie. "We want to teach . . ."

"Gibberish. The devil's gibberish, that's what you . . ."

"Pipe down, Burt," Roy called out. "Let these women speak. They've got that right, whether you like it or not."

Mr. Dolce spat and walked off.

Ann joined Linnie and picked up the pitch. "Every child on this earth deserves to be wanted, loved, and protected. A wanted child has a good chance in life. An unwanted child does not. Hear us, please."

Linnie said, "We fight for a better life. But, we're poor. Many of us have too many mouths to feed. Too many boots to buy. We are dependent on Mrs. Strom. And *the more* children we have, *the more* dependent we are. On her. Now, someday, not too far away, we hope to establish a clinic for women here, in this house."

Scattered applause.

Ann said, "Yes. We want this place to be available to women who want to learn about family limitation. We're working on this and we hope to open the doors in a few weeks."

She then described the column she and Linnie wrote, *The Woman's Informer.* She held up a handful of the publications. "How many of you can read?"

A few hands popped up.

"How many of you know someone who can read to you?"

A better show.

She waved the pamphlets. "Please take one of these before you leave. You won't read much about family limitation because the laws of the land, the Comstock laws, won't allow us to write about it. And to distribute information about this subject is a crime. But we've charted our schedule for the coming weeks and you'll know when and where we'll be. Next Sunday afternoon we'll be at the I.W.W. Hall over in Coldsprings. We plan to go over to Mountain View the following week."

"Teach us," a woman called out.

"Teach us. Teach us." Other women shouted and clapped.

Ann said, "I'll draw pictures here on the blackboard to show you what we mean when we speak of 'family limitation.'" She went to the blackboard and drew a picture of a condom.

Mrs. Elser spoke up. "But how does that work? I don't understand."

Linnie said, "Imagine the male sperm, his seed, if you will, as a tiny fish swimming up river to a woman's womb where it fertilizes the woman's eggs. When the husband wears a condom, that condom provides protection and the sperm is prevented, or blocked, from going anywhere."

"Oh, my land," Mrs. Elser exclaimed. "I can't listen to this."

"I can," said Mrs. Magilly.

Catcalls and jeers splintered the air. "You're preaching against what the Lord wants us to do," a man shouted. Folks echoed their feelings akin to that. A number of people left.

Linnie, recalling Sophie Krueger's words, called out, "Yes, this is difficult to discuss, but let's continue."

Sheriff Mann and two deputies shouldered their way through the crowd. "That's all," the sheriff said. One of the deputies picked up the blackboard, cracked it down on the porch rail and split it in two.

"Mrs. Hearn," the sheriff said, "You and Mrs. Garibaldi are under arrest."

Ann said, "We're here, on my property, and we have the right to say what we choose. This is not public property. It belongs to me."

"Doesn't matter," said the sheriff. "I'm charging you and Mrs. Hearn with spreading obscenity. Mrs. Hearn, you spoke of The Comstock laws. Those laws protect citizens from this kind of nasty thing you're preaching and writing about."

Frank came forward. "Mrs. Hearn and Mrs. Garibaldi have the right of free speech. The information they're talking about is biological fact. The people who came here this afternoon want to listen and learn what these two women have to say. Nobody forced anybody to come. Those who feel uncomfortable are free to leave. Now, please let these women proceed."

"Mr. Dobbs," said the sheriff. "You have no say in this matter." He and two of his men hustled Linnie and Ann to the automobile.

Frank called out to the crowd. "I'll try to continue Mrs. Hearn's and Mrs. Garibaldi's teaching. I have no blackboard and I can't illustrate what I'm about to say, but understand please. In order to prevent the male sperm from fertilizing the female's eggs . . ."

"Dobbs, you're under arrest," said Sheriff Mann. "You must enjoy coming up here and causing trouble." He slapped handcuffs on Frank. Joe swiped all of the literature off the table and stuffed it into a canvas bag.

"Joe Bede," Linnie shouted from the auto. "You think about our mother and ask yourself how can you do what you're doing." She and Ann shouted to the crowd. "We'll be back. Read our pamphlets. Or have someone read them to you." The two raised their fists and pumped the air. Frank joined them. "No surrender. We will not surrender."

✿

Sheriff Mann and Joe locked Frank in one cell, Linnie and Ann in the other. A chipped, stained enamel bucket stood in one corner of the women's cell. A dead sparrow lay under the rusty springs of a bunk. "Will you please take that out," Ann pointed to the dead bird.

"Joe, get that thing out of here and bring in two chairs from my office. These ladies need a decent place to sit. We won't bother with mattresses right now. I have a hunch that someone will post bail, soon."

Joe picked up the dead bird, returned with the chairs and set them down. He put his hands on Linnie's shoulders. "Stop this foolishness."

"You've always talked freely about your beliefs. Why can't I talk about mine?"

"My beliefs are based on the Lord's teachings."

"Then He must be a mean fellow to allow so much human misery."

"A man and his wife are supposed to produce children."

"That's what you choose to believe. But you don't have the right to try to stop me from speaking out on something I choose to believe."

Joe, his face a knot of worry, said, "You're going to find yourself in a whole lot of trouble and I won't be able to help you at all."

"Don't worry about me. I'll be just fine."

Joe and the sheriff left. Linnie went to the barred window. Joe crossed the bridge and started up the hill to Strom's place. His shoulders sagged and he walked like a bent and tired old man.

Late in the afternoon the sheriff returned. "Newt posted bail," he said. "I've got to say that in spite of your ideas, I didn't like the notion of you two being in here."

"Is Mr. Dobbs free?" said Ann.

"Yes. I hope you all come to your senses."

CHAPTER 46

War raged in Europe. Inga Strom's mill produced lumber at a record of over 68,000 board feet a day. But Strom workers were restless. In the camps they cursed the sour milk, the spoiled bacon and meat. Bunks with lice-infested hay. They spoke of clean camps and the eight-hour day as pipe-dreams.

One day twenty-five union workers went out on strike. That night vigilantes drove their rattling automobiles into one of the camps, forced eight men from their bunks, marched them over to Coldsprings and slammed them in the county jail.

The prisoners banged their hands on the bars and chanted, "O.B.U. O.B.U." The next morning the prisoners went missing. Three days later a fisherman found eight mutilated bodies in a backwater of the Blackduck River.

Following the massacre, the tide turned ugly. Company tools—wedges, pickaroons, and climbing irons—disappeared. Blades of bucker's cross-cut saws got bound up in tree trunks and couldn't be removed. Choke setters found cables too short to cinch around a tree. Donkey engines stalled. Planks riding down-flume jammed up. Shingle bolts stuffed with twigs, rocks and mud fell off the conveyor belts. If they made it inside the mill, the dirty bolts clogged the saws.

Mrs. Strom fired her workers. New workers came in, but the Slow-Down continued. Inga Strom was losing money.

One day, with Frank and Bruns present, Inga Strom signed a statement granting the eight-hour day and a promise to build new bunkhouses and a hospital within the year. The Slow-Down came to an end.

One day, with Frank and Bruns present, Inga Strom signed a statement granting the eight-hour day and a promise to build new bunkhouses and a hospital within the year. The Slow-Down came to an end.

After supper on a cool fall evening, Kees and his mother sat in front of a meager fire in the front room. Inga Strom said, "Does the heretic infidel continue her preaching?"

"Yes, and she treats me as if I repulse her."

Inga pulled her black shawl close. "Bear in mind, Kees, she's only a flume tender's daughter. Hardly a prize. She's also a sinner, an adulteress who one day will regret her transgressions."

Kees leaned toward the fire and rubbed his hands over the small flame. "In time something will happen to stop her. I have no doubt about that at all."

CHAPTER 47

On a Friday afternoon in late September, Frank and Linnie were reading in the airy white tent when Frank put his book aside. "I'm driving down to Seattle tomorrow. I'll be back in a couple of days."

"Oh, Frank. I want to go with you. Surely we could take the time to visit Druscilla's grave."

Frank took a long pull on his pipe before he said, "I need to go alone to take care of a personal matter. I'll be home on Monday. Then, let's sit down and plan a trip just for us. Maybe drive up to Canada. Paul says that Banff and Waterton are spectacular."

"Yes. Let's do it. But we must plan around Ann's and my schedule."

He reached over and took her hand. "We'll do that."

She saw him off. The last time she'd watched him drive away was when he'd come out of jail after his arrest. Now, when the coil of dust from his auto settled, a fine, calm sense of pride and love for him washed over her. She was blessed, not only with her love for Frank and his love for her, but with the progress she and Ann were making with their program. Class attendance was higher than expected. And a women's clinic at the Dickerson house was no longer a thought. It would happen and it would be known as *The Druscilla Corrigan Clinic for Women*.

Late that afternoon Linnie went up to Frank's tent to get Havelock Ellis's *Psychology of Sex*. Now that she had a greater understanding of his topic, she wanted to read his work. This evening would be a good time to start.

Frank kept most of his books in the steamer trunk. Linnie opened the heavy, humped lid. An envelope tucked under Ellis's book caught her eye. She hesitated. This was not her business, but she took the envelope addressed to Frank with beautiful cursive handwriting. A sick suspicion got the better of her. The letter was postmarked from Portland only ten days earlier. She opened it and found a letter and a photograph of Sophie and two children. Hit by dull nausea, she sat down on the rock.

September 12, 1917

Frank, Dearest

Word I find most distressing has reached me. I hear you are seeing much of a woman I met briefly some time ago, Mrs. Linnie Hearn. When I first heard this gossip, I laughed. You and I have never kept secrets from each other. Then, I have to confess I wept and felt as if the earth under my feet was slipping away.

In fact we've never discussed such matters, and indeed, I've never told you of my profound love for you. Now I find it impossible to think of you with someone else in a serious situation. If you want me to come home, I'll leave here immediately so we might discuss this together. The children, old as they are, and often left with family members, miss you and ask when they might see you again.

If you don't want me to come home, please write and tell me, even though reading such words will break my heart. I'll wait to hear from you and hope this is nothing more than idle gossip.

Yours, Sophie.

Children! So Frank and Sophie had children and Frank had never said a word about them. She scrutinized the photo. A boy and a girl, maybe five and six years old, handsome, dark haired children, sat with their mother on a bench in a garden. Sophie's dress was simple and elegant with a wide lace collar. Her elbow length sleeves were trimmed with lace cuffs. Her smile was of joy and she had looked directly at the camera, appearing at this moment, to look into Linnie's eyes.

Jealousy, hard, ugly and green, plucked at her heart. Suspicion swept her up in a tangle of anger and confusion. At this very moment Frank and Sophie were no doubt together in their apartment. He would confess his dalliance—nothing more than a fling with a flume tender's daughter—and he'd declare his intention to end it.

Linnie put the letter and photo back where she had found them, closed the trunk, and went walking down the hill toward home.

CHAPTER 48

On Sunday, mid-afternoon, a cool day with gray, misty rain, Linnie and Ann greeted the women trudging up the road to the Dickerson house. Brown Hon, carrying a large basket, was among them. Linnie hadn't seen the Makah woman since the day she'd driven over to Sunnydale. What was her purpose in coming to this meeting?

Women, twelve years to possibly fifty, wrapped in thin coats or jackets, carrying babies or holding the red chapped hands of young children, came. They looked skeptical. Expectant. Perhaps bewildered. And afraid. For Linnie, the work and responsibility brought some relief from dwelling on Frank's heart-breaking deception.

By 3:00 in the afternoon the crowd had grown. A large number of women, a few men and a bevy of children waited in front of the house. During the last two classes the sheriff and his deputies had not come around, but now, once again Sheriff Chester Mann's automobile stormed up the road. And once again Linnie and Ann prepared themselves for jail.

With measured words the two introduced their subject, but Ann was unable to complete her illustration on the new blackboard before she and Linnie were arrested.

"I've got no choice," Sheriff Mann said. "Once again, you're breaking the Comstock Laws of this land."

Once again, Joe hauled two chairs into one of the cells and he hurried, for he was late for work up at the Strom house.

After he left, Linnie wrapped her shawl tight and looked out the barred window. She had once been part of a picnic on a day of red, white and blue and many dimensions. The talk she and Parley had had on the Blackduck Bridge. Her dismay at the thought of marriage. Her envy of her sisters' love for their men. Her own ignorance.

"Union man's in jail." The union man's appearance had brightened her soul that day.

Now her soul was as gray and dull as the sky. The rain had let up, but clouds hung low and the scape lacked color.

Late in the afternoon bail was posted, Ann and Linnie were released and Paul and Bruns took them home. Bruns told the two that this second arrest meant they must appear in the County Court over in Coldsprings to defend their activities. Bruns would represent them. "Pro Bono," he said. "But, it won't be easy. Lots of feelings are out there. Some good and supportive. Some ugly and frightening."

At home, in the silence of deep night, the flume bell rang its erratic, but constant *bong Bong Bong* There was no trouble upstream, but there was a terrible, dark trouble in Linnie's heart.

Tomorrow Frank would be home. If he and Sophie did not have children, the whole situation would be different, but to rob the children of their father was wrong. Yet, what seared her mind and bruised her heart was that Frank had not ever said a word to her about them. Two deceptions. His children. And his reason for going to Seattle alone.

CHAPTER 49
JOE BEDE

The Lord had chosen Joe to lead the way and save his sisters, but he had failed. Years ago Birdie had allowed herself to get in the shameful family way before marriage. Dru, the soiled dove whose soul now burned in hell and would forevermore, was gone. And Linnie, an adulteress, was now talking about how to stop creation. Lord, have mercy on her soul.

After Joe left Linnie and Ann in jail he hurried up to Strom's place. He swept and swabbed down the horse stalls and pitched in sweet, fresh hay. His last chore was to chop a load of clean, dry wood and rack it neatly in the woodshed, saving enough for the fireplace stacked on the back porch.

With his chores done, he leaned against the wall of the woodshed to rest for a moment. A half dozen brown bottles behind a clutter of buckets, shovels, and rakes caught his eye. He picked one up. It was full of liquid and tightly capped. His eyebrows arched in surprise. He'd thought that Mrs. Strom and Kees, religious as they were, didn't touch alcohol. Yet, here was a bottle of shine in their woodshed. But it wasn't his business. He put the pear shaped bottle back where he'd found it, went to the back porch, took his pay of one silver dollar from a tin can and left.

It was his habit—and had been for years—to take the back road from town up to the junction. One road went north to Camp Two, where he lived. The other road went east to the Dickerson place and on down to Joe's father's place. The route Joe chose was a longer route and a little out-of-the-way, but worth it.

At a certain place, he left the road and bushwhacked his way to a tumble of basaltic rocks. He pulled two rocks free, reached into a hidden space and pulled out a large, burlap bag. He added his dollar to the money inside the bag. He'd never taken one dollar to his bunkhouse. He'd given the children silver dollars for Christmas, but he'd not spent another dime. That money had purpose and that purpose was what had led him to seek work at Strom's place, beyond his job as bolt puncher.

With his money properly stashed back, he went on his way. At the junction, where he would swing north up to Camp Two, he stopped. He sniffed the air. His heart quickened. A sickening dread coursed through him. Fire! Leaping, exploding flames could spread for miles, burn everything in its path and the murky, orange glow up ahead meant the Dickerson place was on fire.

He sprinted up the road, his long, lean legs working like pistons. "Oh, Lord, let this morning's rain save the place and thank you Lord for the clearing, clean of trees."

His prayers went unanswered. Sleeves of flames engulfed the old mossy house. Showers of sparks shot up in the sky. Windows popped. Timbers buckled. The walls caved in. But, what was this? Two men cavorted around the awful flames.

"Get away," Joe shouted. "Get away. This is God's revenge. Words of sin were spoken here today."

The roar of fire swallowed his words and Joe's eyes widened at the sight of Kees Strom's curly hair and fine features, and wasn't that Soapy Metzler who always wore a bowler hat? There they were, the two of them etched sharp and clear against the flames. Kees threw his arms high and laughed.

Joe, sensing a terrible, confusing danger, sifted back into the tree shadows. From there, with his heart in his throat, he watched Kees and Soapy do things with each other that he did not and could not understand.

☙❧

Brown Hon saw the fire. Early that morning and with keen anticipation she had mounted her pony and left Sunnydale Valley, intent on hearing Mrs. Hearn and her friend speak. After the sheriff took Mrs. Hearn and Mrs. Garibaldi to jail—as Brown Hon suspected would happen—she rode her pony to the far end of the Dickerson place to peel cascara bark and pick chamomile and she took the herbs to relatives who lived at Green Lake four miles north of Hanksport.

Late afternoon she left her family, but she took time to dig horseradish and nerve root which grew in great numbers.

While passing by the Dickerson place she was surprised to see two men tossing a bottle back and forth between them. Brown Hon's heart beat hard. Didn't the bottle look just like those on her bottle tree? And wasn't one of the cavorting men Strom's son? And wasn't the other man the owner of Metzler's Funeral Parlor? What business did those fellows have on this property? Brown Hon tethered her pony and waited in the thick, shadowed fringe of trees.

Darkness was about to fall. Strom's son struck a match, put it to the bottle, and threw it at the house. Fire burst out.

A third man appeared, briefly, before drifting back into the trees. Brown Hon mounted her pony and spurred him into a trot, away from the burning house and the men who had done the terrible thing.

After passing through Hanksport, she rode up the hill past Strom's house, through the deep forest and down the narrow, twisting Canyon Road to Sunnydale Valley. Once home she lit a lantern and went out to her bottle tree. It was not her habit to pay much attention to the bottles beyond their soft, tinkling music and the play of sunshine that coaxed from them a pretty blue sheen. Now, to her horror, she found a good number of bottles missing. She took those remaining into her house and vowed to stay away from town and white folks for a long time. Someone might have seen her at the fire and when there was trouble, the white man was quick to lay blame on Indians.

While Brown Hon was trotting over to the valley, Joe, on shuddery legs, hurried toward his father's house. Sweat soaked his shirt. Twice he stopped and he looked up—seeking God. Seeking God. Seeking God. A sliver of new moon slid in and out of broken, dark clouds. God appeared. An angry God and he spoke. Joe had seen a terrible fire and an unnatural act performed at the very place where, a few hours earlier, Linnie had spoken against God's intentions. The angry God told Joe that he must not speak of the act that he saw. To speak of it would bring it to light and Joe must keep the act he saw in darkness.

Joe burst in the door at his father's house. His father, seated at the table, pushed a book aside and stood up. "What . . .?"

Joe forgot God's command and he blurted, "The Dickerson house burned down and I saw the fellows who did it and I know them."

"My God! Was anyone in the house?"

"I don't know."

"Who did you see?"

"I . . . I can't say."

"For God's sakes, why not?"

"God told me I can't."

Roy, his forehead knotted tight, paced the room. "What in hell were you doing up there?"

"The money I earn at Strom's . . . I stash it up by the junction."

"There's something wrong with your story," said Roy. "I'll ask you again. You know the men you saw at the fire?"

"Yes. But God doesn't want me to say who they were."

Roy bellowed. "How in the hell will you convince Chester or anyone else that it wasn't *you* who set that fire? Folks know you used to be a hot head. They know you don't like your sister's work. Who in hell will believe your story about two men you saw at the fire and yet you won't identify them because God told you not to? Where is the logic in that?"

Joe's breath left him. He sat down.

His father's hand was gentle on his head. "You let someone else report this business to Chet. As far as I know, you didn't say a word about it to me."

Joe stayed the night at his father's house.

At work the next day, when a couple of fellows asked him if he was all right, he said, "I didn't sleep well." By then, the whole of Hanksport County knew about the awful fire.

CHAPTER 50

In mute disbelief Linnie stared at the long scorched beams thrust skyward and fingers of smoke rising from hissing embers. A speckled blue teapot, whole and unmarked, lay next to a black glove. A journal, in which women's records were kept, was a pile of crumbled ashes. The small printing press and the brown bottle were undamaged.

An automobile came grinding up the road. She braced herself.

Frank got out of the car and came to her and tried to take her in his arms.

She ducked away.

He said, "How . . .? My God . . . was anyone in the house?"

"No. It happened last night. Nobody knows who did it. Or how. Or why."

"I can't believe . . ." He looked tired. Of course he was tired. Balancing love affairs between two women was no small task. Only a few hours ago he had no doubt embraced Sophie, assured her that he would soon be with her and his affair with the flume tender's daughter was only a dalliance.

Again, Frank reached for her.

She moved away. "Any number of people could have done it," she said. "All of us, you and Paul and Ann and I and Bruns have run into a lot of hate." With the toe of her boot, she kicked at the embers. She picked up the bottle. "I have to go home."

"I'll take you," said Frank.

"No. I want to go alone."

"Will you stay with me tonight?"

"I'm bringing the children home. I need to be with them and they need to be with me."

"Something's wrong."

"Dang it, Frank. Lots of things are wrong. We've lost most all we've so carefully put together. Women's records. Our publications and books. Ann and I have a trial coming up and we might have to go to jail. We have to find another place to hold our classes and I hope to heaven Sheriff Mann will find out who did this terrible thing."

"My Lord, so do I. If there's anything, a clue, or anything I can do to help, I'm plenty available. But, when can I see *you*?"

"I don't know. I can't even think straight." With the bottle in hand, she started down the road.

On Friday afternoon, at the end of the dreadful week, Linnie was looking over a bank statement and itemizing expenses she and Ann had incurred. They had made two important decisions. They would continue to print their weekly paper and Paul and Bruns had moved the press to Linnie's house. The women would print *The Woman's Informer* in her living room.

In time, after the trial, Linnie and Ann would build a new clinic on the Dickerson site. Linnie, Paul, Ann and

Bruns would invest in the building. Linnie had asked Joe to draw up the plans and build it. He declined. "I can't do it," he said. "I don't like what you're doing and if I helped you, I'd be working against the Lord."

Linnie thought it was just as well. Joe, always a somber fellow, was now even more so. He kept to himself and rarely joined his family for Sunday dinners. One day, after Linnie confronted him and asked him what was troubling him, he said, "I'm in a dark hole and I can't get out."

But now, once again, Linnie had company and, dreading the moments ahead, she threw a shawl over her shoulders and went out to meet Frank.

He got out of his auto. "You're avoiding me. What's going on?"

"It's time we broke off. You're free from me and you can return to Seattle anytime you choose."

He stared at her. "I don't know what you mean. I can't believe I heard what you said."

"Maybe not, but it's true."

"Am I a toy you're tired of?"

"Of course not." She struggled to keep her voice flat and steady. "This is hard for me, too."

"Why would I want to go back to Seattle?"

"Don't deceive me further, Frank."

"I don't understand. For God's sake, why are you saying these things?"

"Because I have to. And I want to."

"I don't believe you. You don't have to. You don't even want to." His arms hung limp at his sides.

"You don't know what goes through my mind, and I mean it. We have to break off."

"Stop it. You sound like you've memorized lines for a goddamned play." He raked his fingers through his hair. "Marry me," he said. "Please marry me."

"You can't be much interested in taking on four more children when you aren't interested in your own."

"For God's sake, what do you mean? I don't have any children."

"You lie, Frank Dobbs. I'm not proud of what I did, but I read a letter Sophie wrote to you. A recent letter I found in your trunk while you were gone. Sophie's in love with you. And your two children miss you."

"Those children aren't mine," he cried, his eyes stricken. "I've never fathered any children. Those are Sophie's. She had them before I met her. I've never even adopted them. That photo she sent is an old one and those children have nothing to do with me. Or you. Please. You can't do this."

"And what about Sophie?"

"You've always known that she isn't my wife. There's never been a legal binding between us. But with you, it's different. I want us to be together. Always. My God, you're the only part of me that matters."

Was he telling the truth, or engaging her with his charm? Smooth, seductive and forceful, he was a man who succeeded in getting what he wanted. Then the accusation she loathed to say got the better of her.

"I'm sure you saw Sophie while you were in Seattle."

"Yes. That's why I went. I told her I wanted to break off with her. Completely and permanently."

"And how did she take it?"

"She was a good sport."

"I don't believe you. She didn't sound like a 'good sport' in the letter she wrote you. She indicated a broken heart if you broke off with her."

"I can't help that. It's you whom I love and want to be with."

"No. I have to do this."

He stared at her. Neither of them spoke.

"All right," he said. "But I don't ever want to see you again. I don't want to miss you, either. If I leave this place, I won't miss you at all."

"Yes, you will. Just as I'll miss you."

He turned from her, got in his auto and drove off.

❧

During the following week Linnie kept herself busy with her work and the children and she tried to keep memories of Frank at bay. But Sophie's letter haunted her. *I've never told you about my quite profound love for you. The children miss you and wonder . . .*

On a chilly afternoon, when the land was shrouded in fog so thick Linnie couldn't see her father's house, Bruns knocked on her door. "Frank's gone," he said. "He took everything but his tent. It's not my business, but does it have something to do with you?"

"Yes. I broke off with him. Please, Bruns. I can't talk about it."

That evening after dinner with the children, Linnie said, It's hard to know and understand that bad things can happen to people who try to help others. Ann and I can't let the fire stop us from doing our work. But we won't hold any classes until after the trial."

Hugh, his young, handsome face stamped with anxiety, said, "If you're arrested again, will Uncle Newt post bail?"

Linnie reached across the table and ruffled his dark hair. "Yes. It's all arranged."

Meggie, who often had a lot to say, had been silent. Linnie leaned over and chucked her under her chin. "You're alright Megs?"

"I don't want you to go away," she said. "Not ever again."

"If the Judge says that Ann and I have to spend time in jail, we must obey him. But you'll stay with Aunt Birdie and Uncle Newt and you'll be just fine."

Meggie said, "We'll stay with Aunt Baby, too. Don't forget her."

"Of course not."

Meggie got up, went to Linnie and put her arms around her. "I love you, Mama," she said. "And I love second grade."

CHAPTER 51

Three weeks later, Mrs. Dolce, with two little girls in tow, knocked on Linnie's door. "Come in" said Linnie. "Come in and sit down. Will you have a cup of tea?"

"No. Bert's gonna be home soon."

"The children? Would they like cookies and milk?"

"That's kind of you."

Linnie put a plate of oatmeal cookies on the table and poured two glasses of milk. The children's eyes were shadowed with the hollow look of hunger. They grabbed the cookies, ate them and gulped down the milk.

Mrs. Dolce pointed to her slightly swollen belly, "This here will be eleven. Please, help me. Please."

Linnie tried to explain to her that there was nothing she could do. "But after you have this baby, come to our class. That's where you'll find the help you need."

"He's not a gonna let me go. And I can't keep him off me. I'd like to kill him, that's what." She started to weep.

Linnie put a hand on the woman's bony shoulder. "Do you think the two of you might come to talk to me or to Mrs. Garibaldi in private?"

"No. He thinks you're the devil, teaching the devil's words. He says that big house burnt down 'cause of what you teach."

"I'm sorry he feels that way. If he would listen to us, he might change his mind."

"He ain't gonna do it."

"What about your daughter? The oldest one? Might she come to our classes when we start up again?"

"Dora run away. Took off one night and I don't know where she's at. Now I got to go. I got to be home when Bert comes home."

Mrs. Dolce and her children left.

Two days later Linnie learned that the day following Mrs. Dolce's visit, she fixed supper for her family, went to her bedroom, picked up her husband's shotgun and killed herself.

CHAPTER 52

The State of Washington vs. Hearn and Garibaldi. The charges? Obscenity. Illustrating for public observation the use and purpose of the condom and diaphragm. Bruns Wald would represent the two women. And the women began preparing themselves for time they might have to serve in the county jail.

"We can handle it," said Linnie and Ann agreed.

Bundles of letters, addressed to one or both of them, arrived daily from women, and occasionally from men, who had read *The Woman's Informer,* or had heard the two speak.

Dear Missus Hern and Garbaldee. Ive bornd 11 babies and 6 are mareed. The mareed girls have more and more babies. Ever so often those girls try to get rid of another that's coming. One girl got killt when she tried. I tell the others theyll kill themselvs too but they dont care. They say its better to be dead than having any more and cant raise them with no money. Please help.

Dear Mrs. Hearn.

I'm 11. I've had some schooling. My mother has 9 of us. Two died. Every time my mother has another one she goes nuts and her sister comes and gets her and takes her away and when she comes home it aint long before she's gonna have another one. Pleez help us.

Ugly, anonymous letters came from people demanding that Linnie and Ann stop their "anti-Christ crusade and return to the Lord and bosom of hearth, husband, and home."

Nobody should be surprised to find you two dead. Shame. Shame. Shame on you. You should be locked up in prison or hanged from a rope for the evil you're preaching.

Ann and Linnie found the letters disconcerting, yet stimulating, indicative of the necessity in pursuing their work.

Ten days before the trial, a letter from a Mrs. Trude Bleecker arrived.

Dear Mrs. Hearn and Mrs. Garibaldi:

I'm an older woman and I've studied at one of the Rutgers clinics in Holland. I live in Portland, Oregon, am widowed and have no children. When I heard about your endeavors I decided to write and offer my help. I don't need money. I know how to teach and how to fit women with the diaphragm. At your convenience I'd like to drive to Hanksport to meet you. Sincerely, Trude Bleecker.

Ann answered the letter. *We would like very much to meet you. Unfortunately we go on trial next week and we may be sentenced to jail. We'll contact you after we know our fate.*

Mrs. Bleecker sent yet another letter. *I'll drive up and attend the trial. I enjoy big hats. I think you'll know who I am.*

❧

On the day of the trial, a chill nipped the air. Up on the logged off hills—logged off ten or so years ago—vine maple had turned yellow and rust red.

Roy and Colin had informed their supervisors that they would not work on this day. "If she fires us," said Roy. "So, be it. We'll find work somewhere else."

Colin said, "I've told Mr. Wald that Mide and I want to testify."

"We appreciate that," said Linnie.

In front of the Hanksport County Courthouse a group of women, and a few men, including Paul, Roy and Collin, waved placards and chanted, "Free Mrs. Hearn and Mrs. Garibaldi. Free choice. Free speech. No Surrender."

A knot of folks standing across the street also held placards and called out, "Baby Killers. Baby Killers. Return to Husband, Hearth and Home."

A handsome, well-dressed woman wearing a large, brown straw hat with a plume of white feathers was with the group. She gave a measured nod of her head and Linnie knew her to be Trude Bleecker. Linnie and Ann acknowledged the supportive group, who continued to chant: "Free these women and let them speak. Allow us to learn about birth control. Free these women and let them speak. Allow us to learn . . . ."

Linnie and Ann, accompanied by Bruns, went inside and took their seats at the defense table.

Moments later the Bailiff called out, "All rise."

The Judge entered, sat at the raised bench, picked up the gavel and declared the case would be heard.

The state's attorney, a short, balding man, made opening remarks and read the charges. "Drawing obscene pictures and giving a public lecture about conception is a mortal sin and against the laws of this great state of Washington. This sacred act of creation between husband and wife and their loving God is not meant to be flaunted and advertised."

His dramatic, strong remarks carried a sense of power with argument on the necessity to uphold the laws of the land.

After the state rested its case, Bruns, in a calm even tone, began his plea by submitting a condom as Exhibit A.

"Your Honor," he said, "This item is *legally* used by men in the United States to prevent the spread of venereal disease. Thus, I pose this question. Why is it *illegal* for a husband to use this in order to prevent his wife from conceiving? Why is it *illegal* for a woman to learn *how* to prevent the conception of *unwanted* children?"

"Why is it legal for a wife to be denied choice and, in effect, be bound as chattel to her husband? Birth control has been practiced in Europe for years, and the practice goes hand-in-hand with prosperous, healthy nations. This is exactly what my clients are attempting to teach."

At noon the Judge declared recess, after which he would hear from witnesses, followed by closing arguments.

Mrs. Bleecker, a tall, slender woman of middle age with sharp features, a lively smile and green eyes, was waiting at the rear of the chamber. While she and Linnie and Ann went walking to the city park for a picnic lunch, Mrs. Bleecker said, "The Judge will dismiss this case."

Ann said, "Your certainty delights me. And I have to say that my hopes are higher than I'd expected them to be."

Linnie agreed. "If anybody can tell the truth about all of this in plain language, it's Bruns Wald."

"Good," said Mrs. Bleecker. "I'm staying at the Hanksport Hotel. Assuming all goes well, will you join me for dinner?"

"That will be a treat," said Linnie. Ann agreed.

Linnie likened the gathering at the park to a celebration, but she couldn't shake her unease. The prosecutor's attack supported state laws and for anyone to question or resist those laws meant punishment.

By the time court was ready to reconvene, Linnie noted that Joe and Mrs. Bleecker were engaged in a lengthy and apparently enjoyable conversation. Joe's strained expression, brooding eyes and creased brow, had eased a little.

Back in session, Bruns called Mide to come forward. When she made her pledge on the Bible, her tone was even and firm.

Bruns said, "Mrs. Bede. May I ask how old are you?"

"Twenty-five, sir."

"And how many children do you have?"

"Six, sir. Five living. Before I married, my plan was to have two. My husband and I tried to practice the interruptis method. Neither of us cared for it. I enjoy and I love my husband. It wasn't uncommon for me to want our loving, even knowing we might, once more, have another child. The last birth almost did me in. We learned from Mrs. Hearn about using the condom." Her face flushed a little. "And I continue to enjoy my husband's company."

Bruns thanked her and Mide took her seat.

Colin took the witness stand. In his straightforward way he emphasized the need for education on the subject of sex. "Educated people know about it. Why don't we? You might not have the answer, your Honor, but I believe it's because certain people want to keep us poor and uneducated. It makes us easier to control."

"I love my wife," he said. "And she loves me. We enjoy coupling and I will say this. My wife has always had the final say on this matter."

Linnie was proud of Colin and Mide.

She testified to Dru's shattered dreams, emphasizing drugs and abortions as the cause of her death. And she spoke of Mrs. Dolce's despair and suicide.

The prosecutor's closing arguments emphasized the importance of upholding state laws. "Mrs. Hearn and Mrs. Garibaldi have deliberately broken those laws," he said. "In order to prevent future meddling, put in place to protect American citizens, I'm recommending that Mrs. Hearn and Mrs. Garibaldi be sentenced to a minimum of two months in the county jail."

The Judge leaned forward. "The testimony given today by both the State of Washington and by the defense for these women moves me to say that Court is in recess until tomorrow morning. I need time to deliberate on this matter. Court is adjourned until nine o'clock tomorrow." He banged down the gavel and left the bench.

Linnie, Ann, Bruns and Trude left the Courthouse. Linnie asked Trude if they might postpone their dinner to the following evening. "I'm not feeling as chipper about this as I did earlier today," she said.

Trude said, "We'll have that victory dinner together tomorrow. I feel it in my bones."

❧

The next morning Ann and Linnie, their family and friends once again gathered at the County Courthouse. And once again, a knot of women and a few men had gathered both in support of the two, and those in opposition.

Linnie, Ann and Bruns took their seats.

The State's attorney, looking satisfied, took his seat.

The Judge came in and banged down the gavel. He leaned forward. "The testimony given yesterday moves me to say that I find the charges against Mrs. Hearn and Mrs. Garibaldi disgusting. We live in a world of change. If safe methods of preventing conception are used in Europe, America should pay heed. Therefore, this case is dismissed."

Linnie and Ann left the courthouse and faced a cheering crowd. "No surrender. No surrender."

CHAPTER 53

Burgundy velvet drapes and a rich burgundy carpet gave diners at the Hanksport Hotel a feel of unaccustomed luxury. On this evening the drapes were drawn against the chill. Atop each table low, flickering light from small oil lamps with tasseled shades glowed.

Trude lifted a glass of wine. "Birth control is the ultimate challenge in human destiny," she said.

The women touched their glasses.

Trude continued. "It's going to take a long, up-hill battle to convince the public of this educational need, but women working across America can do it. I want to be part of this work up here with you. I have a dependable Oldsmobile sedan, I enjoy driving and I'm a careful driver. In other words, I can get around."

Ann and Linnie expressed pleasure in having her join them.

❧❧

The following day Linnie picked up Ann and Trude and drove up to the charred skeletal ruin of the Dickerson house. An acrid stink of burnt wood and smoke still prevailed.

"You don't know what caused this fire?" said Trude.

Ann said, "No. Someone opposed to our teaching? Maybe. Opposed to the I.W.W.? Possible. An accident?

Unlikely. The sheriff says they have nothing to go on. But we won't be stopped. We'll build a new clinic here, on this site, as soon as we can."

Linnie said. "We want a quiet place where women will feel at ease. Our mission is to educate poor, uneducated people. Especially women."

"Splendid," said Trude. "Linnie, your brother tells me he enjoys drawing architectural plans. He said that designing the house for you and your late husband gave him great pleasure. Would he consider drawing plans for the clinic?"

"We asked him and he declined. He doesn't approve of our work."

"Do you mind if I ask him? I've run into this kind of attitude before and I can be fairly persuasive."

"Do ask him. He's also a fine carpenter."

Ann said, "We don't have a lot to invest, but we'll build it step by step, as we can."

"I'll be happy to add money to the pot," said Trude.

Linnie told Trude about Druscilla's death. The three agreed, on the spot, to name the new building, "The Druscilla Corrigan Clinic for Women."

"But, Trude," said Linnie. "Don't count on Joe. He's stubborn and sticks to his beliefs without bending."

Trude smiled. "I liked him."

Trude Bleecker took up residency at the Hanksport Hotel.

On Sunday evening, a week after the trial, Trude, seated in front of the fireplace, was engrossed in a story in *The*

Hanksport Weekly Gazette. Gavin Corrigan, Superintendent of Hanksport Schools, was asking Hanksport citizens to pass a bond measure for the purpose of building another grade school at the west end of town.

"Mrs. Bleecker?"

Trude looked up from her reading. "Mr. Bede. Hello."

He had on a brown suit, a white shirt and a yellow tie and he held a brown derby hat in his right hand. His curly red hair was combed flat. His brown eyes held a warm light. "Can I . . . As my guest would you have dinner with me? Here in the dining room?"

"Why, yes," said Trude. "I'd enjoy that very much."

While the two enjoyed a tomato bisque soup, chicken and dumplings and baked beans, Joe told Trude a little about the town. "It's time we have another school," he said. "I hope the people will support Gavin. He's a good fellow."

Over a dessert of peach cobbler topped with whipped cream, Trude said, "Aside from Linnie's house, have you drawn plans for other buildings?"

"No. None of the places I've drawn have come to light." He ducked his head and smiled. "Maybe someday."

"Would you consider drawing up plans for the new clinic? And Linnie said you are a fine carpenter. I'd pay you well, Mr. Bede."

I enjoy doing those things," he said, and he sat in silent reflection.

A tall, thin fellow with brown hair and heavy lidded eyes, and a large, overweight man came in and were seated not far from Trude and Joe. Trude recalled seeing them at the trial. The tall blonde man met her gaze.

"Mr. Bede," said Trude in a soft tone. "Who are the men who just came in?"

Joe clenched his hands. His knuckles turned white. "Soapy Metzler and Kees Strom."

"Friends of yours?"

"No. They stay pretty much to themselves. Mrs. Bleecker, I'll have to think about your offer. In my opinion, you all are speaking against God's teachings. But, I'll ask the Lord to send me a sign."

Trude and Joe finished their dinner and when leaving the dining room Trude glanced again at the two men. Kees Strom stared at her and a chill, like a cold breeze, slipped over her.

Out in the lobby, she and Joe sat in front of the fire. "What can you tell me about this fellow, Kees Strom?"

Joe's manner stiffened. "Not much." He stood up. "Thank you, Mrs. Bleecker, for having dinner with me. I enjoyed it." He put on his hat and left.

Trude enjoyed the warmth of the fire for a few more moments before Kees Strom and his friend passed through the lobby. Again, Kees's heavy lidded eyes met Trude's gaze and again, Trude felt an ice-cold breath of a chill.

❧

For the next two weeks Joe prayed and waited for a directive from the Lord as to what he should do. One night, while sleeping, his mother spoke. *Redeem yourself, Joey. Druscilla was abandoned in part because she had too many children. Linnie wants to educate women like Druscilla. And remember, Joey.*

You are responsible for the death of Birdie Mae's first and only child. Atone yourself for the sin of the loss you caused, Joey. Atone yourself.

Joe sat up. "Yes, Mother," he whispered. "I'll do it. And I'll ask Mrs. Bleecker to pay me with silver money."

CHAPTER 54

In May a sturdy, almost-completed building replaced the shabby old Dickerson house.

Early one Saturday morning Joe was setting two-by-fours atop the uprights enclosing a big wrap-around porch. Trude, seated inside at her desk, opened the door and said, "I'm about to make a fresh pot of coffee. Will you come in and have a cup with me?"

Joe smiled. "Thank you, Mrs. Bleecker. I'd like that." He placed his level atop the rail and eyed it. Good. Straight as an arrow. He'd fashioned every detail of the trim structure with its plank-framed windows, steep roof, and deep porch with care and he was proud of his work.

He put his tools aside and went in to join Trude. Over coffee, she said, "Linnie and Ann and I are so fortunate to have this quite lovely building and you've done a splendid job. Would you consider working for us as its caretaker?"

Joe steepled his long, slender fingers. He smiled. "Why not. I can come up on Sundays after work at Mrs. Strom's, and I can stop by after work at the mill most any day."

Trude's eyes and her smile reflected her pleasure. "Thank you. We're in safe hands."

"Thank you, Mrs. Bleecker. I . . ."

"Please," she said. "Call me, 'Trude.'"

"Thank you." He flushed up. "And why don't you call me, 'Joe.'"

"It's agreed."

That afternoon Joe completed setting the porch rails. Folks had been generous. Newt had forked over $200.00 for whatever was needed. Birdie Mae had donated a dozen new towels, a coffee pot, a tea pot, and two sets of pretty cups and saucers. Mrs. Elser over at Coldsprings had hung new curtains at the windows. And Mame Holm had given the women a parlor table and two parlor chairs. But Joe had shuddered when Kees Strom presented the women with a *Barney & Sons* wood stove.

CHAPTER 55

Aweek prior to the clinic's grand opening Linnie, Ann, and Trude distributed announcements throughout Hanksport County. MOTHERS! DO YOU WANT MORE CHILDREN? IF NOT, LEARN ABOUT FAMILY LIMITATION—BIRTH CONTROL. *Safe information can now be obtained at The Druscilla Corrigan Clinic. Grand opening Saturday, June 10. 1:00 in the afternoon.*

Ann made coffee, Trude counted and stacked registration cards, and Linnie made sure that plenty of pamphlets, books, and copies of *The Woman's Informer* were available and for-the-taking on the wide porch rail.

She went out on the porch to catch her breath. Shortly, she would make her speech, to be followed by Trude and Ann.

A haphazard sun shone through churlish skies. To the north, out by Thimble Creek Meadow, dark clouds had gathered. She seldom allowed herself to think about the meadow, the airy white tent and Frank. She kept memories of him in a place to which she rarely ventured.

Some months ago Bruns told her he'd heard from him and Frank had inquired about her.

"Where is he?" said Linnie.

"With the I.W.W. in Chicago. He spoke of joining the Army."

"Oh, Lord, Bruns. I wish he'd stay with his union work."

"So do I."

Linnie had not inquired about Sophie or the children. If she allowed it, questions nagged her. Had Frank told her the truth? The children really weren't his? Yet Sophie's words, *the children miss you and wonder when they'll see you again,* meant that he was at least a strong father-figure in their lives.

Enough of this musing.

She went out to greet the women coming up the road. She mingled with them and asked about their families. She tried to assure them that she and Mrs. Garibaldi and Mrs. Bleecker, as well as women all across America, were trying to teach people about birth control. Whenever a woman's expression softened a little, Linnie knew she had helped quell the woman's fears.

The speeches and information the three women made went well. Late afternoon and into evening Linnie, Ann, and Trude interviewed clients. "How many children do you have? How many are no longer living? How many babies—we call them fetuses—have you tried to get rid of? Have you birthed any babies too early?"

Out of thirty-five women who attended the class, nineteen, with downcast eyes and flushed faces, asked for one of the small packages wrapped in brown butcher paper and tied with a piece of string.

At seven o'clock that evening, after the last client had left, Linnie, exhausted, but elated, said to Ann and Trude, "We gave a few women peace of mind today, didn't we."

CHAPTER 56

Twice a week, during that spring, summer and early fall, Joe went up to the clinic to keep the wood rack full and tidy, the stove clean, the floors swept and mopped. Working after hours and sometimes into dusk, he built a file cabinet and a coat rack. He also crafted two handsome benches, bolted and held fast out on the porch.

In mid-October, before the onset of snow, Linnie, Ann, and Trude locked up the building and hung a sign on the door: <u>Closed. Will Open Mid-April.</u>

That winter Joe and Trude became well acquainted.

On Sunday evenings, after Joe left work at Mrs. Strom's place, he often stopped by the hotel and he and Trude sat by the fire and chatted and had dinner together. Joe learned that Trude had met her late husband at a dinner party. She had also met Mr. Dobbs, Sophie Krueger, and Margaret Sanger at other events.

"Living in New York was an eye opener," Trude said to Joe. "I saw miles of terrible slums and it wasn't unusual for families with over a dozen children to live in two rooms. After hearing Mrs. Sanger's lectures, I joined her ranks. Then my husband and I moved to Portland and shortly after we'd settled, he died of pneumonia."

"I'm sorry to hear that," said Joe.

"It was a difficult time. But, it's good for me to be helping on this program up here. Someday the practice of birth control will liberate women and give them a real voice in today's world."

During the early blustery days of the following spring, Joe continued his work as custodian. He went further by tilling the ground and planting potatoes, carrots, spinach, and turnips. "Some folks might want to take some vegetables home," he said to Trude. He smiled. "Sure can't hurt to have them available."

Linnie, Trude and Ann applauded his work.

One evening he took an old skid road up through one of the abandoned logging camps. He used to go with his mother, brothers and sisters to a place where tall, leafy monkshood grew in abundance. The dark blue flowers formed an arched hood that concealed two tiny white petals. Joe thought the flowers would look nice on Trude's desk.

At the clinic he put the flowers in a jar, added water and wrote a note. *I hope you enjoy these pretty monkshood. I learned about them from my mother. Your friend, Joe.*

On Friday evening, two days later, Joe returned to the clinic and found two notes propped against the jar.

Dear Joe,

Thank you for the flowers. I enjoy them very much and aren't the shapes of the petal interesting. We can see why it's called monkshood. I enjoy wildflowers. Someday soon we might want to go out together and study them.

Would you care to go over to Coldsprings with me tomorrow? I need to use the public telephone in the Western Union office to make a phone call. Shall we have dinner at the Snoqualmie Hotel? Sincerely, Trude.

Joe's heart spiraled high and he answered Trude's note. *Dear Trude. Yes. After you take care of your telephone business, I'd be honored to take you to dinner. I'll surely look forward to that. Joe.*

The other note was from Linnie. *The tree on the south side of my house is a nuisance and blocks the late afternoon sun. Can you come by and help Father cut it down? I'll have supper waiting. L.*

◐◑

"We'll have that sun-blotter out in no time," Joe said to Linnie.

Felling the tree took longer than he'd thought, but shortly before dark it came down with a thundering crack, an ear-splitting crash and a thick spew of dust.

At supper Joe, feeling as fine and satisfied as he'd felt in his life, told Linnie and his father about Mrs. Bleecker's invitation. "Tomorrow morning I'll buy proper shoes, a new coat and a decent hat for the trip," he said.

"And you'll look every bit the gentleman you are," said Linnie.

"It's nice to see you enjoying Mrs. Bleecker's company," Roy said. His smile indicated his pleasure. "I'm proud of you."

Joe left Linnie's house and started up the hill. He'd go up to the junction just beyond the clinic and on up to Camp Two. His thoughts took him to a new and exciting place. A year ago Ollie Holm had asked him to go into partnership with him in an automobile dealership venture. "There's a lot of money to be made," said Ollie. "Everybody is going to eventually buy an automobile."

Joe declined. He didn't have the know-how for selling automobiles. But now he had gained a sense of self-confidence and he viewed Trude's interest in him as a sign that God wanted him to take a fresh look at his life. If Ollie still wanted him as a partner, Joe would accept, work hard and save his money. If he became successful, he would ask Trude if she would consider marriage. Joe could not recall a time in his life when he had felt so at ease with himself, and so happy.

Halfway up to the clinic and junction just beyond, he stopped. His mouth got dry. His legs got weak. Smoke! No. His imagination was getting the better of him. He did *not* smell smoke. But his senses told him otherwise. Fire!

He raced up the road. Fast. Faster. And the nightmare before him rocked his senses. Fire engulfed the fine, sturdy building. Timbers collapsed. Flames crackled and snapped. The walls caved in and showers of sparks flew up in the sky. And, just as before, Kees and Soapy danced and larked around in the light of the flames.

"No," Joe screamed. He raced toward the two. He kicked them. He pummeled Soapy with his fists. He grappled with Kees, landed a punch to his jaw that sent him spinning and he fell, hard. Kees tried to get up. Joe kicked him. But Joe took a blow to his head and the red canopy of sky dimmed.

Late that night Sheriff Mann knocked on Roy's door. "Roy," he called out. "It's me. Chet."

Roy cracked open the door. "What the hell?"

"This is something you're going to have to handle, Roy, and it's going to be tough. Is Linnie over at her place?"

"Yes. Why?"

"You two are gonna need each other. I've got Joe in jail. Linnie's clinic burnt up and he's the suspect."

❧❧

Dawn broke and in a soft mist of rain Linnie and Roy walked up to the burned out clinic. Trude, Ann and Paul arrived at about the same time. They all stood in stunned silence. Embers winked and pulsed like live things. Linnie picked up an expense ledger. Its leaves crumbled into ashes. She kicked a scorched tea kettle. It landed with a dull thud against the charred ribs of the porch rail. The spokes of Trude's umbrella—the green cloth burnt crisp and black— looked like a pile of porcupine quills.

Roy put his arm around Linnie.

"I can hardly breathe," she said. "But Joe didn't do this."

Trude agreed. "We'll hire Bruns to defend him."

Linnie said, "Bruns is in Boston, taking care of his mother. I'll wire him. We'll ask for a delay until he can be here."

❧❧

Joe wakened and his head felt like a swollen eye. He touched the wrap of bandage around his hairline. His world had doubled. Two windows. Two sets of cell bars. He prayed that what he'd seen was a nightmare so terrible he'd lost his senses. He fell back into a dazed sleep.

Linnie, her family and Trude went to visit him. His swollen eyes looked like ripe plums. His left cheek was bruised. Roy, his face like a closed door, stuck his hand through the bars. Joe took it.

"Son," said Roy.

"I didn't do it, Father."

"We know that. No one who knows you believes that you did it."

"We've wired Bruns," said Linnie. "We want him to defend you."

Trude said, "Joe, after you're a free man, we'll drive over to Coldsprings and have our dinner. And we'll take a picnic and look for wildflowers."

"I'll surely look forward to that."

Linnie went directly to Western Union and wired Bruns. Bruns telephoned the Judge and requested a delay. Bruns wired Linnie. *Mother's death imminent. Will return as soon as possible.* The Judge denied Bruns's request on grounds of an unspecified time for return. Linnie hired Tom Macklin, a reputable young lawyer from Coldsprings, to defend Joe.

Joe Bede was charged with one count of arson for destroying the Dickerson house, one count of arson for burning the clinic, one count of assault on Soapy Metzler and one on Kees Strom.

Every week, on visitor's day, Joe's fellow workers, church folks, family and Trude went to visit him.

"You'll soon be a free man, Joe. . . "

"Nobody in Hanksport County thinks you did those things and . . ."

"Take heart, Joe. The smart lawyer fella will see you get treated right."

During the next two months Linnie and Birdie did not allow their father to eat supper alone.

At Linnie's, late one summer afternoon, he slumped down on Linnie's sofa and she appraised him. Creased brow. Grim mouth. Dull eyes, old and lacking. She fixed a plate of Mame Holm's pickled pig's feet, doused them with hot vinegar and gave them to him. She sat beside him and put an arm around his shoulders. "Mr. Macklin will do a good job of defending Joe," she said. "He'll soon be free. And Trude's friendship means a lot to him."

Roy shook his head. "I'd like to think that Joe and Mrs. Bleecker would marry, and I wish I could believe that Joe will soon be free. But I don't."

"Father, that's a dreadful thing to say. Of course he'll be free. And soon."

Roy had nothing further to say.

This was summer vacation, but at supper Roy asked his grandchildren what they most enjoyed in school.

Softball and working on the school newspaper gave Hugh pleasure. Stella looked forward to music classes. Nell, who was reading a book about African tribes, preferred the quiet time when she could read to herself. Meggie liked "all of school. I love my friends Edna and Violet best," she said. "They're twins. I know which one is Edna and which one is Violet, but nobody else at school knows." She giggled. "It's my very own secret and I just love secrets."

"Edna and Violet?" Roy said to Linnie.

"Crupps," said Linnie. "They live a mile or so up-river."

"Billy is a year younger than me," said Meggie. "He's got a wood leg and sometimes he lets me thump it. We laugh and laugh. At recess I always ask him to play with us. And now, we're not in school, but he sometimes goes to Aunt Birdie's with me and we read to Aunt Baby."

Roy reached across the table and patted Meggie's hand. "I'm glad to know that you're a kind girl," he said. "It's important to be kind to those who aren't as fortunate as you are."

"Oh, Granddad, I do feel like that. We have lots of food and Violet and Edna and Billy don't. But Mama puts plenty of sandwiches and cookies in my lunch bucket and I share with them."

Linnie said, "You're showing good traits of a generous, caring girl, Meggie. That's important."

Later, after Roy helped Linnie clean up the kitchen, and the children were in bed, Linnie settled in her chair, plopped a porcelain egg in the toe of a sock and started to darn.

Sudden. Out of the blue, Roy said, "Joe knows who burned down both buildings."

Linnie set her darning aside and turned to her father. "What in the world do you mean?"

"After the Dickerson fire, he told me he'd seen the men who did it. He said he knew them. But he wouldn't tell me who they were."

"Father! Why not?"

"It had something to do with the Lord and he wouldn't talk about it. I'll bet my life that the same people who burned the big house, also burned the clinic, and Joe knows damned good and well who they are."

"This is crazy. He's got to talk. I'll go see him tomorrow."

❧❧

Joe, shackled at his ankles and accompanied by a pudding-faced deputy, shuffled into the visitor's cell. He was hesitant, his eyes deep sunk. But after the deputy left, he said, "I'm glad you came alone, Linnie. I've got something to tell you and it's between you and me."

Relief washed over her. *He's going to talk. Thank the good Lord, he's going to talk.*

Joe said, "When I worked for Mrs. Strom, she always paid me in silver coins." His expression brightened a bit. "And Trude paid me in silver coins. I buried all of the money in a bag under a pile of rocks not far from the junction. You must find it, Linnie. That money is yours."

"That's generous and I thank you, but you know I get Parley's money every month. After you get out of jail, you should spend it on yourself."

"Parley's money isn't enough to pay for the youngsters' college."

"Right now, college for the kiddies is the last thing on my mind. Joe Bede, you listen to me. Father said that *you know* who burned down the buildings. Is he right?"

"Yes."

"You've got to tell Mr. Macklin."

"If the Lord sees me as innocent, I'll get a sign. Until then, I won't talk about it."

"But the Lord wants to protect the innocent. He doesn't want innocent people to die for other folks' crimes."

Joe's smile was thin. "God knows I saw something I shouldn't have seen and I'm guilty of that. But there isn't anything I can do about it."

"Yes, there is. Tell Mr. Macklin the truth. Tell him what you know and who you saw at the fires."

"I'm sorry. I can't do that."

Tears welled in Linnie's eyes. "Joe Bede, you aren't thinking straight. If you die, God will be mad at you for allowing your own death when you are innocent."

"I haven't got an answer to that."

Her voice rose. "You're living in shadows. You need to think about us. Your family. Father puts up a pretty good face when he comes to see you, but he's a lost soul. He hardly eats. He just sits on his porch. Or mine. Or Birdie's. He doesn't even go fishing anymore."

"I'm sorry about Father, but there's nothing I can do about it."

"Remember when we were young, and I was puzzled about you getting so danged religious? Remember?"

"Yes."

"Once I said I was worried because I thought all of your beliefs about God could get you in trouble some day."

"Yes."

"Well, it's happened."

"This is something between God and me and no one else. I'm sorry. It's just the way I am."

When the jailer announced to Linnie that her time was up, Linnie, feeling as drained as a dried-up creek, left the jailhouse and drove home.

❧

On August 10th, the day of Joe's trial, a steady patter of rain wakened Linnie. By 8:30 the rain had stopped, the sun came out and big-bellied clouds sailed overhead. At 9:00 all of the Bede family, including Baby, and many friends, gathered inside the County Courthouse. Linnie and Birdie had instructed Baby to be quiet. If she made any noise somebody would have to take her home.

But for a whispered remark now and then, the crowd was silent. Joe's lawyer, Mr. Macklin, a bald, intense looking fellow wearing eye glasses, strode in, sat down at the defense table, removed papers from his briefcase and neatly arranged them.

The jury, composed of thirteen men, filed in. Linnie knew none of them and a quick study of them told her nothing. The Prosecutor, a tall, firm-jawed man with the suggestion of swagger, appeared.

Joe, flanked by two deputies, came in from a side door. Once a fine looking man, he now had sunken cheeks, hollow, deep-shadowed eyes and a creased brow. His mouth crimped inward, giving him the expression of an old man. But he held his head high and, wearing the white shirt, a dark suit and navy blue tie Linnie had brought him, he looked as if he was on his way to church.

After taking his seat next to Mr. Macklin, he took a deep breath and stared out the window. He'd not been outdoors for over three months. Outdoors today meant scattered, high clouds, pungent smells of fresh milled wood and the earth, damp from rain. Linnie recalled her own brief hours in jail. There were no words to describe 'freedom,' once it was denied.

The bailiff banged down the gavel. Everyone rose. The Judge, a thin, red-faced man with a bulbous nose came in and declared "The State of Washington versus Joe Bede on two counts of arson and two counts of assault is ready to be heard."

In crisp, confident words, Mr. Leach, the Prosecutor, addressed the jury, "Gentlemen, Mrs. Garibaldi and Mrs. Hearn taught birth control classes up at the Dickerson house. Fire destroyed the building. Mr. Joe Bede built a new clinic for Mrs. Hearn, Mrs. Garibaldi and Mrs. Bleecker. A building used for the specific purpose of teaching citizens methods of birth control. These heretic beliefs and methods are counter to beliefs held by every God-fearing citizen in the United States of America. Explosive devices were used to destroy both places.

"Good citizens, the state will show that Mr. Bede was, and continues to be, fiercely opposed to his sister's work. The motive for this crime was clear. Joe Bede wanted to destroy the foundation of that work. Work, he's detested for years."

The Prosecutor began calling a parade of witnesses. A former bunkmate of Joe's testified that Joe had not slept in his bunk on the night of the Dickerson fire. "He was always at camp at night," the fellow said. "But not then."

"Did he show up for work the next day?"

"Yeah. But he was nervous and not himself."

Kees Strom was called to the stand. He said that no one who knew Joe believed he could have done such terrible deeds. "That's why Mr. Metzler and I were shocked to see him at the fire."

Mr. Leach asked, "And what took you there, Mr. Strom?"

"We'd been up at Camp Five to pick up a corpse. That's a big part of Mr. Metzler's business and I often go with him to help."

Chill settled over Linnie.

"We were on our way home," Kees said. "We saw smoke and a red sky. We tore down the road and came to the burning house. Joe was there. He was watching it. We got out of the auto and he saw us and started to fight us. The thing is, I've been a bunkmate of his for years and the only times I've seen him angry was when something came up about his sister."

Mr. Leach said, "And when that happened, Mr. Strom, how would you describe Mr. Bede's behavior?"

"He hated her speeches. He hated the work she was doing. He said, more than once, that Hanksport County would be a lot better off if she would disappear and do something else."

Joe stood. "Your Honor, sir." His voice trembled. "Your Honor, I've never said . . . ."

The courtroom buzzed. The Judge banged the gavel. "Mr. Bede, you'll have opportunity to speak. Please be seated."

Mr. Leach turned to the jury. "Miracles do happen, but do you really believe that a man, known to have a violent temper, is cured by turning to God? A man who comes from a family who, aside from the accused, is known to be agnostic? A family who has no belief in the Lord and does not attend church?"

The state rested its case.

Mr. Macklin began the defense by recounting how Joe, quite by accident, had stumbled onto the first fire. And in May, the night of the second fire, he left his father's house and was on his way up to Camp Two, where he lived, when he smelled smoke and found the building in flames. He saw the same two men at the Dickerson fire. "Mr. Bede knows who those men were, but feeling that he is obeying God's will, Mr. Bede refuses to identify the men. Furthermore, Mr. Bede, swearing by God's word, says he himself, did not destroy the buildings."

Mr. Macklin asked Sheriff Chester Mann to take the stand.

Chester said, "I've known Joe all of my life. I went to school with him and we were friends. I've hunted with him. Fished with him. I've deputized him and I'd do it again, today. I flat out don't believe he has it in him to burn down buildings. Yes, it's true that when he was a young fellow he had a temper, but he got hold of it. And as far as I know, he doesn't even know how to make explosive weapons. He wasn't ever interested in that kind of thing. He liked to build things and draw. Joe Bede would never destroy buildings."

The strong testimony gave Linnie a ray of hope.

The preacher of Joe's church spoke of Joe's generosity and gentle nature. "As a young man of nineteen, he took on religion and asked the Lord to help him overcome his bad temper. I believe he succeeded."

Trude testified that she had known Joe for only a short time. "When I first met him, I judged him to be a gentleman of integrity. He built the clinic for us and cared for it with a great deal of thought. I've never seen him angry. I might add that it's not unusual for young men to have to learn to curb their anger and frustrations."

Mr. Leach objected. "That comment is not germane to this case and I ask that it be stricken from the record."

The Judge affirmed the request.

Mr. Macklin called Linnie to take the stand.

"What do you recall as happening on the evening of the fire?"

"Joe came by to help our father topple a tree on my property. He was happier than I'd ever seen him. I think he'd come to terms with his feelings about our work. We've all known too many women who've birthed two many children."

Again, Mr. Leach objected. "We're not conducting a class in birth control here in court," he said. "I ask that the remarks be stricken from the record."

Again, the Judge affirmed his request.

On cross examination Mr. Leach called Mrs. Bleecker to the stand.

"Mrs. Bleecker, did Joe Bede approve of the work performed at the clinic?"

"I'm not sure. But he's . . ."

"Please, Mrs. Bleecker. Yes, or no. Did Joe Bede approve of the work performed at the clinic?"

"I don't know. He might not have liked what Mrs. Hearn and Mrs. Garibaldi and I were trying to do, but he's got a right to his own opinions. He's a fine carpenter. And I find it odd and coincidental that Mr. Metzler and Mr. Strom just happened to come by the fire.

"It may be coincidental, Mrs. Bleecker, but the alibi stated by men up at Camp Five stands. We rest the case."

The Judge declared Court would reconvene after the Jury reached a verdict.

❦

The jury was out for two days. On the third day, Court reconvened and the Judge said, "The jury has reached a verdict?"

"We have, your Honor. It's unanimous."

"The defendant will rise." To the jury, the Judge said, "Your verdict?"

"Your Honor, we find the defendant, Joe Bede, guilty as charged on all counts."

The Judge hesitated for just a moment before he said, "Mr. Bede, you are sentenced to serve five years in McNeil Island prison. This case is dismissed."

Linnie closed her eyes. This was wrong. So awfully, awfully wrong.

❧❧

Early the following morning once again Chet Mann knocked on Roy's door. Roy opened it and Chester said, "I'd like to come in."

"I'd say by looking at you that you've got rotten news."

Chester came in and took hold of Roy's shoulder. "Brace yourself, Roy."

"I did that two months ago."

"Joe hanged himself. One of my deputies found him early this morning."

Roy, his face pale as death, sat. "My God," he said. "My God. My God."

❧❧

Joe's family, Trude and Joe's fellow workers and friends gathered up at the Hanksport Cemetery. Preacher at First Baptist officiated. Linnie had no idea what he said. When Joe was laid to rest beside his mother, Linnie put a lovely drawing he'd made of her house in the casket with him.

A few thin voices sang, "Rock of Ages, Cleft for Me . . ." Linnie stood, dry-eyed. Trude took hold of her hand and Trude's hand trembled a little.

CHAPTER 57

Some six months after Joe's execution, on a day when a chilly drizzle fell from gun-metal skies, Ollie Holm drove up to Linnie's house. "I'm here to talk to you about an idea Mame and I have come up with."

Linnie made a pot of fresh coffee and sliced some banana cake she had made last evening.

Ollie sat down at the dining table. "Is it alright if I smoke?"

"Of course."

He struck a match and lit his pipe. He drew on it and looked around the room. "This surely is a comfortable place," he said.

"I can't imagine living anywhere else. And Joe added a couple of lovely touches only he could do." She pointed to the kitchen counters. "Those and a nice breadboard."

Ollie sat back in his chair. "Linnie, dear. Anytime you and Ann and Mrs. Bleecker want to start up your clinic again, the upstairs rooms above our store are yours. Rent free. Mame and I have done pretty well with the hardware business, with my dealership and Mame's restaurant. We'd like to help you out."

"That's generous, Ollie. Trude wants to get back to work, but Ann and I are nervous about it. Whoever set those fires is still out there. Whoever murdered Mr. Dickerson and Mr. Knef is probably still out there, too. And I agree with

Trude. It's very strange that Kees and Soapy just *happened* to come by the fire. I also find it disturbing that Kees claimed that Joe said Hanksport County would be a lot better off if I wasn't around. That just doesn't sound like Joe. And when Joe tried to object to Kees's statement, he found he couldn't and he clammed up tight."

"I've thought about that. Kees's and Soapy's presence at the fire is terribly coincidental, but loggers up at Five supported the alibi. Suspicions and conjecture are fine, but something solid has to come up in order to launch any kind of investigation. However, your fears are just what the crazy damned fool, or fools, want and you're playing right into their hands by not continuing your work. Now, you've got lots of community support out there. More than you realize. And the space Mame and I are offering is yours when you're ready."

"That's a generous offer. I'll talk to Ann and Trude. We'll see. Joe's death left a big hole in my heart. And in Trude's. He was such a . . . dang it, Ollie. He was such a foolish innocent."

"He was. Now, there's something else you should know. When Frank was around, he and Mame and I formed a business partnership. He owns stock in the hotel and we three own considerable property around here. Before Frank was shipped overseas, he wrote Mame and me and asked us to . . ."

"Frank's overseas?"

"Yes. He was sent over about 6 months ago. Anyway, he wrote and asked us to do whatever we could, to help you with your work. He asked me to tell you, 'No surrender.' And consider this. The upstairs of the hardware store, as location for a clinic, is a lot more convenient for lots of folks than the Dickerson site."

Linnie toyed with her teaspoon. " 'No surrender' I need to remember that."

"Good. That's what he'd want you to say."

☙❧

That evening Linnie told the children about Mr. and Mrs. Holm's offer. But for Meggie, they agreed it was a good idea. "The bad men will come and hurt you," she said.

Linnie reached over and took her hand. "No, they won't. They're cowards and I'm not. And I'm tougher than they are, too."

Meggie got up and put her arms around Linnie. "I don't want anything bad to happen to you."

"It won't. I promise."

CHAPTER 58

On a cold Sunday afternoon in November, a month after Ollie had visited Linnie, she and Ann, Trude, Bruns, Ollie and Mame sat in the Holm's front parlor. A fire snapped and snapped in the fireplace. Mame poured tea, offered brandy, and passed a plate of sliced dried apples dusted with sugar.

Bruns knocked the dottle from his pipe into the fireplace. "Ladies," he said, "Next spring you will open your new clinic above the hardware store. Folks are pleased, but here are a few repeated words of caution. Because of the Comstock Laws, you must *not* charge fees for any information you utter in speech, or hand out in print. None. If you do, you'll be arrested for selling obscene information and probably slammed into jail. Further, each and every woman who comes in the door asking for advice must sign a paper stating that she's married. And she must *show* proof with a Certificate of Marriage. If you give any information to unmarried women you'll find yourselves locked up quicker than you can blink an eye."

It was agreed.

Ollie said, "Over the last two years, the three of you have paid expenses out of your own pockets. Mame, will you tell them about a new plan we have to offer?"

Mame smiled her pretty smile and, as was her habit, flush rose in her face. "I'll be glad to." She put down her cup and picked up a letter. "Last week Ollie and I had this message from Frank. He asked us to set up a trust fund for the sole purpose of educating women up here. He asked us to serve as trustees. After he learned about your determination to proceed with your plan, he asked that we set up another trust, enabling you three to receive financial compensation."

Mame read from the letter, *"Please tell them. 'No surrender.' They will face obstacles they've never dreamed of. But no surrender. If they are arrested and sent to prison, 'no surrender.' They can do it."*

A sense of wonder settled over Linnie. Because of Frank, her dream of so many years to educate poor, isolated women was now possible. Frank, who had listened to her and worked with her and taught her so much, had not forgotten her concerns and hope that one day she'd be able to reach these women. She would heed his advice: 'No surrender.'

Ann said, "Mame, where is Frank?"

"In France. Linnie, he always asks about you. In his last letter he asked if you had re-married."

Ann said, "And Sophie and the children? How are they?"

Mame said, "Oh, Sophie and Frank haven't been together since Frank left here. Sophie joined the Communist party and I think she and her children live in Russia."

For Linnie, the question loomed. Had she made a terrible mistake in refusing to believe Frank? *Those children aren't mine. I've never even adopted them.* She tucked the thought away. She had work to do.

CHAPTER 59

A discreet sign posted on a door of Ollie and Mame's building read: *The Druscilla Corrigan Clinic for Women. 9:00 a.m. — 3:00 p.m. Closed Sundays and Mondays.* An arrow pointed upstairs. The clinic had been open for a year and a half. It had gone well.

Two large windows in the reception room overlooked the street. The room was furnished with half a dozen ladder-back chairs, a woodstove, a coat rack and a desk. The women's desks and client files sat in a second room. Trude fitted women with diaphragms in a third room, close-curtained for privacy.

On Monday mornings Linnie took advantage of the relative quiet to work at her desk on *The Woman's Informer.* She usually composed it at the clinic and printed it on the press at home.

During the week, after school was dismissed, Meggie, now in fourth grade, came by and waited for Linnie and the two drove home. Stella, Nell and Hugh, often involved with school activities, came later, but Linnie insisted that they be home before dark.

On a warm day in September with a haze of smoke in the air, Linnie finished outlining her column, stoked the fire and put an old battered copper kettle on the stove. Down on the street below, a team of horses pulling a wagon piled with lumber raised a cloud of dust. Folks came and went at the A.D. Dry Goods Store. An occasional auto rattled by. Directly across the street a fellow was putting a coat of white paint on Bruns Wald's large, new two-story house. His law office was attached to the south side. A dray hauling barrels of beer clunked slowly up the street to The Blackduck Saloon. Kees Strom and Soapy Metzler, in Kee's shiny Oldsmobile, pulled up and stopped in front of Soapy's funeral parlor.

Linnie recalled Trude's comments of a few days ago. "The other day I happened onto Mr. Strom at the drug store," she said. "I said, 'Mr. Strom, isn't it nice that we've not had any more buildings firebombed.' He asked me what I'd meant by my remark. I asked him if he enjoyed the sight of fire. He said, 'Mrs. Bleecker, it's not your business what I enjoy and what I don't enjoy.' Oh, my, I dislike that man."

Linnie told her father about her and Trude's suspicions. Roy said much the same as Ollie had said, "Until something solid comes along, there's nothing we can do. But I have a hunch that one day something will turn up and Joe will be found innocent."

The sharp blast of the noon whistle brought Linnie out of her reverie. She took her cup to her desk and re-read a few letters of the past month. Anonymously published in *The Women's Informer,* they gave gritty substance to what Linnie, Trude, and Ann were trying to do.

A poignant letter, received last week, read: *Deer Missus. Im 26 or 27. I live up blackduck valley. My baby is coming most anytime, I have 8. Ive had 4 not live and when my belly gets big I cant move my feet and arms rite. I went to a doctor and he got mad and said I shouldnt have anyothers. I asked how and he said to tell my husbnd to inturupt. what does that mean. pleese help me. I dont . . .*

Linnie heard somebody come up the stairs. She set her work aside. A tall, slender woman wearing a deep-brimmed straw hat came in. "Excuse me, Ma'am," she said softly. "I need help."

"I'm sorry, but we're closed on Mondays. Didn't you see our sign?"

"Yes, Ma'am. But today's the only day I could come to town." With shy, tentative steps she approached Linnie. "My name is Susan Scott. I've got seven children and another just on the way. I'll get rid of this one myself, unless you can help me."

"It's unwise to 'get rid of a baby.' We can advise you about preventing another pregnancy, but that's all we can do."

"That will help."

"Are you married?"

"Oh, yes, Ma'am. Here's my marriage paper." She dug into a little cloth purse, took out a paper and put a certificate on Linnie's desk.

Linnie glanced at it. "Yes. Well, come see us after you've had your child. Right now, there's nothing we can do."

"Do you have something—anything—I can read to help me learn about all this? Something—anything—I can show my husband?"

"Yes. Of course."

Linnie took two pamphlets and a copy of *The Women's Informer* from a drawer. She offered them to the woman. "I hope you and your husband find them helpful. In our publication we try to give as much detail as we feel is appropriate."

"Oh, thank you. Thank you, Mrs. Hearn. How much?"

Linnie waved her off. "Nothing. They're free."

"Oh, my goodness. Thank you." Susan Scott put three pennies on Linnie's desk.

Linnie felt a pang of compassion for the poor woman. Her little and third fingers on both hands were webbed.

A week later seven women seated in the reception room at the clinic waited to be seen. Linnie was interviewing a woman from Coldsprings when a rustle of commotion interrupted her. Startled, she looked up from her work. Four dark suited men strode in and took off their hats. "Mrs. Hearn," said one of the men, his voice strong and hard. "We are Federal Marshalls." He showed Linnie his badge. "We're arresting you, Mrs. Hearn. We're also arresting Mrs. Garibaldi and Mrs. Bleecker for violating Section 1142 of the Penal Code forbidding the sale of indecent written material."

Anger and disgust rippled up Linnie's spine. She slapped a file down on her desk. "The pennies," she said. She pumped her fist high. "No surrender. You can put us in prison, but we will not surrender."

Once again, all of the literature, contraceptive supplies and case histories were swept into boxes and taken to a patrol wagon. Once again the women were hustled out into a waiting automobile. This time, without a chance to contact family or friends, they were driven to Seattle and booked into jail on the fourth floor in the Seattle Municipal Building on Yessler Way.

When a deputy tried to finger-print the women, the women balled their hands tight. "We are *not* felons. We will not be finger-printed. We will not surrender."

The following day Paul, Birdie Mae, Newt and Roy drove down to the city. Birdie brought Linnie a thick quilt, warm clothes and three of her favorite books, Somerset Maugham's *Of Human Bondage,* Jane Hull's *Twenty Years at Hull House*, and Theodore Dreiser's *The Genius*.

"How are the children?" Linnie asked Birdie.

"Hugh, Stella and Nell understand why you're here. Meggie doesn't. She fusses and worries. And she wants a horse of her own. Colin has a young mare he's willing to part with. What do you think?"

"Get it for her, Birdie. And try to assure her that I'm doing important work for young girls who will soon become women."

"I'll do the best I can. She named the horse Stripe because of a long, white stripe on her nose."

Linnie smiled. "A nice name, isn't it. And so like our Meggie. If we're sentenced to prison, or to the workhouse, don't try to drive down again. Please. It's more important for you to stay with the children. We'll be alright."

The following day a sizeable group of women, and a few men, including Roy, Colin, Newt, Ollie and Paul, all carrying placards, stood in front of the Building. BIRTH CONTROL EDUCATION FOR ALL. FREE OUR THREE TEACHERS. WE WON'T GIVE IN. NO SURRENDER. Then, folding their signs, the group went inside.

In the courtroom the District Attorney, Ward Simpkins, said to the Judge, "Just as God rules the world, so does a husband rule his household and wife. Most husbands and their wives—most American people—rightfully believe that methods of birth control are sinful and wrong."

Mr. Simpkins produced a copy of *The Women's Informer* from which he read instructions on how to use a condom for preventing conception. "Your Honor," he said, "it's perfectly clear that selling this type of material, even for three cents, violates the law."

Bruns, arguing that the Comstock laws were obsolete, pointed out that "The citizens of Europe are far more advanced than the self-righteous attitudes of most Americans toward married cohabitation." He called women to the stand who gave stark testimony to the necessity of learning about birth control.

One woman, unable to care for her nine children, put four of them in an orphanage. "Couldn't do nothin' else. Don't figure I'll ever know them."

Earnestine Smit told the Judge that birthing eleven children had not only broken her, but her husband "deserted me after I didn't allow him any more of me," she said in a stiff manner of speaking.

Lottie Haag made a well-spoken, but tearful plea. "I'm a spinster," she said. "Of my own choosing. My sister had six children within eight years. She learned about the seventh and she took her own life and three of her children. All girls. Your Honor, many women need to learn what Mrs. Bleecker and Mrs. Hearn and Mrs. Garibaldi can teach us."

By the third day of the trial the protesters in front of the courthouse was sizeable and the courtroom was packed. On the fourth day the Judge called for order. He looked out over the crowd packed into the courtroom. "I'm sure," he said, "that nobody in here, or out in front, wants to see these women sent to the Crooked Neck Workhouse."

A sharp ray of hope plucked Linnie's heart. She sat forward.

The Judge said, "Mrs. Hearn, Mrs. Garibaldi, and Mrs. Bleecker, I would like nothing more than to see you released. Today. Do you not agree?"

The women sat, silent and motionless.

"You are free to leave this courthouse on three conditions," said the Judge. He allowed a good moment of silence before he continued. "You are free to leave if you promise here today, publicly and openly, that you will obey the laws of this land. You will refrain from speaking publicly on this subject from this day forward. You will close your clinic immediately. And you will not resume your teaching in any fashion. If you promise to take these three steps, you are here and now, released. You are free."

Linnie asked to be heard. Her request was granted. "Your Honor, I speak for the three of us. You say that under certain conditions, set out by you, your Honor, we would be free. But free to do what? Teach about birth control? Pass out literature? Speak out on a subject that would help women? Offer classes? Free to do all of those things only to land in jail or The Crooked Neck Workhouse? Free to build another clinic, only to stumble around in scorched remains? Free to protect records, important to a woman's health? No. Freedom doesn't apply to American women who want to educate poor, uneducated Americans. Women are not free to speak out and make choices about having children. Your Honor, men in power and acting in the name of Christianity will see to that."

"No, we will not obey a law we don't respect. We will serve our sentence and when released we will continue to speak out and teach about birth control. We will not surrender."

The Judge said, "Mrs.Hearn. Mrs. Garibaldi. Mrs. Bleecker. On this 16th day of October you are sentenced to serve six months in the Crooked Neck Workhouse for Women." He banged down the gavel. "Court is adjourned."

A woman sitting in the front row of the chamber slipped out the door. Linnie did not hear her shout out the verdict, but she heard the crowd chant, "Shame on the Judge. Shame on the Judge."

The women were taken to a paddy wagon. "No need to get into the cage," a deputy said. "Sit in the back seat."

Two armed guards sat up front. The trip through deep woods often skirting Puget Sound took over an hour. The wagon pulled up in front of two long, gray, two story concrete buildings with barred windows. It stood on a high point of land above the Sound and in its fifty-two years of operation, nobody had escaped.

A matron, wearing a badge on her dark blue dress, took Linnie, Ann and Trude to a large room in which six bath tubs lined one wall. Linnie caught the strong scent of Lifebuoy soap. Four light bulbs in the ceiling did little to heighten light from a narrow band of windows high on the walls.

Another matron appeared and the two whacked off the women's hair. After Linnie, Ann and Trude finishing bathing, each was given a gray, wool sack dress. Slippers, made of strips of thin rope, pinched Linnie's feet. The three were separated.

Linnie was taken to the bottom half of a chilly, two-tiered cell. A bucket of water stood in one corner. A thin gray blanket covered a metal bed frame bolted into the concrete floor.

"You will come to supper," the matron said. "Daylight, from seven o'clock to five o'clock in the afternoon, you will sew dresses and undergarments. You will clean cells. Hallways. The Common room. Dining room. Kitchen. You will swab out latrines at each end of the halls. You will do your share of cooking and serving food. If it was up to me, I'd see you stoned to death." The matron spat at Linnie's feet. "Shame on you."

Linnie, Ann and Trude had other plans.

Bruns visited each of them the following day.

"No, Bruns," said Linnie. "We will not appeal. If we go on a hunger strike and refuse to work, our efforts might get the attention it needs. Months ago we decided that if we were arrested again, we'd do just that. We start today."

Bruns paled. "For God's sake, don't go on a hunger strike. No work is fine, but you have no idea how sick you'll get if you refuse to eat. I guarantee you'll be force-fed and that's a living hell that can end in death."

"We're determined, Bruns. We won't change our minds. We will *not* surrender."

There was little relief from the smells of Lysol and the chill of the place. All inmates, wearing the sack dresses and rope slippers, gathered in the common room for meals. Bread, coffee and cold mush or scrambled eggs for breakfast. Mid-day supper, a watery stew. Canned peas or string beans. Potatoes. At the end of the day, bread. Canned peaches or applesauce. Silence was the rule. Spoons scraped against the metal plates.

Linnie, Ann and Trude appeared at each meal and sat with their hands in their laps. They drank the water. They ate nothing.

All inmates gathered in the common room to work from seven in the morning until noon and from one o'clock until six. Talk, speech, singing was forbidden.

Sewing. All inmates pumped on the treadles of the sewing machines and guided the cloth under the needle. Seams and hems on hundreds of sack dresses and big aprons. Linnie, Trude and Ann, each seated at a machine, kept their folded hands in their laps.

They refused to cook in the big, chilly kitchen. A matron dealt sharp, stinging slaps to their faces. The three didn't bend. They refused to clean, pick up a broom or a mop. They were taken back to their cells and their arms were chain-locked to one of the higher bars, a torture exquisite in pain to the arms, the neck and head. The three endured.

At some point, Linnie lost track of time. Needle-sharp pains pierced her belly. One day, too weak to leave the thin mattress on the iron frame, she was surprised to see Birdie float in between the bars. Linnie sat up. "Birdie! You came alone? Where are the children?"

"You've got to stop this awful business."

"No. Bruns came. I think I . . . told him . . .I'm bald. A cap. I wish I had one of your knit caps."

Birdie disappeared.

Tosstles came in and gave her a package and she opened it and she picked up a blue knit cap. "Thank you," she whispered.

Linnie was home, but why couldn't she hear the flume bell? "Father," she cried. "Bell's down. There's trouble upstream." A burnt man floated by. "Do you know who he is?" she called out. "Do you?" And here came Kees holding a picnic basket. "Please, share my picnic with me. I want to be your friend. I like to look at corpses. No, I don't know why." Long sleeves of flames shot up behind him and he disappeared. She was in Frank's tent. "Tomorrow I have to go to Seattle," he said. "Let's both go," she said. He floated away. Parley, his eyes like gold balls, sat down beside her. "I've got to talk to you," he said. "Just you and me." Linnie whispered, "You want to tell me about Baby, don't you. Well, Baby had a beautiful little girl and I named her Meggie, and I love her and she loves us all and yes, that includes Baby. Meggie believes that Baby is her aunt and we allow her to think this, but someday we must tell her the truth. Can you be with me when I tell her? Oh, I hope so. I . . ."

Linnie was back in her cell. A tall, thin woman with a beaky nose and ice blue eyes came in. A big, tubby man with blotched, drooping cheeks and arms big as logs was with her. "You're sick," he shouted. "You're sick. Sick." He and the woman wrapped Linnie in a tight blanket. ". . . can't let her die, can we," said the man.

"Sinful women," said the woman. "All three should die."

"Well, we did the others too and now . . ."

Linnie, unable to move in the tight blanket. . . oh, yes, a straight jacket was what it was . . . clamped her mouth shut tight. Fingers pried her lips open. A sharp ache shot through her head. A fire-like pain burned her ears. She clenched her jaws. Something hard and cold parted her teeth. A thick liquid was plunged down her throat. She gagged and swallowed. Plunge. Gag. Swallow. Sleep. The woman and man came back. Again. And again. Pry. Plunge. Gag. Swallow.

Wretched nausea. Vomiting into the bucket. Again. Again and again.

Day after day the forced feeding. Was it raw eggs . . . the thick warm liquid forced down her throat? Gag. Swallow the awful stuff. Vomit. Try to vomit in the bucket. Sometimes couldn't make it. Aching, weak limbs. Cold. Always cold.

And one day, sleep. Blessed sleep wrapped her. Sleep. Blessed sleep.

❧❧

The touch on her shoulder was gentle. "Mrs. Hearn. Mrs. Hearn. Merry Christmas, Mrs. Hearn."

Linnie opened her eyes.

A nurse's white flat hat floated above her. "Oh, Mrs. Hearn, I'm so glad you're awake."

A crucifix loomed on a gray wall. "Where am I?" Linnie whispered. "Where are Ann and Trude?"

"You're all here in Providence Hospital. You were brought by ambulance."

"From where?"

"From Crooked Neck. People want to see you. You were released early."

"Early?"

"Yes. Your attorney got your six month sentence reduced to two. It's December 15. And you're famous, Mrs. Hearn. You and Mrs. Bleecker and Mrs. Garibaldi. You're really famous."

Linnie wakened to sounds of rustling paper. Across the hospital room Bruns was leafing through a notebook. "Bruns?"

He put his papers aside.

She touched her cap. "Am I still bald?"

"You'll want to wear the cap for awhile."

She touched her throat. "It feels blistered."

"Don't try to talk. You'll feel better in a few days."

"My family? And Trude and Ann?"

"Your family is fine. You won, Linnie. All three of you are free."

Linnie closed her eyes for a moment. A dark wing of fear hovered over her. "Bruns?"

"Yes."

She tried to sit up.

"Don't," said Bruns. "You need to rest and you're doing fine."

She collapsed back on the pillow. "I have to talk to Father. Somebody is out to get the children. Father. Me. You. Trude and Ann. I've got to talk to Father."

Linnie reached out and took her father's hand. She whispered, "With Parley's money and my own you don't have to stay on with Strom anymore. I need your help. I don't want the children walking home from school alone. Whoever set the fires, also devised the trick for Susan Scott. They're after all of us. Trude, Paul, Bruns, Ann. All of us. I need . . ."

"Shhh, shhh," Roy said. "I quit Strom right after the trial. Newt, Birdie or I take the children to school and pick them up afterwards. Day after tomorrow, Bruns and Paul will bring all three of you home." He leaned over and kissed her forehead. "I'm proud of you, Daughter."

CHAPTER 60

Frenzied snow ticked against Linnie's front window. Wind whistled around the eaves. The flume bell was silent. Logging operations had ceased.

Ann and Trude had fared a little better than Linnie and they often drove over to visit her. They all wore knit caps. Stick thin, their faces gaunt with hollow cheeks, they sipped tea and talked about going back to work. "When," not, "if." But the clinic remained closed.

Now, slowly, bent like an old woman, Linnie eased herself up from her chair in front of her parlor fireplace, stoked the fire and went to her kitchen. After pouring herself a cup of tea, she held the cup close to her face, inhaling the steam and savoring the warmth.

She'd been home from the hospital for almost two months and she spent most of her days in front of the fire. She was cold. Always cold. Violent shivers often overcame her. She often found it hard to breathe. She'd lost all sense of taste and smell. She seldom left home.

She glanced at the clock. Two-thirty. In a little over an hour the children and her father would be home.

She set her cup down, wrapped her shawl tight and went to the front window. It had stopped snowing and weak sunlight shone over the broad reach. Not far from Linnie's front door a large cedar tree, burdened by heavy snows, had fallen. Ice and snow crusted the enormous, tangled root wad. Come spring the pale, green fronds of bracken and fern on the wad would emerge. Tough, thought Linnie. Not easily destroyed.

She pulled her cap tight and put on a pair of thick wool gloves. She took Joe's old sheepskin coat from a peg and slipped it on. Sinking her chin into the fuzzy, thick fleece she set out for the barn. The low arc of winter sun broke out from behind a cloud's black wing.

Her boots squeaked in the snow. A walk in snow. The smell of snow. Tea with Frank in the little café. A sleeping cat. *I like winter. The smell. Cold and clean.*

That was long ago.

A stiff wind slapped against her face. At the barn she pulled the door open—a feat that left her exhausted— peered into the low light and went inside. Leaning into Stripe's long, warm neck, she cried, "Oh, Lord. I've lost my stuffing." With her fingers she combed Stripe's coarse, black mane.

Stripe's calm warmth seemed to steady her turbulent thoughts. What had Frank said all those years ago? *You mentioned your sister, Druscilla. You could give her no finer tribute.*

Dru, the lovely, young girl who had sung at weddings, funerals, and Fourth of July picnics. A trusting young girl devastated by a husband, the handsome, dashing gambling man, who had deserted her and their three children.

Lantern light cast shadows on the thick timbers Parley had hewn all those years ago. *Go to Seattle and learn what you need to learn . . .*

She straightened. "No surrender," she whispered. She stroked Stripe's muzzle. "No surrender."

She climbed the loft. She struggled to toss a bale of hay down close to Stripe's stall. She climbed down and pulled off a flake. She used a pitch fork to break the ice in the water trough. And she left the barn. She had cared for Stripe. She had done something.

Snow sifted down from the trees and she, buffeted by the high wind, stopped for a moment to look out over the snow covered reach, brilliant at this moment, with the low winter sun. She vowed to give herself back to her family. She vowed to trump her fears and get back to work. *No Surrender.*

At the house she washed up and stoked the fires in the kitchen and parlor. After pouring milk into a pan, she added a little honey and set it on the stove. This year, until this moment, she'd not made the winter-after-school-treat for the children.

She sat down to rest. She couldn't remember when the spindle-legged trestle up on Wildcat Mountain had been repaired and the mill up at Camp Five had started up again. Long long ago, while Parley was still alive? Or maybe after she'd moved into her house?

Who tended the flume bell now? She had a vague notion that somebody across the river tended it. Colin? Yes. Colin and Mide lived in a newer place and Colin was tender on this stretch of the Blackduck River.

She went to her bedroom closet, reached up and took a box from a shelf. She opened it and lifted out Dru's rabbit-skin muff and the scarf. She wrapped them separately in tissue, labeled one for Nell, one for Stella, and put them at their places on the table.

It wasn't long before her father, with Stella, Nell, and Meggie crossed the reach. Hugh, editor of the school newspaper, had Linnie's permission to come home a little later.

Roy and the children came up on the back porch and stomped their feet. Their banter and laughter chimed like bells.

"Stella's got a boy friend," Nell sang.

Stella laughed. "Cecil Collier hangs around you like a bur caught on your coat."

"I have a boy-friend, too," Meggie said. "Billy Crupps is my boy-friend."

"That's right," said Nell. "We all have boyfriends."

"I hope Mama is feeling better," Meggie said.

Roy said, "After she reads her mail, I have a hunch she will."

They trooped inside and, with anxious eyes, looked at her. "Take off your wraps," she said. "I've made our winter treat."

"Wonderful," said Nell. "I've always loved coming home in winter and having that to drink." She picked up the package at her place. "What's this?"

Stella picked up hers. "A present!"

"Open and see," said Linnie.

"Oh," said Stella. She lifted the scarf from the tissue. "This belonged to Mother. I remember when she got it and Nell, she put it on and picked you up and we danced around the room. All of us. And we sang 'Jingle Bells.'"

Meggie said, "Didn't I get to dance, too?"

"You weren't born yet," said Linnie. "After you were born, we all danced."

Stella wrapped the scarf around her neck. "Oh, so nice, Auntie. When I move to the city and become a famous singer, I'll wear this scarf and a long fur cape. Thank you. Thank you."

Nell snugged her hands into the muff. "I wonder if Eskimos wear fur muffs. I don't think so, but someday, when I'm a famous anthropologist, I'll visit the Eskimo people.Yes, Auntie, thank you. Where have these things been all these years?"

"In my closet. I knew I'd give them to you when you were old enough to appreciate them. Your mother would want you to have them."

"Where's mine?" said Meggie. "Why didn't she want me to have one, too?"

"Auntie Dru left here before you were born," said Linnie. She poured the honey-milk into thick cups and they all sat at the table. "Now, all of you, tell me about school today."

Roy sat back, fattened his pipe and smiled.

Meggie would soon read *The Secret Garden* aloud to her class. Stella had been asked to sing "The Star Spangled Banner" at the next school assembly. And Nell was reading a book about American Indian culture. It had been a long time since Linnie had heard such laughter, warmth, and love inside her house.

Roy handed Linnie a canvas bag. "Lots of letters," he said.

Five days a week they came. Invitations to speak. Invitations to be a dinner guest at a party. Invitations to attend a suffragist rally. Ann, Trude and Linnie had not felt strong enough to accept. Not yet.

She opened the bag, leafed through a dozen letters, paused and looked closely at a letter with Frank's handwriting. "Excuse me," she said to her family. Letter in hand, she went to her room and sat down on the old platform rocker.

October 20, 1918 -

Dear Linnie;

Responding to my inquiry Bruns wrote that you have not re-married. While it's presumptive of me, I hope you will read this letter. I also learned, from Bruns, about your hunger strike. I hope all of you have recovered. He says you have, but I would like to hear this from you. Hunger strikes are vicious, as you now know.

I'll soon be shipped home, but I have to spend a little time in a hospital. I have what's called 'battle fatigue.' After I'm discharged I plan to settle in Seattle. I'll be driving up to see Ollie and Mame. May I come by to call on you?

I want to write so much more. Bruns wrote that you know about Sophie and her children. I have no attachments to her, or to anyone, and I love you as I always have. Please answer this letter, even if it's to tell me not to write to you again.

Yours always, Frank.

Holding the letter close to her breast, Linnie closed her eyes and for the first time in years she allowed herself to think about him. The way he looked at her while making love. The taste of him. The touch of his beautiful hands and how well and complete he had loved her. His laughter, warm and strong. His profound good mind and beliefs. Honesty, courage and tenacity. *No Masters. No Gods. No Surrender.*

CHAPTER 61
SPRING - 1919

Hanksport gained another bank, the new grade school, an Episcopal Church and a boarding house. Strom Lumber Company purchased two large tracts of timber, including a logging camp two miles east of Sunnydale Valley.

Classes at *The Druscilla Corrigan Clinic* had grown and now, with the Great War over, Linnie sensed a feeling of well-being. Women, whom she recognized as former clients, appeared less anxious. The warmth of spring and steady correspondence with Frank brought her renewed strength. And while she still tired easily, she enjoyed her work.

In late May, Ann drove down to Seattle to visit her mother and participate in a suffragist conference. She would be gone for a week.

One bright, windy day Linnie opened a letter addressed to *Missus Hern, Missus Garbald Missus Bleekr,* signed by *Missus Tibbs.* Mrs. Tibbs wrote about herself and five other women whose husbands worked for Strom. They lived in the logging camp east of Sunnydale Valley and among them had a total of 32 children. *Will you all three come to my house on Monday morning and tell us about this birth control? We need so bad to learn what to do. We'll serve coffee and cake. Thank you. Mrs. Agnes Tibbs.*

On that Monday afternoon Meggie was to play the part of Little Red Riding Hood in a school play. While Linnie was committed to see the performance, she and Trude decided to act on Mrs. Tibbs's request. Trude would gather up pamphlets and copies of *The Women's Informer,* drive over to the camp, and talk to the women.

Before leaving town that morning, she said to Linnie, "I'll be back no later than three o'clock"

Linnie said, "The children are spending the night at Newt and Birdie's. I'll join you for dinner at Mame's."

"Yes. Good idea. I'll have lots to tell you."

Meggie was excited about the play. Birdie made a red, hooded cape for her to wear and Meggie, who was learning how to bake, baked a batch of sugar cookies. After she picked a bouquet of violets that grew beside Linnie's front door she tucked the cookies and bouquet into a wicker basket and was ready to play her part.

Linnie enjoyed the play and felt a fine burst of pride. Meggie displayed genuine distress for the grandmother and her voice soared high with fear and horror when she learned that the wolf had eaten her. Meggie's concern for those like the Krup's boy would no doubt lead her to find and enjoy a life helping others.

Mid-afternoon Linnie was back at her desk, waiting for Trude's return. She took Frank's latest letter from a pretty, blue and white letter box. She re-read it.

May 4, 1919

My darling girl,

Your good letters give me such happiness and I read them every day, several times over. I'm so proud of you. I enjoy hearing about the children. Yes, college is important and I'd raise my hat—if I had one on—to your fine spirit. More on this later.

I'm mending nicely at this veteran's hospital not far from Chicago. In three months I'll be discharged and I'll come straight to you. Don't think for one moment that I won't ask you again to marry me. Having four children to help you care for is just fine. I love you, dear girl. Yours, Frank.

A rush of pleasure washed over Linnie. She folded the letter and tucked it back into the box with all the letters she'd received from Frank. She picked up her pen, dipped it into the ink-well and wrote.

Good Mercy, Frank Dobbs, you do know how to woo a girl! How can I resist your loving words? Yes, I will marry you . . . She wrote him details about work at the clinic and news about Hanksport and its citizens. In closing she wrote, *I look forward to the day when you come home and become a part of my life again. I love you, Frank, dear.*

Linnie.

After going over her letter a second time put it in an envelope and addressed it. She glanced out the window. Ollie Holm, driving a new automobile, parked in front of Hart's Grocery. Brown Hon, whom Linnie hadn't seen in years, came up the street, stopped at Bruns's office and tried the door. It didn't yield. The woman looked around. She seemed uncertain. She crossed the street and started up the stairs below.

Linnie met her at the door. "Come in," she said.

"Excuse me. I don't want to bother you, but do you know when I can see Mr. Wald?"

"I think he's over at Coldsprings. He probably won't be home until evening. Can I give him a message?"

Brown Hon frowned. "I saw . . . I need to talk to him, myself. Thank you." She hesitated for a moment, turned and left.

This was a puzzle but it wasn't any of Linnie's business.

Four-thirty. No Trude. Linnie tried to read information about a Marxist doctrinaire on which a particular Socialist Labor Party was founded. She intended to be educated in these matters and she envisioned lively conversations with Frank and their friends.

Late afternoon brought dark clouds and gusting wind. Linnie put her shawl around her shoulders and, in spite of a nagging worry, she put her head down on her arms to catch a few winks.

The chill of evening along with scattered rain on the window woke her. She looked at her watch. 5:55. She paced the room. She counseled herself. Trude was cautious and wise. She would drive up any moment now, have a logical explanation and she and Linnie would have a fine supper at Mame's.

She tried to get back to her reading. She couldn't concentrate. She sharpened pencils. Filled inkwells. Trimmed lamp wicks. Time and again she went to the window. At six-thirty Trude had yet to return. Lamps began to glow. Across the street Bruns drove up and parked his auto. Linnie grabbed her shawl, locked up, and hurried over. The two went to see Sheriff Mann.

He was skeptical. "She might have stayed for supper with those folks," he said. "With the rain and all, she's probably spending the night."

"No," said Linnie. "We don't stay out after dark, and we never stay over in a stranger's home."

Chester Mann said, "If she hasn't returned by early morning I'll round up some deputies and go up to the camp."

"We should go now," said Bruns.

The sheriff shook his head. "Hunting for someone up in that rough country in the dark and in rain doesn't make sense. We'll leave at first light."

Linnie spent the night in Bruns's guest room, but sleep eluded her. Before dawn she crept down to the kitchen to make herself a cup of tea. Bruns was already up. "Come on," he said. "I couldn't sleep either. Let's go."

Bruns cranked up his auto and the two started out in drizzle and thick fog, They crossed the Blackduck Bridge and drove up the hill past the looming shadow of the Strom's house. From there they drove up through deep woods to emerge in high open country. Bruns shifted into low gear and started down Canyon Road. An oncoming auto pulled aside to give Bruns room to pass. Linnie knuckled her mouth and tried to push the dreadful image of crashing over the side of the road down into the canyon out of her mind.

Once in the valley Bruns drove past Brown Hon's place and Linnie said, "I forgot to tell you that Brown Hon came to see you yesterday. She came over and asked me when she might see you."

"If it's important, she'll come back."

Bruns, usually conversant and easy, didn't have much to say. His expression was grim. At the camp, in the first dim light of day, a pall of smoke and fog hung over the Company Store, a mess hall, jerry-built shacks, a two-story dormitory and a blacksmith shop. Men and older boys were off to work. Bruns parked in front of the mess hall. He and Linnie went inside. Smells of coffee and rancid bacon assailed Linnie. A scrawny, slack-jawed woman was clearing tin plates, silverware and mugs from one of six long trestle tables.

"Excuse me," said Bruns.

The woman looked up. "Yeah?" She wiped her hands on her stained apron.

"Where might we find Agnes Tibbs'?"

"Who?"

"A woman by the name of Agnes Tibbs."

The woman shook her head. "Never heard of her."

Tightness gripped Linnie's throat. "Do you know anyone who might know of her?"

"No."

Linnie persisted. "Do you know who asked someone from Hanksport to come over here to talk to a group of women?"

The woman laughed. "Talk to women? Up here? That's some joke. Who the hell are you after anyhow?"

"A woman from Hanksport," said Bruns. "She left town yesterday morning to come over here. Said she'd be home by mid-afternoon, yesterday, and she didn't show up."

The woman shrugged. "Mister, I don't know nothin' about it. We got Ada Byerly who runs the store. Me and some girlies. The girlies live in the box cars down t'the end of the road. Maybe one of them's the one you're looking for. But I don't know why they'd ask some woman to come over here to talk."

Linnie said, "Are there children living here in the camp?"

"Nope. Men and Ada and the girlies and me. That's all."

The black wing of fear gripped Linnie hard. She and Bruns left the mess hall and got back in Bruns's car. He drove to the end of the road and parked. Thin ropes of smoke rose from the metal cylinder chimneys of three boxcars. Bruns knocked on one of the doors. A woman slid it open. Her loose shift exposed her breasts and dark nipples. She smiled a gummy smile. No, she didn't know anyone named Tibbs. "Honey," she said to Bruns, "There ain't no women up here but us and Ada Byerly and cookie. We was hired to do what we do best and that's all I know."

Bruns thanked her, tipped his hat, and he and Linnie left the camp where Trude Bleecker had never been.

∽∾

Linnie phoned Ann from Coldsprings. Ann drove home the next day. The women closed the clinic and joined Chester Mann and his deputies on a county-wide search. On the third day a hunter found Trude's body and her crushed automobile at the bottom of the canyon. The assumption was held that she'd missed a sharp curve in the road and plunged over the edge.

Trude Bleecker was buried beside her husband in Portland. More than two dozen folks from Hanksport attended the service.

Linnie, sure that she herself and Ann had been marked to die along with Trude, held fast to her resolve to defeat the black wing of fear. But, she said to Bruns, "Trude didn't miss that curve. She was a careful driver and she never drove fast. Someone was out to get her and Ann and me. That invitation to come over to the camp was addressed to all of us."

Bruns said, "I share your feelings. We'll stay alert."

CHAPTER 62

The following summer Linnie threw herself into her work and anticipated the day when Frank would settle in Seattle and life for her and the children would take a splendid new turn. She said nothing about her plans. She would wait until after he was home and the two of them, together, would tell her family.

On a Monday morning in early August she stopped by the post office to pick up the mail. An invitation to a women's meeting over in Coldsprings. A request to speak to a Suffragist club in Seattle. The latest issue of *The Call*, *The Seattle Union Record*, and *The Industrial Worker*. No letter from Frank.

Disappointment and worry picked at her her. Frank's habit had been to write at least twice and often three times a week. Now, eight days had passed and not a word. Tomorrow she would drive over to Coldsprings and wire the hospital in Illinois.

She went up the street to the clinic and let herself in. After settling at her desk she leaned back in her chair and tried to think through a new and vexing concern. One day last week, when Linnie was home running editions of *The Women's Informer* through the press, Meggie, breathless, her blue eyes sparkling, burst into the room. "Mama, guess what happened."

"Stripe asked you to come and ride her for awhile."

Meggie laughed. "No." She danced around. "When Edna and Violet and Billy and I were walking home from the ice-cream parlor, Mr. Strom stopped his fancy auto and asked us if we wanted a ride. We got in and I got to sit in the front seat and he drove fast and my hair flew."

"And he let you out first, and then took the twins and Billy home?"

"No. He took them home first. Then me. I got to ride the longest."

"I don't want you to ride in his auto again."

Meggie's mouth drew down in a pout. "Why not? He's nice."

"Perhaps. But you're not to go with him again."

"Why not?"

"I have my reasons and there's no point in arguing."

Linnie counseled herself that Kees had done nothing wrong, but after school started she would revert to her old plan of either picking Meggie up at school, or Meggie would come to the clinic and the two of them would drive home together.

The sound of the noon whistle brought thoughts of Mame's black-eyed pea soup and silky biscuits to her mind. She was about to lock up and leave when she heard slow, plodding footsteps come up the stairs. She rose from her desk. Big, red-headed Tosstles stood in the open doorway. He held his hat in one hand, a gray, metal box in the other.

"Tosstles!" Linnie said. "Oh, it's good to see you. Come have lunch with me. There's so much . . ."

He stood as if rooted, his blue eyes fixed on her. "Flu got him, Linnie. Flu got Frank."

She held on to her desk. Air left her.

Tosstles came to her. He gave her the box and he took a letter from his vest pocket. "This came yesterday. I got here quick as I could. Flu grabbed Frank a week ago." He handed her the letter.

She opened it. Her hands shook. *Please see that Mrs. Linnie Hearn of Hanksport, Washington state is notified of Sergeant Frank Dobbs's death. Sgt. Dobbs died from influenza on August 2nd, 1919. Please convey my regrets to Mrs. Hearn.*

Prior to Sgt. Dobbs's death, he asked that I convey to Mrs. Hearn, through you, that he wishes his ashes to be scattered in a certain Thimble Creek Meadow. A tent may still be on the premises. Mr. Dobbs wishes for the tent to be taken down and given to Mrs. Hearn.

Sincerely,

Father Patrick O'Brien, St. Mary's Parrish.

For Frank, and for Tosstles, Linnie held her head high.

❧

Fleecy clouds floated in a clear blue sky. Linnie stood on the Thimble Creek Bridge and took a handful of ashes from the gray metal box. She scattered them and they disappeared in the white scribbling waters.

She saw him everywhere. Coming out of jail, fedora set rakishly on his head, his eyes briefly on her. Driving away in his mud-spattered auto with the smashed windshield. Clenched fist pumping the air. *No Gods. No Masters. No Surrender. Organize.*

She saw him at the union hall. Speechifying. Raising hopes. Generating ideas. Listening. In the white tent, bent over a book, looking up at her, smiling. Sitting on her porch and talking with her father. Arguing. Laughing at a joke. Fattening his pipe and asking questions about the old I.W.P.A. Talking politics. Socialism, Marxism, Democracy.

She allowed herself to flow into the sense of him and the clear, bright memories of the long, high-crowned summer days they'd had together and she would cherish and guard those memories for the rest of her life.

While slowly making her way across the meadow she scattered the remaining ashes among tall strappy grasses, withering pink pussy paws, and monkshood's hooded blue-violet petals. She stood for some moments in front of the tent. Stained, weathered and slumped. She pushed the flap aside, ducked her head and went in. Musty and damp. Chunks of mattress stuffing, pink and green with mold. Squirrel and small animal scatter. She would ask Bruns to take down the once lovely, airy white tent.

She left, crossed the meadow and the road and stopped at the site on which the Dickerson house and the handsome small clinic had once stood. A chunk of brown glass glinting with sunlight caught her eye. She picked it up. Odd. It had the same faint, blue-brown sheen as the bottle Linnie had seen at the luncheon party all those years ago. A sheen like the glass bottles on Brown Hon's tree. Like the bottle she'd used to fend off Kees. And like the pear-shaped bottle she'd taken home with her after the first terrible fire.

Something was wrong. Prior to building the new clinic, Joe had excavated this place so clean one could have swept it with a broom. And Linnie couldn't recall using anything at the clinic made of this kind of glass. She looked closely at the ground and found half a dozen shards that matched the chunk she held. She picked up three of the larger shards, one of which was slightly flared. She put the pieces in the metal box.

Her heart kicked up. She was on to something. She had no idea what it was, but she suspected it had everything in the world to do with the terrible fires and with Joe's knowledge of who had destroyed the house and the clinic, and ultimately Trude's "accident."

Bruns had invited her to have dinner with him at Mame's restaurant that evening. He had something important to tell her. Well, she had something important to tell him, too. She hurried down the road toward home.

From Mame Holm's hotel kitchen came rich smells of good food and, for the first time in days, hunger nudged Linnie. She and Bruns dined on delicious slow-cooked string beans and ham, macaroni and cheese. For dessert, a luscious molasses pie. While sipping a cup of strong, black coffee Bruns took off his glasses and set them beside his plate. "When do you want me to take down the tent?"

"As soon as possible, please. I may clean it and use it someday. But, Bruns, can you come for dinner on Sunday? I've invited Father over, too. I have something to show both of you."

"You have my curiosity running full steam." He looked thoughtful and then he said, "The important thing I have to tell you, Linnie dear, is this. Frank left his entire estate to you."

"What?"

"Yes. I don't mind telling you that you're a very wealthy woman."

Wealth! Money! No need to worry about how to pay for the children's education. No need to worry about her family. She could buy her father an automobile. She would have financial security she'd never dreamed of having.

"It's interesting," said Bruns. "Frank's father, like Strom, made his money in the lumber business. But, he made it in Northern California. Frank's union work displeased his parents, yet he was an only child and he was left a fortune in stocks, bonds, and real estate. He dipped into a little of it, but the rest is intact."

"Good mercy, Bruns. What should I do? I'm ignorant of such things."

"Invest. We'll find someone to advise you."

"But I'll be a capitalist."

"There are generous capitalists, like Maude Easton and Frank and Ollie and Mame. And there are greedy capitalists. I have a hunch you will be most generous."

"What a strange twist of fate. Frank came home from the war, but died from the common old flu."

"This 'common old flu' is vicious. Over twenty cases were reported when I was in Seattle last week. Five people died."

"I doubt it will spread up here. We're too tough."

On Sunday, after supper, the older children were in their rooms studying, and Meggie was curled up in front of the fire with a book. Roy, Linnie and Bruns, seated at the dining table, spoke quietly. Bruns leaned his big, loose frame back in the chair and looked closely at the bottle sitting in front of him. The shards of glass Linnie had found lay beside the bottle. Bruns picked it up. "Of course I remember this. None of us know where it came from. And you found it in the ashes the day after the Dickerson house burned down."

"Yes. One day, a long time ago, I saw several bottles, just like this, hanging on one of Brown Hon's trees. But, Bruns, we didn't have anything of the kind at the clinic Joe built. Dang it, Bruns. We just didn't."

"I smell a rat," Bruns said.

Roy said, "You find that rat and I'll die peaceable."

Bruns reached in his pocket and tossed two quarters on the table. "Linnie, every now and then I see you use money, when scrip is still most commonly used up here. Where'd you get the coins?"

She told him about the bag of money Joe had hidden, and where they'd come from. "He never talked about his work up there," said Linnie. "His work at Mrs. Strom's."

"Interesting," said Bruns. "Never?"

Roy said, "He told me once that he was surprised to find moonshine in the woodshed. Said he thought Kees and Mrs. Strom didn't approve of whiskey."

Bruns's eyebrows shot up. "Joe found shine in Strom's woodshed?"

Roy nodded. "*Bottles* of shine."

Bruns tapped a pencil against the bottle. "Can I borrow this? Tomorrow I'm going to take a look at the site of those two fires."

"Of course, you can borrow it," said Linnie. "Does it hold a secret regarding Joe?"

"Maybe." Bruns stood, put on his rumpled fedora and tucked the bottle in his coat pocket. "I'm also going to go over to the valley to visit Brown Hon. And before I come home I may stop by Strom's place and pay Mrs. Strom and her son a visit."

Linnie said, "Do you think something will come of this?"

Bruns said, "Maybe."

CHAPTER 63

A week later Linnie sent her children over to her father's house, cranked up her auto and left for town. Fingers of sunshine touched gold and scarlet vine maple that blazed in an old grow-over. Linnie saw none of September's beauty.

Last week Ann learned that her mother had succumbed to the flu. Ann was still in Seattle. Linnie was unable to attend Maude's service. The flu had a firm grip in Hanksport County.

A sign posted outside of town read: THIS TOWN IS QUARANTINED. DO NOT STOP. Yesterday four adults, including Mame Holm, and two children died. Gavin Corrigan closed the schools. On Main Street white arrows pointed the way to the I.W.W. Hall, converted to a makeshift hospital. Businesses closed down. Because folks believed that germs, borne on fresh air spread the disease, many victims died in dark rooms with heavily curtained windows. For some, the sickness lasted up to three weeks, followed by recovery. For some, the disease was brief, perhaps a day or two, and a return to health. For others, health blessed them in the morning; death cut them down a few hours later.

Linnie parked in front of the hall and tied a white, medical mask over her mouth and nose. Linnie and other volunteers, men and women, nursed the sick day and night at the "hospital."

Gavin Corrigan, his face the color of robin's eggs, came staggering up the street. Linnie helped him inside and settled him on a cot. His skin was hot as live coals, his kind, brown eyes fearful. Linnie gave him cascara tablets, followed by a sugar cube, damp with drops of turpentine. She tied a sack of camphor balls around his neck and moved on to tend another patient.

By noon five more people had come seeking help and in the terrible cacophony of hacking coughs the women volunteers did what they could. Linnie gave Gavin two more cascara pills and offered him lemonade. She propped him. He couldn't swallow. He fell back. Gasped for breath. Gagged on blood-streaked phlegm. Linnie and Mrs. Elser cleaned him and held him to try to calm his floundering, but gentle Gavin Corrigan died.

"They're drowning," Rebecca Elser cried. "Their lungs are swamped and nobody knows what to do."

During the following week, twenty-four more folks came to the I.W.W. hall for help. Birdie Mae organized a soup kitchen in Ollie's hotel. Ollie decreed all food coming from the hotel was free for those at the hospital. Birdie ran the place and stayed in a hotel room for days at a time before returning home for a day or two of rest. Newt and Roy shared the care of Baby.

Healthy people, including older children carried soups, lemonade and puddings to the hall and to private homes. They learned to minister cascara tablets, camphor, sugar cubes, and ammonium carbonate. They applied cold cloths on fevered bodies, cleaned patients, held them, propped them, and spanked their backs to try to dislodge the deadly mucous.

Every day brought a new onslaught. Logging came to a halt. The mills closed down. One morning when Linnie was on her way to the drugstore, she came upon four little girls jumping rope and singing in the otherwise quiet street:

> I had a little bird
> Its name was Enza
> I opened up my window
> And in flew enza.

Day and night, Soapy Metzler's death wagons rattled through town and out into the hills to pick up the dead.

Every day, at noon, Birdie Mae brought kettles of hot soup into the hall. She hadn't been home for over a week. Mid-afternoon, Newt was to drive into town and pick her up. She needed a day or two of rest. But until he arrived she helped two recovering patients wash themselves. A hoarse cry came at the open door, "Birdie."

"No. Oh, no." she cried.

Newt, his face a mass of blisters, came crawling across the room, leaving a trail of vomit, blood, and loose waste behind him. In a frenzy, Linnie and Birdie did everything they could, but, like Gavin Corrigan, Newt died quick.

Birdie Mae covered him with a sheet. "I don't know that I can go on."

Linnie took Birdie home with her that evening and the two, wrapped in thick wool shawls, sat out on the porch. The children joined them and they talked about Newt's gentle nature, his goodness and his profound love for Birdie. At one point Birdie hugged Linnie and the children. "I'm lucky to have all of you," she said. "I'm lucky to have Father. And Baby. Newt would want me to go on and that's what I'll do."

At the "hospital," four days later, Roy, holding Stella in his arms, came in. Stella, her blue eyes glassy and unfocused, gasped and strained for breath. Linnie tended her and when she saw her fade, she held her and tried to sing to her, but Stella stopped gasping, fell forward, limp as a rag doll, and was gone. At home, just the night before, she and Meggie had laughed and sung: *"I had a little bird; its name is Enza . . ."*

"Will it never end?" Linnie sobbed while holding Stella's body. "Oh, dear, dear Stella."

Two days later the family buried her beside Parley. Nell put the white rabbit fur scarf beside her inside the wooden casket. "Maybe the scarf is a part of Mother," she said. "Indian tribes do that kind of thing."

That evening Meggie lit a candle and put it in one of the living room windows. "This is for Stella," she said. She knelt on the floor. "She sees it from heaven. I know she does." Meggie stayed beside the burning candle at the window for some time. When she told Linnie good night, she said, "Will you get sick, too?"

"No. Remember, I'm tough."

"Oh, Mama, I love you."

The following day, a cold, gray day, Kees, his face tight-pinched, brought in two women. "My mother," he said to Linnie. "And our housekeeper." His sleepy brown eyes glinted with tears.

Linnie helped Kess settle the women. The housekeeper's eyes were glazed and she was violently ill, vomiting and floundering. There was little Linnie could do. She cleaned her, time and again, and the woman grasped Linnie's hand and held it tight. "I don't want to die," she whispered. "Please. I don't want to die."

Moments later, she drew her last breath. Linnie had a bit of trouble disengaging her own hand from the woman's strong grip with the woman's two webbed fingers. *Do you have something—anything—I can read to help me learn about all this? Something—anything—I can show my husband? Oh, my goodness. Thank you.*

Susan Scott was the Strom's housekeeper, or the housekeeper took on the identity of a woman named Susan Scott. Linnie would worry about it later. Susan Scott was dead. Linnie had work to do with the living.

She instructed Kees on what he could do to help his mother. He ministered medicines to her and fed her soft puddings. For two nights he slept on the floor beside her cot and paid scant attention to anyone else. She died early morning of the third day. Kees sat on the floor beside her cot and Linnie left him alone.

That afternoon, during a pouring rain and sleet, Roy brought in Meggie. Deathly pale. Vomiting. Diahrrhea. Skin hot as flames. Linnie sprang into action and applied every conceivable and known method of doctoring that she knew.

Late that day Baby, wearing Joe's old fleece coat and an old watch cap, clomped into the room. Her heavy shoes were caked with mud. She looked around, galumphed over to Meggie's cot and sat, silent and humped, on the floor beside her. She kept her eyes riveted on Meggie.

Roy came in and he said to Linnie, "I didn't know she'd gone. I'm sorry."

"We'll let her stay, Father."

Kees had not yet had his mother's corpse taken away and Linnie told him, in no uncertain terms, to "make the arrangements." Seated beside his dead, shrouded mother, his eyes locked on something, or somebody across the room, he did not appear to hear Linnie's request, but by evening the corpse of Inga Strom was gone.

Linnie put a mattress beside Meggie's cot and Linnie and Baby slept on it together.

Early the next morning a damp sheen covered the child's face and she was cool to the touch. "Her fever broke," Linnie said to Baby. "She'll be alright. I promise she will." Meggie opened her eyes and smiled at Baby and Linnie. Baby got up and clumped out of the building.

Later that morning Kees said to Linnie, "I should do something to help. What can I do?"

"Your housekeeper. What was her name?"

"Marta Olsen. She was a good sort. But please, let me help out. I didn't know it was so bad."

Once again Linnie set the thought about the housekeeper with the webbed fingers out of her mind. Once again, she reminded herself that she had work to do with the living.

She put Kees to work running errands, ministering medicines and reading aloud to recovering patients.

Kees did as he was asked to do and he did it well, but he turned most of his attentions to Meggie.

During the next two days he brought her ice-cream sodas, a new doll, and a beautiful edition of *Black Beauty*.

"Meggie," he said late one afternoon, "What is your favorite game in the whole world?"

"Jacks."

He left and returned with a pretty red velvet bag and he gave it to her. "For you," he said. "Let's play."

She laughed with delight and poured a shiny red ball and a dozen bright red jacks from the bag. She and Kees spent a good part of an hour playing the game and Meggie beamed when she beat him. "Let's play it again," she said. And they did.

The next morning Linnie told Meggie that she'd be able to go home in the afternoon. Meggie said, "After I play jacks with Kees. Not until then."

"You mean, 'Mr. Strom.' "

"No. He told me to call him 'Kees.' "

Linnie would correct Meggie later, at home. Now, she let the matter go.

Mid-afternoon Kees and Meggie settled down to their game. Linnie waited. Late-afternoon she told Meggie it was time for her to gather up her things. "You've played four or five games and it's time to go. We're having a nice celebration dinner at home just for you."

Kees said, "Meggie, tomorrow, being as it's Saturday, would you like to come see my horse, Helga? You can ride her if you'd like. She's very gentle. And I'll ride my mother's horse. We could ride over to Tat Meadow. Bee plants are coming off their bloom, but I'll bet some persnickety bees will be there looking for nectar."

"Oh, yes!" Meggie's eyes danced with pleasure. "Yes. I do want to ride your horse to the meadow and look at Bee plants. Mama. Please."

"I think not." She turned to Kees. "But thank you for thinking of her."

"She'd find Helga a fine treat," Kees said. "And the Bee plants are still quite pretty. I can drive her home, or bring her here. Whatever suits you."

"No," said Linnie. "Surely you have more important things to do than take little girls for horseback rides."

"You're stopping her from having a great lot of fun."

"My decision stands. Now, if you'll excuse us, we're eager to get home."

The red spot bloomed on Kees's forehead. "You'll regret this, Mrs. Hearn. You'll regret snubbing me, like you've always done. You'll regret it for the rest of your life." He turned from her, his back ram-rod stiff, and left.

"You're mean," Meggie cried to Linnie. "You're real mean."

Linnie knelt and took hold of her shoulders. "It's been a while since you've ridden Stripe and her feelings might be hurt if she knew you rode another horse."

"She wouldn't even know."

"There's no point in fussing. You're not going to ride Mr. Strom's horse and you're not going to ride in his auto. Now, come. It's time to go home."

During the drive home, Meggie did not engage Linnie in her usual busy chatter. Once there, she stormed into the house without saying a word about the sign on the front door. WELCOME HOME MEGGIE.

At supper she sulked. When Hugh asked her what was wrong, she said, "Mama won't let me ride Mr. Strom's horse. And she won't let me ride in his auto. Mama doesn't like him and she doesn't want me to have any fun."

"That's not true," said Hugh. "If she doesn't like him, I'll bet it's for good reason."

Linnie said, "You don't need to ride Mr. Strom's horse when you have one of your own. And one of us can ride with you to Tat meadow to look at the bee plants."

"But I want to ride Kees's horse and *he* asked me to ride her."

"Meggie, you will not. The matter is settled."

❦

Three months later the numbers of those taken ill with the dread disease slacked off. Late one afternoon, Linnie said to Ann, "We didn't have a single new patient today. Thank God. Thank God."

The scourge that had whipped through Hanksport County, through the state of Washington, through America and Europe, vanished as quickly as it had come. In Hanksport County, 176 people had died. Folks called it, "The time of horror."

CHAPTER 64

Spring up in Hanksport County. Torrents of rain had washed out the Blackduck Bridge, replaced by temporary wide, sturdy planks, but no railing. Citizens of Hanksport and Coldsprings slogged through mud, put up with wind and hail and welcomed the bright day and occasional arc of a rainbow.

Linnie told Ann, Birdie, Bruns and Paul about the housekeeper's deception. They decided to forget it. Marta Olsen, alias Susan Scott, was dead; there was nothing to gain by pressing Kees for information when there were too many other matters to tend to.

One day Birdie Mae said to Linnie, "I've got to learn to enjoy the days I've got left on this earth." Within a week she was working in the kitchen of Ollie Holm's hotel and it wasn't long before the dining room once again prospered.

One sunny afternoon Kees happened to drive through Coldsprings and he spotted Linnie's auto parked in front of the I.W.W. Hall. He slowed. A sign propped in the front window of the hall read: <u>Meeting this afternoon with Mrs. Hearn. 2:00 - 5:00. Learn about birth control and family limitation.</u>

Kees's eyes narrowed. Linnie Hearn, the adulteress and messenger of sin. Linnie Hearn, the flume tender's daughter, who for years had spurned him, and now suspected the Susan Scott ploy, hadn't yet met her fate. She wouldn't be coming home until after 5:00. It was time to see her undone.

Arriving in Hanksport at 3:30, just as students were dismissed from school, he slowly drove down the street. Meggie and the twin girls and the boy with the wooden leg were walking together. Kees drove up beside them, stopped, leaned out the window and smiled. "How about ice-cream cones and a ride home on this pretty day?"

The twins and the boy giggled. "Yes. Yes." They hopped in the back seat.

Meggie hesitated. "I'm not supposed to," she said. "Mama says I can't."

Kees said, "That's all right. After we get our ice-cream cones, we'll wave to you when we pass by."

"Oh, no," Meggie cried. "I do want to come, too. But Mama mustn't know."

Kees turned to the children in the back seat. "Can we keep it a secret?"

"Yes. Oh, yes."

"Good. We don't want Meggie's mama to get mad at her, do we."

"No. No."

Meggie got in the front seat and Kees drove to the ice-cream parlor. "I'll be right back with your ice-cream cones."

He returned and after he gave the children their treats they were on their way. He drove fast and the children squealed with delight. Approaching Meggie's house he said,

"Duck, Meggie. Your grandfather is sitting out on the porch. You don't want to get caught and I'll go even faster."

Meggie crouched low in the front seat. Kees pressed down on the accelerator. Fast. Faster. The auto slowed, a little further Kess stopped and dropped off the Krupp children. He turned his auto around. "Let's drive by Tat Meadow," he said. "I'll bet lots of flowers are in bloom."

"Oh, goodie. Let's do that." She sat up straight and said, "I feel grown-up and important."

"It's fun to feel grown-up and important, isn't it." He pulled off on an old spur road and drove to the meadow. Blue larkspur and pink trillium buds had burst. Kees stopped the auto and cut the motor. "What would you like to do more than anything else in the whole world?"

"Ride your horse. See bee flowers."

"What else?"

Meggie looked off at the meadow. "Pick flowers for Mama."

"Come on, then. Let's pick a bouquet just for her."

Meggie scrambled out of the auto and she and Kees wandered about the meadow while picking a pretty bouquet. When they returned to the auto, Kees said, "Now we have a secret, don't we."

"Yes." Color rose in Meggie's cheeks.

Kees started the auto. "Do you want to know another secret?"

"Oh, yes. I love secrets."

"Your mama doesn't like me."

"I know that." Meggie tossed her head. "That's why she didn't let me ride Helga. That's why she doesn't want me to ride in your auto."

"Yes. You're right. But you know what?"

"What?"

"She's not your mama."

Meggie's brow puckered. "Yes, she is."

"No. Your Aunt Baby is your real mama."

"She is *not* my mama. My mama's my mama."

"Your mama wants you to *think* she's your mama, but she's not."

"I don't believe you. My mama doesn't tell lies."

"Maybe not. Maybe I'm wrong, but we'll keep it a secret, won't we."

"I don't like this secret."

"Then you can pretend it isn't true."

He drove down the road while Meggie, clutching the bouquet with tight hands and white knuckles, sat in silence.

When Kees pulled up in front of her house, the old man rose from his chair and approached him. Kees got out of the car, went around and opened the door for Meggie. He turned to Roy. "Hello, Mr. Bede. I happened to pass Meggie and her friends down in town and I gave them a ride home." He nodded toward the flowers in Meggie's grip. "We picked those, too."

"Linnie won't like you bringing her home, and neither do I. I saw you high-tailing it past this house, but I sure as hell didn't know you had Meggie with you. You come near her again, and there's going to be a helluva lot of trouble. I'm telling Chester Mann that I've warned you, so take your fancy auto and get out of here."

"All right," Kees said amiably. He turned to Meggie. "Goodbye, Meggie. No more rides. I'll always think of you as my friend and I hope you'll think of me as your friend too. Always."

CHAPTER 65

A week later, late evening, Kees warmed his hands over the high snapping fire he'd built in the parlor fireplace. The clock in the vestibule struck eight. Early that morning a spring gale had brewed and by late afternoon it struck full force. Wind beat about the house and whistled around the deep eaves. A loose shutter banged. What a miserable evening to do the task Kees and Soapy planned to do, but the fire tonight would be the end of it.

Kees had sold the mill and logging operations to Thurson Brothers and was free to go anywhere he chose. He didn't know where that might be, but he would leave this cold, dark country. And to hell with Soapy. The once plump, rosy cheeked boy, now an overweight pompous fellow, no longer interested him. Soapy had served a purpose. He'd been his friend, his only friend, and an innovative lover with exciting ideas. But now all he liked to talk about was embalming and sex. So the fire tonight would be the last for Kees. And there would be no ride on Soapy's fat butt.

Kees looked around the room. He hated this chilly house of shadows, gray walls and shuttered windows. How many endless prayers had he endured in this parlor with the enormous crucifix on the wall? Hundeds of hours, during which he'd put his mind to daydreams. Had he been able to become a botanist, his life might have been different. But enough musing.

He turned from the fire and went through the kitchen to the back porch. He held a match to the wick of a lantern. It flamed bright. He put on a black duster and hat and struck out across the muddy reach to the barn in which his horse and his mother's horse chomped on fresh mounded hay he'd pitched that very afternoon. He hung his lantern on a hook. He'd always found the barn comforting. At night he liked the shadows flung up on the rafters and walls. He liked the smells of hay and grain and the sounds of the animals eating and their occasional blow and whinny.

Rain peppered the roof. The stiff wind blew the door shut. "I'm sorry," Kees said to the animals, his words choked and tight. "But I can't take you with me and I don't know anyone who would give you proper care. I don't know anyone at all. I hope somebody will find both of you and take good care of you."

For a moment he wept softly into his horse's warm hide. He straightened and wiped his eyes and nose with the cuff of his coat. He filled the feed bin, made sure that the horses had plenty of water, and picked his lantern from the hook. He closed the barn door behind him.

Bent into the sweep of the storm, he hurried to the wood-shed, rummaged around in a corner behind shovels, pitch-forks, and buckets and pulled out a brown bottle. Fighting the brutal wind and rain, he went back to the house, wrapped the bottle in newspapers and put it in a satchel. After shedding his duster he sat in front of the fire. In an hour he would walk down the hill, cross the river and go on to town to meet Soapy in front of the Holm's Hardware Store.

Fatigue, like a deep, troubled sleep, flowed through him. He and Soapy had had fine adventures together. It had started with stealing bottles from the Makah woman's bottle tree, filling the bottles with kerosene and a cloth, hurling the big, pretty bottles up at Wildcat trestle. Why, those big, spindle-legged trestle sticks must have blown a good half-mile high and the deep booms that echoed up and down the canyon might have been canons in a bloody war.

It had surprised Kees and Soapy that nobody raised much fuss after Kees and Joe found the union fellow, Les Knef. But one evening, shortly after that happened, the sheriff came calling at Kees's house. Kees's mother sent Kees to his room. She would handle the matter.

Back then, a part of Kees yearned to be caught. He wanted to rid his tortured mind from the terrible lust that drove him to do such dreadful things. After the sheriff left, Kees's mother asked him if he knew anything about Mr. Dickerson's murder. Did he have any information about the explosion that destroyed the trestle up on Wildcat Mountain? What about Mr. Knef's murder?

"Someone saw you and Soapy not far from where Mr. Knef was found," she said. "On the same day." She was pale, more so than at any time Kees had known her to be, and her hands trembled a little and her brow was creased.

"Sure, someone saw us at the time of Mr. Knef's murder," said Kees. "We'd been up at Camp 5 and were on our way home. I don't know anything about any of that terrible business."

"I didn't think you did, but I had to ask."

Kees allowed himself further musings.

Yes, the fire at the old Dickerson place had been spectacular. So was the show at the clinic. But neither those fires, or sending Marta to pose as informer for the Federal Marshall's, or stumbling on the luck of nailing Joe Bede—Joe, who had snubbed Kees for years—or crafting the plan to force the suspicious Mrs. Bleecker off the road—had stopped the haughty red head. Tonight, it no longer mattered. If the fire at Ollie Holm's building didn't do it, the flume tender's daughter would soon be distracted by another matter, and no doubt distracted for the rest of her life.

He had dull-witted Baby to thank. The secret was exposed when she came in to be with Meggie at the make-shift hospital. Kees had long been aware of the child's blue eyes and blond hair, so like Baby's. And she had a thoughtful expression that was surely the late Parley Hearn's. Kees figured Parley to be the child's father and Baby her mother and the child herself, did not know. Had no idea.

But now Bruns Wald, the Jew, was on to him. Just last week he'd come calling and he'd shown Kees a brown bottle. "You know anything about this?" He'd kept his probing eyes steady on Kees.

"No, sir."

"Last spring, on May 28th to be exact, what took you and Soapy over to Sunnydale Valley?"

"I . . . Soapy had business and he likes to ride in my car."

"Did you happen to see Mrs. Bleecker in her Oldsmobile?"

"No, sir."

"That's odd. A friend of mine said she passed you up on Canyon Road. The same friend told me that Mrs. Bleecker passed my friend, going east, within a couple of minutes of each other. So, you and Mrs. Bleecker must have passed each other. You, driving west up that steep road coming back here. Mrs. Bleecker traveling east, down the road to the valley. There aren't many automobiles in the entire county and very few on the road over to the valley."

"Sir, I'm sorry, but I don't remember seeing her. Not at all."

"I'll be back," said Bruns, the Jew.

Kees and Soapy's secrets would soon be revealed, but Kees didn't care. He'd taken his revenge on the flume tender's daughter and in doing so, he was the victor.

The clock struck 11:00. Kees put on his duster, picked up his hat and satchel and left the house. He didn't bother to close the door. He leaned against driving rain. Slipped on the road, slick with mud.

He stopped at the make-shift bridge and listened to the roaring white water below. He stepped out onto the wide planks and he found solid purchase. He started across. Midway he stopped. Two black dogs with orange eyes and tiny ears stood between him and the other side. He turned to flee. Rain. Sheets of rain. Trapped in rain. He held his lantern high. He blinked. Blinded by watery light on the canopy of dripping trees above and black waters below, he reached out to grab the rail. It wasn't there. "Mother," he cried. "Help me. Please help me."

The next morning Brown Hon did not want to leave her house. Last night's rain had ceased, but the road to town would be a misery. However, she'd promised her relatives over at Green Lake that she'd come to visit, so she mounted her pony and started toward town.

She approached Strom's big house, blackened over the years by sun and rain. She thought it strange that the front door was wide open, but the house had always had about it a sense of evil.

She reflected on the talk she'd had with Mr. Wald just before the terrible sickness came. He had come to her house and he'd had with him a bottle like those she used to keep on her tree.

He said, "Years ago Mrs. Hearn picked this up after the fire at the old Dickerson place. Mrs. Hearn said that at one time she'd seen similar bottles on one of your trees."

"Yes. A long time ago when Mrs. Dickerson was living, she came over here to buy herbs from me. One day she noticed the bottles and she liked them. That very day I put the herbs she bought in one of the bottles and gave it to her. I saw Mr. Strom and Mr. Metzler at the Dickerson house on the night of the first fire. Mr. Strom put a flame to a bottle, like that one." She pointed to the bottle Bruns held. "Mr. Strom threw the bottle at the house. I saw another man at the scene, but I didn't know who he was until later, after Mr. Bede was convicted of the crime. Mr. Bede, Joe Bede I believe is his name, had nothing to do with the fire. Mr. Metzler and Mr. Strom did it."

After Mr. Wald left Brown Hon's house, she was relieved of the burden she'd carried all these years.

Now, on this chilly, wet early morning she approached the makeshift bridge. A tangle of loose logs and fallen trees was jammed against the foot of it. Brown Hon dismounted and led her pony across. At the far shore, she stopped. "Oh," she said.

In a swirling eddy, Mr. Strom, face up and hatless, afloat and buoyant, moved with perfect rhythm. Sticks and chunks of mossy mud and bark were caught in his wheat-brown hair. Crawdads crawled in and out of the gaping mouth. Clutched in one hand was a little suitcase. Brown Hon climbed down the riverbank and she took the suitcase, climbed back up to her pony and in the clear, watery sunshine went on her way.

CHAPTER 66

Two weeks later Linnie, on her way home from the clinic, stopped by the post office. A poster of Soapy Metzler hung on one wall. <u>WANTED. DEAD OR ALIVE.</u>

How long would the turbulent thoughts connected to the dreadfully known facts about Soapy and Kees tumble around in her mind? The two had killed Joe. She often talked to herself. "Where's the justice? My God, when will I find some peace? And what am I going to do about Meggie?"

At the Company Store—now owned and operated by the Thurson Brothers—her final stop, another poster of Soapy was prominently displayed. She bought a newspaper, bacon, potatoes, a cut of pot roast and went home.

After getting supper underway, she sat down to read *The Hanksport Weekly Gazette*. Soapy Metzler's face was on the front page. Headlines: *Pyromaniac Gets Life*. Linnie allowed herself to think back on what had happened to reveal Soapy and Kees's evil deeds.

The first crack in Trude Bleecker's "accident" and death came from Brown Hon. She'd seen Trude driving her automobile east, up the steep grade toward Sunnydale Valley. Brown Hon, riding her pony, traveled on the road's narrow shoulder going west, toward Hanksport. Moments later, Kees Strom and the man who owned the funeral parlor, passed Brown Hon. He drove fast. She heard a terrible crash. An auto had tumbled down the steep grade. Brown

Hon tried to get down to the automobile, but brambles and rocks and the steepness made sure footing impossible. She got back up on her pony and rode in a hurry to town. She would go see the lawyer, Bruns Wald. But, Bruns was over in Coldsprings, so Brown Hon went home.

The "suitcase" Brown Hon turned over to Bruns provided a solid link. Bruns snapped open the satchel. Inside the bottle a rag floated in kerosene. The bottle matched the shards found in the burned debris and the bottle Linnie found at the scene of the first fire.

Soapy Metzler disappeared.

Bruns took all of his information to the District Attorney over in Coldsprings. A search warrant for Soapy was issued. Two bottles, identical to the bottle in the little suitcase, were found in Soapy's basement. Two days later Soapy was caught at a bus station in Portland. While in the city he'd set two warehouses and a church on fire. Oregon turned him over to the State of Washington authorities and he was charged with five counts of arson and found guilty. He was sentenced to fifteen years in the McNeil Island Penitentiary.

For days Hanksport County citizens talked about Kees's death. Buzzards had eaten his ears and pecked out his eyes. Had he been murdered? No. He'd jumped off the bridge on purpose after his terrible crimes had been exposed.

You can thank Brown Hon for her suspicions, and Bruns Wald for pursuing the case. But, Joe Bede took the rap for the two despicable hoodlums and lots of folks wouldn't forget it.

When Meggie learned of Kees's death, she closeted herself away in her bedroom and wept as if her heart had been split in two.

Linnie tried to talk to her. "He wasn't a happy man, Megs. Sometimes a person doesn't care if they live, or die."

"How do you know what he thought? You hated him. And I'm going to go to his funeral. I don't believe all the bad stuff that's been said about him. He never did anything bad to us."

"Yes, he did. Uncle Joe hanged himself for something he didn't do. Hanged himself for something Kees and Soapy *did* do. Kees and Soapy burned down buildings. They blew up a trestle and put lots of folks out of work. They murdered two men in cold blood. They forced Trude off the road and killed her, too. They . . ."

"Stop it." Meggie covered her ears with her hands. "I don't believe you. He *couldn't* have done those awful things and I'm going to go to his funeral and you can't stop me."

Linnie took a deep breath. "I'll take you. I don't want you riding Stripe all that way alone."

On the day of the funeral Meggie picked a bouquet of lupine and scarlet creeper. Linnie made no comment. She drove Meggie up the hill to the Hanksport cemetery. It was a bleak place with a few pines and fir trees, but it lacked pretty plants. She wished that her mother and Joe, Johnny Corrigan and Dru's little boy, Newt and Parley were buried somewhere far away from Kees Strom.

Soapy's assistant buried Kees. A man from Thurson Logging Company was also there. Meggie, her blue eyes wide and dry, held her bouquet tight. After the coffin was buried, she put her flowers atop the grave.

Linnie went to pay thought at her family's and at Johnny's graves.

On the way home, Linnie tried to engage her in conversation. Meggie had nothing to say.

CHAPTER 67

On Sundays, mid-afternoon, following a custom of many years, Roy and his family gathered either at Birdie Mae's or at Linnie's house for mid-afternoon dinner. Of late Ollie Holm was among them. At table everyone took their accustomed places, Meggie seated between Linnie and Baby.

One mid-summer Sunday, some two months after the Kees incident, Meggie said to Linnie, "I won't sit by Aunt Baby ever again."

"Don't be silly," Linnie pointed to the chair beside Baby. "That's your place, now sit down."

"No," Meggie shouted. She slammed out of the house.

Tears pooled Baby's eyes.

Hugh started after Meggie, but Linnie said, "Let her be. She still grieves over Stella's passing and she's still upset over Kees's death."

Birdie said, "I don't understand why that man paid all that attention to her. It wasn't a good thing at all."

Roy said, "I never liked the fellow." Ollie agreed.

After a dessert of rhubarb pie, Linnie went out and found Meggie twirling around in the swing. "We're through with dinner and now I want you to go inside and apologize to Aunt Baby. You've hurt her feelings."

"I don't care. I'm not ever going to sit beside her again."

"This isn't like you. You've always loved her a lot."

"No, I haven't. She's dumb."

"That's a cruel thing to say and you know it. She can't help the way she is."

"Why not?"

"She was born that way."

Meggie stopped her spinning. "Will I get to be dumb like her?"

"Of course not."

"How do you know?"

"You were born perfectly normal. Aunt Baby wasn't even a year old when we knew she wasn't right in her head. And here you are. Nine, going on ten years old. Now get a wiggle on, go in and make your apology."

With slow, dragging steps Meggie went into the house. The family and Ollie were still at table. Meggie, standing on the far side of the room, called out, "I'm sorry." She turned and ran back outside.

Linnie put her arm around Baby. "Be patient. By next Sunday she'll be fine."

But in the days to follow Meggie grew increasingly sullen and withdrawn. After two weeks of this behavior Linnie suggested that next Saturday the two of them drive over to Coldsprings and have lunch at the Snoqualmie Hotel.

Meggie brightened. "Oh, yes. Just you and me and nobody else?"

"If that's what you want, yes. Just you and me and nobody else."

During the drive to Coldsprings, Linnie said, "Let's sing a couple of our favorite songs. 'In the Good Old Summer Time' is always fun." She was pleased when Meggie, with her old playful exuberance, joined in. Perhaps all she needed right now was a little special attention.

Linnie had never been inside the hotel. The dining room had a rosy pink carpet and pink upholstered chairs. Heavy, dark pink drapes dressed the three large windows. At each place crystal goblets and heavy silverware sat on snowy white table linens.

After being seated, Meggie, with a sweet smile, asked for pork chops, sweet potatoes, and baked lima beans. Linnie would have split pea soup, chicken and dumplings and cole slaw. While they dined Linnie kept the conversation focused on Stripe, the books Meggie enjoyed, and how were Edna and Violet and Billy Krups?

Meggie frowned. "They're so poor and I feel bad for Billy. He's got an infection and the doctor might have to cut off more of his leg. When I grow up, I want to help people like Billie and Violet and Edna."

"Then you should do it," said Linnie. "After high school, go on to college and find a career in helping people."

"I will. Yes, I will."

Over a dessert of angel food cake, Meggie said, "Mama, when was the photo of Auntie Dru and Stella and Nell and Hugh taken?"

"Well, let's see. It would have been 1914 when Dru was eighteen years old. Her husband took the photo. He also took the one of Dru alone."

"Why don't you have a photo of Baby?"

"We do. She's in the family picture."

"Hugh is standing in front of her and you can't even see her and nobody wanted her in the picture because she's dumb."

"That's nonsense. We simply lined up and Buzz took the photo."

Long moments passed and Meggie had nothing to say. Linnie leaned across the table and said, "It's fine to have secrets, but if those secrets hurt you, they hurt those who love you, too. And it usually helps to talk about that hurt. Please, Meggie. Tell me what's bothering you."

Linnie's plea was met with silence. And it was a silent ride home.

In the days to follow, Meggie became churlish. She balked at doing her chores and refused to have anything to do with Baby. If Baby and Birdie Mae came over to visit, she left the house.

One day Meggie's teacher called Linnie in for a conference. "Meggie no longer completes her lessons," she said. "She won't go out at recess to play with her friends and her desk is a mess. I don't understand it. She used to be one of my best students."

Linnie tried to talk to Meggie about it, but Meggie had nothing to say.

During the last week of the school year, Mr. Lawton, the principal, came to the clinic to talk with Linnie. Meggie had deliberately pushed Billie Krups and the boy had taken a mean fall.

Appalled, Linnie said, "I can hardly believe this. It isn't like her. She's always been protective of Billie."

"I have the full report, Mrs. Hearn. Billie and a number of students made up a ditty about Kees Strom." He handed a piece of paper to Linnie. "Read this, if you like. It was a bratty thing to do and I let the students who did it, know it. If it happens again, I'll talk to their parents. But Meggie lashed back. I won't tolerate this behavior, Mrs. Hearn. I hope that over the summer you'll find out what's bothering her and we'll start next year with a clean slate."

It was warm that evening and Linnie opened all the windows. The rushing sounds of the river and the *bong bong bong* of the bell helped calm her deep concerns.

After Meggie went to bed and Nell and Hugh were studying at the dining table, Linnie, lamp in hand, went into Meggie's room. She set the lantern on the bedside table and sat down on the edge of the bed. "Because you aren't willing to talk to me about what's bothering you, and because you're causing trouble for others, like hurting Billie Crupps, I'm taking you to a doctor in Coldsprings."

"I don't have to go."

"Yes, you do have to go. We have to find out what's troubling you. When I was young, my mother was very sick and when something bothered *me*, I wished, more than anything in the world, that I could talk to her. But I couldn't. Now something has happened to you, and because I'm your mother I need to know . . ."

"But you're *not* my mother." Meggie sat up. "You *aren't* my mother and you storied to me and everybody did. Aunt Birdie and Granddad and everybody. Kees said that Aunt Baby is my mother and I shouldn't ever tell." She lay back down, turned, put her face in her pillow and sobbed.

A tangle of thoughts raced through Linnie's mind. She reached over and put her hand on Meggie's arm.

"Go away," Meggie shouted. "I hate you."

Stunned, Linnie tried to collect herself. She sat quietly. Best to let Meggie weep. And she did for some time. Linnie sat and waited. Meggie quit sobbing but she lay with her back toward Linnie.

Linnie said, "Yes. Aunt Baby is indeed your real mother. Your birth mother. Parley is your father, as you've always known. But, Aunt Baby knew she couldn't take proper care of you and the minute you were born, she gave you to me. At that moment I loved you then, as I love you now."

She put her hand on Meggie's head. Meggie moved away from her. "If you loved me," she cried. "If you loved me, you'd . . ."

"There isn't any 'if,' Meggie. I've always loved you and thought of you as mine. And I've always known that when you turned eighteen or nineteen, old enough to understand, I'd tell you that Baby is your birth-mother. I'm your mother in every way, but for birthing you. And you've always known that Hugh and Nell and Stella are Dru's children and not mine. But I love all of you more than anything or anybody in this world."

Meggie sat up. Her eyes were swollen, her mouth drawn and ugly. "But Baby and Parley weren't even married, so how could they be my mother and father?"

Linnie's heart felt ripped. Her mouth got dry. "Those things happen. But please remember that you have a family who loves you very much."

"I knew about Stella and Nell and Hugh," Meggie said, again with big, gulping sobs. "But I didn't know about me. You should have told me. I didn't like it when Kees told me. At first I didn't believe him, but then I did. Now, go away."

Linnie left Meggie and went to the dining room. She sat down beside Nell and across from Hugh. "What you heard is true," she said. "I'd always planned to tell Meggie the truth when I felt she was old enough to understand. I'm sorry it happened this way."

Hugh said, "Stella and Nell and I figured it out some time ago. We admire you for doing what you did. It must have been hard."

Nell said, "Meggie will soon realize she's lucky to have you. Your love for her. For us."

Hugh agreed. "She'll think this through and be fine. But why did that fellow, Kees Strom tell her this business? It was a darned cruel thing to do."

Linnie agreed, but she gave no answer.

Nell and Hugh went off to bed. Meggie continued to whimper. Once more Linnie went to her, but Meggie hissed, "Get away from me. Go away."

Linnie left the room. She took the paper Mr. Lawton had given her and she sat beside one of the open windows and she read.

> *Poor Kees Strom lives up on the hill.*
> *Poor Kees Strom is a dirty old pill*
> *Up on the hill lived poor Kees Strom*
> *Poor Kees Strom can't throw another bomb.*

Linnie tore up the paper and threw the scraps in the fire. She returned to her chair by the open window and she stayed until the first gray hint of day. *You'll regret snubbing me. For the rest of your life, you'll regret it.*

CHAPTER 68

Linnie and Ann, reaching out to women and men through-out Hanksport County, enjoyed two more successful years in running *The Druscilla Corrigan Clinic*. They added three rooms and they bought books, a piano and the clinic became known as "Dru's Center." Women and men came, not only for birth control education, but for borrowing books about geography, history, politics, and fiction, books contributed by friends and through Maude Easton's estate.

But, Linnie's great sorrow and concern was Meggie, now twelve years old. Twice a week, after school, she took her to a doctor in Coldsprings. For a time these sessions appeared to help, but during the rest of the year, and well into the next, Meggie see-sawed back and forth, functioning fairly well some weeks, turning angry, sullen, and inward on a whim.

One day Mr. Lawton paid Linnie another visit. "Do you know where Meggie is?"

"She's not in school?"

"No, Mrs. Hearn, she's not. Nor was she in school yes-terday. She was sent to my office twice last week for using inappropriate language and speaking badly about her family. Something is still very wrong. She's such a bright girl and, if headed in the right direction, she shows a lot of promise."

After Mr. Lawton left, Linnie, acting on a hunch, climbed the steep trail up to Horsetail Falls. Meggie, her hair loosened from its ribbon, sat on a boulder overlooking the hissing, cascading waters.

Linnie sat down beside her. "Isn't it pretty up here."

"It's my favorite place in the world."

"This was your grandmother's favorite place, too."

Silence.

"Did you know that Aunt Birdie and Ollie are getting married on June 22nd?"

Meggie shrugged. "He's always around. That was quite a Christmas present he gave her. I'll bet she's got the biggest diamond ring in the county."

"Well, they're both smitten with each other."

"Will Baby live with them in that big, fancy house?"

"Yes. And Birdie and Ollie hope you'll come to visit. There's plenty of room."

"I won't go if Baby's there. It sickens me to think she's my mother. Parley coupling with her nauseates me so much I want to puke. What a fool. Coupling with an idiot."

"I won't defend, or accuse either of them, Meggie. There are too many other things going on in the world. For instance, Mr. Lawton came to see me today."

Meggie covered her face with her hands and cried, "I don't care. I wish Kees was here. *He* was my friend. More than you, or Granddad, or Aunt Birdie. More than Hugh or Nell. Or Stella or Uncle Newt when they were alive."

"Hugh and Stella and Nell were very young when you were born. I didn't ever tell any of them about Parley and Baby. But Nell and Hugh now know, just as you do. They understand. And you're old enough to understand that we all did what we thought was best for you because we love you."

"But, Baby isn't Hugh and Nel's mama. And she wasn't Stella's mama. And Baby's photo isn't *any*where because nobody took one of her because she's dumb. And all of you were shamed by her. Now, none of you understand that I don't *like her being my mother* and I'm never going to call *you* mama again. Linnie. If Kees was alive, he'd tell me what to do. Linnie."

Linnie decided to act on a significant decision she'd made during the past few months. "I want to ask you something," she said. "Something that's important for you and Hugh and Nell and me."

"What?"

"How would you like to leave here and move to Seattle?"

Meggie's eyes widened. "If we move away, I won't have to see Baby at all."

"At times you'll see her, yes, along with the rest of our family. Meggie, at least try to accept her."

"Don't *tell* me that. How would you feel if you learned your mother was a dumbbell?"

"People often must come to terms with family members who have problems. I had to accept the fact that my mother had a broken mind."

"Like Baby's?"

"No. Baby understands some things, but she doesn't know what to do, or how to act. My mother shut her family away. She often didn't know where she was. Or who we were. None of us. Not even Granddad. But, we loved her and took care of her the best we could."

Meggie lowered her head. "That doesn't mean anything to me. I don't even want to be around Baby."

"She knows that, and you've hurt her feelings a lot."

"I don't care. If we move to Seattle, when will we go?"

"At the end of the summer. One of these days soon I plan to drive down to look for a house close to good schools. I also want to visit Dru's grave. Do you want to go with me?"

"Just you and me?"

"Nell and Hugh would like to look at houses and they'd want to visit their mother's grave."

Following a long pause, Meggie said, "Yeah. I suppose so. Do you love them more than me?"

Linnie tweaked her nose. "Silly goose. Of course not. Now, stay in school. Please. Promise me?"

"I promise. *Linnie.*"

Birdie chose to be married in Saint James Episcopal Church, followed by a sit-down dinner party and dancing at the hotel.

On the morning of the wedding, the family set out for town. Linnie, Birdie, Meggie, Hugh and Nell piled into Linnie's auto. The rest of the family rode with Roy or Colin. Wildflowers—lady slippers and dog-toothed violets had burst into bloom.

Birdie Mae broke out in song. *"Oh, Ollie, Oh, Ollie, how you can love . . ."*

Linnie joined her and from the back seat came Hugh and Nell's voices. Finished, Birdie laughed and said, "What a beautiful day it is for my wedding."

"And you surely deserve it," said Linnie.

"Well, Ollie's a fine man."

"He's getting a fine woman. And I like to think of you living in that splendid house."

"That house is too fancy for me. Ollie and I will build our own house, plenty big for a family. Who knows? Maybe my bad luck will change." She turned to Nell, Hugh and Meggie in the back seat. "Tell me about your schools in the city. Aren't you looking forward to it?"

Nell and Hugh launched into a description of the school they would attend and oh, how they loved their new house. "And Aunt Bridie, you must go with us someday to visit Mother's grave," said Nell.

Meggie sat in silence and stared out the window.

CHAPTER 69

In August, Linnie and Ann locked up the clinic and visited for a few minutes. "We're lucky to have Emma join us," said Ann. "And thanks to you she was able to go on to college."

"It was the least I could do for Mide and Colin. Nursing is what Emma wants to do."

"I can't quite believe that you leave next week. I'm going to miss you."

"And I'll miss you more than I can say, but I'm making this move, in part, because of the children. Dru wanted her chicks to go to school in the city. And I feel that Meggie will make new friends and prosper. But, you'll see me once a month. I don't want to be away from my work up here for too long. And of course we'll be back to see the family."

While driving home Linnie passed Soapy Metzler's large, fancy ginger-bread house. A new family now occupied the place. Linnie had found it hard to believe that Soapy, the fat, innocuous fellow, and the handsome, but odd and lonely Kees had done such terrible things. She didn't hate them. Something had been wrong with them. Just as something was now wrong with Meggie.

Once home Linnie popped a ham in the oven. And she had time to pack up a few things before her family arrived for a pot-luck supper. She would store a lot of her possessions over at her father's house. Her own house would be used, rent free, by Ted, Mide and Colin's oldest son, Ted's wife, Susan, and their two children.

She picked up a framed photo Ann had taken of her and Frank. They were standing in front of the white tent. Linnie had on a pale blue chemise. A dark blue scarf was tied around her neck. Frank was wearing sporty, tan summer pants. His white V-neck sweater was trimmed with navy blue. He was smiling and his eyes crinkled. Linnie was turned slightly, looking at him.

She put the photo in a steamer trunk along with the photos Buzz had taken of the family. Odd. The photo of Meggie astride the pony—the one Birdie had sent to Linnie in Seattle—was missing. Perhaps Meggie had taken it. Linnie would let the matter rest.

From Meggie's room came sounds of her humming songs. Linnie had left the task of packing her things entirely to her. To advise, or make suggestions meant trouble. But at this moment, she opened the door. She held up the ugly Santa Claus puppet with the stained clothes Dru and Buzzie had sent their children as a Christmas present years ago.

"What's this?" Meggie said. "I found it at the bottom of Stella's wardrobe. It was just . . . just there."

Linnie told her about its history. "We'll toss it," she said. "It's nothing anybody would want."

"So, that's what you do when something is ugly, worn out and old? Toss it out? Well, I'll keep it myself. Somebody loved it once, a long time ago."

"That's fine," said Linnie. "Whatever suits you."

Just as the clock struck 5:30, Ollie wheeled his big Buick sedan up beside the house and parked. He and Birdie got out.

Baby followed. Birdie retrieved two pies from the back seat
and gave one to Baby to carry into the kitchen.

Colin, Mide, Emma, Ted, Susan and their two children arrived. Mide set a large bowl of buttered string beans
and a platter of tomatoes on the table. Emma contributed a
bowl of steaming whipped up potatoes. Susan added bowls
of relish, pickles and watermelon pickles to the feast. Roy,
who had taken to baking bread, brought three loaves, still
warm from the oven. It wasn't long before they all sat down
to eat.

Meggie sat at the far end, as far from Baby as possible.
Before anybody could say a word, she said, "You should see
our new house. It's big and beautiful and I mean *big*. It's up
on Queen Ann Hill, not far from the place where Linnie
lived when she first learned about . . ."she spit out the words,
"birth control. And our house is even bigger than Mrs.
Easton's house and everybody and I mean *everybody* will know
we've got lots and lots of money. I mean we're really putting
on the dog."

"It's a comfortable place," said Linnie. "I felt that we . . . "

"In fact," Meggie interrupted. "If you . . ."

"Hold on here." Birdie held up one hand. "Just hold on.
I'm the one with big news today." Her dimples flashed. Ollie,
seated beside her, beamed. Birdie said, "Ollie and I are going
to have a baby."

Whooping cheers. Busy talk. Names for boys. Names
for girls. Knitting sweaters, booties, caps, blankets. Sewing
rompers and gowns.

Ollie had hired an architect in Seattle to draw up plans
for the new house up on 7th and Pine. "Birdie wants a plain,
but a nice house," he said. "And what Birdie wants, she gets.

Two stories. Big kitchen. Lots of bedrooms. I have a hunch we're going to have a large family." He put his arm around her and gave her a nice kiss on her cheek.

Cheers. More talk. Teddy bears. A play pen. A crib. "I'll make a sand box," said Ollie. "And we'll have . . ."

Suddenly Baby slumped forward. Her head struck the table with a sickening thump and she sprawled, inert, saliva leaking from her gaping mouth.

Cries. "Oh, my God. My God."

Attempts to rouse her failed. The men carried her to Linnie's room and they laid her on the bed. Ollie left to fetch the doctor. Meggie went to her room and closed the door. The remaining women cleaned Baby's face, picked pieces of mashed potatoes, ham and beans out of her hair and sat with her.

Linnie suspected she'd suffered a stroke. And what would this mean? If Birdie Mae, finally starting the family she'd longed for all these years, was to be saddled with Baby's care, how could she enjoy the pleasures of caring for her own children? And, because of Meggie, it would be impossible for Linnie to take Baby with her. What a gnarly, unexpected problem.

Ollie returned with the doctor. After examining Baby, he confirmed Linnie's fears. "She's had a stroke."

Birdie Mae said, "But, she's too young."

"Stroke can hit people of all ages," said the doctor.

Ollie said, "What can we expect?"

"It's hard to say. She might improve. She might get worse."

Ollie said, "She'll continue to live with us. We'll see that she gets proper care."

A short time later the men carried Baby to Ollie's car, laid her on the back seat and covered her with a blanket. The big sedan's blinking red lights on the rear of the car disappeared in the night.

After the women cleaned the kitchen, Linnie made a fresh pot of coffee and the remaining family sat by the fire. Ted asked Linnie if there was anything she wanted him to do while he and his family lived in her house. "Keep it as it is now," she said. "And make yourselves comfortable and at home."

Susan said, "How can Birdie manage her own family now that Baby is sick? To speak honestly here, I wonder if we should take her for six months out of the year."

Linnie said, "No. Baby wouldn't do well being moved about. If she could think clearly and talk to us, I think she'd tell all of us to stay with our plans. I'm going to ask Birdie and Ollie to hire a full time nurse. I can afford that."

After Ted and Susan and their two children left, Nell and Hugh bade Linnie good-night and went off to bed. Linnie settled in her reading chair. Lamp light glowed across the reach at her father's house. Loss. While still a young man he lost the love, the help and companionship of his wife and mother to their children. He lost Lily, the infant who had lived for only two days. He lost Joe, his grown son, and Parley and Newt, his sons-in-law. He lost Druscilla, his beautiful grown daughter. Four grandchildren—Birdie Mae's tiny thing, Dru's infant, Colin and Mide's deformed baby. And Stella. Now his youngest, nameless daughter, the one with the twisted mind, had suffered a crippling stroke.

SEATTLE
CHAPTER 70

At three o'clock in the afternoon Linnie left work at *The Annette Johnston Women's Clinic* housed in a well-kept, brick Victorian home on 15th and Pike. Annette Johnston, who had come from a wealthy Seattle family, had met a fate similar to Dru's. Her family had established the clinic two years prior to Linnie's move to the city. Linnie did volunteer work at the clinic five afternoons each week.

It had been two years since she'd gathered her family and moved to the city. Hugh was now a freshman at the University of Washington. Nell was a junior in high school. Meggie was a freshman.

When they first arrived, Linnie gave Meggie her full attentions. Visits to doctors and psychiatrists did not help. Nothing was physically wrong with her and doctors had no doubt that while Kees Strom's information had shocked, angered, and confused her, she should have come to terms with it by now. Doctors also pointed out to Meggie that she was surrounded by a loving family and had opportunities many young people did not enjoy.

More than one psychiatrist said to Linnie, "Her problems are part of a larger psychotic disorder. She wants to hurt you and has found a way to do it. She's highly manipulative. Don't allow yourself to fall victim to her games."

While the counseling sessions did little to help, Linnie clung to her hope that love, attention, and financial security would bring Meggie out of her bitter, dark world. It hadn't happened. She had disliked school from the first day on. She'd had no interest in going with Linnie, Hugh, and Nell to the theater, to museums and concerts.

One Sunday in mid-summer, Linnie asked all of the children if they'd like to drive up to visit Druscilla's grave. Nell suggested that they buy lilacs to plant. "Mother would have loved lilacs."

Meggie shrugged. "Why should I go? I didn't even know her."

"We'd like to have you with us," said Linnie. "On the way home, we'll stop for an ice-cream treat."

"The only gravesite I'd consider going to visit would be Kees's."

Linnie, Hugh and Stella bought two lilac plants, drove up to the site and planted them. They would grow into beautiful trees. Linnie felt a surge of pride—Dru's two living children were doing well and Dru would be proud of them.

Time went on and Meggie continued to show discontent. Her friends, older boys and girls, most of whom had dropped out of school, lived in dingy houses or flats down around 2nd Street. And Meggie, who had stopped calling Linnie by her first name, now called her, "Hearn."

In spite of Meggie's deep-seated trouble, Linnie enjoyed Seattle. During her first winter in the city she drove to the café not far from the library. She sipped tea while sitting

DEB MOHR

beside a frost spangled window and she thought back to the pleasant winter afternoon she and Frank had sat at the same table. Linnie had known at that time that she was in love. She hadn't known that Frank was also in love.

Once a month or so, she and Hugh and Nell joined Tosstles for lunch, either at the Union Hall, where he still worked, or in a restaurant not far from the Ballard Locks. Boats fascinated Tosstles and he told stories about the time in his young life when he'd worked as a deep-sea Pacific Coast fisherman.

But, while Linnie enjoyed these opportunities, she missed her family. She missed Ann and her own work and her home, the river and the bell. Every third week of the month she drove up to Hanksport to work at "Dru's Center." On weekends, every other month, Hugh and Nell and Linnie drove up to visit family. Meggie had never gone with them.

Now, on this early spring day after Linnie left the clinic, she stopped at the Bon Marché, bought a necklace of crystal beads and had it gift wrapped in tissue and tied with a silver ribbon.

She drove up Queen Anne Hill to her two-story home, passed through a high, wrought-iron gate and parked her Packard sedan in the Porte cochére. After gathering up her purse and the package, she took a moment to look out at her garden. Fat buds studded the lilacs and forsythia. Sap had begun to rise in the elms. She enjoyed the quiet feeling of it, but the nag of worry took hold. Was Meggie home? If so, what was her mood? If she wasn't home, where was she?

In the kitchen, Nese, Linnie's housekeeper and cook, was busy spooning dark chocolate frosting on a cake. "She's up in her room," she said.

Linnie passed through the dining room. Two birthday presents for Meggie, wrapped and tied with bright ribbons, lay on the table. In the adjoining living room a vase of pussy willows and camellias stood on a grand piano. French doors opened out to a verandah, beyond which was a sweeping lawn and flower beds.

Linnie went to her study, a small room with a gas fireplace. The photo of herself and Frank stood on her desk. After taking a piece of creamy white paper from a drawer she sat down and penned, *Happy Birthday, Meggie. Lots of love, Linnie.* Her package and Hugh's and Nell's on the dining table looked festive.

She went up a wide, spacious stairway and down a hall. She knocked on Meggie's door. "Happy Birthday, Megs."

Meggie, a large girl with high color and stern eyes, opened the door. Her loose, blue shift was stained, her blond hair hung lank and stringy. "Come on in, Hearn." Romance and movie magazines littered the room. The old puppet was propped up at the head of Meggie's unmade bed. A box of salt-water taffy sat on the dresser.

Linnie said, "I hope you'll come down for supper at five-thirty. You'll find presents and Nese's made a beautiful chocolate cake."

"Really?" She picked up the box of salt water taffy, "Want one? By the way, I'm going to church tonight. You want to come with me?"

"I'd . . . well, yes. I'd be happy to. What time?"

"Seven o'clock."

"Yes. That will be fine."

Early that evening Linnie, Hugh, Nell and Meggie gathered around the dining-room table to eat. Meggie had on a white pleated skirt and a loose, hip-length blue sweater. She'd washed her hair and tied it back off her face with a pink ribbon. After taking her place, she opened her gifts—from Nell, two jeweled combs. From Hugh, a lavender silk scarf. And from Linnie, the crystal beads. "These are nice," she said. "They're the cat's meow."

She pushed the gifts aside. "Oh, my. Here we are living in this mansion and eating all this food while millions of people have nothing to eat at all and here I am, getting all these presents, when so many people live in deserted buildings. Or in tents. Or in doorways. Doesn't that bother any of you?"

"Yes," said Hugh. "The food drives a couple of times a week help. And you know that Linnie gives a lot to charities."

"Yeah," said Meggie. "Those food drives are all over the place. But, it's more than that. Look at how we live. Pretty nifty, huh. Hearn, don't you feel a twinge of guilt, living like we do when there's so much poverty?"

"No. But if it bothers you, you're more than welcome to help Nell and me in the soup kitchen on Saturdays."

Meggie slapped one hand on the table. "Oh, my God, that's right. The soup kitchen. Everything you do is *so* important." She sat back in her chair and yawned. "Hughie? Nell? Hearn and I are going to church this evening. You want to come, too?"

"I've got homework," said Nell.

"Which church?" Hugh asked.

"St. Mary's Catholic," said Meggie. "I like being with people who are against birth control."

"Thanks," said Hugh. "But no, I won't go."

❧

Inside the high-spiraled church Linnie was struck by the beauty of the statues, the candles, the jeweled stained windows, incense, and pageantry. But the whole of it evoked the ancient, iron-fisted rule imposed on millions of people world-wide, the dogma that kept wives dependant and in bondage to husbands with the stern and binding beliefs prohibiting birth control.

Was Meggie using the church as a means to taunt her? Maybe. Or maybe she was sincere with her professed interest in Catholicism. If so, even though Linnie found such interest repugnant, she would give Meggie unconditional support.

❧

That spring Linnie observed that Meggie fully embraced the religion. Evenings, when Nell and Hugh studied their lessons, she studied the catechism. Three or four times a week she went to confession.

One day she said to Linnie, "I told Father Ragazzo about your work on birth control. He says if I moved out of your house, I wouldn't feel so ashamed about what you do. He said he'd look for a suitable family for me."

Linnie didn't flinch. "I hope you won't go, but if you'd feel more comfortable living with another family, you're free to leave."

CHAPTER 71
1932

A year later on a Sunday in May, Linnie went downstairs to the dining room, poured herself a cup of coffee and sat down to read *The Seattle P.I.*

Nese set platters of sausage, eggs and toast under shiny domed lids on the sideboard.

Linnie said, "Listen to this." She adjusted her glasses, held up the paper, and read, "President Hoover decided last week that employing economy in the White House kitchen would be bad for the country's morale. Each evening the President and First Lady, heralded by men playing glittering trumpets, enter the White House dining room. Dressed to the nines, the President in black tie, the First Lady in a long gown, the two, often the only diners present, enjoy seven-course dinners. It is said that Mrs. Hoover sets the finest table in White House History."

Linnie slapped the paper down on the table. "Can you believe it? This country is in a terrible depression and the President and his foolish wife behave like that? Yesterday I passed four long soup lines downtown, but the Hoovers dine like royalty."

Nese said, "People like that can't see beyond themselves."

Hugh joined them. "Morning, Linnie. Nese." He glanced at the paper. "Well, we won't have to put up with Hoover much longer. FDR is going to beat the pants off him."

"My Lord," said Linnie. "I hope you're right."

Meggie came in, poured coffee for herself and, while carrying her cup to the table, the coffee sloshed over on the pale blue carpet. Ignoring the brown seeping stain, she sat down and said, "Church, anybody?"

Linnie said, "Meggie, you know we're going up to Hanksport. Baby is very ill and probably won't live much longer. I know she'd like to see you."

Meggie hooted with laughter. "All these years and you still don't get it, do you, Hearn. Well, I've got other plans. Church and my friends."

Nell, holding two baby dolls, came in. "I bought these for Aunt Birdie's little girls," she said.

"I bought these for Aunt Birdie's little girls," Meggie mocked. "Aren't' you the Miss Goody-Two-Shoes?"

"And these for the boys," said Nell. She took a small, bright red fire truck and a black model "A" automobile from a sack. "When do we leave?"

Hugh said, "Right after breakfast."

With Hugh at the wheel of Linnie's car and Nell beside him, Linnie took the back seat. This was her preference on drives with Nell and Hugh up to Hanksport—to enjoy and appreciate the countryside without the worry of driving.

Today, the return to this country brought her a sense of loss. Johnny Corrigan. Her mother. Dru. Dru's infant son. Mide and Colin's baby boy. Parley. Mame Holm. Trude Bleecker. Joe. Newt. Gavin. And Frank. Each person had affected her in a unique way. Now she would soon lose Baby.

Baby, who had caused so much trouble for the family. Baby, who unwittingly had brought enormous pain to Linnie. Baby, Meggie's mother, and Meggie, the sweet-faced little girl with the sunny disposition, now unpredictable, angry and manipulative.

While following the muddy road down the south fork of the Blackduck River, Linnie wondered how had her mother and father felt when they first arrived in this land of dark forests and rain? Linnie suspected they viewed the move into the small, cramped cabin as an adventure. Unexplored country. A challenge to be met and conquered. But, after having too many children, those dreams faded away.

However, Linnie felt a longing and strong identity with this place. She wanted to come back and live in her own house. In a couple of years it should be possible. Next month Hugh would graduate from the University of Washington with a degree in Journalism. He had applied for a job writing for *The Nation* and if he landed the job he'd live in Washington D.C.

Next year Nell, a major in Anthropology at the University, would live in a woman's dorm on campus. That would leave Meggie and Linnie at home. Meggie didn't have grades for college and had declared, more than once, her intent to leave home. "This is such a vulgar, pretentious place. I'll find work and rent an apartment downtown."

Linnie hadn't objected. Meggie hadn't moved out.

In Hanksport, Hugh drove down Main Street and stopped in front of *The Druscilla Corrigan Center.*

"I'll be just a minute," Linnie said. She went in and greeted a number of women patiently waiting in the reception room. She gave the receptionist/secretary a note. *Dear*

Ann, I'll call you from Birdie's. I don't know when because Baby is very ill. Eager to see you. L.

Back in the car she said to Hugh. "Before we go up to Birdie's and Ollie's, let's drive by the park. I've not been there in years."

The municipal park now boasted two swing sets, teeter-totters, a large sandbox and a good size wading pool. New bleachers faced the bandstand. Thank goodness the large white oaks and aspen groves had been saved. Such beautiful trees.

"It looks well used," said Hugh.

On the other side of The Blackduck River the jail looked as it always had. Squat and solid.

Union man's in jail.

You know who they've got?

Dobbs.

No Gods. No Masters. No Surrender.

Hugh drove down Main Street. New buildings had sprung up, including an Andrew Carnegie Library. Birdie and Ollie's big, two-story bungalow was up on 7th and Pine.

A Swedish woman, whom Birdie had hired years ago, was still with the family. And the nurse Linnie had hired still tended Baby.

Hugh pulled up in the back driveway. Two dogs of a medium size and of no particular breed, wagged their tails and came to greet them. A vegetable garden grew beyond the large sandbox. Two swings hung from the sturdy limbs of an oak tree.

Birdie and her three older children, ages seven, five and four years, came out to greet Linnie, Hugh and Nell. A two-year-old girl and a seven-month-old boy completed the Holm's family.

Linnie, holding the hands of two of the children, went into the house. The wide, screened back porch led into a large kitchen with an electric stove, black and white tiled counters and floor. From there, through the spacious dining room to the front room. Books filled the glass fronted bookcases flanking the fireplace. Upton Sinclair's *The Jungle* and an unfinished jigsaw puzzle were atop a heavy, library table. A young boy's cap lay on an easy chair. A toy train sat in one of the bay windows. And a large orange cat snoozed on the sofa. It was a room of mild disarray, a room of love and comfort and good thought.

After the rush of greetings, Birdie shooed her children outside.

"Sit down, please," she said to Linnie, Hugh and Nell. I have news and it isn't pleasant."

Linnie's thoughts spun out. Was Birdie ill? Ollie? Had Baby died? Was something wrong with one of the children . . ."

Birdie said, "There's no easy way to tell you that Buzzie is dead." She picked up a newspaper. "Here's the story I read early this morning." She handed the paper to Hugh and he read aloud.

Last week Busby Corrigan, well known on the West Coast for his connections with bootlegging and gambling, was stabbed to death in a New York speakeasy. Mr. Corrigan, who once lived in Seattle, honed his skills since a young man with gambling. He was known as a good sport, win or lose. When he won, he lavished his family and friends with gifts. When he lost vast sums of money, over a long period of time, he lived in flop houses and worked on the docks. He was known as the man with the smile and in spite of his shady

connections, he was well liked. His dying request was to be buried in
a Seattle cemetery next to his wife.

Linnie kept her silence.

Hugh said, "I hardly remember him. Taking the photos, I guess. Saw him for a minute at Mother's funeral. He didn't know us at all."

Nell agreed. "He's only a name to me, but I know he broke Mother's heart."

Birdie said, "How do you feel about being put to rest beside your mother?"

Nell shrugged. "It's fine with me." She smiled. "Maybe Mother would like it."

Hugh said, "Yes. Let's let it be."

Birdie gave them both a big hug. "Good for you."

Hugh and Nell left to go downtown. They both wanted to stop by the library and Hugh wanted to visit a friend who worked for *The Hanksport Weekly Gazette*.

Birdie and Linnie went up to Baby's room. The nurse excused herself and left the three sisters alone. Baby, no longer heavy, lay under a sheet. Her once beautiful skin was loose and wrinkled. Her scalp shone pink through her thin blond hair. Paralyzed on her left side, her left eye permanently closed, she cast her wide, watery right eye on Linnie. She grunted.

Linnie bent to her. "Meggie?" she said softly.

Baby blinked her one open eye.

Linnie smoothed back Baby's hair. "Meggie's just fine," she said. "She's busy and sends you her love."

Baby died that night. Her two sisters, her father, her one living brother, Colin and his family, her brother-in-law,

Ollie, and the Holm's two older children—Baby's niece and nephew—were with her.

Later, seated at Birdie's dining room table, Colin sketched out a picture of a headstone the family would buy and have inscribed, *Alice Bede.1893-1930. She was loved.*

She was buried beside her mother up in the Hanksport Cemetery on a day of breezy sunshine. Linnie recalled other burials held in smoke, mud, and rain, but the sun shone bright and clear for Baby.

The following day, when Linnie and Birdie Mae were going through Baby's few things in her dresser, Birdie Mae handed Linnie the photo of Meggie astride the pony. Labored letters at the bottom of the photo read: M Y G I R L.

CHAPTER 72

Meggie took to wearing a large, gleaming silver cross around her neck. Her long, gray skirts, middies and sweaters emphasized her blue eyes. She was well groomed and she wore her blond hair tied severely back off her face with a large bow.

Delbert Fromme, a gangly, nice looking boy with a beaming expression, started coming around. Three months later Meggie announced with a smug pride to Linnie, Hugh and Nell, "I'm *very* pregnant."

"And what are your plans?" said Linnie, careful to remain calm as counseled.

Meggie shrugged. "Stay home and take care of the kid."

"And Del?"

"Oh, he isn't in the picture anymore. I've found other fish to fry."

"You're young to be taking on this responsibility."

"No younger than Baby was, when she had me. Hearn."

Linnie, holding her head high, left the room.

❦

The birth of Meggie's baby was relatively easy. She named him John, but she paid him scant attention.

Two weeks passed, during which time the care of the child fell primarily to Linnie and Nese. One afternoon, after

Linnie had fed the baby, she took him up to Meggie's room for his nap. Meggie, seated in a rocking chair, was eating chocolates and reading a movie magazine. After Linnie laid the child in his cradle she said, "I'm hiring Nese's daughter to take care of John so you can return to school."

Meggie hooted. "Jeepers, Hearn. I'm never going back to school. I plan to have another kid just as soon as I can. Why, we'll have a whole house full of brats, one after the other."

Keep calm, Linnie counseled herself. Don't reveal emotion. Just take the news as an ordinary event. A trivial announcement. But once in her bedroom she sat at her dresser and wept.

᭢᭢

A year later Meggie gave birth to another boy. A month after his birth it became her habit to stay away from home for days at a time, leaving the care of her children to Nese's daughter.

One cold January day, when Meggie had been away from home for over a week, Linnie went looking for her. At the police station she learned that there had been no unusual, adverse reports regarding a young girl. "Just the usual, Ma'am. Girls working the streets. Stealing. Drunks. Dope. Nothing out of the ordinary. You might take a look down at the waterfront."

Linnie drove slowly past taverns, brick warehouses, the ferry terminal, the docks. These streets held thousands of stories about broken people, like Dru, unable to cope with life, and troubled people like Meggie.

On First Street she parked in front of The Bread of Life Mission. And there she was, walking up the block just ahead. She carried a satchel and she had on an orange and black plaid coat—not the pretty navy blue wool with the fur trimmed collar Linnie had given her last Christmas. She entered a two-story brick building in which a dim light shone in a window on the second floor.

Linnie got out of her car. She hesitated. The confrontation would be ugly. But with a firm step she went to the building, passed through the doorway and up a flight of stairs. On down the hall, a door opened. Greetings. "Hey, Megs." Laughter. "Megs, you got some hooch?"

"Got the goods. Got the hooch."

Linnie knocked on the door.

Sudden silence. Then, a male voice. "Yeah?"

"Please open the door," said Linnie.

"Jeepers," said Meggie. "I know who that is. Let her in." She laughed. "Let her see how I *like* to live."

A man who looked to be in his twenties opened the door and Linnie stepped into a big, drafty room crowded with old furniture. A number of girls and older men, all wearing heavy coats, lounged in chairs and smoked. Empty wine bottles, cigarette butts, and pieces of clothing—a scarf, caps, a pair of overalls—lay scattered about.

A tall, pug-nosed girl with a head of brown curls, said. "Hey, Megs. Better go home with your mama."

The group snickered.

"She's not my mother," said Meggie. "I learned that a long time ago. But not from her." She slung her arm around one of the men and said to Linnie, "Meet Carl. He's swell. And these folks," she said with a wave of one hand, "They taught me how to steal. I'm good at it, too. When I'm arrested and sent to jail, I'll play the martyr. Just like you once did." She rolled her eyes and turned to her friends. "Oh, boy. One of the family's favorite tales. Linnie Hearn in the Crooked Neck Workhouse. Linnie Hearn on a hunger strike. Well, you can bet your bottom dollar that if and when I'm hauled into jail, she will bail me out."

Linnie turned to leave.

Meggie said, "Hearn, you need to know this. If Kees had lived, I would have been his mistress and we would have had a whole slew of kids."

"I'm sure you would have," said Linnie and she left.

Once in the car she sat for a moment, her forehead pressed against one hand on the steering wheel. Who was this girl who preferred to live with thieves, pimps, and prostitutes, instead of living a decent life at home? And Linnie steeled herself for what she was sure would come.

Three months passed without a word from Meggie. Then, one Sunday evening Linnie was working in her study when someone knocked on the front door. She wasn't surprised to see Meggie and Carl.

"Come in," she said. She did not usher them into the living room. She would make her stand in the foyer.

"I want to come home," said Meggie. Her sweet smile nearly broke Linnie's resolve.

Carl whistled. "I can understand why. Wow. What a swell house."

"Where are the kids?" said Meggie. "Carl wants to meet them. He loves kids."

"Your children are in bed."

"Well, I'm pregnant again and, as I say, I want to come home. Carl can live here, too. There's plenty of room and he's nuts about kids."

"No. Under certain conditions, you alone, are welcome to come home. If you do, you must leave the streets, go back to school, and help care for your children."

"Hey," said Carl. "I can take care of the babies while Meggie here goes to school."

Linnie said, "Carl, understand this. If Meggie agrees to come home, she comes alone and she accepts her responsibilities."

"Where's your big heart, Hearn?" said Meggie.

"I have nothing else to say. Either accept my offer as it stands, or leave."

"You're kicking me out?"

"If you don't take care of your responsibilities, yes, I am."

"Let's get out of here, Carl. Hearn, tomorrow we'll come and get the kids. They *are* mine."

The following day when Linnie came home from *The Annette Johnston Clinic*, Nese said, "Meggie and the older fellow came by. They took the little tykes and all their clothes and toys. And that old puppet."

Linnie said, "I'm not surprised."

CHAPTER 73
OCTOBER, 1935

In the basement of the First Christian Church, Linnie poured a cup of thick, split-pea soup into a bowl and handed it over to a young man. His eyes reflected hopeless despair. The soup would no doubt be his only hot meal for the day.

Next in line were two young boys, and behind them was Meggie. She held the hand of a little girl beside her. The child carried a strong resemblance to Meggie as a child. Blond curls. Blue eyes. A sweet, dimpled smile.

Meggie, quite overweight, her hair pulled back and tied with a dirty pink ribbon, said, "Hello, Hearn. Still helping the down-and-out?"

"I've hoped you might show up. I'd like to talk to you about a plan I have."

Meggie's eyebrows lifted with surprise. "*You* want to talk to me?"

"Yes."

"I'll come by the house this evening."

"I sold the house years ago. How about having dinner with me tonight? I can pick you up and we'll go to the diner on 12th Street? Six o'clock?"

"Yeah. Well . . . yeah. I mean . . . sure. Carl will stay with the kiddies. No, you don't need to pick me up. I'll be there."

❧❧

At five-fifty that evening Linnie drove to the diner. Meggie, seated in a booth had on a worn, but clean pink dress and she'd pinned her hair back with the sparkling combs Nell had given her some years back. She looked curious, wary, and a little expectant.

Linnie sat down. The two ordered the Blue Plate Special of mashed potatoes, gravy, steak and string beans. They spoke of the weather. Yes, it had been a cold winter. Linnie asked about the children. John was in third grade. Les was in first. Two year old Carol-Ann was a lively child. Meggie asked no questions of Linnie.

Over a dessert of bread-pudding, Linnie said, "Next year I'm moving back to Hanksport. Please write once in a while. After all, you're still part of the family."

"Family?" Meggie shook her head. "No, Hearn. You lost me years ago. My family is Carl and my boys and my daughter. We get by. Carl's a longshoreman. Active in union. She smiled. "You also might like to know that I don't plan to have any more kiddies."

"May I ask, where are you living?"

"Sure. An apartment on Second Street. It's okay. This is the life I choose. It's where I belong."

"I respect that, Meggie."

Meggie took Linnie's coat from a hook and held it for Linnie to slip into. "I've got a question," she said. "The photo of me on the horse? Taken when I was little?"

"Yes? We found it with Baby's things."

"Good. Years ago, when you told me we were moving to Seattle, I know I'd never go back to Hanksport and I'd never see Baby again. Just before we left I took the photo over to Birdie and gave it to her. I didn't say a word. I hoped she'd give it to Baby."

"She did. And that was kind of you. Thank you."

"You don't need to thank me, Hearn. Not ever." She turned and walked away.

CHAPTER 74

A year later Linnie climbed the long flight of stairs to the fourth floor of the apartment house, in which she lived, went down the hall, unlocked the door of her place and went in. She took off her hat, coat, and gloves. She flipped through the mail. A flyer announcing a union rally at Ballard Hall. *The Nation* magazine where Hugh now worked. *The Call.* And a letter from Nell, who was studying anthropology at The University of California.

Linnie sat at a small table at one end of the kitchen and read Nell's letter.

Dear Linnie;

I can't, in good conscience, allow you to pay for the rest of my schooling. Selling our house in order to send Hugh and me to school was bad enough. Now, it's time for me to go to work for awhile. I've withdrawn from my classes and will be home in a week. My professors are allowing me to take my finals early this term and then when I come back, I'll be that much ahead. And I will come back. Someday, after I'm a fine anthropologist like Ruth Benedict, I'll pay back every cent and then some.

I'll take the train from San Francisco to Portland, then on to Seattle. I'm sure I can find work. Much love, Nell.

Only one more year and Nell would have her Ph.D. Too often Linnie had seen students leave school and, in spite of good intentions, not return.

She put on her hat, her coat and gloves. At Western Union she wired Nell. *I'll find the funds Will send within the week Do NOT quit school*

While on her way home she pondered her dilemma. From whom could she borrow the money? Banks, including Linnie's, had stopped making loans. Ollie and Birdie were putting money aside to send their own children to college. Linnie's father had no cash to spare. And Ann and Paul had been hard hit by a decline in the Real Estate market. To whom could she turn?

While eating supper, she read in *The Call* that Carl Sandburg's play, *The People*, would be performed the following night at the Union hall on Yesler Way. Linnie put on her coat, her hat, and gloves, left her apartment and drove to the Ballard Union Hall.

∞

"Oh, my health is as good as any old man my age," Tosstles said. "Sit down. I'll pour coffee."

Linnie sat at the same long, trestle table covered with faded red oilcloth she had sat at many times over the past years. I.W.W. posters covered most of the walls. The big dining hall smelled faintly of boiled chicken and it was chilly, even though flames snapped in the large woodstove.

Linnie set her cup down. "I'm in a dilemma," she said. "Nell is a top-notch student at the University of California, but I no longer have the means to keep her in school. If I can find means to keep her there, she'll graduate with a Doctor's degree in Anthropology in June. Can you help me? Or might you have an idea or two?"

Tosstles ran his fingers through his thick, red beard, now sprinkled with gray. "Too bad money isn't spread around to the masses," he said. "I read recently something that Thomas Jefferson said. 'The tax which will be paid for the purpose of education is not more than the thousandth part of what will be paid to kings, priests, and nobles who will rise up among us if we leave the people in ignorance.' I like that. Got it pinned on my wall in my room. Jefferson's words get right to the belly of the beast. The rich get richer while the poor get less and less. It's now to the point where lots of young folks can't afford to go on to school at all." He paused. His eyes were thoughtful. "Let me think about this."

"Thank you, Tosstles."

Two days later she found an envelope with a check for $400 under her door. More than enough to keep Nell in school. Linnie would send Tosstles small checks every month and she wrote the first check that evening.

CHAPTER 75
JULY, 1936

Just before noon Linnie pulled up in front of Ollie and Birdie's house. She sat for a moment to contemplate the place. As children—she and Dru and Birdie Mae, Joe and Colin, growing up in the small, dark, shanty—who among them dared dream that one day one of them would live in a home as lovely as Birdie's?

She rang the buzzing doorbell.

"Come in," Birdie called out.

Mouth-watering smells came from the kitchen. When, in all of Linnie's life, had she not known Birdie to be busy in her kitchen? Three of the Holms's children ran to greet their "Aunt Linnie."

Moist eyed, her dimples flashing, Birdie appeared, dried her hands on her apron and the two sisters hugged. Birdie said, "Oh, my, it's good to have you home." She put one hand atop one of her son's blonde hair. "Take Aunt Linnie's jacket and purse and put them in the front closet. Linnie, come help me in the kitchen. Dad and Colin and his family are due in about an hour."

The big dining table was stretched out to full length. To accommodate the large family a second table had been set up at the end of the room. Both tables were set with Mame's heavy, ornate sterling. A large bouquet of peonies and lilacs sat on a built-in sideboard.

In the kitchen Birdie pulled a good-size pork roast from her stove. Linnie slipped an apron on over her head and went out to the back porch to shuck a good two dozen ears of corn. Finished, she watched Birdie sprinkle sugar and cinnamon on the golden crusts of three blueberry pies, "It's good to be home," Linnie said.

"It never felt right with you down in Seattle."

"There were good times. Hugh and Nell prospered. But now it's time for me to get back to my own work. My desk is still at the center. At one time I thought I'd move it down to Seattle, yet I think I knew all along that once the children were through school, I'd come back. Things have a way of working out, don't they."

"They surely do. At one time we didn't know if we could keep this house. Or the hardware building. But now Ollie's business is picking up and we've bought more property." She fell silent. Then, "Have you heard from Meggie?"

"Not for over a year and I doubt I'll hear from her again." She told Birdie about the dinner she'd had with Meggie.

"You did more than enough to help her," Birdie said.

"Maybe. I hope so. I don't feel guilty, but Kees, in death, is the victor."

"Look at it this way," said Birdie. "If Kees hadn't told her, and we had, she still might have turned on us. Or on you."

"I've come to the same conclusion. And I keep my thoughts on Hugh and Nell. Dang it, Birdie. I wish they could be with us today."

An hour later Colin and his family arrived, but Roy had yet to drive up. It wasn't long before a car honked out front. Linnie said, "There he is." She hurried out to greet him.

"Linnie? Surprise!" Hugh and Nell, along with their grandfather, piled out of the car.

"Oh," Linnie gasped. "What a surprise. What a *splendid* surprise."

"We couldn't let you come home without us here too," said Hugh.

"How on earth did you get here? Both of you without my knowing it?"

"It took some doing," said Nell. "We took the train to Seattle. Hugh from the East Coast, me from the West. We met at Nese's house, spent the night, caught the train this morning and Grandfather met us in Coldsprings."

"This makes coming home just right," said Linnie.

Mid-afternoon, nineteen members of Roy Bede's family sat down at Ollie and Birdie's bountiful tables. Politics—the adults were Socialists or Democrats—was discussed—Pleasure in F.D.R.'s Second New Deal Policy. The CCC (Civilian Conservation Corps) was working on roads and building an enormous lodge up in the Cascade Mountains. Their work brought new businesses to Hanksport County. The recent Revenue Act specifying an increased surtax on citizens with incomes of over $50,000 a year was applauded.

At one point Linnie said, "Tosstles quoted something Thomas Jefferson once said. 'The tax which will be paid for the purpose of education is not more than the thousandth part of what will be paid to kings, priests, and nobles who will rise up among us if we leave the people in ignorance.' "

Applause. "Yes. Yes. I like that. And he's right."

After the children were excused from the table, Birdie Mae poured sherry into pretty cut-glass flutes.

Memories of loved ones. Parley, coming around Roy's house to court Linnie. Parley's work with union. The gifts he'd made for the family. Linnie pulled out the small wooden owl from under the collar of her blouse. "I still wear this," she said.

Frank arguing politics with Roy. Negotiating settlements with Mrs. Strom. Helping Linnie and Ann with their work. Meara's love of books and nature. Her care and love for her family "before," Roy said, "She lost her stuffing."

Dru's keen eye for beautiful things. Her rich voice, her love for her children and her dreams. Newt, courting Birdie, scouting for good land, agreeing to take Baby in when the rest of the family could no longer handle her.

Gentle Joe, always with a pencil or hammer in hand. His friendship with Trude Bleecker, and thank God he was gone when Trude met her terrible fate. Stella, so like her mother in looks and bestowed with the gift of a beautiful voice. Mame's generosity, good nature, and wonderful food. And Baby's unrecognized perceptions of her own difficult place in her world. Gone now. All gone.

No one spoke of Meggie.

Nell offered to help with the dishes, but Birdie Mae would have none of it. "My girls know how, and I know you're all eager to get home."

Nell said, "I wish we could stay for a week, or longer, but we don't have much time. Day after tomorrow Hugh and I have to leave."

Linnie said, "On the way home we'll take the road that goes up to Thimble Creek Meadow. I'd like to stop for a few minutes."

"Coffee tomorrow?" Roy asked her.

"Yes," said Linnie. "I'd like that. Come on over, please."

∽∾

At Thimble Creek Meadow Linnie sat on the big rock. Hugh picked a daisy and said, "I remember Mother wearing flowers like these in her hair."

"She did," said Linnie. "She was lovely and an inspiration to me. Were it not for her, I don't know that I would have taken the path I chose to take."

A breeze rippled the meadow grasses and flowers. Linnie smiled. Perhaps Frank's spirit lived in this beautiful place.

She and Hugh and Nell returned to the car and Hugh drove home.

Cut wood was stacked neatly beside the hearth. There was no other scent as welcome as that of fresh cut pine. Linnie opened the windows through which came spangles of late afternoon sun. The rushing Blackduck River and the soft, erratic *bong bong bong bong* of the flume bell meant there was no trouble upstream. But Linnie had work to do and she had a good hunch that her work wouldn't be easy, nor would it cease.

THE END

Made in the USA
Charleston, SC
12 June 2012